SUSAN ... ...DS:
TH...
C...

... BY

ALISON J. LINDSAY

Jean Evans (Jane Shaw) and Alison Lindsay in 1994. Photograph: Ernest Marchand

Bettany Press

2002

First published in Great Britain
by Bettany Press 2002.
8 Kildare Road London E16 4AD.

Text © The Authors/HarperCollins.

British Library Cataloguing in Publication Data.
A catalogue record for this book is available
from the British Library.

This book is sold subject to the condition that it
shall not, by way of trade or otherwise, be lent,
re-sold, hired out, or otherwise circulated without
the Publisher's prior consent in any form of binding
or cover other than that in which it is published
and without a similar condition including this
condition being imposed on the subsequent
purchaser. All rights reserved.

ISBN 0 9524680 6 9

Printed and bound in Great Britain
by LSL Press Ltd, Bedford.

CONTENTS

CHAPTER   PAGE

Acknowledgements and Dedication

JANE SHAW: HER LIFE AND WORK

I: Jane Shaw: One of the Great 20th-Century Writers for Girls ROSEMARY AUCHMUTY   1

II: A Glasgow Girl: The Life of Jane Shaw   22
ALISON J. LINDSAY

III: Builders of Books: A Career in Publishing   32
JEAN B. S. PATRICK [JANE SHAW]

IV: Dedications and Connections: Glimpses into the Personal Context of Jane Shaw's Books   36
IAN M. EVANS

V: Fifi and the Fish: Susan in Sweden   48
EVA LÖFGREN

SUSAN IN SHORT BY JANE SHAW

VI: Susan's School Play   53

VII: Susan and the Home-Made Bomb   67

VIII: The Wilsons Won't Mind   82

IX: Susan and the Spae Wife   95

X: Susan in Trouble   110

JANE SHAW'S SCOTLAND

XI: Starting from Glasgow: Jane Shaw's Scotland ALISON J. LINDSAY   116

XII: Amanda's Spies JANE SHAW   128

XIII: Crooks Limited JANE SHAW   139

CHAPTER	PAGE

JANE SHAW'S ENGLAND

XIV: The South Country: Jane Shaw's England ALISON J. LINDSAY	153
XV: Family Trouble JANE SHAW	162
XVI: Jumble Sale JANE SHAW	175
XVII: A Girl with Ideas JANE SHAW	192

JANE SHAW'S FRANCE

XVIII: Sands Across the Sea: Jane Shaw's France ALISON J. LINDSAY	266
XIX: Sara's Adventure JANE SHAW	277
XX: The Picture JANE SHAW	290

JANE SHAW'S ALPS

XXI: Adventures in the Alps: Jane Shaw's Austria, Switzerland and Italy BEVERLEY GARMSTON	303

JANE SHAW'S SOUTH AFRICA

XXII: With Jane Shaw in South Africa POLLY WHIBLEY	319
XXIII: The Matchmakers JANE SHAW	326
XXIV: A Jane Shaw Bibliography ALISON J. LINDSAY	338
Photograph Album	345

ACKNOWLEDGMENTS AND DEDICATION

My first acknowledgement must be to Jean Evans (Jane Shaw) herself, whose friendship I enjoyed for six years. She was always happy to respond to my queries, despite her incredulity that anyone should now be interested in her work. I would like to think I repaid all of her kindnesses in some measure by showing her how many people still appreciate her books. Jean's children, Jane and Ian, have been equally helpful in seeing *Susan and Friends* through to its conclusion: I am particularly grateful to them for permitting me to look through their mother's surviving papers; and for allowing me to reproduce much hitherto unpublished material in these pages.

I thank the various contributors who have given generously of their specialist knowledge: Rosemary Auchmuty, who draws on her own awesome familiarity with children's fiction to place Jane Shaw's work in its context; Ian Evans, whose essay on dedications elegantly outlines his mother's wide interests and capacity for friendship; Beverley Garmston, who wrote about Jane Shaw long before I did; Eva Löfgren, who discusses Jane Shaw's works in translation; and Polly Whibley, who knows and loves South Africa.

Over the years, my research into Jane Shaw and her books has brought me into contact with many people, all of whom were generous with their time and knowledge. Dr W. J. Ainsley Patrick first put me in touch with his aunt, and Jean's old friends Joyce Aitken, Anne Buck and Nan Murchie willingly shared their recollections. Mrs Myatt, Mrs Ritchie and Mrs Midgeley of The Park School, and Mrs Surber of Laurel Park School, helped in tracing Jean's early education. Peter Doughty, of Dulwich, welcomed a group of Jane Shaw enthusiasts to his home without a qualm, and provided us with a fascinating account of his home area. Alison Gould of the Dulwich bookshop was equally welcoming. In Binic, Madame Françoise Villané was an ever-present advisor. I have been in touch with many Jane Shaw fans over the years, and I would like to thank them all for their willingness to share their enthusiasm and information with me.

The assistance of Jane Shaw's publishers, William Collins and Sons (now HarperCollins), Thomas Nelson and Sons Ltd, and The Lutterworth Press is gratefully acknowledged: all responded willingly to my queries. Particular acknowledgements are due to HarperCollins, who have permitted the quoting of material on which they hold the copyright.

Finally, I would like to thank Gill Bilski, Sharon Brown and Jane Jamieson for their hard work in typing much of this book; Reena and Ernest Marchand and Alison and Norman Brown for their unstinting help and generous offers of accommodation as I toured Jane Shaw sites; and Joy Wotton, Fen Crosbie and Ju Gosling for the sympathetic audience they provided.

Jean Evans dedicated her first book *Breton Holiday* to MWP and JP, her mother and father. Like her, I consider that one's first book should be dedicated to one's parents, and so, with thanks for their unfailing love and support, I inscribe this with gratitude to my mother, and to the memory of my father.

Alison J. Lindsay

I: ONE OF THE GREAT 20TH CENTURY WRITERS FOR GIRLS

ROSEMARY AUCHMUTY

No one else writes quite like Jane Shaw. If asked to read a story and guess the author, I think I would always know if she had written it. No one else has Jane Shaw's particular combination of dotty humour and affectionate engagement with different settings, the whole forming the background for a tightly plotted mystery. Yet, for all her novels are distinctive, they are also clearly representative of their time and genre. If you were not familiar with Jane Shaw's work, you could still locate the books in British children's writing of the period after the interwar years: the period when the school story was in decline; and children's librarians and critics were demanding more sophistication and 'social realism'. Shaw's output cleverly bridges the gap between the tried and true preferences of children and what the critics thought they should have. It's a transitionary style, combining the best elements of the classic interwar girls' story and the beginnings of a more modern approach to writing for children.

CONTINUITIES

Where Shaw is most representative of the new era is in her choice of story-line. She published five full-length school stories, in an era in which the school story was in decline, but her preferred plot was the mystery, often concerning the theft or loss of a valuable object, and generally not of a dangerous nature. Unlike some of her contemporaries (Mabel Esther Allan and Viola Bayley, for instance), who specialised in 'young adult' stories for the mid-teens which were quite definitely thrillers, Shaw wrote for a range of age-groups, and therefore produced some novels at the thriller end of the juvenile market (for example, *The House of the Glimmering Light*, 1943), but a great many more which were simply adventure/mysteries. The latter are probably the more successful, since the thriller genre (at which these other writers excelled) did not sit well with her sense of the ridiculous. That said, *The House of the Glimmering Light* is a splendid read, and the opening pages of *The Man at the Villa Carlotta* (reproduced on the Bettany Press website), again aimed at older readers, promise similar suspense: it's a great shame this novel was never completed.

The school stories are a relatively minor part of Shaw's output — five out of 42 published books — and she is not regarded as one of the major exponents of the genre. But they are excellent of their type. It is interesting that she did not start off writing school stories and then switch to family and holiday books in line with critical pressures at the time. Her first book was published in 1939, but she only entered the school-story market in 1950, relatively late in the genre's history, albeit contemporaneously with another important writers in the field, Antonia Forest. In fact, *Susan's Trying Term* (1961) and the two splendid Northmead novels (1961 and 1963) were among the last published examples of the traditional school story in Britain.

As an established author, Shaw seems to have embarked upon writing school stories because her publishers asked for them. It was not her preferred genre, largely because she had not enjoyed her own schooldays very much, but hers were successful because they incorporated the very features — mystery, sense of place and humour — which made her holiday stories so popular. Significantly, her first school story, *The Moochers* (1950), was followed by *The Moochers Abroad* (1951), a holiday tale. (The manuscript of a third Moochers novel, *The Moochers and the Prefects*, was lost by the publishers.) This mixture of school and holiday books in the same series was, in fact, uncommon. It was a formula successfully adopted by Elinor M. Brent-Dyer and Antonia Forest, who have been praised precisely for their more rounded portrayal of the various parts of a child's life, school and home; but Shaw did it too, and her characters, though undeniably middle-class, lead much less rarefied lives than those of Brent-Dyer or Forest and in consequence are arguably more accessible to her readers.

The two school stories in the Susan series were likewise interspersed with the holiday tales which make up most of the series. We know a little about their genesis from surviving correspondence between the author and her publisher. Shaw first wrote about Susan at school in a short story, 'Susan's School Play', which appeared in *Collins' Girls' Annual* 1957. She later proposed addding a school novel to the series and, when the publisher replied requesting four or five, she decided she should start at the beginning of Susan's schooldays, setting *Susan at School* in her first term at St Ronan's. That is why it appeared out of chronological order in the series. After *Susan's Trying Term*, however, the school story project was abandoned, perhaps because the genre was on the way out by then.

In some respects Shaw's school stories were typical of the genre, but it depends on what you mean by 'typical'. They have the usual emphasis on team and house loyalties and are underpinned by traditional school values, but Shaw's heroines are not particularly devoted to school. They tend to be misfits, and spend a great deal of their time seeking lost treasure and solving ancient mysteries rather than concerning themselves with school matters. In this sense she follows more in the tradition of Rita Coatts, say, or the early Oxenham Abbey stories, than in that of Elinor Brent-Dyer or Enid Blyton, whose interest lies more in school-centred relationships and rivalries. But Shaw's characters' concern with extra-curricular activities such as fêtes and plays harks back to the earliest prototypes established by Angela Brazil and Elinor Brent-Dyer, as does the focus on the new girl and, as Alison Lindsay puts it, "the theme of redemption or of making good after an unfortunate start [which] underlies many of the endings".[1]

Jane Shaw could emphatically not be described as a social realist: her world is a cosy middle-class one, and she resisted almost all efforts to introduce the new cultural manifestations and critical demands of the 1960s into her writing (the juvenile delinquents in *No Trouble for Susan*, 1962, are a rare exception, and they are rather tame). She does not focus on boy-girl relationships the way Mabel Esther Allan and Viola Bayley do, though Alison (in *Anything Can Happen*, 1964) is permitted a boyfriend, and Clare in the sequel (*Nothing Happened After All*, 1965) actually gets engaged. But Susan and Co stay resolutely girlish till the end. I wonder if it was because she was unwilling to move with the times that Shaw ceased to publish in 1969.

SENSE OF PLACE

The second feature Shaw's stories share with other works of her time is the importance of location. Travel stories dominated the children's market in postwar Britain: both the overtly didactic, like the Young Traveller or Kennedys Abroad series, and the adventure story set in a foreign location, such as the Shirley Flight Air Hostess series or Dorothy Clewes's novels. Shaw set her stories in places she knew and loved: her native Scotland; Dulwich Village in south-east London; and later South Africa where she lived; Cornwall, Brittany and other holiday destinations. Perhaps surprisingly, Kent is the most popular setting of all, but even this is the Kent of romance: village life, orchards, country houses, archaeological sites and endless summer days (though there is a good deal of rain in *New House at Northmead*). The setting is always integral to her plots, and is used in a way very characteristic of writing for children at this time: part local colour, part instruction, and part wish-fulfilment. Reading accounts of time spent in Scotland, Paris, Venice or Switzerland made the young reader long to do the same. Years later, of course, we did, travelling as adults with children's novels in our luggage, seeking out the sites which so attracted us when we were young. As I write this, I am sitting in a Paris hotel room with a copy of *Looking After Thomas* beside me, wondering what it was about Shaw's books (and also those of other authors whose work shares this sense of place, such as Viola Bayley, Elinor M. Brent-Dyer, Elsie J. Oxenham, and Dorita Fairlie Bruce) which inspired me and stayed with me, when so many other worthy tales of travel that I read as a child did not.

The answer lies, I think, partly in Shaw's choice of

location, and partly in her ability to convey not only what she loved about it, but also what she thought would appeal to children. With the exception of South Africa, she wrote about places that many other authors were writing about at the time. Scotland, France and Switzerland were places of history and romance, as well as (to the English, and to colonials like myself) quaint customs or foreign ways, but they were nevertheless familiar; they were imaginatively, and increasingly in reality, accessible to child readers. When Shaw was writing, stories set in Scotland were quite popular (for example, Sheila Stuart's exactly contemporary Alison series), and France and Switzerland were probably the most common 'abroad' settings for British children's books of the period. Apart from Brent-Dyer's Chalet School series, whose latter half was not coincidentally set in the same part of Switzerland as that depicted in Jane Shaw's novels (the Bernese Oberland has been associated with the British since the mid-nineteenth century), girls' annuals regularly depicted a skiing or skating scene on their covers in the 1950s, illustrating an appropriately Alpine tale within. (In the 1960s, the covers showed air hostesses and the stories ranged further afield — as did Shaw's novels.)

At the same time tourism, a minority activity before the second world war, expanded to enable those British children whose families could afford it actually to go abroad with their parents or a school party. Of European destinations, France and Switzerland were once again the most popular: France was just across the Channel; and as mountain walking and skiing increased in popularity, the Bernese Oberland continued to be the obvious place for Britons to go until new resorts developed in later decades in other parts of Europe.

That is why Shaw's Swiss stories, based on her honeymoon stay in the 1930s, continued to have relevance in the 1960s.

In her descriptions of foreign settings, Jane Shaw managed to meet the critics' requirements for more realism and a more educational approach to children's literature, while maintaining the level of entertainment that children had come to expect from their now despised (by the critics, that is!) school stories. Local colour is particularly evident in the Breton tales (*Breton Holiday*, 1939, *The Moochers Abroad*, 1951, *Twopence Coloured*, 1954, and *Susan's Kind Heart*, 1965); and Shaw lets her readers learn with her characters how other people live, and how interesting (and occasionally challenging, or even frightening) different cultural experiences can be. In later books, instruction never lies far beneath the surface: here is the narrator of *Looking After Thomas* (1957), David, on French hotel breakfasts:

> It was very late when I lifted the telephone next morning and ordered two *cafés complets s'il vous plait*. That's what you say when you want breakfast for two, and for that you get coffee (sometimes we ordered chocolate, scrumptious!) fresh rolls, butter, jam and *croissants*, which are a cross between rolls and pastry (p.30).

This is precisely the sort of information which the envious child reader stores away for future use, to dazzle her teacher in the French class, or to produce when she finally gets to visit the place in the book — as assuredly she will! It's a technique used by many other children's authors, of course, but where with a writer like Brent-Dyer you can never be sure she got the details quite right, Shaw's books seem to me to be an accurate guide to bourgeois manners in her chosen society.

At its best, the sense of place arises out of the dialogue and the needs of the plot (as in *Crook's Tour*, 1962). At their worst, Shaw's stories seem to me to read rather like a travelogue, with whole pages of narrative sounding as if they have been lifted from a guidebook or her own holiday diary (*Venture to South Africa*, 1960).[2] But these low patches are rare in Shaw, not nearly so common in Shaw as they are in The Young Traveller, We Go To and other earnest series of the time — not to speak of late Brent-Dyer!

HUMOUR

There remains the third characteristic: humour. Although Shaw's particular brand of humour is idiosyncratic, the actual presence of this quality in books for girls is characteristic of a trend in the period in which she began writing. Of course there have always been funny books for children, and funny episodes in otherwise serious books including many school and adventure stories. But whereas you could not really call Elinor Brent-Dyer or Dorita Fairlie Bruce humorous writers, despite the existence of many amusing scenes in their books, most people would describe Jane Shaw in this way, as they would Jessie McAlpine, Joanna Lloyd or Nancy Breary. These three writers are representative of a thread of iconoclasm which entered in the school-story genre towards the end of its ascendancy. Many people would regard it as evidence not of a decline, but its high point. As Sue Sims explains, it was only when girls' education and the girls' school story were fully established that writers could afford not to take themselves terribly seriously, and could start to laugh, with their readers, at some of the more ridiculous aspects of life.[3] By the time Jane Shaw produced her first novels, writing for girls was a respected and sophisticated activity, and she approached it with the confidence of one who is assured of a public. As the school story gave way to the holiday-adventure story, the humour was easily transferred, the 'abroad' setting providing a fertile site for amusement based in unfamiliarity and misunderstanding.

But if Shaw's humour is representative of a trend, it remains highly individual: indeed, it is probably this quality which most plainly marks out a piece of writing as hers. Shaw's humour tends to the slapstick: she juxtaposes eccentric and straight characters, the funny guy and the fall guy, the one who gets involved in ridiculous situations and the one who gets her out of them. Often the story is told from the straight character's point of view (for example, Alison in *Anything Can Happen* and *Nothing Happened After All*), a clever device, much used by greater writers, which enables the ordinary reader (who believes herself to be uninteresting) to identify with the heroine's position, including her ability to rescue the more brilliant character. Likewise, in the Penny books, the central character is depicted as shy and dull compared to her more assertive younger sister, Jill; but it's to Penny that the adventures happen, and increasingly, as the series progresses, it is Penny who brings about the successful conclusion.

But sometimes the main character, and the person who solves the mystery, is the lovable eccentric herself (Susan, of course, and Sara in the Holiday series). In some ways these stories are potentially more radical than those which reward the 'ordinary' character, since they send a message to readers that it's all right to be 'mad'; that you can be different and still beloved; even that eccentric people are the ones who succeed. For girls growing up amid the pressures of conformity to a passive, self-denying femininity, and especially for those who seek escape or freedom from social constraints in reading, such a message is a godsend.

'LIGHT' ENTERTAINMENT?

It's rare for Jane Shaw to get involved in deep feelings. Her novels are generally regarded as light entertainment, the presence of instructional elements notwithstanding, since these are generally well integrated, arising from the action and dialogue. Shaw's characters may suffer moments of crossness and irritability, but they are rarely desperately unhappy. There are no tragedies, no one dies, and the ending is always neatly happy — the treasure is found, the family fortunes are restored or, at the least, a solution is found to the problem: in *Fivepenny Mystery* (set in the Austrian Tyrol) the treasure is not found but the impoverished Graefin adopts Penny's suggestion that she convert the Schloss into a hotel.

One exception to this general rule is the ambivalent novel *Venture to South Africa* (1960), which concerns a family removal to a new country. The book centres on Jennifer, who doesn't want to go and is determined not to like it, but who gradually becomes reconciled to her new home. Clearly *Venture to South Africa* is different from most travel stories, including most of Shaw's, in that the characters are not mere tourists but seeking to become nationals of the destination country. It's one thing to view a country's cultural traits as detached outsiders, quite another to have to adapt oneself to them on a permanent basis. Moreover, this style of character study — the emphasis on Jennifer and her reactions — is unusual for Shaw, who tends to focus on story-line rather than character-development, and it is more revealing than, perhaps, she intended.

Obviously based on her own move to South Africa, the book contains the usual travel-story introduction to the setting's sights and culture. But South Africa in the time of apartheid is not a site where it is possible to suspend value judgments in the same way as one can with Paris, say, or Switzerland; or rather, the value judgments concern rather more important things than food or manners. It's quite clear that Shaw had difficulty accepting the social system in South Africa; her characters voice their dismay, but that's the end of the matter. There was nowhere for critique to go, not just because this was a children's book (and therefore supposedly apolitical), but also because Shaw had to live in that society, and must have felt her powerlessness to change it. In the circumstances, it was brave enough to draw her readers' attention to the injustices.

Unlike stories like *Breton Holiday* and *Bernese Holiday*, which are pure escapism and fun, and where the plot romps along at a spanking pace, *Venture to South Africa* attempts to chart Jennifer's change of heart about the country through a series of leisurely episodes in which she is exposed to its attractions. The trouble is that, despite Shaw's best efforts, Jennifer never does really settle down. "I'll go back — sometime, I'll go back [home, to Britain]," she vows in the last sentence of the book. These words negate the intended conclusion, Jennifer's successful assimilation. They seem to me to express a sadness and a longing which came straight from

Shaw's heart. I feel sure she grew to appreciate, even to love South Africa, but it never really felt like home — and she, too, eventually came back to Britain. For all its contradictions, this uncomfortable book nevertheless suggests that had Shaw concentrated more on character and less on plot, the description 'light' might not have been so appropriate for her output.

That said, I'm not sure that I, for one, would have liked the books any better. The lightness is part of the attraction for me. When you pick up a Susan novel, for example, you know that you are going to accompany Susan and her cousins upon a blundering crusade full of ridiculous situations and mildly anxious moments, to arrive at a triumphant resolution, not only for Susan and her cousins but for the people they were trying to help. The very titles of the books reflect their unthreatening nature: *Susan Interferes*, *Susan Rushes In*, *Susan Muddles Through*. So certain is the reader that all will turn out well that even quite awful situations (for instance, where Susan is left bound and gagged in an empty house in *Susan Pulls the Strings*) are stripped of their terror. The long-standing feud with the Gascoigne family, who weave in and out of the Carmichaels' lives from the moment they move next door in *Susan Rushes In*, is extraordinarily cleverly done. As children — even as adults — have we not all known people like the Gascoignes, who are good at everything, including making you feel stupid and ordinary and unsophisticated? What makes the Gascoignes' depiction so remarkable is that they never really get their come-uppance; if occasionally — very occasionally — they are worsted, or rise above themselves (as on the last page of *Susan's Trying Term*, when Gabrielle finally confesses it was not she but Tessa who wrote the school-song music), they usually they get away with murder, and always bounce back, blissfully unaware that Susan and the Carmichaels really hate them. The characters may be broadly drawn, as are the actual incidents, but the resolution or, rather, lack of resolution, is most unusual in children's literature. In a Chalet book, for example, Gabrielle Gascoigne would certainly have been brought into line, to become a 'real Chalet girl' in the end.

THE OEUVRE

Across a writing career of thirty years (1939-69), Jane Shaw published forty-two books. These include a few books for very young readers, a re-telling of *Heidi Grows Up* and some folk tales, edited and non-fiction work. Of the rest, some 35 titles, all but six belonged to series or pairs (a book and its sequel). This partly accounts for their popularity, since we know that readers who have liked a novel about one set of characters will often want to meet them again in another.[4] Shaw also wrote a number of short stories — for years she was a mainstay of the Collins Annuals — and many of them featured characters from the series.

The six single titles comprise two early novels, *The House of the Glimmering Light* (1943) and *The Crew of the Belinda* (1945); two late ones, *Venture to South Africa* (1960), which has already been described, and *Crooks Tour* (1962); and two novellas which she published in 1967 under the name of 'Jean Bell' for Collins 'Spitfire books' series, *Paddy Turns Detective* and *The Penhallow Mystery*. These last small-format paperbacks for pre-teen children are, despite the fairly obvious mysteries, vintage Shaw in language and construction, though perhaps rather old-fashioned for the time. The thriller *House of the Glimmering Light* (1943), atmospherically set on the west coast of Scotland, was a personal favourite of Shaw's. It is very hard to find these days, but fully justifies its author's approval. *The Crew of the Belinda* (1945), a personal favourite of Alison Lindsay's, is on the other hand quite easy to get hold of. Set in a houseboat on Loch Lomond, this book has many similarities to Nancy Breary's almost exactly contemporaneous *The Snackboat Sails at Noon* (1946): the absent parent, no money, children go into business — using a boat — to survive, stumble on a mystery, and solve it — all told with much humour, well-drawn characters, and breathless action. The setting, however, has more in common with the Scottish tales of Elsie Oxenham and Dorita Fairlie Bruce.

Crooks Tour introduces the trio of Glasgow schoolgirls — Ricky, Julie and Fay — who were to appear again once only in a short story, included in the present volume. The title, a classic Shaw play on words, refers on the one hand to the school trip to the Bernese Oberland and Paris which forms the setting for the girls' adventures and on the other to Ricky's anxious determination to find a 'crook' in every situation. Inevitably, she suspects a good many innocent people and makes many embarrassing and amusing mistakes. Of course, when she meets a real crook in the last chapter, she fails to recognise the fact; in a double irony, however, through an innocent act of her friend Julie, the unlikely crook is unmasked. This is a light, undemanding novel, but absolutely typical Jane Shaw, with its wacky Scots heroines, beautifully evoked locations, episodic construction concealing careful plotting (involving the characteristic little old lady and stolen jewels), and really clever twist at the end. Published by Collins in the Children's Press imprint, *Crooks Tour* is one of the easiest Shaw titles to find, but it is worth looking for a copy with its dustwrapper, the cover picture depicting the three girls in gay summer frocks strolling towards the reader. In the first edition their skirts are full and gathered, in the second, pencil-slim. Both look exactly like a dressmaking pattern from the period.

Shaw wrote three pairs of books: the two about the Moochers (1950, 1951; as already mentioned, there was a third, now sadly lost), the two Northmead novels (1961, 1963), which are school stories; and the symmetrically-titled *Anything Can Happen* (1964, set in Paris) and *Nothing Happened After All* (1965, set in South Africa). These three pairs all have their devotees, and all are worth reading. But it is for her series that Jane Shaw is most loved; and of these, the best known are the books about Susan Lyle, partly because they constituted the longest series she wrote — eleven books in all, plus several short stories published in Collins annuals — and partly because the early volumes were widely disseminated in Children's Press editions. Those of you who know only the Susan books, however, should not imagine that all Jane Shaw's stories are in the same vein. Shaw wrote three other, shorter, series, and each one is distinctive.

SARA AND CAROLINE

Surely as well known as the Susan books are *Breton Adventure* and *Bernese Adventure*, which circulated in their thousands in Children's Press editions in my childhood and were among my own favourite reading. These books are slightly abridged versions of Shaw's first two novels, *Breton Holiday* (1939) and *Bernese Holiday* (1940), and had a sequel,

Highland Holiday (1942), which is much less commonly found. *Breton Holiday*, Shaw's first novel, lays fair claim to being her best. A gentle, episodic tale of a summer vacation in Brittany, with the barest hint of a mystery element, resolved in the last chapter, the book introduces cousins Caroline and Sara Storm, their contrasting characters emerging affectionately from the action and, especially, the dialogue. There are some genuinely funny incidents, and also some pathos. The girls interact sympathetically with the Breton community, at once foreign and not so; cultural differences are so gracefully observed that Shaw's love for the place shines through. After such a promising beginning, *Bernese Holiday* is less subtle, though as a child I preferred it, perhaps because of its Swiss setting which reminded me of the Chalet books. In *Bernese Holiday* the mystery element is much more to the fore, and maintains a gripping hold on the plot throughout the story. Vanessa's dottiness and John's masculinity are brilliantly caught, and the humour is mostly unforced.

Highland Holiday, the third of the series, never enjoyed the success of its predecessors. I can only assume it was not reprinted in such quantities because it features a German spy for a villain. This dates it as a wartime novel (which, of course, it was), and had it reappeared alongside *Breton Holiday* and *Bernese Holiday* it would have caused them to appear dated, too. As it was, I read these in the 1960s with no sense that they were old-fashioned (not, of course, that I knew anything about travel in France or Switzerland at the time). I don't think that *Highland Holiday* is as good a book as the other two because I find the characters overdrawn and some of the humour, too. Still, there are some nice touches: the Arran setting is lovingly depicted and the end of the feud between Sara and her cousin Jane is told with a (very British) reserve which is quite touching. As in *Breton Holiday*, the mystery is pushed to the background, with the foreground occupied by a series of holiday episodes; but to this familiar formula Shaw added the evolving relationship between Jane and her cousins, an unusual emotional element in her writing. If you like Dorita Fairlie Bruce's wartime novels, you will like *Highland Holiday*, whose plot has much in common with *Toby at Tibbs Cross* (though with younger heroines and, therefore, no romance), while the setting resembles those of *Dimsie Carries On* and *Nancy Plays the Tune*.

PENNY

The six Penny books were written for Nelson between 1953 and 1958. Each features a mystery in an attractive (and by now, usually familiar) setting: Arran, Brittany, and so on. There is less slapstick in these novels than in some other Shaw stories, a factor which may make them popular with readers who find the obvious humour of Susan or Sara wearing at times. The English-based stories in particular have the peaceful just-postwar atmosphere of Brent-Dyer's novels of the period, the Lorna books, for example. The focus is on the heroine's developing confidence and self-reliance in the face of ever more threatening danger. In *Fivepenny Mystery*, for example, a book noteworthy for being set in the Austrian Tyrol, with one chapter devoted to a visit to Brent-Dyer's Achensee, Penny weathers a kidnapping with astonishing equanimity. Shaw deliberately plays down the danger (often by treating it with humour), thereby enabling Penny to emerge as a sort of British Nancy

Drew. By the time we get to *Crooked Sixpence*, Penny has finally conquered her fears; her sister's mockery no longer touches her. This well-plotted mystery, involving the discovery of a Roman villa in a field near Bath, provides a satisfying end to a series many readers regard as Shaw's finest.

THOMAS

In 1957 Nelson published Shaw's *Looking After Thomas*, the first of a trio of mystery stories intended for a slightly younger readership. *Willow Green Mystery* and *The Tall Man* followed in 1958 and 1960. These are unusual for Shaw in being written in the first person, and by a boy. Though I generally dislike narratives in children's books which purport to be first-person accounts (for who knows what goes on in the mind of a child?), these are cleverly plotted, and the settings (Paris, the Kent countryside, and Lake Brienz) are well-drawn, varied, and significant in terms of the mysteries. The humour, though of the more obvious type designed, no doubt, to appeal to young people of both sexes, is nevertheless not intrusive.

SUSAN

I am sure I am not the only reader who mixes up the Susan books because I can never remember which title belongs to which story. The individual novels are, however, more distinctive than the confusingly similar titles would suggest. The series extends over three years of fictional time from the Christmas when Susan comes to live with her cousins in South London in *Susan Pulls the Strings* (1947) to the Christmas she spends with her parents there on their return from South Africa (*A Job for Susan*,

1969). The full circle suggests a kind a closure, but there is nothing else in the last novel in the series to indicate it was meant to be the last. We now know that Jane Shaw started writing the next title, which was to take Susan and Midge to the United States and Mexico.[5] These are countries known to Shaw through family connexions, which she never wrote about anywhere else; for me, as a constant visitor to those countries (and a collector of books set in them), the fact that the project was never carried through engenders a tremendous sense of loss.

In between, apart from two terms at her Kent school, Susan enjoys an Easter break on a Kent farm (*Susan's Helping Hand*), one summer of three holidays — at home with the Carmichaels (*Susan Rushes In*), in Switzerland (*Susan Interferes*) and on Arran (*Susan Muddles Through*), another Christmas at home (*No Trouble for Susan*), a summer holiday in Brittany (*Susan's Kind Heart*) and another the following year in Venice (*Where is Susan?*). It's a pity that the later books were not reprinted in such quantities as the earlier ones, as they show no decline in quality — a remarkable feat when you consider the later work of Elinor Brent-Dyer or Elsie Oxenham. Neither, I suppose, do they show much advance: Shaw's heroines act rather young for their advancing years and, as I have already noted, she certainly resisted critical pressures to introduce more social realism into her stories. Modern developments (apart from travelling by aeroplane) are all but absent from the last three novels in the series. *Susan's Kind Heart* is a throwback to *Breton Holiday* and *The Moochers Abroad*, published years before, but *Where is Susan?*'s Venetian setting is unique and the plot, though it hinges on the usual coincidences and blunders, is nevertheless very satisfying. The awful cover illustration, however, depicting Susan and Midge in Mary Quant-inspired sundress and stretch trousers respectively, more than makes up for the writing's old-fashioned feel.

THE HERITAGE

What has happened to Jane Shaw's reputation? She died in 2000, when this book was in preparation, but, even though she hadn't published anything new for three decades, her books were never out of circulation in all those years. You could find a copy of *Breton Adventure* or *Susan Interferes* on any second-hand dealer's list, in any charity shop; you still can. I read her as a child and I collected her as an adult. For me, and for other women of my generation, Jane Shaw was a household name.

But turn to the critical literature on children's books and what do we find? Apart from Alison Lindsay's articles in *Folly* and *The Encyclopaedia of Girls' School Stories*, there is no reference that I can find — *no reference at all* — to Jane Shaw's work in any historical or critical study of children's literature ever published. She isn't even mentioned in Cadogan and Craig's panoramic survey of girls' reading *You're a Brick, Angela!* (1976, 1985). So I repeat: What has happened to Jane Shaw's reputation? How can she have been so comprehensively overlooked, when her books continue to be so much in evidence?

When I embarked on this project, I really thought that I would no longer have to protest against the silencing of women's cultural heritage. As we enter the twenty-first century, you'd have thought that the importance of girls' reading was pretty well accepted by now, and that the contribution of the main writers in the field had been noted and evaluated. Clearly, however, there is much more naming and (re-)instating that needs to be done. If only because her books sold so well in their time, as evidenced by the thousands of reprints still doing the rounds, Jane Shaw deserves to be right up there with the handful of twentieth-century writers for girls who have received critical recognition so far.

But, as I hope I have demonstrated, there are many more reasons for celebrating Jane Shaw's work than this. The Susan series on its own represents a substantial achievement, the Penny stories are probably even better; but *all* her books are cleverly plotted and, most unusually for a fairly prolific author, there are no weak links. Above all, Jane Shaw's novels are illuminated by their sense of place. There are few novelists for children who could capture the physical landmarks, the people, the culture, and the thrill of exploring a new or familiar setting as well as she did. She made her readers want to go there themselves and, when we did, made us feel we knew them already.

1) Alison Lindsay, ,"Jane Shaw", in Sue Sims and Hilary Clare, *The Encyclopaedia of Girls' School Stories*, Aldershot, Ashgate, 2000, pp.295-6..
2) But Polly Whibley, who knows South Africa much better than I do, disagrees with this assessment; see her contribution to this volume.
3) Sue Sims, *Introduction* to *The Encyclopaedia of Girls' School Stories*.
4) Sue Sims, "The series factor". In Rosemary Auchmuty and Juliet Gosling eds. *The Chalet School Revisited*, Bettany Press, 1994, pp.253-81; Victor Watson, *Reading Series Fiction*, London and New York, Routledge, 2000.
5) The surviving fragment is included in this volume.

II: A GLASGOW GIRL

ALISON J. LINDSAY

Jane Shaw was born Jeanie Bell Shaw Patrick in Glasgow on 3 December 1910, the youngest child of Dr John Patrick and his wife Margaret (née Shaw). Jean, as she was known, was born into a professional, middle-class family; like his father William, John had studied medicine at Glasgow University, graduating MB, CM in 1893. John began his professional career working alongside his father as a general medical practitioner at their surgery at 18 Bridgeton Cross in Glasgow, a working-class area on the north side of the River Clyde. On their marriage on 7 September 1899, John and Margaret moved to 23 Westercraigs Street, Dennistoun, a pleasant avenue of villas off Duke Street, east of Glasgow Cathedral. Their four boys — William, John, Harry and Robert — were born here, but shortly before Jean's birth, the family moved to No 9 Newton Place, an early Victorian terrace just off Sauchiehall Street. John was now lecturing on surgical techniques to medical students in various hospitals in the north and west of Glasgow, and the move meant that he would be closer to Glasgow University.

Jean was at first taught at home by a governess, but when she was eight her parents sent her to Park School at 25 Lynedoch Street, about five minutes' walk from their home. The Park School had been founded in 1880 to provide an academic education for girls and, like Jean, many of its pupils were the daughters of Glasgow University lecturers. Park was considered one of Glasgow's leading girls' schools, and when Jean started there in 1919 there were 371 pupils on the roll. In 1926 the headmistress, Miss Margaret P Young, introduced a 'house' system, and Jean became a member of Bruce House (all the houses were named after famous Scots). In all, Jean spent nine years at Park School, and in her two final years was editor of the school magazine the *Park Chronicle*. Her 1928 editorial already reveals traces of her mature style: "How you hate the thought of starting [any unpleasant duty], and how you put it off and off — unless, of course, you are one of those brisk, purposeful characters who do not." In her final year, Jean was Vice-Captain of Bruce house and a member of the Bruce First Eleven. Jean insisted that she had not liked school very much, but she always sent the *Park Chronicle* news of later events in her life, and contributed two or three short articles to it. In 1996 Park School merged with another private Glasgow girls' school, Laurel Bank, to form Laurel Park, and left Lynedoch Street to move into Laurel Bank's premises at Lilybank Terrace near the University. Five years later, in 2001, Laurel Park was taken over by Glasgow's leading private school, Hutchesons' Grammar School, to become Hutchesons' Lilybank.

The Patrick family had long been connected with Glasgow University: as noted above, Jean's father and grandfather studied medicine there, as did two of her brothers, William and Harry. The Patricks' third son, John, studied engineering and worked on projects all over the world, while the fourth brother, Robert, became an accountant. The family's emphasis on higher education, a very Scottish trait, perhaps explains why Jean, too, was able to attend university at a time when relatively few young women had the opportunity to do so. She studied English and French in her first year and Moral Philosophy and English in her second year, before concentrating on English Literature and Language. She graduated with a Second Class Honours Degree in the summer of 1932. It may have been her university education which nursed Jean's passion for Shakespeare: references to his works appear throughout her books. While a student, Jean played golf for the university: she was secretary and treasurer of the women's golf section for the session 1930-31; and after her graduation she served as its captain for the session 1932-33.

After graduating, Jean spent a year training to be a teacher at the Maria Gray Training College in London, where her headmistress Miss Young had trained. Although she completed the course, Jean realised that she had no desire to teach. London, however, she loved, and she remained there for a year or two working for the Times Book Club, which she described as a very upmarket lending library, before joining William Collins Sons and Co Ltd, the Glasgow-based publishing firm. Jean wrote an article on publishing as a career for the *Park Chronicle* of 1937, based on her experiences there, although she owned that this had not been well received by her employers. It was at Collins that Jean started writing, encouraged by their children's editor, Jocelyn Oliver, who died in October 1993. There was a strong bond between the two: Jean inscribed his copy of her first book, *Breton Holiday*, "To Jocelyn Oliver, paragon of publishers". When he later moved from Collins to Nelson, Jean (or at least her books) accompanied him: this explains why Collins continued to publish the Susan books, but the Penny stories were published by Nelson.

On 10 May 1938, in Glasgow's Wellington Church

where her father served as a church elder, Jean married Robert Evans. Robert was three years older than Jean (he was born on 29 August 1907) and his family had lived in Burnside, once part of the Royal Burgh of Rutherglen and now a suburb of Glasgow, before moving to Dulwich. The Evans family, like the Patricks, spent their summer holidays on the island of Arran, which was to be the setting for several of Jean's books. Robert had trained as an accountant and was then living in Dulwich, where Jean moved after her marriage.

A sense of place characterises most of Jean's stories. Her first book, *Breton Holiday* (1939), which featured the Scottish cousins Sara and Caroline Storm, used as its setting the Breton village of Binic, where Jean had stayed while at university. Jean had travelled in Europe before her marriage, and she and Robert spent their honeymoon at the Hotel Schweizerheim in Schwendi, near Grindelwald, the setting for a 1940 sequel, *Bernese Holiday*. The last Sara and Caroline book was *Highland Holiday* (1942), based on memories of summer holidays in Arran during her childhood. Other holidays in Connel Ferry, on the west coast of Scotland near Oban, inspired *The House of the Glimmering Light* (1943). This and *Highland Holiday* are Jean's only spy novels, which may explain why they were not reprinted after the war.

Jean gave birth to the Evans' first child, Margaret Jane, on 9 April 1942. While pregnant with her second child, their home in Dulwich was bombed and she and Jane sought sanctuary with friends in Bath, where Ian was born on 23 June 1944. Later, Jean and her children moved to a farm in Kent, although Robert remained in London and served as a fire warden in addition to his accountancy work. The family managed to move back to their top flat at 11 College Road, Dulwich, after the war. Jean was very fond of this house, and it appears as the Carmichaels' home in the Susan books. Besides her published work, Jean was developing links with the British Broadcasting Corporation, who broadcast several of her short stories on Children's Hour. The longest of these was *Wullie*, which was broadcast over several episodes in 1949. Unfortunately no script or recording of this can be traced by the BBC. Some of these stories may have subsequently been used as the inspiration for her books: for example, *Christina's Left Handed Brownie*, sold for 5 guineas to the BBC in March 1949 and broadcast on 13 May 1950, may have been turned into *Left Handed Tumfy*. Jean had stories broadcast on the daily children's programme Listen with Mother, too, and *The Tale of Three Little Puppies* was later published in *Five Listen with Mother Tales No. 6*. When she moved to South Africa, she continued to offer material for broadcast, and had stories for younger children accepted by the South African Broadcasting Corporation and the Australian Broadcasting Commission.

In 1952, Robert Evans took up an accountancy post in Johannesburg. Jean, with their children Jane and Ian, sailed to the South African port of Cape Town on the *Warwick Castle* to join him. The journey and the settling in to a new life formed the basis for *Venture to South Africa*, the most clearly autobiographical of Jean's novels. Although not published until 1960, Jean evidently wrote it soon after their arrival, since Lutterworth paid her £90 for a manuscript entitled *Venture to Africa* in June 1953. Nothing seems to have been done towards publishing it, and in 1958 her editor Jocelyn Oliver, by now at Nelson, bought the manuscript from Lutterworth (as with most of her contracts, Jean's work was bought outright for a fixed sum — it was not until the 1960s that she began to receive some royalty payments on her later Susan books). Her old school magazine, the *Park Chronicle*, in 1954 carried Jean's *Letter from South Africa*, and it is clear from this that she admired the South African scenery. "The winter is unbelievably lovely, with hot sun during the day and unvarying blue skies, while the mornings are crisp and cold and the nights are often frosty... I think that one of the things settlers miss most is the Scottish or English countryside. You have to go a long way from Johannesburg to find tolerable scenery, for everywhere round the city stretches the vast and featureless veld. Yet people say that the veld grows on you, and I can begin to see that that is true, for the space is refreshing, and the colours are always changing under the wonderful skies, and the hills in the far distance are a deep, amazing blue." The Evans settled in Johannesburg, in a three-bedroomed bungalow at 7 Congo Road in the pretty suburb of Emmarentia. Relieved of many household cares by two live-in servants (as was common with most White South Africans at the time), Jean quickly found the ideal job selling books at the Children's Bookshop. This was housed on the ground floor of Grenville House in Rosebank, one of the northern suburbs of Johannesburg. Jean joined the bookshop just four years after it had been founded by Sylvia Klugman, and spent over twenty years there.

Fan letters were regularly forwarded to South Africa by her British publishers, and Jean was scrupulous about replying to these and sending a copy of one of her books. One or two draft replies have survived in her own papers: these give additional information about her career and show that she treated her fans' letters seriously, although she did not supply the signed photographs which many requested. In 1960, in reply to a letter from Joan Friar, Jean wrote "Chang [Susan's cat] is a real cat but unfortunately he doesn't belong to me. We have a white cat called Puff and I'd love to have a Siamese as well, but as we also have an Airedale [Biddy] and a dachshund [Mitzi] who hate cats and only just tolerate poor Puff, I'm afraid that's not possible." In the same year, she wrote to Sandra Rowsthorne "you ask how I first started writing books — well, I always meant to, ever since I was about your age, writing stories for the school magazine, but I was too lazy to start until one day, when I was working in a publishing firm (Collins, as a matter of fact) I thought, why not write a girls' book, so I wrote a book called *Breton Adventure* [the reissued title of *Breton Holiday*] and I was off!" One of Jean's most characteristic literary devices is the extended sentence: that last one has 70 words.

Jean travelled back to Europe once or twice during these South African years, but her contact with publishers was now and inevitably made mostly via letter. Perhaps it was this element of distance that prevented her books being promoted more by her publishers, in spite of her regular production of titles for both Collins and Nelson. Collins in particular evidently saw her as a good writer to keep in mind for various projects: Hugh Hastings, her editor there, commissioned her to rewrite *Heidi Grows Up* and the Uncle Remus stories about Brer Rabbit on a very limited timescale. The latter required Jean to produce 12,000 words in about ten weeks, and Mr Hastings must have been satisfied since she was later asked to produce a second volume. She enjoyed this commission very much, and her son Ian remembers Jean making frequent contact with the American

Embassy to discuss Southern dialect while she was writing it.

Her Susan books made up a popular series, and Collins were happy for Jean to produce a new story every year or two. When *Susan at School* was published in 1958, it took the characters back in time to Susan's first term at school, immediately after *Susan Pulls the Strings*. This was at Jean's suggestion, but accepted by Mr Hastings since "I can quite see that it is going to be difficult to bring Pea-Green back into the picture" (letter from Collins, 31 January 1957). Susan had made her first appearance at school a little earlier, in a short story in the 1957 *Collins' Girls' Annual*, *Susan's School Play*. Jean took her publishers' comments and criticisms seriously, and in 1960 made a number of changes to the manuscript of *Susan's Trying Term* in response to readers' reports. Mr Hastings was concerned that "your characters are caricatured to a much greater extent nowadays and that consequently they don't emerge so strongly as 'real' people and that this tendency does perhaps affect the humour of the stories to some extent" (letter from Collins, 4 February 1960). Jean responded "I do agree that the next 'Susan' book should not feature the Gascoignes. The fact of the matter is that although *Susan at School* seemed to go quite well, I don't really like writing school stories, as adventures seem to be more in my line than day-to-day school events...if you remember, I had started on a plot when you reminded me that this book should be a school story, and that seemed to me to be promising quite well (little or no Gascoignes, by the way, I'm a bit tired of them)."

Jane Shaw might have been better known today if plans for paperback publication had gone ahead. Collins were finding hardback publication increasingly expensive, and hoped that issuing some of the older Susan stories in paperback would generate interest in the new titles. In 1967 Armada had contracted to publish three Susan books in paperback (*Susan at School*, *Susan's Trying Term* and *Susan Muddles Through*). Jean heard nothing further on this for years, and it was not until she wrote to Collins in 1976 that she discovered the project had lapsed. Susan's possible appearance on television was discussed in the mid-1950s in correspondence with Pamela Brown, author of *The Swish of the Curtain* (1941) and then working at the BBC, but although she wrote favourably about the idea, nothing came of it. Jean then attempted to interest other producers, although this proved unsuccessful and indeed resulted in the loss of the unpublished manuscript of the third Moochers book, *Moochers and Prefects*, which Lutterworth had sent to West Regional TV in the 1950s. Jean had been paid £80 on delivery of the manuscript in 1951, but its disappearance prevented the publication of the book.

The Evans moved to 21 Cradock Heights, Rosebank, five minutes from the Children's Bookshop, in 1967, and Jean continued with her writing and bookshop work. This included two shorter novels for younger children, *Paddy Turns Detective* and *The Penhallow Mystery*, for Collins' new Spitfire series of small paperbacks. At the request of the publishers she used a pen name, Jean Bell, part of her real name, for these. Her parents had followed Scottish tradition by naming their first daughter after her mother's mother, Jeanie Shaw née Bell, and Jean drew on her imposing collection of surnames for her two pen names. In 1969 Jean was one of the guests of honour at a lunch hosted by the South African PEN Centre (Poets, Essayists, Novelists). In the following year the *Johannesburg*

Star carried an interview in which Jean admitted that she needed a deadline hanging over her to force her to work: "If you knew the schemes I devise to avoid getting started...like cleaning cupboards, which is always a sign in our home that I should be working." A *Sunday Times* review of *A Job for Susan* by the unidentified "MMW" on 14 June 1970 observed: "As a writer of teenage fiction, indeed, this author outclasses most of her contemporaries in this field." It is all the more strange, therefore, that her books received almost no contemporary recognition, a theme expanded on by Rosemary Auchmuty elsewhere in this volume.

As the political troubles in South Africa grew, friends and family in Scotland became concerned for the Evans' safety. However, it was not until 1978, and Robert's retirement, that Jean and her husband left South Africa, and moved back to Scotland to renew their acquaintance with friends from their Glasgow and Arran days. They bought a bungalow at Balmichael, in Arran's Shiskine valley. At Robert's request the builder reversed the plans so that the sitting room looked north up the valley towards Goatfell, which they knew so well from their childhood stays. Robert died very suddenly in 1987, and Jean carried on living by herself at Balmichael, absorbed in reading (including her lifelong favourite Jane Austen as well as vast quantities of detective stories) and needlepoint. Family and friends kept in close touch, and Jean especially enjoyed the visits of her children Jane and Ian, and the latter's daughter Kim, her only grandchild. After a very short illness, Jean died in her sleep on 19 November 2000; she and Robert now lie buried beside each other in the little cemetery at Shiskine on Arran.

III: BUILDERS OF BOOKS

JANE SHAW WRITING AS JEAN B. S. PATRICK

Perhaps it is inevitable that publishing, one of the most delightful careers in the world, should be also one of the most difficult in which to get a start. For there is no specific training and clearly defined procedure in it as in medicine or teaching: a publisher will scorn an unknown applicant (very politely, of course, for they are a charming body of men, but very firmly) if you have no experience, yet the only real training for publishing is publishing – a fine little vicious circle. Never, by any chance, do you see a publishing job advertised, for the sad truth is, most people get into a publishing house because they "know a man", and the acquaintance of someone already established who can introduce you is unfortunately worth more than all the MAs and B Litts ever conferred.

The only alternative to influence is nagging: circularise the publishers: call on them: pester and harry them. If you manage to convince one that you will be useful he may agree to send you a manuscript to read; that is a great step and the rest is then up to you. But experience of some kind is essential: it is no manner of use going to a publisher with nothing but a "love of books" and editorship of the school magazine as your qualifications. Knowledge of the retail trade is always an advantage, in fact, being in the book trade in any capacity is more than useful; apart from the experience itself, it puts you in the way of those so-helpful introductions.

There is one other possible mode of entry into the charmed circle, namely, through a secretarial course, the only trouble being, if you prove in any way efficient as a secretary, your chief will grudge you to the publishing side proper. But whatever your method, the great thing is, get in. Never refuse any job in a publisher's office on the grounds that it is not just what you want: once inside, you can start to pick and choose, and find the work to suit you.

And what tremendous fun that work is! In this rather depressing modern atmosphere, when most people you meet or work with fairly hate their jobs, it is an absolute joy to find some who really enjoy their daily toil, which most publishers, and their minions, do. Because publishing is creative, important, varied, and offers great scope, particularly nowadays when the demand is so tremendous, and facilities for producing really beautiful books to satisfy it are unlimited.

The actual work depends, naturally enough, on the particular publishing house and its particular speciality – whether fiction, children's books, biography, educational books, and so on. In a large firm, too, the work will be divided into editorial, production (that again sub-divided according to the class of book), the complicated negotiations and agreements between author and publisher, publicity, royalties, and all the routine work involved in the financial side,

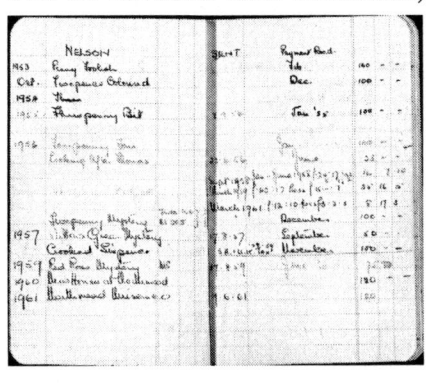

Notebook recording JS's sales

and other departments.

Editorial is probably the line towards which the literary will gravitate, perhaps because of the idea that it will be so nice to sit reading manuscripts all day; but that is by no means all fun, for although there is some prodigious rubbish published, it is absolutely nothing to the rubbish that is mercifully sent home again.

When a manuscript has been accepted, it is your job in editorial to prepare it for press – tidy up the punctuation for example, restore order out of the chaos of the author's spelling, or, if it chance to be a children's book, remove anything that any single grown-up could possibly take exception to. Later, when the material has been set, proofs will come back for you to correct – and the third or fourth time of reading is not just so enthralling. Perhaps, if the house does educational books, you may help to prepare readers, and writing poems in words of one syllable can be so difficult, particularly straight after doing an encyclopaedia!

Editorial is only to be equalled in variety and interest by production, which is perhaps more thrilling, but is certainly more nerve-wracking, for although you can edit most beautifully, the newcomer meets countless snags in production. Imagine the anguish if you have ordered paper (a horrid business, by the way, involving the most shocking calculations, and the most obscure formulae) for a whole printing, only to discover, when you put the book on to print, you have ordered the wrong size. It seems to your inflamed and terrified imagination that you have wasted thousands of pounds of the firm's money; but fortunately such dramas don't happen often.

The whole process, actually making the book, is exciting – deciding the format; choosing cloth, perhaps, for the case and designs to be stamped on it; having the dust-jacket designed and blocks made for reproduction; commissioning artists to illustrate the book and worrying the life out of them to have the drawings done on time. And then more work on the jacket – to "paste it up" as it will appear when finished, with advertisements arranged and "blurbs" written. Next the text must be made up in imitation of its finished form, and the illustrations too – and the whole thing sent, with much relief, to the printers and binders. And if your firm does its own, your troubles are only beginning, for the printers and binders and casers and packers will keep running to you with queries you will certainly not be able to answer.

But somehow or other, the book is ready for its publication date, and seeing the lovely thing, which you have helped to make, complete, is a thrill not so easy to find in other jobs.

IV: DEDICATIONS AND CONNECTIONS: GLIMPSES INTO THE PERSONAL CONTEXT OF JANE SHAW'S BOOKS

IAN M. EVANS

"It's a pity you're not having the cold cure theme, because there's your happy ending—"
"Oh, that's all right," Sara assured her. "I have my ending: it's the beginning I'm worrying about. As a matter of fact," she added rather coyly, and stopped.
"Yes?" said Jane.
"Would you mind, I mean, may I—oh well, can I dedicate my thriller to you along with Caroline?" Jane blushed. "Sara," she said, "I'd be honoured—"
(p. 256, *Highland Holiday*, Collins, 1942)

My mother, Jane Shaw, dedicated her first book, *Breton Holiday*, to her parents MWP and JP, who had made possible her first overseas excursion, to the Brittany coast of France. Her mother was Margaret Wilson Patrick, maiden name Shaw—the origin of the pen name. Once, so the family story went, when Margaret was asked about her children she replied proudly: "Yes, I've got four sons." When *Breton Holiday* was published, her father, John Patrick (born 1869), had recently retired as a surgeon at the Glasgow Royal Infirmary. In his obituary in the *Glasgow Medical Journal* (July, 1944, Vol. XXIV, No.1), it states "He was never quite happy far from his many interests in Glasgow, but when he did go away, Arran was his favourite choice when on holiday" (p14). There is much evidence that John Patrick doted on his only daughter, and must have been delighted with her writing accomplishments although he lived to see only a few of them: he died just 10 days after Jean gave birth to me in 1944. For unknown reasons, when this novel was re-issued as *Breton Adventure*, the dedication to Jean's mother and father was not reprinted.

Her first book had been written while Jean was working for Collins, a publishing house in London: "one day I decided to have a bash" (newspaper interview with Jean Evans, *Johannesburg Star*, 1970). One of the editors at Collins, Jocelyn T Oliver, greatly encouraged her, and her third book, *Highland Holiday*, was thus dedicated to Nancy Oliver (NO) and Jocelyn (JTO), nicknamed Ollie. Jean and Ollie had a close relationship and even in his business letters he always addressed her as "Dear Wee Jean". The correspondence, although light-hearted and bantering, is amazingly blunt and harsh at times. He was a conscientious editor and made detailed suggestions, such as requiring the spelling "Ugh" in earlier works to be changed to "Och" as a common Scotish expression roughly equivalent to "Oh!". He also wrote once, "I am pleased to see that I am now immortalised as Mr. Parfit". This character is a true curmudgeon in *Crooked Sixpence*, being described as "a gaunt old man with a close beard and savage eyebrows" (p59).

In 1938 Jean Patrick married Robert Caldow Evans (Caldow being his mother's maiden name), a company secretary (accountant) she had known most of her life, as the Evans family also holidayed annually in Blackwaterfoot on the Isle of Arran. When his parents moved from Glasgow to London, Robert, as the youngest child, moved with them and started working for his father's shirt manufacturing company, adding the name "Fleming" to avoid being taken as Welsh! So the dedication in *Bernese Holiday* uses his full initials: R. C. F. E.

The events and scenes depicted in *Bernese Holiday* were drawn extensively from a car trip to Germany and Switzerland that Jean had undertaken a few years earlier. Quite daringly for the time, she went with Robert, her fiancé; John Patrick, her brother; and a university friend, Joyce Moffett. From this time on the dedications can be seen sometimes to relate to people associated with the setting of the story, and sometimes to an important relationship. In the latter category, her fourth book, *House of the Glimmering Light*, is dedicated to two of her closest and lifelong friends (and bridesmaids at her wedding): Jane Gibson (JBYG) and Nancy ("Agnes") McCutcheon (NBMcC). Nancy McCutcheon — or Ag, as she was known to us — had a sharp sense of humour and a strong personality. She was an English teacher, and became deputy headmistress of Craigholme Girls' School in Glasgow. She retired to the Isle of Arran, and it was she who convinced Jean and Robert they too should settle in Arran upon leaving South Africa, a decision that gave them both wonderfully happy years in Shiskine. After Robert died in 1987, Jean and Ag spent much time together, regularly meeting with their other old friends to have lunch and a few drinks at Duncan's Bar in Brodick.

Jane Aitken (the large Aitken family had also holidayed in Arran, and again all of these individuals knew each other as children) had married a doctor, Bert Gibson, and moved to Bath, establishing another long association with that city, which Jean always loved for its connections with her favourite author, Jane Austen. Because of the V1 air raids and some bomb damage to their house in

Dulwich, Jean went to stay with the Gibsons in Bath to deliver me, her second child. As an indicator of her closeness to the Gibson family, Jane Shaw gave her first dedication to any child (after her own daughter) to Jane Gibson's daughter Christine (*The Moochers Abroad*, 1951). Christine, now Claydon, is married to a vicar, actively involved in the church, and has herself published books of prayer.

Although Jane Shaw obviously enjoyed the idea of a dedication, not every book has one (*The Crew of the Belinda*, for instance). There are hints in the correspondence with her publishers that cheaper editions, or limited production methods due to the impact of the war, played a role in these omissions. In a letter to Hugh Hastings, children's book editor at Collins after Ollie moved to Nelson publishing company, she complained that her dedication (we don't know to whom) had been left out of *Susan's Helping Hand*, and worried that perhaps they were going to omit it from *Susan Rushes In* as well. She wondered if this was due to the low cost of the series — both books sold for only two shillings and sixpence. In fact, however, the dedication to "Joan Lucy Wilmoth, who used to live in Tollgate Road" did appear in *Susan Rushes In* (1956).

Joan Lucy Wilmoth is an accomplished artist whom Jean met in Dulwich ("Wichwood Village"). They became good friends, and although the Wilmoths moved to the Midlands, they remained in close touch. Not long ago Joan visited Jean in Arran and produced a number of quick watercolours that really captured the light and mood of the Arran hills as seen from her little house in Shiskine. Joan's daughter Caroline was Jean's goddaughter, and *Susan's Trying Term* was dedicated to Caroline in 1961.

Jane Shaw's own daughter Jane (full name

Margaret Jane Patrick Evans) received the dedication to *The Moochers* in 1950 at the age of eight. Always known in the family as "Paddy" (a name that crops up in later Jane Shaw writing), Jane retired from the BBC reference library and now contributes to research on properties held by the National Trust. This is the first dedication when someone's full name was used rather than initials. I see the use of initials as being a more modest, private kind of connection to the person: "you'll know who you are". Jane is the first child to get a dedication and the first more confident use of a full name.

In 1950 and 1951 the Evans family went on holiday to France and Switzerland respectively, a change from our usual annual holiday to the pebbly beaches of Cornwall. We were accompanied by one of Jean and Robert's friends: Katherine McGowan, an old pal from Glasgow. The French holiday was to Binic on the Côtes-du-Nord. *Twopence Coloured* is set in Binic (given the name "Kerdic") and dedicated to "Katherine, remembering Binic". Kath also visited us in South Africa, and when in 1955 Jean made an extensive return trip to the UK and the Continent, revisiting their many old haunts in Brittany and the Bernese Oberland, she was accompanied by Kath and a friend of hers, Mary Hill Jack. Mary and Kath have a dedication in *Susan Interferes* (1957).

That Kath McGowan should have had two dedications is very fitting. She was an enthusiastic and observant traveller. Small events delighted her and Continental customs and phrases would give such pleasure that they would be repeated in our family for years. Much of the richness of observation and verisimilitude of the settings, particularly in France and Switzerland, is due to Jean and her friend Kath sharing experiences and memories, although my father Robert also enjoyed observing the little peculiarities one noticed, especially when foreign travel was still such a novelty. And in those early post-war years there were many complications involving currency exchange, excise duty (hence the frequent smuggling themes in Jane Shaw!), and language barriers, few of which exist today.

Moving to South Africa involved travel of a different and more stressful kind. In the upheaval and her reluctance to leave Britain, it is not surprising that Jane Shaw would have set the first Penny story in the intimate comfort of the Isle of Arran, and dedicated it to the equally comforting Murchie family (*Penny Foolish*, 1953). It was to the Murchies' farm, High Feorline, that the Patrick family relocated summer after summer. Many years later, when Jean and Robert retired to Arran, Bessie Murchie's champion baking provided wonderful treats, and her daughter Nan would never fail to look in on Jean. The third generation Murchies, brothers Charlie and Jack, are still farming in the windy valley, which Jean constantly liked to remind us is the meaning of "Shiskine".

After the first Penny book, the pattern of dedications for that series relates to another set of associations. In Dulwich, Jean's greatest friend was Clare Fisher, whose daughter Rosemary was born the same time as Jane, with son John coming a few years later. Clare, who still lives in the Dulwich area, was very knowledgeable about antiques, so she and Jean would prowl the London antique shops together. On one occasion they bought a George III penny and twopenny piece, dated 1797 — both huge heavy bronze coins, with the sort of chunky feel to them that Jean loved. She gave them to her son Ian, which, together with the Roman Britain coin issued by HADRIANUS (*Crooked Sixpence*), began my interest in collecting old British coins, and readers will know that this was what Penny did too. In Bath, Claire and Jean found the pewter tobacco jar mentioned in *Threepenny Bit*, and gave that to me as well (although being just seven, I used it for pencils only). This latter book was appropriately, therefore, dedicated to Rosemary (Fisher, now Bagley) and Ian "who were born in Bath". And John Fisher received a dedication in *Fourpenny Fair* (1956).

While living in Dulwich, and the mother of two young children, Jean had the luxury of help from Mrs Doris Nicholson. Known to us as "Nicky", there was an enduring attachment, and in later years Nicky and her second husband Jack Cheall often visited Robert and Jean and stayed in their house on Arran. When talking to her on the phone after giving the news of Jean's death, Nicky commented to me that Jean had been "like a sister" to her. She considered having *Susan Muddles Through* dedicated to her to be a great honour, and as it was published in 1960, eight years after Jean left London, the dedication reflects the close bond.

From 1958 onwards the pattern of dedications shifts again, this time to South African connections, the first being for sisters Sandra and Gail Tyrrell (*Susan at School*). The Tyrrells had become bosom family friends, a relationship originally based on the friendship between Sandra and Jane, who went to school together in Johannesburg. The Tyrrell parents, Alec (Uncle Alec in *Venture to South Africa*) and Betty, were fairly typical of the English-speaking, Anglophile, middle-class Johannesburg families the Evanses started to meet and associate with. Alec was a wonderful raconteur, banjo player, and amateur military historian. We went on holidays with the Tyrrells to the Natal north coast, the Kruger National Park, and other parts of South Africa that the Evanses began to explore. Sandra and her parents have all since died, but Gail continues to live in Johannesburg.

One of the major elements of Jean's new life in South Africa was her work at the Children's Bookshop, located in Rosebank in Johannesburg's exclusive northern suburbs. Among the first specialised bookshops for children in the world, the "CBS" was a thriving business founded by Sylvia Klugman. Jean respected Sylvia greatly for her business acumen, but believed that she did not actually have a great feel for children's literature. Instead Sylvia hired staff who were extremely knowledgeable, such as her sister Flora Cohen, and employee Norah Hampton, formerly a children's librarian, whose family owned the farm in Rustenburg mentioned in *Venture to South Africa*. These work colleagues became a circle of loyal friends, and the staff collectively received a dedication in 1962 (*No Trouble for Susan*). Of course, hiring Jane Shaw, children's author, also benefited the success of the shop, but Sylvia Klugman was most generous and supported Jean's travel to visit her daughter Jane, working in New York, and her brother and sister-in-law John and Nina Patrick, who were living in Italy. The dedication to Sylvia in *Where is Susan?* reads: "who made it possible." As a measure of her closeness to the Klugmans, Jean dedicated *Fivepenny Mystery* (1958) to Sylvia's daughter Susan, and *Venture to South Africa* to her son Jonathan.

Working full-time at the CBS meant that Jean did all her writing in the evenings and some weekends. She never retreated to a study, just sat in the living room with a few pencils and a lined writing tablet on her knee, eventually typing the final manuscript on a flimsy portable on the dining room table. About the time I started high school (St. John's College) in 1957, I was beginning to take a greater interest in her books while they were being written and Jane and I would sometimes get to read the initial drafts and occasionally be asked for comment. In 1958 *Crooked Sixpence* was dedicated to me: "W. I. M. E." There is a small family joke in this set of initials, since my actual first names (after my grandfather and uncle) are William, John, Martin. Being Scots, however, my parents simply used Ian as a substitute for John, and, they claimed, to avoid confusion with John Fisher in the early days in Dulwich. My school calendar, therefore, usually listed me as W. I. M. E., and my nickname at school became Wymie, sometimes with the added schoolboy embellishment that I thought quite unjust, of Slimy.

My various school friends, who like me loved camping, the game reserves, wildlife, and South African history and cultures, gave my parents endless amusement and I was always slightly shocked to discover these boys referred to in the stories: Bush-pig (*Nothing Happened After All*) was the nickname of my closest friend Martin Bennett; the twins were my other good friends the Pettifor twins, David and John (who went with us on trips to what were then the Rhodesias); and the "orphan" Sid (*Crooked Sixpence*) was based on one of my school mates Johnny Orpen, whose hyperactivity when visiting our house for parties totally amazed my parents. Although there is little hint of any romantic relationships in Jane Shaw's books, boys become more central as characters rather than just younger brothers about this same era.

Two remaining dedications are worth explaining. One is to a young girl Sally Thom (*Nothing

Happened After All). The Thom family were ex-pat Scots, quite a bit younger than my parents, whom they came to know well because Mr Thom had started a plastics factory in Johannesburg, where Robert worked for some years as company secretary. My father, who was totally scrupulous in all financial matters, disagreed with the management over some business practices and was fired as a result. There was such a significant falling out with the Thom family that we never had any further contact with them, which is very different from all the other people receiving dedications.

One final dedication, however, is something of a mystery as it is to someone whom we know very little about. *Susan's Kind Heart* (1965) is dedicated to Marilyn Scott. Neither my sister nor I, who were no longer living at home by then, can remember who this was, nor any family by that name. However, by scouring through Jean's Christmas card and gift list (for a relatively disorganised person she kept meticulous lists, including notes on her foreign travels), we discovered that Marilyn was given a book in 1959 (not a Jane Shaw, but the *Tall Book of Make Believe*), and the Uncle Remus book in 1960. In 1961 Marilyn got *Susan's Trying Term* and *New House at Northmead for Christmas*, and seven additional Jane Shaw's in subsequent years. By 1966 she only got a bookmark (presumably being close to about 17 by then) and by 1969 she no longer appears on the list at all. We then vaguely remembered that Jean knew a family of this name employed at a rest home called Randjeslaagte, and Marilyn was presumably their daughter. Given that she had received a total of ten Jane Shaw works, we hope that she was indeed a fan.

Even though living in South Africa, so long as her own children were still young adolescents Jane

Shaw did have access to teenage jargon and ideas. But by the time we went off to university it was extremely hard for her to keep pace with young people's rapidly changing vernacular, values and attitudes, especially those of British children. Her ear became better attuned to South African children's slang, with its occasional mixture of Afrikaans and African words. Her plots, which are of course pure fantasy, were drawn from real stories, culled from overseas news reports in South African papers. All of Jean's old scrapbooks and files have clipped newspaper stories relating to daring jewellery heists, lost masterpieces turning up in surprising places, treasure troves unearthed in some home county field, and those actual events gave a slight measure of the plausibility to the themes of unexpected discovery that Jane Shaw enjoyed so much.

The South African settings themselves are as authentic as those of Europe and Britain, since, with their enjoyment of adventure, Jean and Robert travelled quite boldly by an ancient and frequently breaking-down Peugeot 403 to places such as the Victoria Falls, Wanki Game Reserve in Rhodesia, and Gorongoza Game Reserve in then Portuguese East Africa. They also enjoyed the Drakensberg mountains in Natal, Loch Vaal, the Kruger National Park, and other places mentioned in her books. And though the political discussions (who could write even a children's story set in South Africa without some mention of apartheid and race relations?) now seem somewhat naïve, they nevertheless represent a certain openness to important issues facing South African society in all its diversity. The Klugmans and others at the Children's Bookshop, for example, were probably the first Jewish families with whom the Evans became really close friends, and in many ways South Africa, while so isolating from the peaceful British settings of the Highlands, the Cotswolds, or Cornwall, allowed Jean's social and cultural horizons to be considerably expanded.

With so much of her writings drawn from direct observation, there were very many people — family members, friends, and members of her various communities — who shaped Jane Shaw and her works. Although only briefly mentioned here, my father Robert's wit and quiet enthusiasm provided constant encouragement, not to mention his whipping up batches of Russian toffee — yes, the recipe in *Fourpenny Fair* really works. There were numerous chance factors determining who in this wide and caring network happened to receive a dedication, although some clearly had earned the privilege through their special contribution to the theme or setting of the book. Mostly their importance was a function of the significance of these individuals at that particular time of her life. In this brief survey I have provided a glimpse of the context for each of the individuals appearing in dedications. But it is not a biography of influences, as there were many other important and valued friends and beloved relatives who enhanced her life: in particular her readers and those, like Alison Lindsay and all in the present volume, who have continued to express appreciation of her work. To you, this essay is dedicated.

V: FIFI AND THE FISH: SUSAN IN SWEDEN

EVA LÖFGREN

Susan's adventures never brought her to Sweden, but most of the books about her came here in translation. I first found the Swedish edition of *Susan at School* when I was looking for girls' boarding school stories, and what caught my eyes was not the rather uninteresting title, *Farligt fiffel, Fifi!*, but the cover with three girls in what a Swedish reader — or publisher — might take for an English school uniform. I was disappointed that only one more book in the series is a school story, and so didn't start collecting the non-school stories until many years later.

The first eight Susan books were translated into Swedish between 1965 and 1972. They were published by B. Wahlström, well known publishers of popular books for children and young people since 1914, including many famous series like Nancy Drew and Biggles, many of Enid Blyton's books, and more recently Sweet Valley High. As they were translated by four different people, styles of writing differ slightly in different titles.

There are two mysteries about the Susan books in Swedish; the titles and the name of the heroine, together making the books appear even more comical than the English originals. Susan is an ordinary name and the nickname, Susie, often used by her friends, is not any more humorous, but the Swedish nickname, 'Fifi', is certainly meant to be funny. The publishers, B. Wahlström, are known for their various series of books identified by the name of the principal character, but they were already publishing a 'Susan' series by Judith M. Berrisford, which, confusingly, were 'Jackie' books in the original. And the English short form might perhaps have been confused with the 'Susy' series from another publisher. But why Fifi? Originally it was a short form for either Sofia or Josefina but it is now a funny and endearing nickname in general — sometimes even used for dogs. But it may also be related to the colloquial adjective 'fiffig', meaning 'clever' or 'ingenious'. A hypothetical explanation might be found in the construction of the titles; once somebody had settled on the 'F' titles, they had to include a name beginning with 'F' — although Susan remains her real name even in the Swedish translations.

The 'Fifi' titles follow the pattern set by several original Swedish series of humorous books for children published by B. Wahlström in the 1960s and 70s, with the same kind of catchy, almost proverbial, titles often addressing the protagonist, though none of them are as consistent as the 'Fifi' books, with their alliterative titles largely consisting of words beginning with 'F'.

The title of the first book, *Fina fisken, Fifi!*, may have been inspired by Bill's words about the fish used to lure Chang, the cat, out of the empty house. This expression 'fina fisken!' literally means 'fine fish', but may be translated just 'Fine!'. This first title sets the pattern. The fish reappear when *Susan Middles Through* is translated as *Fula fiskar, Fifi!*, literally 'ugly fish', but in this case rather 'ugly customers', alluding to the villains of the book, in which fishing plays some part. The real names of the characters remain unchanged, but a few more nicknames were translated. 'Midge' becomes

'Myggan' (same meaning); 'Peagreen' is 'Grinus' ('whiner'), a good short form for Peregrine and one better suiting his character, in my opinion. 'Dotty' (Miss Johnson) is 'Tokan' (same meaning again) in *Farligt fiffel, Fifi!*, but 'Dotty' in *Fiffigt, Fifi!*.

I have only two of the Susan books in English, *Susan at School* and *Susan's Trying Term*, so here is only a short comparison between *Susan at School* and its Swedish version, *Farligt fiffel, Fifi!*, which is still my favourite of the series. The translation, by Gunvor Håkansson, is more or less faithful, but slightly abridged, probably not more than approximately 10 percent. Most of the cuts have little impact on the plot; but there are a few longer passages omitted, especially in the middle of the book, like parts of the plot about Miss Johnson's car. The most deplorable cut is perhaps in the episode when Susan helps Diana to dress up as an outer space monster and then leaves her behind upstairs. The absence of Diana's lonely musings, gives a slightly different impression of those two characters in the Swedish version. The special features of a British boarding school — prefects, houses etc. — are explained quite clearly for a foreign reader, without major adaptations of the text. But it is a minor mystery why the translator insists in rendering the new Hall as 'gymnastiksal' ('gymnasium'), as most Swedish secondary schools by that time had separate assembly halls and gymnasiums.

All the Swedish covers were illustrated by Heidi Lindgren, one of the most prolific artists of the period for covers and illustrations of children's books. Like almost all Swedish juvenile books until the last two decades, they have fronts and backs in cardboard and only the spines in cloth — red cloth for Wahlström's girls books. There are no dust wrappers or inside illustrations, but the covers are illustrated in full colour, with lists of other books from the same publisher on the backs. As the Swedish editions are printed on thinner paper with smaller print, they are much slimmer than the English originals, even considering the cuts. *Farligt fiffel, Fifi!*, with its 141 pages, is less than half the thickness of the original *Susan at School* with 192 pages.

Heidi Lindgren must have seen and been inspired by some of the original dust wrappers, as she chose the same episodes for at least two of her covers, but in a more expressive and less realistic style. She more or less copied Miss Johnson's old car for the cover of *Farligt fiffel, Fifi!*, although turned in the opposite direction, and with the characters dressed differently. Dotty herself stands behind the car, dressed in the practical tweed suit of the proverbial English spinster. The three girls in the car — presumably Susan, Midge and Tessa — wear short narrow blue dresses with sailor collars, which was a common Swedish notion of English school uniform. With its plain white background, this is one of Lindgren's most effective cover pictures, the sense of speed and movement reinforced by the hockey sticks and boots flying into the air over the heads of the characters. On the cover of *Susan's Trying Term*, the same sailor dresses are red. For *Fritt fram, Fifi!* Lindgren chose the episode with the lawn-mower, depicted on a later edition of *Susan's Helping Hand*, but once again with a greater sense of speed. Susan wears jeans and T-shirt, unlike the striped summer dress in the English picture. One humorous detail is the name of the author, Jane Shaw, on a low sign post partly hidden in a shrub in the lower right corner.

JANE SHAW TITLES PUBLISHED IN SWEDEN

Fina fisken, Fifi!, transl. Helge Åkerhielm, cover Heidi Lindgren. Stockholm: B. Wahlström, 1965. 140 p. (B. Wahlströms flickböcker; 1258) (*Susan Pulls the Strings*)

Fritt fram, Fifi!, transl. Helge Åkerhielm, cover Heidi Lindgren. Stockholm: B. Wahlström, 1966. (B. Wahlströms flickböcker; 1308) (*Susan's Helping Hand*)

Fara på färde, Fifi!, transl. Helge Åkerhielm, cover Heidi Lindgren. Stockholm: B. Wahlström, 1967. (B. Wahlströms flickböcker; 1356) (*Susan Rushes In*)

Det fixar Fifi!, transl. Helge Åkerhielm, cover Heidi Lindgren. Stockholm: B. Wahlström, 1968. (B. Wahlströms flickböcker; 1414) (*Susan Interferes*)

Farligt fiffel, Fifi!, transl. Gunvor Håkansson. Stockholm: B. Wahlström, 1969. (B. Wahlströms flickböcker) (B. Wahlströms ungdomsböcker; 1466) (*Susan at School*)

Fula fiskar, Fifi, transl. Eva Larsson, cover Heidi Lindgren. Stockholm: B. Wahlström, 1970 (B. Wahlströms flickböcker) (B. Wahlströms ungdomsböcker; 1520) (*Susan Muddles Through*)

Fiffigt, Fifi!, transl. Eva Larsson. Stockholm: B. Wahlström, 1971. (B. Wahlströms flickböcker) (B. Wahlströms ungdomsböcker; 1573) (*Susan's Trying Term*)

Full rulle, Fifi!, transl. Solveig Karlsson, cover Heidi Lindgren. Stockholm: B. Wahlström, 1972 (B. Wahlströms flickböcker) (B. Wahlströms ungdomsböcker; 1634) (*No trouble for Susan*)

The publishers are correctly written B. Wahlström, in order to differ them from another publisher Wahlström. 'B. Wahlströms flickböcker' ('girls' books') is a sub-series of 'B. Wahlströms ungdomsböcker' ('books for the young') and the numbering is common to the main series, not only to the girls' books.

VI: SUSAN'S SCHOOL PLAY

JANE SHAW

Susan and I were horrified. We couldn't believe our eyes. "Yet there it is!" I said. "In Aunt Lucy's letter! In black and white!"

"In green and white I'd say," said Susan. "Where do you imagine Aunt Lucy got that awful green ink?"

"Never mind the ink," I said. "It's what she has written that's worrying me—"

We looked again at the ominous words. *I am bringing Mrs. Gascoigne and Peregrine with me on Saturday to see your school play*, she had written.

"What can Aunt Lucy be thinking of?" I said.

"She has just gone off her head," said Susan calmly.

"That's all very well," I said. "But what about *us*? We'll be disgraced for ever if that boy comes to the school. We can't go around explaining to everyone that unfortunately our aunt has gone off her nut and brought a ghastly small boy with her to the school play!"

"Of course not. But don't worry," said Susan confidently, "I'll deal with that dreadful boy—"

These Gascoignes, I should explain, live next door to us at home, and more awkward neighbours it would be difficult to imagine. They're all simply awful and they all behave in the dottiest way, but Peregrine, whom we call Pea-green in order to relieve our feelings, is the worst. If ever a boy should have been left on a bleak hill-side to perish like the Spartans of old, he's the one. To begin with, he's allowed to do exactly as he likes in case his personality should get stunted or something, and the first time that Susan ever saw him he jumped on her from a great height dressed up in a moth-eaten old fur coat pretending to be a gorilla. Susan thought he was a gorilla and has never quite got over this and is always expecting the worst from Pea-green. She is, I may say, seldom disappointed. Oddly enough, Aunt Lucy seems to like these dreadful Gascoignes — Auny Lucy, by the way, looks after us since we have no mother; she's Susan's aunt too. Susan is our cousin, she is living with us at the moment while her people are in Africa. Oh, and I'm, Marjorie Carmichael, but I'm always called Midge. I could tell you plenty about Susan's character only she happens to be reading this over my shoulder. So I shall say that she thinks it is her mission in life to interfere in everybody's business and try to organise their lives and change things for the better. The annoying thing is that she sometimes succeeds, but she hasn't so far ever managed to change Pea-green for the better.

Under any circumstances it would have been pretty disturbing to have the Gascogines come to our school but this event that they were coming to was rather a special occasion. To put it quite bluntly we were having this play (two plays really, one house doing scenes from *A Midsummer Night's Dream* and our house doing scenes from *The Tempest*) to try and wheedle money out of the school governors for a new hall. Ours is a nice school — as far as school is ever nice — it's in Kent, in an old rambling Tudor manor-house, but we haven't a hall, we have gym and school plays and Founder's Day and so in an old barn, so that the audience sit with ropes practically round their necks and the people sitting at the side are more or less hanging on to the rib-stalls. Worse than that, there is no proper stage and for plays, the school handy-man rigs up a temporary sort of platform out of what feels like old orange-boxes, and the fear of going through them is always worse than the fear of forgetting lines so that the cast in our plays always have a slightly strained expression when they're acting. Everybody says that the chairman of the governors, a benevolent old boy called Lord Dulwich, who had a daughter at the school away back in the dark ages, would give us a hall right away but that he is restrained by the clerk to the governors who is a very disagreeable lawyer called Pennington-Smith and who says that the school can't afford any extras like building a hall. We know he's disagreeable not only because of not letting us have a hall, but also because his daughter Hermione is a prefect in our house and she's ghastly. She had the part of Ariel in our play and we all said that she only got it because of her father being clerk to the governors. We wanted a girl called Elizabeth Rogers to have the part, she really can act and she would have been marvellous as Ariel (who, in case you don't know the play, is a sort of weird fairy creature) but as it was, she was only the understudy. She was frightfully fed-up about this because she wants to go to a school of dramatic art only the old aunt with whom she lives doesn't hold with the stage and says that in any case Elizabeth can't be a very good actress or she would have been chosen for this part of Ariel. Elizabeth say it's not use explaining to *her* about Hermione's father being clerk to the governors, or even telling her the reason old Crummy (that's Miss Crumbles, who is producing the plays) gave for choosing Hermione — that Elizabeth being younger would have plenty of chances of having good parts later on, whereas it is Hermione's last year.

Susan, of course, was in a great state over this situation and had thought of various schemes for getting rid of Hermione, from pushing her downstairs to sending fake telegrams from dying grandmothers, none of which were any good at all. When Aunt Lucy's letter with the bad news came, Susan became really worked-up. "Now I'll have two of them to get rid of!" she said. "I wish I could think of something –" and she brooded on this problem constantly. It wasn't as if she had even a part to learn to keep her mind occupied, for although she was in the play she had very little to say. She was to be the goddess Juno in the masque which the old Duke, who is a sort of magician, puts on to celebrate the marriage of his daughter Miranda to Ferdinand. Susan looked the part all right, being rosy-cheeked and cheerful and healthy looking. She was supposed to be let down from the heavens in a cloud but this was beyond the resources of our orange-box stage, so instead some shimmering curtains were pulled back to reveal her seated on her cloud with a couple of cherub-like juniors playing at her feet. Charlotte, my elder sister, was Miranda, but I was only taking part in the ballet that had been pushed in to give as many people as possible something to do even if they couldn't act, for Crummy imagined that everybody was dying to get into these plays. Don't ask me why, for when you got it, it only meant rehearsing and practising for hours every day, which wasn't my idea of a nice peaceful end of term.

The day of the play dawned clear and cold with a nip of frost in the air. Susan had been hoping for snow in sufficient quantities to make the roads impassable, failing that, dense fog, but these proved vain hopes. It was as nice and clear and bright a day as the twentieth of December possibly could be. The governors and other V.I.P.s were having lunch with the Head in her house, the school had early lunch in hall, such of them as weren't too nervous to eat, and the ordinary parents began to trickle in about two o'clock. We gave Aunt Lucy an affectionate welcome which was very forgiving of us seeing how cross we were with her, greeted Pea-green's mother civilly even although she was wearing trousers, and behind their backs scowled at Pea-green who made hideous faces at us. Then he said in his high, affected voice, "I suppose you're going to be Caliban the savage and deformed slave in *The Tempest*, Susan?"

"No, of course not," said Susan, unwarily, "why should I be?"

"Because you wouldn't need to be made up at all," said Pea-green.

I led Susan away before she could think of a suitable reply to this, and we made our way backstage. Our play came on second in the programme but I couldn't stand Pea-green another minute. So you can image our horror to find that Pea-green had followed us to a little room we like to call the green-room but which is only a little place where sacks used to be kept when our hall really was a barn. Pea-green, I must admit, is a very handsome little boy with great big eyes and black curls, and a lot of the girls who should have known better began making a fuss of him and somebody even produced a bar of chocolate which is strictly forbidden and must have been smuggled in by a parent. Crummy of course would have got rid of him in two shakes of a dead lamb's tail, for she wouldn't have stood any nonsense from a nine-year-old boy, but Crummy was backstage with the cast of *A Midsummer Night's Dream*. Charlotte told him to buzz off, but supported by the fuss the others were making of him he ignored Charlotte. He got more and more above himself and began rummaging among the costumes and getting them disarranged and grabbing sticks of grease-paint and even began reciting some of Ariel's speeches — that's the kind of stuck-up little show-off he is.

"I'm going to be sick," I whispered to Susan. "Can't we get rid of him?"

Susan put her mouth right to my ear and began whispering. It tickled like anything and I couldn't hear a thing. I pushed her away and she looked over at Pea-green nervously. "Come outside," she said. "Don't want him to hear. I've got a plan —"

Susan's plan was to get hold of some cakes and stuff from the dining-room where they were all arrayed ready for the parents' tea and with these, entice Pea-green to an old shed which was right at the other end of the grounds and there lock him in until the plays were over.

I had grave doubts about this scheme. "He'll yell the place down, of course," I said.

"So what if he does?" said Susan. "No one will hear him."

"We won't be able to get the cakes," I said. "Matron will be hovering around watching them like a hawk."

"You go and get Pea-green and I'll get the cakes," said Susan confidently.

So I said all right and went back to the green-room. Pea-green was having the time of his wicked young life by then, wearing a spare nymph's tunic over his jersey and shorts, with his face made up like a cherub's, but at the promise of a feast of cakes he came with me readily enough. "We have to go where no one will see us," I told him and led him past the hockey pitches and the lacrosse pitch to the gardener's shed.

Susan meantime wasn't having nearly such an

easy job. She told me about it later and said really she didn't know how on *earth* people managed to take to a life of crime, stealing a few miserable buns was difficult enough. When she reached the door of the school dining-room she peeped cautiously in. The coast seemed clear so she slipped inside. The sandwiches, scones, cakes etc. were all in tins on the long trestle tables, waiting to be put on to plates. The simplest thing, Susan thought, would be just to grab a tin and run. But it would be unlucky if she happened to take a tin of scones, she thought, for she couldn't imagine Pea-green being persuaded into the gardener's shed with only a large tin of scones for company. She glanced round quickly and then opened a tin — sandwiches. The next one was little iced buns, which was better. The next one revealed a most heavenly cake with whipped cream in the middle and icing on the top covered with chocolate worms. (There is a proper name for that sort of stuff but we always call it chocolate worms.) That should fix him, Susan thought and just to be on the safe side went back to the first tins and tucked a few egg sandwiches and little buns into the corners round the big cake. She was just putting the lid back on when a voice said, "Well, Susan?" and there was Matron standing staring at her.

"Oh hallo, Matron," said Susan, dropping the lid with a clatter.

"Hallo," said Matron, mighty grim, Susan said. "Were you looking for something?"

Susan gave a mad sort of laugh. "Looking for something?" she said. "Oh *no*, Matron! Just looking, you know, to see what kind of a tea you were going to give us. I was too jolly nervous to eat any lunch –"

Matron grunted and began putting out cups and saucers. "Hadn't you better be getting back to the barn?" she said. "It's nearly half-past two –"

"Oh yes. Yes of course," Susan said, hopping from one foot to the other and making no move to go. "There's heaps of time actually, I'm not on till the second play and near the end of that. Couldn't I get out the cups for you while you go and have a rest or something?"

Matron looked at her sharply. Old Susie can look jolly innocent when she likes, but Matron knows all the tricks. "Susan," she said, "if you want a bun or a sandwich for goodness sake take one and stop jigging about there. You're giving me the fidgets –"

"Oh but I don't, Matron," said Susan, looking slightly offended. One cake was no use to Pea-green.

"Then please be off," said Matron.

Susan reluctantly went, in slow motion, then watched Matron through a crack in the swing-doors. She thought, she told me, that Matron was stuck there for the afternoon and would never go, when suddenly she came banging through the doors nearly knocking Susan senseless (not that that would be difficult, I told her) and hurried off. Her head still reeling from the blow, Susan darted in, grabbed the tin, moved the others a little to fill up the gap and ran.

She nearly knocked into a prefect who had her arm in plaster and couldn't be in the plays, but she reversed round the corner of the form-room block in time, only unfortunately stumbling and letting the tin fall in her haste. The cake, cream buns and sandwiches were a bit mixed up by the time she picked the tin up again but really, she thought, she didn't see that Pea-green had any cause for complaint there — he was lucky to get anything at all, she felt.

Pea-green was beginning to be slightly restive by the time Susan appeared. Rude too, but Pea-green's cheek doesn't worry me the way it does Susan. After all I have a young brother of my own. Anyway Susan eventually pitched up, looking rather red in the face and flustered. She showed the cakes and stuff to Pea-green who asked her if she had been sitting on them and graciously consented to go into the shed and eat them.

Seeing him well started on the cake (he always ate in that order, sweet things first, then plain) I said, "Well, we'll have to go now, Pea-green, sorry, Peregrine. We'll come back for you later."

"Very well," said Pea-green in his pedantic voice, his mouth all smeared with cream. So we went.

"We'll shut the door," Susan called, "Safer—". Pea-green didn't answer and we shut the door, then very, very cautiously drew the bolt. Hugging ourselves with glee we ran round the edge of the lacrosse pitch. We were in plenty of time too, because there were still girls and parents walking about. We saw Hermione Pennington-Smith and her disagreeable father in earnest conversation.

The peace of the green-room without Pea-green! The school orchestra was playing Mendelssohn's music for *A Midsummer Night's Dream* and any minute now the curtain would go up for School House's piece. It was a pity that we couldn't see it, but we had seen it at the dress rehearsal and actually we didn't think it was nearly as well done as ours. However we could hear the audience laughing, which was all to the good, and anyway the School House parents would think it was wonderful.

Then it was the interval, and the school choir singing madrigals and other Elizabethan songs, and I was feeling so sick I thought I'd die — and wished I could, really. I was sure we'd get the ballet all muddled up or one of my shoes would fly off or I'd trip over a crack in the orange boxes and fall flat on my face. I was just trying to swallow the ghastly great lump in my throat and looking at Susan and thinking what a peculiar colour she was, sort of pale green, when Crummy burst in and she was pale green too.

"Hasn't anyone seen Hermione?" she demanded.

Well we all said that we hadn't, not since the play started, and Crummy said why had no one told her and we said we had seen her ages ago, with the father, and somebody else said she had noticed that Hermoine wasn't there but that she had thought that Hermione must have had special permission to sit with her father and Crummy made furious noises and sent the back-stage helpers and the School House people, all laughing and chattering excitedly, thankful their bit was over, to look everywhere for Hermione, while we looked at each other and at Elizabeth Rogers and we all went greener than ever.

But the searchers came back empty-handed. Hermione couldn't be found.

"Then we can't wait," snapped Crummy." "Elizabeth, get into the costume –"

A message was sent to the choir to spin out the songs a bit and even sing another if they knew one, and Elizabeth was pushed into Ariel's costume, fortunately only a few wisps of green gauze, and her face made up. "Are you all right?" said Crummy, "Can you do it?"

Elizabeth nodded without speaking. She told us afterwards that if she'd opened her mouth she'd have been sick right there at Crummy's feet; but the choir had sat down amidst applause, as the saying is, and the audience had stopped whispering and rustling and shuffling their feet and the curtain was going up and Ariel was on.

Even back-stage we could sense the effect that Elizabeth had on the audience. She just wasn't like the rest of us, a schoolgirl mumbling her way through lines which we knew were beautiful but which were jolly difficult to say and to understand — she *was* Ariel, a creature of fire and spirit. Whenever she spoke in her lovely voice a stillness came over the audience. Besides, she seemed to inspire the others — Miranda, Prospero and Ferdinand acted as they had never done before.

Then at last it was the masque — rather a silly bit we all thought, with goddesses blessing Miranda and Ferdinand, but a good way to fit in a lot of girls without much to say — and of course the ballet. Well, we were on and we danced and all went well and then we tripped daintily — I hope — to one side and the moment came to reveal Juno on her cloud, and the silken curtains drew aside and revealed Juno, not simpering prettily as we expected but standing with a look of fury on her face tugging with both hands at Pea-green's black curls and muttering through her teeth, "Get off, you little fiend, get *off* —!"

The audience roared. Susan glanced up, and at the expression on her face when she saw the curtains had been drawn the audience roared again. We were all considerably shaken, I can tell you. Someone had the presence of mind to draw the gauzy curtains, and, feeling idiotic, the ballet did a few uncertain steps. We didn't know how long to go on like this and were still weaving about rather helplessly when the curtains jerked back again and Susan, looking regal, delivered her few words. As her piece couldn't have been called amusing by any stretch of imagination she must have wondered why the audience were shrieking with laughter, but she couldn't see Pea-green mopping and mowing behind her stately skirts, and the audience could.

As Susan's words were being completely drowned in laughter she suddenly remembered Crummy's instructions about pausing for laughs and prepared to step off her cloud to give the audience a chance to recover. She didn't succeed in doing that, for what she didn't know was that Pea-green was standing on her draperies. As she tried to take a step she found herself jerked back, she lost her footing and collapsed on the cloud. It had never been designed to stand Susan's full weight, it tipped up — and cloud, Pea-green and Susan disappeared backwards over the edge of the platform. Gales of laughter surged up at us from the audience.

Crummy's voice whispered urgently from the wings, "Go into the last ballet routine and then we'll drop the curtain. Last ballet routine –"

We went into the stately pavane with which the masque was to end. There should have been the bit after that where Prospero gives his fairy servant Ariel his freedom but Crummy obviously wasn't risking that. The curtain came down to an absolute thunder of applause.

"Take a curtain," Crummy muttered and we drew up in our lines as arranged. Then Pea-green, his nymph's tunic half torn off to show his shorts and grey jersey, darted on to the stage pursued by a furious Juno, holding up her draperies with one hand and reaching for Pea-green's curls with the other. At that moment the curtain went up. Pea-green disappeared into the wings, Juno gasped, hesitated, then picked up her skirts in both hands and *ran*. There was a tremendous crash off-stage, we felt the platform heaving under us, then it slowly collapsed under a jumble of legs, arms, curtains, cast, and the curtain mercifully came down...

Old Lord Dulwich was in front of the curtain addressing the audience. Crummy shushed us furiously as we crept off the collapsed platform. "...most enjoyable afternoon" the old boy was saying. "Not only did we have the charming rendering of *The Midsummer Night's Dream*, we had a really outstanding Ariel followed by a most joyful burlesque which showed us all too clearly that there is a crying need in this school for a proper hall with a proper stage —" (Loud and prolonged laughter.)

Susan whispered to me, "What's the talking about? What's a burlesque?"

"Burlesque means making a fool of something on purpose," I whispered back. "They all think we did it on purpose!"

Susan couldn't believe it. "They think I carried on like that *on purpose*?"

"Yes. Better than thinking it was all a mistake —"

"Jings!"

"Sh!"

Lord Dulwich was continuing, "...unexpected absence of my old friend, your estimable clerk to the governors, who keeps such an admirable, necessary and tight hold on the purse-strings —" (laughter) "—still I can promise you that your board of governors will help you to build a new hall where a contretemps like that which we have just seen portrayed so appropriately —" (laughter) "—cannot occur ..."

Loud sounds of cheering came from the hall and Susan said, "Does all that blah mean we're going to have a new hall?"

"Yes. The dear old man, bless him, is taking the chance to promise it to us in public while horrid Mr. Pennington-Smith isn't there to put a stop to it."

Then Susan said, "Where on earth did he and Hermione get to, not that I care?"

Elizabeth appeared at our elbows then we both slapped her on the back and I said, "Your old aunt can't stop your being an actress after this!" And Liz nodded, absolutely radiant.

Susan said, "Sorry I mucked the whole thing up and you didn't get saying all your part, Liz —"

"It didn't matter," said Elizabeth. "It was better to bring down the curtain then, but Susie, why did the platform collapse anyway?"

"Pea-green, that limbo of Satan, crawled under there to get away from me when I was chasing him — he knocked over some supports or something and the whole thing gave way —"

At that moment the limb of Satan himself tugged at my skirt. "I say," he said. "I think somebody ought to go and release the old man and the girl I locked up in the shed —"

"*You* locked up in the *shed*?" I breathed.

"Yes. When I shouted, they let me out. Then they went into see what I'd been doing so I locked them, in. They were shouting like anything when I left so I should think they'll be rather cross by this time. I think somebody ought to go and let them out —"

Susan and I looked at each other.

"Bags not me!" we both cried together.

Susan couldn't see Pea-green mopping and mowing behind her.

VII: SUSAN AND THE HOME-MADE BOMB

JANE SHAW

"Don't tell Susan!" said Charlotte in an alarmed whisper.

"Don't tell Susan what?" asked Susan, coming into the room at the wrong moment.

"Oh, just a hard-luck story," said Charlotte in an off-hand voice. "Nothing to worry about."

For Susan's most awkward trait was an insatiable desire to help people. At the first sign of trouble in the lives of any of her friends or relations, Susan was on to it like a terrier at a rat-hole. And while sometimes her efforts were highly successful, sometimes they were anything *but*, so that on the whole her cousins Charlotte, Midge and Bill Carmichael, with whom she was staying at this time, thought it best to keep Susan and the troubles of their friends as far apart as possible.

"Well, you could just tell me about it, surely?" said Susan.

Her cousins found Susan very hard to resist — that was one of the dangers. "It's Jennifer Harding," said Midge weakly, "she has just been awarded a scholarship to the Sloane School of Art —"

"I don't call that a hard-luck story," said Susan. "If anybody awarded me a scholarship to anywhere, even to an Institute for Backward Brains, I'd put the flags up."

"Well, naturally," said Charlotte. "That's not the hard-luck bit. The hard-luck bit is that she can't afford to accept it."

Susan looked puzzled. "Can't afford to accept it?"

she said.

"No. The scholarship only covers the cost of the fees, of course, and apart from the money it will need to keep her for three years, there is the money she won't be earning while she's at the Sloane. She thinks that she'll have to give up art as a career and train as a secretary or something so that she can earn a lot of money soon and keep herself and even help with young Michael's school fees. They have no father, you see, and ever since her old grandfather died they have been frightfully hard-up and Mrs. Harding has had to get a job and —"

"But they live in that huge house!" said Bill. "Why don't they sell that and get a lot of money?"

"Yes, but that's half the trouble," said Charlotte. "I met Jennifer in the village this morning and she was telling me all about it. She was nearly in tears—" She glanced at Susan, whose usually round and rosy face became woebegone and looked as if she wasn't far off tears herself, and hurried on, "— you see, her old grandfather was absolutely bats —"

"He was not!" said Bill indignantly. "He was a nice old boy! He gave me a goldfish once. It escaped down the plughole in the bath the very next day when I was giving it some exercise, but still —"

"Oh, I know," said Charlotte, "he was sweet, but when he died his money died with him and the will he left was absolutely bats. He was madly proud of his family — it seems Hardings had lived in that house ever since it was built in the eighteenth-century — and he said in his will that the house mustn't ever be sold, and that if Mrs. Harding tried to sell it, it was to pass to a distant cousin who was to keep it going as a sort of memorial to the Harding family! It makes my blood boil!"

"I should think so," murmured Midge. "A living Harding is more important than a whole lot of dead ones, I should have thought."

They all agreed with Midge and said what a disgusting will it was. Susan said, "But must they do what the will says? Can't it be broken or whatever you call it?"

"Well, naturally Mrs. Harding has got her lawyer on the job but it takes time, and Jennifer has to let the Sloane School know by Wednesday if she's taking up the scholarship," said Charlotte.

"Oh jings!" said Susan, thinking that that didn't give her much time, for this was Friday.

"Now, Susie!" said Charlotte. "Don't you start anything!"

"As if I would!" said Susan virtuously. "I don't even know the girl!"

"You will to-morrow," said Charlotte, "because she's asked us all to tea."

The situation was desperate, Susan thought. She must do *something*, but how could she work out a way of getting round the old man's silly old will by the next day?

Long before the next day, in the next half-hour as a matter of fact, all or nearly all thoughts of Jennifer Harding's troubles were put out of the heads of Susan and the Carmichaels by their own worries. Aunt Lucy, who was the Carmichael's aunt as well as Susan's and kept house for them, came into the sitting-room.

"Er —" said Aunt Lucy, "Selina Gascoigne has gone away for the weekend and I promised that we'd keep an eye on her family —" She had the grace to be slightly apologetic because it had been borne in on her at last that her family didn't much like their next-door neighbours, the Gascoignes, in fact they hated the sight of them, in spite of all that she could say about their being a charming, handsome, talented, clever, original and gifted family.

This announcement was greeted with rebellious mutterings which swelled into roars of rage and disgust as soon as Aunt Lucy had hurried back to the kitchen to get on with her chores.

"No, it's too much!" cried Charlotte. "As if it wasn't bad enough living next door to the creatures, we have to keep an eye on them as well every time their mother goes away!"

"The only way I'd like to keep an eye on them would be with a very, very long-distance telescope," said Midge. "If the Gascoignes were in the moon, say, I wouldn't mind keeping an eye on them."

"It's too much," said Charlotte again. "What could Aunt Lucy be thinking of?"

"It's all very well for you, Charlotte," said Bill. "That drip Adrian will take you to the pictures — but catch him taking us to the pictures. I'll have to play with Pea-green, the boy monster."

"Leaving us," said Midge in the gloomiest voice, "with Gabrielle, the ghastliest of the ghastly Gascoignes —"

They relieved their feelings for the next five minutes by calling the Gascoignes all the names that they could think of, from Peregrine, the poisonous pest and Gabrielle, the smug, self-satisfied, stuck-up snob to Adrian, the adenoidal ape. "Except that he isn't," said Charlotte in the interest of truth, "he's very handsome." The others glared at her and she blushed. "Well, he is. And you know that you like him best of the three —"

"Help, that's not saying much," said Midge.

Aunt Lucy popped her head round the door again. "I've asked them to lunch," she said. "One of you go over and fetch them. They might be shy."

"Shy!" said Midge faintly. "The Gascoignes are about as shy as a herd of stampeding elephants.

Bags I don't go and fetch them!"

"Bags I don't!" "Bags not me!" Charlotte and Bill yelled simultaneously. Everybody looked at Susan.

"Och, you can't send me to fetch them," Susan said. "I'm only a visitor myself —"

"Oh, Susie, you're not!" said Bill, looking quite hurt. "You're one of the family, you know that!"

"Well, thanks, Bill —" Susan began.

"Besides, you're always wanting to do things to help people," Charlotte said, rather nastily Susan thought. "Now's your chance. You can do this to help us —"

Susan looked at Charlotte reproachfully, heaved herself out of her chair and went with dragging step through the garden, ablaze with dahlias and chrysanthemums in the September sunshine, to the little gate that led to the Gascoignes' property next door.

Her steps became slower as she approached the door that led straight to the Gascoignes' "rumpus-room" as they called it and where she was most likely to find the family being original, gifted, talented and clever, making clay models or getting up a play or writing stories or composing music. It was ridiculous, she thought, to be frightened of a nine-year old boy, but, she thought, let's face it, I'm terrified of what that awful Pea-green will do next. One minute he's pretending to be a gorilla, nearly frightening me out of my wits not to mention tearing my hair out by the roots, and the next minute he's pointing a gun at me and all his mother does is smile admiringly and even she won't be there to-day to keep him from actually killing me, not that she would, probably, it would be bad for darling Peregrine to be stopped from killing me if that's what he felt like doing. And of course that stuck-up Gabrielle will only laugh — gosh, the others will be sorry they sent me, when I'm dead —.

At this point she began to giggle to herself and felt better. Honestly, she thought, she was *bats*, what could that Pea-green, even if he was the wickedest small boy in England, actually *do* to her? Calling, "Yoo-hoo, anybody at home?" she banged on the door and went into the rumpus-room.

She told the others later that she must have had a premonition that something terrible was going to happen to her and that was why she had been so unwilling to go near the Gascoignes (Bill said what's a premonition and Charlotte said it was a feeling some people got of bad things to come but she doubted if Susan had really had one, the fact that Pea-green was around was a better warning of bad things to come than any premonition) and the first terrible thing that happened was the smell that met her as soon as she opened the door of the rumpus-room. It was like rotten eggs she said afterwards, and drains, and that time at school when the poor old rat went and died under the floor on the Upper Fifth form-room. She reeled back and made to shut the door.

"Who's that?" called Peregrine. "Oh, it's you, Susan. Do come in and shut the door," he went on in his high pedantic voice, "you're spoiling my experiment."

If she had any sense, Susan thought later, she would have rushed away as fast as she could, banging the door behind her, but her curiosity was too much for her. She came in and shut the door, and holding her nose she said, "What experibet?"

"Oh, just something I'm doing," said Peregrine carelessly, "to find out what happens when you combine H_2O and $NaH(CO_3)$ and H_2SO_4 with a few ideas of my own. My discoveries may revolutionise the whole world of chemistry."

Cocky little beast, thought Susan, I'll bet that you don't know what all these letters mean, goodness I don't myself, although H_2SO_4 is sulphuric acid — I think — which would account for the smell. She looked across the room. On a bench were spread out test-tubes and retorts and glass jars filled with noisome-looking liquids and heaps of coloured crystals, winking and sparkling in the eerie light of a Bunsen burner.

"I bought this chemistry set with my own money," Peregrine was saying, "it cost two pounds. It's rather babyish of course but Selina got me some quite decent stuff as well from a friend of hers who is an extremely famous chemist. She had this bench fitted up for me too and the Bunsen burner."

Of course, Susan thought, irritated as usual by the way the Gascoignes called their mother by her first name, all the Gascoignes' friends are famous, I'd forgotten that, but how can you be a famous chemist? Unless of course you're Boots or Andrew's Liver Salts or Mr. Enoor —. "You bead he bakes fabous pills or cough-bixtures or sobethig like that?" she said.

"Not that kind of chemist," said Peregrine scornfully. "A scientist. Come over here and hold this for me."

Still holding her nose, Susan gingerly approached the bench and at arm's-length held the test-tube as ordered.

"Not like that. Over the flame," said Peregrine. "I'm going to pour in this" — he held up another test-tube half-filled with a filthy liquid. "It's a special chemical combination that I've invented. If the stuff in your test-tube turns green it means —"

It turned green all right, a strong vivid green something like the colour of the scum that forms on stagnant water. Not only that, but as Peregrine added his recently invented chemical combination to Susan's test-tube and she leant over to watch this surprising change, the liquid began to fizz and suddenly spurted up over Susan's hands and face. She dropped the test-tube and yelled. She tried to wipe her hands on her handkerchief, but the spots remained, obstinate, livid green. Oh help, my face! she thought hopelessly. I suppose I'm disfigured for life!

"Oh really, Susan!" said Peregrine in an exasperated voice. "You've ruined my experiment!"

"Of course it's a pity that Susan looks such a sight," said Gabrielle during lunch. "Worse than usual, I mean, but it's too annoying that she messed up Peregrine's experiment. I don't know as much about chemistry as I do about most things, it's not really my line, but I do know that a gifted little boy like Peregrine might easily have hit on something really important, and now perhaps it has gone for ever —"

Not like my spots, Susan thought savagely.

Midge and Charlotte were quite certain from the expression on poor Susan's green-spotted face that any minute now she would start bashing Gabrielle over the head with a plate of salad if Gabrielle didn't stop talking about the gifted Peregrine, who in his spoilt way was walking round the room looking into Aunt Lucy's sideboard drawers and eating his cold meat in his fingers, so they began quickly and rather incoherently to tell Aunt Lucy about Jennifer Harding's troubles. They didn't in the least want to talk about Jennifer in front of those ghastly Gascoignes, but still less did they want old Susie to brain Gabrielle in the middle of lunch. When they got her alone afterwards it would be a different matter.

Gabrielle was diverted immediately. "The Sloane

School?" she interrupted Charlotte in mid-sentence, "do *you* know someone going to the Sloane School? Selina has a great friend who is a director of the Sloane. Perhaps she could put in a word with him for this friend of yours — if she has any talent — that is —" Her voice expressed doubt.

"She doesn't need anyone to put in a word for her," said Charlotte acidly. "She has great talent and she already has been awarded a scholarship. So unless this friend of Mrs. Gascogines' is likely to cough up enough cash to keep Jennifer for three years besides helping to educate her young brother, I don't see that a word to any director is going to be much help."

"We'll go with you for tea to-morrow," said Gabrielle, "and talk to her."

"You haven't been asked," murmured Midge.

"I should think an introduction to Tootsy Fitzgerald is worth a cup of tea," said Gabrielle. "We could take some buns with us if these people Harding are likely to be short," she added insultingly.

Susan and the Carmichaels were red with rage — red and green in Susan's case — but before a real row could develop Peregrine caused a diversion by dancing over to Susan and tucking a piece of lettuce behind each ear. "To match your spots," he said. "You look too sweet. Like a comic rabbit in a baby's picture book."

"That's enough, Peregrine," said Aunt Lucy firmly, taking a hand at last. "Come and sit down at once if you want any pudding —"

Peregrine drew Susan aside after lunch. "Of course," he said, "the only thing to do to help your friend is to blow up the silly old house. One of my home-made bombs would be just the thing."

Susan looked startled. "You make bombs?" she

said.

"Naturally," said Peregrine.

Just the way I'd talk about making toffee! Susan said to herself, and for a wild moment thought what a wonderful idea it would be — a nice harmless explosion — then she blushed at these terrible thoughts and said, "Honestly Pea-green, sorry, Peregrine, you can't do things like that. Besides, I don't expect your bombs work."

Peregrine didn't answer directly. "My secret combination of H_2O and $NaH(CO_3)$ and H_2SO_4, etc. worked, didn't it?" he said. "Just glance in a looking-glass if you don't believe me."

Susan had had courage for only one bitter hasty look as she brushed her hair before lunch. Disfigured for life, she thought again. "Pea-green, sorry, Peregrine," she said in a more ingratiating tone, "what about trying an experiment to get *rid* of these green spots? I should think that would be a pretty unique experiment and make you famous —"

"Oh well, next week if I've time," Peregrine said, strolling off in the direction of his garden gate. "And if," he added over his shoulder, "you're a bit more polite to me and stop calling me Pea-green."

The next day, Charlotte, Midge, Bill and Susan unwillingly accompanied Gabrielle and Peregrine to the Hardings'. Adrian had announced that he wasn't coming, he was taking a girl to the pictures, so none of the Carmichaels was in a very sunny temper. The day matched their mood; it was cold, wet and blustery, reminding them that winter wasn't far behind.

The Hardings' house was in the middle of Wichwood Village, set back a little from the road, a gaunt ugly house built of yellow brick and certainly not, Gabrielle said disparagingly, worth all the fuss that was being made about it. The Carmichaels and

Susan instantly said that it was a lovely old house, and they were still arguing about it when they climbed up the short flight of steps to the front door. But it wasn't, it was a hideous house, and the argument lacked conviction.

But inside, in the old-fashioned drawing-room, there was a fire burning cheerfully, warmly lighting up the dark old pictures on the walls (the work of an early Victorian Harding) and the heavy solid furniture that crowded the room. The Hardings, warned by telephone of the Gascoignes' invasion, had a sumptuous tea waiting for them — tomato sandwiches and scones and home-made plum jam and fruit cake and chocolate biscuits — and although Peregrine was his usual disgusting self, starting with cake and finishing with cake after a lot of cake in the middle, Gabrielle, who could behave properly when she set her mind to it, talked quite sensibly to Mrs. Harding and Jennifer about the Sloane and said that they must come to tea when Selina got home and she would have Tootsy Fitzgerald to meet them.

Jennifer thanked her very much and added sadly that she was afraid that that was the nearest she would get to the Sloane and then changed the subject, while Susan clenched her teeth in rage and thought that life was horribly unfair and why *couldn't* she think of some way to help Jennifer?

After tea Bill and young Michael Harding went off on some boyish pursuit like meccano or Dinky cars and forced Peregrine to go with them, so the girls were left in peace and played canasta nosily and cheerfully and Gabrielle cheated but Midge spotted her so she didn't gain any advantage from her dastardly behaviour — rather the reverse because they all watched her like hawks after that. And they were just reluctantly dragging themselves away from the drawing-room to go home and Susan was thinking that everything had gone much better than you would have expected with Gascoignes around, when she noticed Peregrine slipping out from behind the big wing-chair at the side of the fireplace and nonchalantly joining the others as they were putting on coats and macs in the hall.

Something — another of her famous premonitions, Midge said afterwards — made Susan go back into the drawing-room and look behind the chair. There, lying on the floor, was what looked like a dry wrinkled old orange — but issuing from it was a length of pyjama cord, the end of which was alight and smouldering briskly.

That Pea-green! Susan thought. Honestly! Him and his home-made bombs! But all the same, the little fiend, that lighted "fuse" will burn the carpet —

She picked up the object which, sure enough, was an old dried-out orange, cut in half and joined round the middle with scotch tape. Serve him right if I showed everybody what he's been doing, she said to herself, but I won't give the little perisher away — and she bent down and poked the orange into the fire.

She watched it burn briskly for a second — and then there was a roar like a thousand cannons and a sheet of flame leapt out at her. She yelled and flung herself face downwards on the floor.

The others crowded round the door in horrified silence. Then Mrs. Harding darted to Susan. "Susan!"

Susan slowly raised herself from the floor. She put a hand up to her face, felt the hard burnt stumps of eyelashes and eyebrows and brought away a handful of charred hair. She looked round her in shocked dismay. The whole room was covered with soot, a window was blown out, a pair of lustres lay smashed on the ground and across one of the dark old pictures was a wide, light-coloured scar. Susan hurriedly shut her eyes again.

Peregrine, dancing with rage, shouted "Susan! What did you do to my bomb?" Everybody began to talk at once, Susan was led away to have some soothing ointment put on her face, Charlotte said helplessly hadn't they better start to clear up the mess and Midge said what on earth had happened?

Bill said severely, "Perhaps Pea-green can tell us that?"

"What d'you mean? Gabrielle asked. "*Per*egrine had nothing to do with it!"

Susan, with Mrs. Harding hovering anxiously round her, came back.

"Heavens," said Gabrielle, "you look awful."

This was no more than the truth. Apart from the remaining green traces of Peregrine's chemical discovery and a horrid bald look where the explosion had removed her hair and eyelashes, she was white and shaky. She had caught a glimpse of herself in the bathroom glass when Mrs. Harding was putting on a burn remedy and it had been a disheartening sight but, she felt, she didn't need Gabrielle pointing it out. "Well, I dare say I do look awful, but you can hardly blame me for that!" she snapped, indignation getting the better of her usual sunny temper. "I'm only the victim! Why don't you blame *him* for lighting bombs in people's drawing-rooms?" and she pointed a quivering finger at Peregrine.

"It's not my fault," Peregrine said coldly. "How could you be so silly, putting my bomb in the fire?"

"How was I to know it would go off?" demanded Susan. "Home-made bombs don't usually."

"Mine do," said Peregrine.

"You should remember," said Gabrielle, "that everything Peregrine does, he does well —"

Charlotte said, "I can't *think* why anybody should bring a bomb into the house at all! Mrs. Harding, I'm so terribly sorry!"

Susan looked round the wrecked room again and shuddered. "Och, Mrs. Harding!" she wailed. "I don't know what to say!"

"Don't *worry*, Susan," said kind Mrs. Harding, "it will all clean!"

"Except those dangling glass things that were on the bookcase," mourned Susan. "And the picture!"

Jennifer had taken the picture — a gloomy study of Highland cattle — down from the wall. A piece of flying glass from the lustres had scraped across it, leaving a long streak across the dark paint. "There's something queer here!" said Jennifer, excitement in her voice. "There seems to be another picture underneath!"

They all crowded round and Gabrielle, know-all as usual, said, "It looks like an Italian Primitive."

Bill nudged Susan, "What's an Italian Primitive?" he whispered.

"I haven't a clue," Susan whispered back, "but jings I hope it's something valuable!"

"Old Ludovic Harding did that one," Mrs. Harding was saying, "he painted about a thousand pictures and all of them pretty terrible. I suppose that he ran out of canvas one day and painted over an old picture that he didn't like much anyway!"

"Isn't it exciting?" cried Jennifer. "I wonder what the old picture is —"

"Selina has a great friend at the National Gallery," Gabrielle said, "he's absolutely *the* authority on the cleaning and restoring of old paintings. Why not take it to him and he'll have all that muck properly cleaned off and be able to tell you what the picture is. But I think," she added, "that you'll find it's one of the Italian Primitives."

"Don't *tell* me," Midge muttered under her breath to Susan, "that one of Selina's friends is going to come in useful at last?"

A few days later Jennifer came along to the Carmichaels' house bursting with news.

"The picture!" said Jennifer. "That great-great-great-uncle Ludovic had the cheek to paint over! It's a Fra Angelico!"

Charlotte gasped. "But that's an Old Master!"

"Yes! Isn't it wonderful? The National Gallery people are wild with excitement! They've offered us seven thousand pounds for it!"

The Carmichaels and Susan nearly fainted.

"I'd like to keep it," said Jennifer a little wistfully. "Fancy owning a Fra Angelico! But of course it would be mad. We'll sell it — and actually I don't mind selling it so much when it's going to a picture gallery where everybody can look at it and enjoy it — and I'll be able to go to the Sloane and Mother is going to shove in a couple of bathrooms and convert the house into flats and we'll be able to manage Michael's school fees —"

"It's a good thing that your old grandfather didn't know about the Fra What-ever-his-name-is," said Bill "or he would have put it in his will that you mustn't sell that."

Jennifer nodded happily. "And it's a good thing," she said, "that Susan heaved that home-made bomb in the fire, or the Fra Angelic would still have been hidden under Highland cattle!"

The Carmichaels looked at the blushing Susan solemnly. "She's done it again!" Midge said.

"Done what?" asked Jennifer

"Helped somebody," said Midge.

VIII: THE WILSONS WON'T MIND

JANE SHAW

The Carmichaels thought ruefully that they should have know better than tell their cousin Susan about the misfortunes of the Wilson family. There was a strong streak of the knight errant about Susan — at the drop of a hat, Midge said gloomily, she'd dash out and rescue somebody or help somebody, or poke her nose into somebody's misfortunes, and these rescuings and helpings and pokings usually turned out to be extremely uncomfortable for the rest of the family and very exhausting. Of course, the Wilson misfortunes were enough to keep any knight errant busy for weeks — father ill and out of a job, mother worn out with nursing him, taking in sewing and looking after four children, who as often as not were ailing in some way or another too. They were patients of Dr. Carmichael's and kept him busier than three ordinary families put together. He was always saying that they ought to move away from Wychwood, the London suburb where they lived, because it was much too damp and low-lying and not at all suitable for a family that went in for bronchitis as much as the Wilsons did. And now, to crown all, the children were going to be done out of the visit to the pantomime that they had been promised this Christmas because there simply wasn't enough money to pay for the seats, even if Mr. Wilson did get them a bit cheaper on account of being a stage carpenter — or had been until he lost his job.

Susan gazed at her cousins with big anxious eyes. "But that's *awful*!" she said. "Not to be able to go to the pantomime, poor wee souls! Can't we do something about that?"

Midge was lying back in her chair with her feet almost in the fire, scratching the chilblains on her heels occasionally. "What d'you suggest?" she said in her lazy voice.

"Well," said Susan, "surely we could do *something*? Club together and pay for their seats — or something —"

"Mrs. Wilson wouldn't like that at *all*", said Midge. "She's a madly proud and independent sort of person."

"Oh," said Susan. "Oh well, we'll just have to think of something else. Couldn't we put on a show for them ourselves, then? Have a party and put on a show, a little pantomime or something? Couldn't we do that?"

"We *could*, I suppose," said Bill doubtfully. "But d'you think that the Wilson kids would think us as good as a pantomime?"

"Not *quite* as good, perhaps," Susan admitted, "but wouldn't we be better than nothing?"

"I doubt it," said Bill.

Midge and Charlotte thought that a home-made pantomime was a horrible idea, and said so. "Not even the Wilsons," said Charlotte, "starved of treats all their lives, would want to watch us larking about."

"Oh," cried Susan, "*surely* they're not so blasé as all that! What age are they, anyway?"

"Elvira must be twelve or thirteen because she's in our class at Sunday School," said Midge, "but she looks about nine. And Stevie must be ten, I suppose, and the twins are younger still."

"Well then," said Susan emphatically, "they'll be

thrilled with anything."

Charlotte who was the eldest Carmichael, now changed her mind and said that a party for the Wilsons was a wonderful idea. She would make the cakes for it, she said.

The others glanced at each other with raised eyebrows. Charlotte was always having wild enthusiasms for one thing or another, and her latest was baking. As she baked with a reckless disregard for the cookery-book the results were sometimes slightly peculiar. Still —

"The Wilsons won't mind," said Susan. "Now, what pantomime are we going to do? We must decide, so that Midge will have lots of time to write it."

Midge moaned slightly, settled farther back in her chair and savagely scratched her chilblains. "Let's do *Mother Goose*," she said, "and Susan can be the goose."

Charlotte said quickly, "What about *Babes in the Wood*, and then we could use the woodland scenery that's lying in the garage? I could slosh some paint on it and cheer it up a bit."

"Oh, good idea," cried Susan. "Bill and I can be the Babes and Midge can be the Fairy Godmother and do a dance in the middle and Charlotte can be the Wicked Uncle. And I know how to make leaves out of crêpe paper — fig leaves, actually, but the Wilsons won't mind."

Everybody seemed to think that if they must do a pantomime, and Susan insisted that they must, then *Babes in the Wood* was as good a one as any. The only thing to settle now was the date, and they finally decided that Saturday the sixteenth of January, the last Saturday before they went back to school, was the only possible date. But when they consulted Aunt Lucy, who looked after the

Carmichaels because they had no mother, she shook her head. "That's the afternoon that I'm going to the ballet with Madame," she said, "and coming back here for dinner, so I shan't have time to do anything for your party."

"Who's Madame?" Susan whispered to Midge.

"Madame Polinski or some such name," said Midge. "She owns that ghastly ballet school that Aunt Lucy wanted to send me to last year. Can't you go to the ballet at night, Aunt Lucy?" she said.

Aunt Lucy said no, they couldn't because one of Madame's pupils was dancing that afternoon and naturally she wanted to see her. But, said Charlotte, did it matter if Aunt Lucy wasn't at the party? After all, she was going to bake the cakes and so on; and Aunt Lucy said that in that case, she'd just leave the whole thing to the young people, and would Midge *please* stop scratching her chilblains or they'd go septic. And Susan said that of course it was a pity that Aunt Lucy wouldn't see the pantomime, but she didn't suppose that the Wilsons would mind.

So it was settled; and Charlotte, who was the artist of the family, did a very grand invitation card with babes and robins and wicked uncles in the corners, and they took it up to the Wilsons' very picturesque but damp little house overlooking the old mill-pond, and the Wilsons said that they'd all be delighted to come.

From then on, Susan and the Carmichaels were very busy writing the pantomime and rehearsing and making clothes with the help of the dressing-up box, but what with Christmas and parties and outings coming in between, there still seemed a great deal to be done at the dress rehearsal on the Saturday morning.

The Carmichaels very luckily had sliding doors between their dining-room and sitting-room, so there was no trouble about stage and curtains — the dining-room would be the stage, while the audience sat cosily in the sitting-room.

The doors were open now, and Susan was feverishly cutting out leaves from crêpe paper — green and brown and red. Bill was up a step-ladder, experimenting with a powerful spotlight that his father had let him have from the car. Charlotte, in cloak and slouch hat and very sinister curly moustache, was slapping paint on to the woodland scenery. Midge was sitting on the floor, her white *tu-tu* unbuttoned, one ballet shoe on and the other dangling from her hands. She looked up at the others and there were tears of pain in her eyes.

"It's no good," she said. "I just can't get this shoe on!"

"That's what comes of scratching those chilblains," said Charlotte absently. "We all warned you."

"But, Midge," said Susan aghast, "you *must* get your shoe on! You're the Fairy Godmother and you have to dance!"

"Then I'll have to dance in my bedroom slippers," said Midge. "But the Wilsons won't mind."

"Of course they'll mind!" said Susan indignantly. "Dance in your bedroom slippers! I'd rather dance myself and let you be the Babe —"

"Well dance then," said Midge, whose painful chilblains were making her rather short-tempered, "because I can't. Come on, try on my *tu-tu* — "

"But I can't dance, you know I can't —" began Susan, who hadn't expected to be taken literally. But Midge took off her *tu-tu* and forced her reluctant cousin into it. Susan wasn't fat, but she was sturdy; the *tu-tu* didn't meet at the back by a good three inches.

"Never mind," said Midge ruthlessly, "we'll tie it

together with string and you must just not turn your back to the audience, that's all. Here's the wand. Start the gramophone, Bill." She thrust the fairy wand into Susan's shrinking hand and Bill, grinning broadly, started the *Dance of the Sugar-Plum Fairy*. Susan jumped unhappily across the floor.

"We'll need to change the programme from Fairy Sugar-Plum to Fairy Elephant," murmured Midge.

Susan, clutching her wand like a weapon of attack, raised her arms and executed a pirouette — new style. The floor shook and the scenery rocked dangerously.

"Hi, *Susan*," yelled Charlotte, "you can't do that, you'll knock my scenery over!" She grabbed at the swaying scenery, Susan lowered her arms and her wand knocked Charlotte's villainous slouch hat into the poster paints.

The door opened and Mrs. Taylor, the daily help, poked her head round.

"Charlotte, lovey," she said, "there's a smell of burning, something awful, but you told me not to touch the oven —"

"My cakes!" wailed Charlotte, and cloak flying, she rushed to the kitchen. The others trailed interestedly after her, in time to see her snatching a tray of round, smoking objects, burnt quite black, out of the oven. "Wouldn't it *madden* you!" she raged, flinging the tray on the kitchen table.

"What's this mush?" said Bill, poking an inquisitive finger at another tray.

"Oh, these are rock cakes," said Charlotte, "but I thought that the recipe needed cheering up, so I put in lots more butter and sugar than the book said. They're a *tiny* bit crumbly and you'll have to eat them with a spoon but they taste divine. And look at this," she added proudly. She displayed a beautiful layer-cake, smoothly covered with white icing.

"Yum-*yum*," said Midge, playfully advancing with a knife.

"Don't you dare!" cried Charlotte. "That's for the Wilsons —"

"But what are you going to do with the burnt offerings?" said Bill.

"Oh, I'll cover them with icing — if there's any left. I used all that was in the sugar tin, but I think I saw another bag in the cupboard."

"How delicious," said Midge. "Iced cinders —"

"I'll cut the burnt bits off," said Charlotte with dignity. She did so, and was left with a dozen small cakes about the size of marbles.

Midge turned up her nose. "I'd say F.K.O. to that little lot, *definitely*," she said.

"F.K.O.?" said Susan.

"Family Keep Off," said Midge.

Charlotte snatched a tray of round, smoking objects from the oven.

THE WILSONS WON'T MIND

But the harassed cook's patience was now exhausted. "Will you please all get out of my kitchen and let me ice the beastly thing!" she said, and pushed them out and firmly closed the door on them.

Back on the stage, Susan reluctantly picked up her wand while Midge wound the ancient gramophone. "What *are* we to do?" said Susan. "I can't do the dance!"

"Well, I think you can," said Bill tactfully, "if you don't mind being slightly — er — comic, instead of pretty —"

"Oh, *I* don't mind," beamed Susan. "And I'm sure the Wilsons won't mind!"

"Help, these Wilsons seem to be an insensitive lot," Midge muttered.

Bill, who had been itching to try his hand at scattering leaves all morning, climbed up the step-ladder once more with the basket of leaves. He let a handful flutter down, calling to the gyrating Susan to be careful not to stand on them. The Elephant Fairy was having enough trouble trying to be funny and keep on her feet without having to avoid a whole lot of paper leaves, and her steps became more elephantine than ever. Bill leant over the top of the step-ladder shrieking with laughter.

"The Wilsons will love you, you'll knock 'em cold," he called, and knocked the basket of leaves over with his elbow.

It caught Susan on the head, and she, taken unawares by this attack from above, staggered back into the woodland scenery. This, not very steady at the best, was quite beyond supporting the full onslaught of the Elephant Fairy — it wavered for a second or two, then collapsed gently on top of her.

"Help!" yelled Susan, from below scenery, leaves and basket. "Help! Get me out!"

When Midge and Bill had recovered from the first paralysing gust of laughter, they noticed a slight little figure, pale-faced, big-eyed, hovering just inside the sitting-room door.

"Oh, hallo, Elvira," said Midge, pulling herself together and wiping her eyes. "Do come in. We were just rehearsing the pantomime —"

Bill gave another cackle of laughter and went to Susan's assistance.

Elvira advanced a timid step or two. "I — I'm sorry," she said. "Mrs. Taylor told me to come in; she said you were here. I — I just came to ask what time we were to come this afternoon, the invitation didn't say —"

"Oh," said Midge, "Charlotte *is* a dope not putting the time. Five o'clock. Tea first then the pantomime."

The Elephant Fairy struggled painfully to her feet. "There isn't going to *be* a pantomime," she said, feeling her head tenderly. "Not one with a fairy in it, anyway."

Midge explained the situation to Elvira, giggling again at the picture that Susan had presented.

Elvira's thin face looked eager. "You — you wouldn't like *me* to do the fairy, would you?" she said. "I can dance a bit. In fact, I've always wanted to be a dancer, but of course when Dad got ill we couldn't afford the lessons any more. I'd love to — if you think I'm good enough."

"You'd be good enough for this pantomime," said Midge, "with your legs tied together. Here, try on my *tu-tu* —"

While on the big side, the *tu-tu* still fitted Elvira much better than it had fitted Susan. "Mum could take a tuck in it," said Elvira, " if you don't mind —"

"Do what you like with it," said Midge airily. "As you see, Susan has already burst a couple of buttons off it and it's covered with paint. I hope poster paint washes off or Aunt Lucy will slay me."

Bill switched on the *Dance of the Sugar-Plum Fairy*. "Can you dance to this, Elvira?" he shouted over the sound of the music. "D'you know it?"

"Yes I do," said Elvira. "But have you the music of *Swan Lake*? Because I can do a dance to part of Act One —"

"Aunt Lucy has the record," said Bill. "I'm sure she'll let us borrow it."

It was settled that Elvira would hurry home to ask her mother to sew the *tu-tu*. "And thanks a ton for letting me dance!" she said. "I'd better go now, Stevie and the twins are waiting in the garden —"

"Oh, poor wee souls!" cried Susan. "Where are they?" Bring them in —"

"The twins," said Midge musingly. "You know, they'd make much better Babes than Bill and Susan. Just the right size —"

"Oh gee," said Elvira, "they'd love it! They love acting!"

"Go and get them," said Midge.

Stevie came too, his round face, red from the cold, beaming. Elvira said apologetically, "He says he'd like to be the Broker's Man — and make jokes."

"Okay," cried Susan, carried away, "we'll put him in! But," she suddenly realised, "this pantomime was for *you*! Who's going to be the audience if you're all in the cast?"

"*We'll* be the audience," said Midge thankfully. "The Wilsons will do the pantomime and the Carmichaels will be the audience!"

"The Carmichaels won't mind," Susan giggled ...

The tea could hardly be called an unqualified success. Mrs Taylor had, fortunately, made piles of sandwiches, and the little Wilsons spooned eagerly at the extra-rich rock cakes, but after one bite of the beautiful frosted layer-cake, Charlotte noticed that they unobtrusively put down their slices. She couldn't help feeling slightly offended, and passed the plate of iced cinders. They didn't look at all bad, she thought, although she had had a lot of trouble with the icing — first it wouldn't set, and then it set too much and was now as hard as bricks. Still — Stevie and the twins each took a cake and popped it whole into their mouths. Bill took a bite of layer-cake and immediately and rather disgustingly spat it out. "Charlotte!" he said accusingly. "No sugar!"

"Elvira!" a twin suddenly yelled. "I'm going to be sick!"

"Elvira!" yelled the other desperately.

"*Elvira!*" yelled Stevie.

Elvira grabbed a twin in each hand and hurried them out, followed by an anxious Stevie. Bill cautiously licked one of the little white cakes. "No sugar in these either," he said.

"Of course there's sugar in them!" said Charlotte indignantly. "They're all sugar, icing sugar!"

"Taste them then," said Bill.

Charlotte tasted. "They're not *bad*," she said defiantly.

"I hope we never have to eat any of Charlotte's downright failures," said Bill.

Susan was cautiously examining the cakes. "I think it's starch," she said.

The Wilsons came back, pale and shaken. Charlotte apologised abjectly. Elvira said it didn't matter, that the kids were all right now, and Midge said, "Well, if no one's poisoned let's get on with the pantomime."

The twins were such angelic Babes and played their parts so touchingly that Susan watched them through a mist of tears. And Stevie was so funny that she cried again, this time with laughing. Bill was up the step-ladder working the spotlight and dropping leaves, and when the Babes were cosily covered, Charlotte put on the record of *Swan Lake* and Elvira floated in.

Midge and Susan gasped. "*Is* it Elvira?" whispered Midge.

She's — she's sort of *glowing*," Susan whispered back. "And Midge, what a dancer! Nearly as good as you," she added loyally.

"As good as me!" said Midge. "She's a thousand times better than me! In a different class."

The sitting-room door opened gently and two shadowy figures slipped in. Midge and Susan were too intent on Elvira even to turn their heads, but at the intervals they could hear a strange voice crackling excitedly and Aunt Lucy's soothing whispers in reply. At the end of the pantomime the stranger darted forward, grabbed Elvira and held her hands.

"My child!" she cried. "My dear-r-r child! Who have teach you to dance? Never mind, now *I* teach you, Polinskaya herself will teach you! You will come to my school —"

Aunt Lucy was heard to mumble something about fees.

"Fees!" shrieked Madam Polinskaya. "Fees, pah!" I will teach her for nothing. Already she is a million times better than that hopping clod we saw this afternoon. Never-r-r will I forget those ar-r-r-abesques! How she wobble! And how she thump! This child is like — like — how you say it — eiderdown?"

Midge, giggling a little, said, "Thistledown?"

Madame shrugged. "Thistledown, eiderdown —! Ah, if she wor-r-k and if she do what I tell her, I shall make her a dancer —"

Elvira stood dazed, her eyes bright. Aunt Lucy

now began to explain in a low voice the circumstances of Elvira's father, but she didn't get very far. "Come!" cried Madame Polinskaya. "You will take me to this child's father-r-r-r this instant. A stage carpenter!" she shrieked. "Out of a job! And there is my little theatre in Surrey falling in pieces, but falling in *pieces* I tell you, for want of a stage carpenter! Take me to see him! Now, this instant minute!"

Aunt Lucy, completely swept off her feet, wrapped the Wilsons up in their scarves and coats and bundled them into Madame's car. As they went Madame could be heard exclaiming that there was even an empty cottage in the school grounds. "A dancer-r-r *and* a carpenter-r-r!" she exulted. The car door slammed, and they were gone.

Susan and the Carmichaels, feeling as if they had been out in a high wind, collapsed into chairs. Bill began to giggle quietly. "D'you realise," he said, "that she's done it again?"

"Who has done what again?" Midge asked,

"Susan!" said Bill. "Really helped somebody! This dotty Madame will swish them all off to the country and they'll have a job and a house and Elvira will go to ballet school and they won't have bronchitis any more—!"

Susan giggled happily. "I'll bet the Wilsons won't mind!" she said.

IX: SUSAN AND THE SPAE-WIFE

JANE SHAW

"Well, of course," said Midge, "the great mistake was letting Susan have anything to do with the fête."

"Oh, I don't know," said Bill, who always stood up for Susan, "she was only trying to help."

"Help!" said Charlotte. "That's the one thing that Susan should never be allowed to do. We should all know by this time that Susan is about as helpful as an atomic bomb."

Susan smiled at her three cousins. "Och away, you daft scones!" she said. "This time I was more like a wee damp squib than an atomic bomb —"

This fête and sale of work was to raise funds to repair the church roof and Susan and her cousins the Carmichaels, who were on holiday in Scotland, in the Isle of Arran, had, like most of the other visitors in the place, been roped in to help. It was going to be an outstanding affair, with a cake-and-candy stall, a white elephant stall, a produce stall; there were to be competitions for the best scones, the best cakes, the best honey, the best butter; Mirren Macalister from Auchenlochan, who was the seventh child of a seventh child and a real spae-wife with second-sight, was going to tell fortunes at half a crown a time; biggest draw of all, Rock Carlisle, who was staying with Lady Alison at the Big House, was going to present the prizes.

"Who is Rock Carlisle?" Dr. Carmichael asked mildly.

Susan was shocked. "Uncle Charles! Rock

Carlisle! He's *famous*. He writes thrillers."

"Tough ones," said Charlotte.

"I expect that he'll arrive with a gun under each arm and a switch-knife between his teeth," said Susan with relish. "I wish I could meet him. I could help to show him round, maybe —"

Midge said coldly, "You've already offered to help at the white elephant stall, the fancy-work, the cake-and-candy stall, the produce. You've offered to take the money at the gate, to run the Wheel of Fortune, to judge the best entries in the baking competitions, to tell fortunes instead of Mirren. It's a wonder that you didn't offer to open the thing."

Susan giggled. "I did," she said, "but the Minister thought that Lady Alison could manage that fine by herself —"

In the end, Susan and Midge were given the job of taking the money for the spae-wife. At first Susan was a little disappointed; she doubted if this gave much scope for her talents — but she cheered up at the thought of getting her own fortune told for nothing.

While all the fever of preparation was going on, only the day before the fête the district was thrown into an uproar by the bank robbery. The whole village seethed with excitement. Such a thing had never happened in the Isle of Arran before. Daring burglaries and armed hold-ups were quite unknown; robbing hen-houses or a bit of quiet poaching in the burns was about the extent of the criminal activities on the island, and the last man who had gone for higher game and robbed the post office at Lamlash had been caught as he tried to board the steamer at Brodick pier. And now, in broad daylight, at eleven o'clock in the morning, a man had walked into the bank, pointed a gun at young Jessie Kelso the cashier and cleared off with a haul of five hundred pounds. And worse than that, he had not yet been caught.

Susan, in her helpful way, immediately turned her attention from the fête, and decided that it was her allotted task to capture this daring criminal and restore the five hundred pounds to her friend the bank manager.

Midge said plaintively that she wouldn't mind Susan turning herself into a ghastly sort of amateur detective running round like a terrier after a rat, if only she wouldn't expect her to run round as well. "Besides," she said, "it's so embarrassing when Susan asks the Minister if he has an alibi for the time of the robbery."

"Yes, well, that was just a wee mistake," said Susan, blushing. "That wasn't one of my successful interviews. I did better with Jessie Kelso. You must admit that I got a lot of information from her. That interview went jolly well —"

"Och," Jessie Kelso had said, "I'd know the rascal again anywhere —"

"Gosh, would you, Jessie?" asked Susan. "I thought that he wore a nylon stocking over his face which disguised him completely?"

"Aye, he did, right enough," said Jessie, "but he had a wee scar on his hand, across the knuckles of his right hand; I'd know yon scar again anywhere."

"Gosh!" said Susan, wide-eyed. "That's a wonderful clue! Did you tell the police?"

"I did," said Jessie, "but when the police iss only yon daft Mackenzie I am not very hopeful of an early arrest."

"Leave it to me," said Susan, her round rosy face unusually grim.

And after that, as Midge said, it wasn't only embarrassing, it was a downright nightmare, with Susan inventing the most ridiculous excuses to look at the hands of every stranger in the neighbourhood. It was just as well, said Midge, that the fête was coming along to take Susan's so-called mind off bank robberies and scarred hands.

The fête was held on the golf course, with the various stalls inside the club house and the sideshows scattered about the last hole. The spae-wife's eery little tent was in a secluded corner under the veronica hedge by the tennis courts. The weather for once was perfect. It was a golden day, with scarcely a breath of wind to stir the flags and gay bunting, and the sea at the edge of the golf course was smooth as satin. Susan and Midge put up a notice:

THIS WAY TO THE SPAE-WIFE
Admittance 2s. 6d.

and Bill walked about with a placard, devised by Susan, which said on one side: WHAT DOES THE FUTURE HOLD FOR YOU? and on the other: VISIT THE SPAE-WIFE AND FIND OUT.

They made the inside of the tent as dark and mysterious as possible and festooned it with black and purple and deep red hangings, which they had borrowed from the long-suffering farmers' wives in the valley. Mirren wore a tartan shawl over her head and a black veil swathed round her face, leaving clearly visible only her eyes, which were dark and piercing and very spae-wife-ish, Susan said admiringly. Mirren was just as anxious as Susan to have the tent dark and mysterious. "I do not want them all to be knowing it iss me," she said in her soft Highland voice, "telling them such daft blethers."

Susan looked surprised. "Don't you believe in it?" she asked.

Mirren glanced away. "Och," she said, "I would

not be saying that. Queer things happen, whiles."
She paused and then added, "Even this forenoon I
was not wanting to be leaving the farm —"

Susan was very much interested in this instance
of Mirren's second sight and questioned her eagerly,
but Mirren either wouldn't, or couldn't say any
more; and as a few prospective customers were
beginning to cluster round the tent, peering and
prying and trying to catch a glimpse of what was
going on inside, Susan and Midge thought that it
was time to get organised and start raking in the
cash. They sat Mirren behind her little table and
put a chair ready for the clients and went outside to
form the customers into a queue.

Trade was exceedingly brisk and Midge's cash-box
was growing delightfully heavy, Susan and Midge
were standing guard at the entrance to the tent
while Bill kept the queue under control at a safe
distance so that no one could overhead what was
going on in the tent, when Angus Macalister from
Auchenlochan, one of Mirren's six brothers, came
hurrying towards the spae-wife's tent. He was quite
out of breath. "There has been a message from the
farm," he said. "It iss my mother. She was chust
crossing the stack-yard to take in some clothes that
were bleaching on the green when she fell and broke
her leg. The doctor is with her now, but she needs
Mirren. Can Mirren come away home?"

Susan was staring at him with her mouth open.
"But — but —" she stammered at last, "Mirren
knew that something was going to happen! And it
happened!"

"Och aye," said Angus impatiently, "Mirren aye
kens when something iss going to happen. But it iss
a great pity that she could not be telling us chust
exactly what iss going to happen for then my mother
could have kept away from the green and saved

herself a broken leg —"

"Gosh, Angus," said Susan indignantly, "I think she did jolly well—," but before there was any further argument, Mirren's customer came out of the tent beaming with delight at the fortune she had been told, and Susan and Midge and Angus crowded into the tent.

Of course there was no help for it, Mirren had to go home to look after her mother. She took off her shawl and the veil, and Susan said carelessly, "Mirren, you had better slip out the back way, if you don't want anyone to know that you're the spae-wife. Oh, and you'd better leave your shawl and veil —"

Midge glanced at Susan sharply, but was unable to read her expression in the dim mysterious light of the tent. Susan lifted up the back flap. "Hope your mother will soon be better," she whispered, and Mirren and Angus slipped away.

"Now!" said Susan and pounced on the veil.

"Susan!" Midge said. "What are you going to do?"

"Well," said Susan, draping the veil across her face, "I'm going to be the spae-wife, of course —"

"Oh, help, Susie —" Midge began in a hopeless voice.

But Susan interrupted eagerly, "Well, gosh, Midge, look at the rows of customers! We can't just go out there and send them away! Think of the church roof!"

"But Susie," said Midge, in a slow and patient voice, "You... can't... tell... fortunes."

"I can tell these people's fortunes," said Susan. "I know all about them, Especially the visitors. Better than Mirren. Maybe Mirren has supernatural powers, but I've known these people for ages, all my life, practically. I bet Mirren couldn't tell Elsa Henderson that she had a birdie two at the fourth yesterday."

"Oh, heavens," said Midge, "if you're only going to talk about golf —"

"No, I'm not," said Susan. "I'll tell them all who they're going to marry."

"Worse and worse," said Midge. "I wash my hands of the whole thing."

Susan put the shawl round her head and shoulders and crouched behind the table. "How do I look?" she said.

"Awful," said Midge crossly. "Like a horrid old spider waiting for a fly."

Susan gave a little giggle. "Okay," she said, "go and fetch in the flies —"

Midge need not have worried. Susan was an outstanding success as a fortune-teller; she even helped on one promising romance by judicious hinting to both parties. As far as she could make out, none of her friends and acquaintances suspected for a moment that she was the spae-wife. They came out of the tent quite dazed with astonishment at the fortune-teller's miraculous powers; the news of it went round the fête like wildfire and crowds came flocking to join the queue. Susan was having the time of her life. One of her early customers was Charlotte, who came in looking sceptical and smiling in a superior way. I'll soon fix her, Susan thought, and began with a non-committal sing-song mumble, her assumed Highland

accent very pronounced. "Och, the bonnie lassie, with the sunlight in her hair and her lips ass red ass the rowan berries —" It wasn't a very accurate description, but it would put old Charlotte into the right mood. She took Charlotte's hands and studied them closely. She was dying to put in a word for herself, to tell Charlotte, for example, to be kind to her cousin, who was a girl of noble and sterling worth, but she didn't like to risk it; better to keep to Charlotte's own character, she thought. "Och, there iss a fine nature here," she mumbled, "sweet and kind and gentle — most of the time. But there iss a fault, there iss a grave fault —round and round she goes, birling round like a peerie, now birling one way, now birling the other."

Charlotte blushed in the dim light of the tent. She didn't consider that she was quite as giddy as a top, but she was well-known in her family for her sudden mad enthusiasms which stopped as suddenly as they started, although she hadn't expected it to be obvious in her hand. Susan smiled to herself and didn't belabour the point; after a few further insults she dropped Charlotte's left hand and turned her right hand this way and that and looked at the back and the front and the side and made her double her hand into a fist — she toyed with the idea of telling Charlotte to stand on her head, but reluctantly decided against it. "Och, there iss a long, long life here," she said, "long and happy, with great riches too —"

Charlotte looked pleased. "What about a husband?" she asked.

"Och, a husband," murmured Susan. "Some are good and some are bad, but in your hand I am seeing two —"

"Two husbands?" said Charlotte, startled.

"Or mebbe three," said Susan, now anxious to

please. "There iss a young man in your fortune now," she said, slowly and consideringly as if searching for the truth in the lines of Charlotte's palm, "a young man with a queer-like occupation, who digs in the earth —"

"Goodness!" Charlotte was greatly impressed, because her young man of the moment was a budding archaeologist.

Susan nearly ruined everything by giggling; and when Charlotte's turn was over she heard her at the tent door telling Midge that the spae-wife was sensational. "She saw Andrew McPahil!" she said.

"Where?" said Midge, looking anxious. "A sort of apparition, you mean?"

"No, of course not, in my hand!"

Susan congratulated herself on being a very successful clairvoyant, and grinned to herself but, as she told Midge later, the next customer took the grin off her face; she had never seen him before in the whole of her life.

He was a little fat bald man, with glasses and an anxious expression. Susan was in a panic. She thought of fainting, she thought of ducking out of the tent and running for her life, she thought of announcing that her inspiration had packed up for the day — which, she thought, would be no more than the truth. But this, she thought, wouldn't be fair — after all the poor little man had paid his half-crown like everybody else.

The little man was beaming at her kindly and saying in a gentle voice, "Delightful, quite delightful! The tent is excellently contrived. I am indeed looking forward to a peep into the future, or an analysis of my character although there, I fear, you will find little scope for the exercise of your skill, for there is nothing deep or subtle there —"

Just as well! Susan thought, severely curbing a

hysterical giggle. Across the table she took his two hands in her trembling ones and gazed at them long and earnestly. She had never seen such a conglomeration of meaningless lines in her life and she was just thinking that there was absolutely nothing else for it but to tell him so, when she noticed the faintest possible smudge on the second finger of his right hand. "The pen is mightier than the sword!" she announced in her most solemn and Highland voice — after all, that didn't commit her to anything — and glancing up at him quickly caught the ghost of a smile on his face. A lucky shot! she thought, but before I go on with this, I'd better make sure that the smudge is really ink, she thought, and folded his fingers into a fist. Across the knuckles ran a white scar.

Susan felt her brain reel. The Robber! The Bank Robber!

Afterwards, she never knew what rubbish she muttered, half under her breath — absolute rot about the lure of gold and the vanity of riches — while she wondered desperately what to do. The little fat man was looking decidedly uncomfortable — he half-rose from his chair — what could she *do* — she tore at her shawl and flung it over his head meantime yelling, "Help! Help! Midge! Bill! *Help!* HELP!" at the pitch of her lungs.

Uttering strange muffled shrieks, the little man pawed at the folds of the shawl. Susan dived for his legs and brought him down with a most efficient rugby tackle. Midge and Bill, colliding in the opening, stumbled into the tent.

"Sit on his head," yelled Susan, hanging grimly on to the legs of the Bank Robber as he kicked and struggled.

Midge looked at the writing mass on the ground in horror. "Susie!" she cried. "Have you gone *mad*?

What are you *doing*?"

Susan panted, "It's the Bank Robber... I've caught him... But I wish you would...sit on his legs.... I can't hold on...much longer... Sit on his head —"

Midge wasn't at all sure where the man's head was, nor did she fancy sitting on it. She gingerly leant across the flying legs and arms and pulled at the tartan shawl. The mild face of the little man, wispy hair on end, glasses gone, gazed at her in indignation, like an infuriated sheep. Midge put her hand to her head. "Susan!" she whispered. "What have you *done*?"

There was a rush of feet outside and the Minister and Lady Alison, followed by a number of interested onlookers, crowded into the opening.

The little man looked round him in a daze; Lady Alison gazed at him in horror. "Mr Carlisle!" she exclaimed.

There was a horrid silence. Susan, her head still wrapped up in the black veil, turned and gazed at the little man too. She said in a shock whisper, "Not Mr *Rock* Carlisle!"

The little man began to crawl about on his hands and knees. Lady Alison said, "But my *dear* Mr Carlisle, what are you *doing* grovelling there?"

The little man turned his head and looked up at her. "I am endeavouring to find my spectacles," he said, "which became dislodged in the recent — ah — fracas."

"But — but — but — but how did you get into the fracas?" Lady Alison stammered.

Bill and Midge, not liking the turn that events were taking, went down on their knees and also began to hunt around for the glasses, their faces averted. Susan, feeling sick, dragged herself to her feet. "Lady Alison —" she croaked. She began again, "Lady Alison, I'm sorry, I'm *sorry*, but I went for Mr

He turned his head and looked up at her.

Carlisle."

"What an extraordinary thing to do, Susan," said Lady Alison coldly.

"Yes, I know," Susan gulped. "But you see, I didn't know that he was Mr Carlisle. I thought that he was the Bank Robber!"

Midge gave a little moan; she handed a rather lop-sided pair of spectacles to Mr Carlisle who put them on his nose and gravely regarded Susan through them. "I am gratified," he said.

But he didn't sound gratified. He sounded, Susan thought, as mad as a snake. Babel broke out, everybody talking at once and most of them abusing Susan. Susan — it was the least that she could do, she felt — apologised abjectly to Mr Carlisle, to Lady Alison, to the Minister, to practically everyone. "It was a terrible mistake," she said in a small voice.

Eventually Mr Carlisle, with Lady Alison and the Minister in attendance, went off to be tided up and brushed down and comforted with cups of tea; and as the excitement was apparently over, everybody gradually drifted off. Silently, Bill and Midge picked up the table and chairs knocked over in the "fracas." Susan just stood there in hopeless dejection. Eventually Midge could stand this dreary silence no longer. "But Susie," she said, "what made you *do* it?"

"Well, it was the scar," said Susan. "He had a scar across his knuckles, like Jessie Kelso said, and naturally I didn't stop to say, 'Excuse me, but are you the Bank Robber,' I just went for him —"

"Naturally," murmured Midge.

Bill burst out, "Well, I don't care what any of them say, I think that you were hang of a brave, Susie. Gosh, he might have whipped out his gun and shot you dead!"

But even this kindly thought didn't cheer Susan up. "Well, thanks, Bill," she gulped again, "but I don't think I was anything but plain daft. But" — she added indignantly — "who would ever have thought that that little rabbity man was Rock Carlisle! Where are the guns? Where are the knives? Where's the tough American slang? How could that little man *ever* write those terrific blood-and-thunders?"

No one was able to answer these questions. Midge handed Susan her tartan shawl.

"What's this for?" said Susan.

"Well, ducks," said Midge, "for the spae-wife. There's still a queue about a mile long outside."

"You don't think that I'm going to tell any more *fortunes*!" Susan demanded.

"The Show Must Go On," said Midge, striking an attitude. "Remember the church roof."

Susan muttered a few rude remarks under her breath, but in the end gave in and agreed to go on with her fortune-telling. "But," she said, "if any more strangers approach, for goodness' sake come in and warn me first and tell me who they are before I start telling them their fortunes..."

When the fête was over and the piles and piles of money were being counted and Mr Rock Carlisle had presented the prizes for all the various competitions, and all the young people were thinking of hurrying home to change for the dance that was to follow, Mr Rock Carlisle came to the spae-wife's tent to look for Susan who had refused to attend the prize-giving. "Go and stand there in front of everybody and feel a fool?" she said. "No fear!"

" 'Mm, perhaps better not," Midge agreed. "They say he has a black eye —"

It wasn't a very black, black eye, Susan noted as she took one quick, self-conscious look at the famous author before turning her eyes shame-facedly to the ground, but perhaps that would come later. She didn't know what he had come back for, unless to hand her over to the police for assault or something, and she wished that he would go away.

Mr Carlisle didn't seem to know what he had come for, either. He hummed and hawed and clasped and unclasped his hands nervously and eventually said, "Miss Susan, I owe you an apology."

Susan looked up then, in amazement. "*You* owe *me* an apology?"

"Yes, indeed." Mr Carlisle went on humming and hawing and clasping and unclasping like mad. "You see," he finally burst out, "I *am* the Bank Robber!"

At the expression on Susan's face he hurried on, "Oh, not a *real* Bank Robber, naturally, but you see, Miss Susan, in my books I do like to have my detail as accurate as possible, so I have to commit the most extraordinary crimes and carry dead bodies across moors and hide corpses in cellars — not *real* dead bodies," he put in soothingly, "and this time I had occasion to perpetrate a bank robbery. And I must say," he added in a pleased voice, "that it all went off very successfully, very successfully indeed, when one considers that the weapon was no more than a water-pistol." He paused and gave a little happy smile at the recollection; and then he hurried on more seriously, "But unfortunately, I must admit that I am a very great coward. Not only a physical coward but a moral one as well — and this, my dear Miss Susan, is where I owe you an apology, for with Lady Alison and the good Reverend Mr McLeod standing by, I just could not confess to what I had done."

Susan burst out joyfully, "Oh, gosh, Mr Carlisle, how wonderful! I mean not that you're the Bank Robber, I think that's a bit steep, actually, Jessie Kelso nearly had a heart attack, but that I was right after all and didn't really make a fool of myself! Och, *please* don't apologise, Mr Carlisle, I'm a dreadful coward myself about things like that and *please* may I have your autograph?"

Mr Carlisle beamed. " I shall send you an autographed copy of my next book," he said kindly. "With the bank robbery in it."

"Oh, thank you," said Susan. Mr Carlisle said not at all, raised his hat politely and turned away.

Then suddenly Susan gasped and said, "But Mr Carlisle! What about the money?"

"Dear me, yes, the money," said Mr Carlisle in a vexed voice, "how forgetful I am." He fished a huge wad of notes out of his pocket. "I was debating with myself how best to return this, but perhaps you can help me? I leave on the early boat to-morrow, so if you would be good enough to delay the return of the money until after I am gone?" He thrust the notes into Susan's limp hands, then gravely raising his hat once more he turned and walked gently away across the golf course.

X: SUSAN IN TROUBLE

JANE SHAW

There was great excitement when Tessa got the letter about the USA from her father. At least, no one, according to Susan, had ever seen Tessa more excited than a half-dead fish in an aquarium at feeding time — "she opens her mouth a little wider than usual, that's all" Susan maintained — but Susan was excited enough for two anyway.

The letter came at breakfast time just before the Easter holidays, when everybody was pretty sick of school anyway and any diversion was welcome. Midge, Susan and Tessa were dallying over breakfast, reluctant to leave the warm dining room and face the icy March winds outside on their way to prayers, when the post was handed round by a prefect. Tessa read her letter in her slow deliberate way and Susan, who had no letters herself that morning, fidgeted. "Well, go on, tell," she said eventually, when Tessa had been given enough time to read a *book*, "what's the news, Tessa?"

As usual, Tessa didn't answer directly. "You know my father?" she said.

"Of course I don't know your father," said Susan. "I've never met your father. He's always abroad, never even comes to Speech Day — ."

"No, well, but you know who I mean — ."

"Och, I know who you *mean*."

"Yes, well, you know that he is in the Foreign Service?"

Susan said that she did know that, but that she'd often wondered if Tessa hadn't made some sort of mistake about that, because *she* had always thought that these diplomatic types were supposed to be very clever, diplomatic and all that jazz, yet how could a clever diplomatic father have a dim daughter like Tessa?

Tessa was indignant. "Well of course I haven't made a mistake," she said. "Surely I should know what my own father does?"

"Well, you would think so," said Susan, "but you know what you're like, Tessa, you never know what's going on half the time."

Tessa said she jolly well knew what her own father did and this time she could prove it because this letter was from him saying he'd stopped being a first secretary and had become an ambassador.

"Wow," said Susan, impressed in spite of herself.

"Ambassador to where?" asked Midge.

"He's been appointed ambassador to Mexico," said Tessa, referring to her letter, "and I'm to go out there for the summer hols instead of going to Granny in Cornwall as usual."

"Lucky you," said Susan.

"He and Mum will meet me in New York," said Tessa, "and we'll sort of have a quick look at the USA first and then go to this place in Mexico."

"Sup-er," said Susan, nearly ill with envy.

"Wish you could come too," said Tessa vaguely.

"Some hope," said Midge, and Susan got very excited at the mere idea and plied Tessa with questions about New York, the USA and Mexico which she certainly couldn't answer until a prefect told them to make less noise and to get over to prayers right away if they didn't want an order mark or a fine or a few lines to keep them quiet...

At Easter, Susan told her parents about Tessa's fantastic good fortune, and her parents glanced at each other and her mother said, "Well, that's a funny coincidence because there's a chance, just a chance mind you, that you and I might go with your father when he goes to New York for this engineering conference. If we do go, Tessa could travel with us — ."

Susan could hardly credit her good fortune. Her ideas of life in the USA were sketchy in the extreme and derived, naturally enough, from the pictures, but she was sure that it was a country which would please her extremely. "For one thing," she said, "no boring old museums and picture galleries like in Italy and even in London for that matter." The Statue of Liberty and the Empire State Building were about the extent of her knowledge of the sights of New York and she was prepared to examine them with enthusiasm. "The only thing is," she said, "Midge. Any chance of old Midge coming too?"

Susan's mother didn't think so. "The fare, after all — rather expensive," she said.

"Couldn't we stand that?" Susan suggested helpfully.

"No, we could not," said her father. "D'you think I'm made of money?"

Susan hadn't given the matter much thought. She had just got used to being with her cousin Midge most of the time, having lived with the Carmichaels while her parents were in Africa — going to the same school and everything. She put a coat on (it was a very late and cold spring that year) and went off down Tollgate Road to the Carmichaels' house to discuss this fantastic news with Midge.

She found Midge, as usual, lying supine in a big chair in front of the fire in the room that everyone except Charlotte, the eldest of the family, called the schoolroom.

"Midge," said Susan, losing no time. She threw off

her coat and edged Bill, who was doing something to his stamps on the hearthrug, over a bit with her toe and knelt down at Midge's feet. "Midge, d'you remember that story you once wrote and Charlotte illustrated and some dotty publisher gave you twelve pounds for it, well could you do another one, only bigger and better?"

"No," said Midge.

"Oh go on, you could," said Susan persuasively. "There's nothing to it, no running about or anything, just sitting there writing a story — ." Susan had no illusions about Midge's energy, which was non-existent.

"Even if I could, which I can't, why should I?" said Midge. "I'd rather read stories that other people have written than write one of my own. More fun, you don't know what's coming. Why should I write a boring old story?"

"Because you need the money," said Susan.

Well, that was all too probable, the Carmichaels always apparently needed money, but was there some urgent need of money just at that moment? — "What do I need it *for*?" Midge said cautiously.

"Your fare to New York," said Susan. Midge didn't go so far as to sit up, but she did raise an eyebrow. "We're all going in the summer vac," said Susan. "Tessa too, *you* remember, and Daddy won't pay your fare — ."

"That doesn't altogether surprise me," said Midge.

" — so I thought," said Susan, "that perhaps you could write a story or something and pay your own fare." She sat back on her heels triumphantly. "Nothing to it."

"Nothing to it!" Bill interrupted his philatelic labours to snort. "Look at all the trouble I had raising a measly ten pounds at Christmas for Oxfam! And I bet the fare to New York's more than

£10."

"I bet," said Midge. "And you can cut out this writing lark, Susie my pet, you know I can't stand it. I'd as soon stowaway or hijack a plane or something — ."

There was a momentary gleam in Susan's eye. "D'you think you could?" she began eagerly, kneeling up again, but at the sight of Midge's expression she sank back on her heels again. "No, I suppose not," she said. "After all, I don't imagine you've got a gun."

Midge couldn't help feeling that that would be one of the least of her problems if she were contemplating taking up hijacking, but if she so much as mentioned this she was sure that Susan, in her helpful way, would produce a gun for her in no time. So she said, "What's all this about New York anyway?"

"Well," said Susan, "can you believe it, but we're *going*. I was telling Daddy and Ma about Tessa and Ma said that there was a chance we might go. Daddy has some old engineering conference and Ma thinks that we might go with him, isn't it really something?"

Midge cast her mind momentarily on all the thousands, indeed millions, of unsuspecting Americans whom Susan, in her bossy way, would be longing to help, organise, reform and generally alter, and gave a small shudder. "Heaven help America," she said.

"Och, away, you daft scone," said Susan giggling. "It's none of *my* business what Americans do."

"It's none of your business what *any*body does," said Midge, "but does that stop you?"

"Midge," said Susan earnestly, "you *know* that I've given up interfering in people's lives and all that jazz — ."

"What d'you think you're doing at this moment?" Midge asked wildly, "nagging away at me to write stories?"

"Don't you *want* to go to America?" said Susan.

"Well, natch," said Midge, "but my chances are slender. Nil if they depend on my literary abilities."

"It doesn't have to be a story," said Susan. "You could win a competition. There are thousands of those. You can't open a paper but there's a competition. 'Write a slogan for Bang-on toothpaste and win a free trip to the Costa del Sol and five hundred pounds spending money' — ."

"You could win a beauty competition," said Bill, entering into the spirit of the thing. "Oh, well, no," he added, glancing at Midge, "perhaps not — ." Midge certainly wasn't looking her best.

"How can anyone who looks like a midge, all big eyes and pointed chin, win a beauty competition?" said Susan. "Charlotte, now — . We'd better find another sort of a competition for Midge."

She became, in the days that followed, a bit of a bore with her competitions, from the rather highbrow efforts in the back of the *Spectator* to the two guineas for every recipe published in the *Woman's Weekly*. Not that she hadn't other schemes as well, of course, from backing the Derby winner at tremendous odds and the expenditure of a few paltry shillings, to something like the Great Train Robbery, only easier and, preferably, more honest, there was no shortage of schemes. "Just the basic unlikelihood that I'd ever make a more successful punter and/or train robber," said Midge.

"Well, just like I said," said Susan, "you should write a story. No skills, energy, exertion, brains, required."

"You write a story," said Midge. "You've got all the qualifications plus energy — ."

XI: STARTING FROM GLASGOW: JANE SHAW'S SCOTLAND

ALISON J. LINDSAY

As befits an author born and brought up in Glasgow, all of Jane Shaw's Scottish books are set on the west coast of Scotland; and her chosen sites are, conveniently, easily accessible by public transport. Her home town is the starting point for journeys to Loch Lomond, Arran and Connel; but there is much more to say about Glasgow as the setting for Jane Shaw's own life than for her writings, since she set only one short story, *Crooks Limited*, there. Several of her books do begin in Glasgow, but the participants lose little time in moving the action elsewhere. Nonetheless, Jane Shaw spent all of her childhood in Glasgow, in the family home at 9 Newton Place, and all of her education was obtained within ten minutes' walk of this house. Newton Place forms part of Sauchiehall Street, just west of its crossing over the M8 motorway and No. 9, like its neighbours, now houses offices although the attractive frontage retains its ironwork balconies and railings.

A short walk up the adjoining Woodside Terrace leads to Lynedoch Street, formerly home to the private Park School, which Jean attended between 1909 and 1928. Park's school uniform included a navy blazer with olive-green collar, and both *Crook's Tour* and *Crooks Limited* mention this unusual colour combination, although the book refers to striped blazers: Fay's inquiry of Mr Rushton if he has seen two girls in "blue and green blazers" is closer to Park's own uniform.

Following its merger with another Glasgow girls' school, Park's building at 25 Lynedoch Street was converted to flats, but the imposing sandstone portico remains and the gates still bear the legend "Park School". From here, one can follow the route taken in *Crooks Limited* "down the hill" from school and along Woodlands Road. Rushton's "famous antique shop" may have been inspired by the real J. E. Rushmer, Complete Home Furnisher and specialist in antiques, whose shop once occupied 228 Woodlands Road, on the right hand corner of its intersection with Willowbank Crescent. At this part of the road, various streets provide short cuts to Great Western Road, where Fay sought help from young PC McPherson and along which Jean used to drive to reach Loch Lomond.

Over the river Kelvin is Glasgow University, where Jean's grandfather, father and two brothers studied medicine. Jean spent four years here, between 1928 and 1932, at a time when relatively few women were able to attend university, and graduated with honours in English Literature and Language. No doubt inspired by this, the Macfarlanes' father in *The Crew of the Belinda* lectures at Glasgow University on English literature and bibliography. Jean was married in Wellington Church, whose Greek portico entrance faces University Avenue, where her father was an elder.

After graduating, Jean spent a year or two in London, but then returned to work for the well-known Glasgow publishing company, William Collins Sons and Co Ltd. The office premises at that date were at No. 144, on the north side of Cathedral Street: these were demolished some years ago; and the grassy land which replaced them is now part of the Strathclyde University complex. Although the firm no longer has premises in the centre of Glasgow, its name is commemorated in the university's nearby Collins Gallery.

Loch Lomond

While she was living in Glasgow, Jean and her mother made many motor trips out to the countryside that lies around Glasgow. Great Western Road is the main road which leads west from Glasgow: it takes travellers out to Balloch, Loch Lomond and Luss, the setting for *The Crew of the Belinda*. To join *Belinda*, Lilias, Fanny and Pips took a bus from 'Little Drumbles' to Luss. Fanny's dirge began near Balloch at the foot of Loch Lomond: Balloch lies on the road around the loch, which means the girls could have been arriving from Glasgow or round from the north east. I've always thought of Drumbles as being to the north of Glasgow, perhaps somewhere like Drymen, which too is "a lovely little village, only twenty miles from Glasgow".

Luss is now by-passed, but a path leads from the bus-stop on the main A82 road to the Colquhoun Arms Hotel, where Mr Macfarlane found accommodation. In the past twenty years, Luss has acquired a new fame as the original of 'Glendarroch' in the television soap opera *[Take the] High Road*, and the Glendarroch Tearooms stand beside the hotel.

The road down to the pier from the Colquhoun Arms is lined with single-storey cottages (red sandstone rather than the white houses which Fanny admired), each with a tiny garden in front. The trim appearance is emphasised by the well-polished brass door knobs, letterboxes, and neat nameplates which brighten each front door. Halfway down the road on the right, as it curves towards the pier, is the post office, most of which is now given over to tourist souvenirs. Luss's size suggests that it could never have supported a bookshop, let alone one with an upstairs room: but this seems the likeliest location for Margaret Scott's shop since the girls interrupted their walk through the village to the pier to go in and see her.

Loch Lomond is the largest single expanse of enclosed water in Britain, over 27 square miles in extent. The Macfarlanes' morning row up to Tarbet and Inveruglas would have taken several hours more than the book suggests. Along the promenade to the right is the church, built in 1875 to commemorate the drowning of Sir James Colquhoun of Luss off Inchtavannach two years previously. It lies close to the water's edge, above the jetty which also serves the Loch Lomond Rescue Boat. The church is a neat stone structure, built on a miniature scale, and the aisle up which the anguished Fanny had to walk is no more than a few paces long. The girls' surname, MacFarlane, is one well-known in the area: on the north wall is the 'MacFarlane stone', dated 1612, with its inspiring aphorism 'after deathe remains virtue', and there are a number of Macfarlane memorial inscriptions in the graveyard.

Parallel to the A82, now the main route north, runs the Old Military Road. This passes in front of the Colquhoun Arms and along it, about a mile south of Luss, is Aldochlay, which consists of half a dozen cottages and a yacht club. The Buchanans' houseboat, *Clairinch*, was moored in the little semi-circle of Aldochlay Bay and it still holds a variety of pleasure craft, now yachts and dinghies, many of them moored beside the little island Liz mentioned. The scale is startlingly small: Aldochlay Bay is crowded with a dozen boats, and "the steep green slope" Robert climbed to greet the girls is only about six feet from the shore to the road. Inchtavannach, also known as Swan Island, guards the bay, and its peculiar humped shape was noticed by Lilias when the MacFarlanes arrived. Between it and Inchconnachan (Inch is Gaelic for island) lie Luss narrows, called "the straits of Luss". *Belinda* was moored "just round the corner", on the Luss side of Aldochlay Bay's sheltering arms, by ground now owned by a private yacht club. Jean spent some time here as a university student with a group of her girlfriends, on a houseboat owned by a male friend; she based her book on this stay.

Connel Ferry

Both Arran and Connel Ferry may be visited by train: with of course, in Arran's case, an additional ferry journey. Glasgow now has just two railway stations, Queen Street and Central Station, and it is from the former that trains run two or three times a day to Connel Ferry (now Connel, once South Connel), a place of family holidays in Jean's youth, and the setting for her wartime thriller *The House of the Glimmering Light*. Its station, confusingly still called Connel Ferry, is the penultimate stop on the Glasgow-Oban section of the West Highland Line. Although the action in *The House of the Glimmering Light* does not start until the train is nearly at Dalmally, the entire journey provides a fascinating and beautiful introduction to the scenery of the west of Scotland. Beyond Dalmally is the head of Loch Awe, and Kilchurn Castle on its rocky islet: its rugged grey walls suggest Jean's description of Tighanleys, "an ancient house, tall and grey, with crow-stepped gables and high narrow windows. It had begun life as a fortress; on one side its walls went down almost sheer into the Loch..."

At Taynuilt, the railway joins Loch Etive and runs

alongside it until reaching Connel Ferry which, despite considerable new building, remains a small and quiet West Highland village. From the station, the road sloping down to the left leads to the only shop in the village, which serves as Post Office and General Store combined. The original Post Office lies to the left and round the corner, and is now a terracotta-coloured guest house called Taigh Òsda Loch Èire. This road carries on to the lochside, past St Oran's Church with its noticeboard featuring a carving of Connel Bridge. The church is on the corner of the main road to Oban: the right-hand section leads towards the house of Dunfiunary on its promontory, the original of Tighanleys, and ten minutes' walk from the village.

Dunfiunary, "the big house" as it is still called in the village, is smaller and more modern in date than its description, but it is still much the largest house in the village. Built of grey, rough-cut granite, with red sandstone window surrounds and crow-stepped gables, it is just two storeys high: lower, one infers, than Tighanleys with its "top storey" where Miss Gill slept. The house stands some ten or twelve feet higher than the road, and on the Connel side a footpath descends to a little white gate giving on to the main road, where Angela, racked with toothache, met Noel one morning. Further along the road is the drive for cars visiting the house. On the north side, Dunfiunary's windows overlook but do not overhang the loch. The "east wing" where Fiona slept, has its basis in fact: between 1903 and 1910 the then owner, Captain Norman Macalister, virtually doubled the size of the house by building an extension and turret onto the original property on the eastern side. This addition lies nearest to the road, and includes the round turret on the eastern side of the house: there is another turret on the north-west corner of the house overlooking the loch.

Much of the activity in the book takes place around the boathouse and garage. As described in the book, these buildings lie on the Connel side of the house, but Dunfiunary's garage, built around 1910 by Captain Macalister, lies further from the house than the boathouse, not between the two. The 'jetty' would more correctly be described as a slipway, a stone ramp which descends at a shallow angle into the water and a more practical solution when launching in tidal water. The land on this side of the house is more overgrown, although the tall pines which cluster here offer little cover for watchers between their slim trunks.

Walking back into the village, the view to the west is dominated by the light grey girders of Connel Bridge. Surprisingly, this is never mentioned in *The House of the Glimmering Light*, although as it was built in 1903 Jean must have known it. The bridge originally carried the railway north to Ballachulish, and so would have been closed to pedestrians. Now, with the railway gone, it carries the road north over the Falls of Lora: shallow but dangerous tidal rapids, not a waterfall. From the bridge there are superb views down the loch towards Dunfiunary on its promontory and Ben Cruachan.

Arran

Arran is the setting for three Jane Shaw stories: *Highland Holiday* (1942), *Penny Foolish* (1953) and *Susan Muddles Through* (1960), as well as the short story *Susan and the Spae-Wife*. *Highland Holiday* is the book most closely based on Jean's memories of summers spent there before the Second World War, when the island was a popular holiday spot for thousands of Scots. The familiar holiday joys of sniffing the peat-scented air for the first time and meeting old friends at the club house recur throughout the Arran books, but Jean's strongest holiday memory may well be the six boiled eggs eaten at various farms on an afternoon of farewell visits: both Midge and Caroline recall the event vividly.

Trains run from Glasgow's Central Station to Ardrossan Harbour and are timed to meet the Arran boats. The *Glen Sannox*, which served the route between 1925 and 1954, would have carried the Patricks across, and in turn takes the Storms, Penny and the Carmichaels. It was replaced by another *Glen Sannox*, this one a car ferry, but in 1970 she was replaced by the larger *Caledonia*. The crossing is now made by M.V. *Caledonian Isles*, the largest car ferry operated by Caledonian MacBrayne. Ardrossan to Brodick takes about an hour, and as the ferry sails into the encircling arms of Brodick Bay, the neat triangular peak of Goatfell can be seen to the north. Lower down its slope are the Victorian turrets of Brodick Castle, once home to Arran's aristocratic owners the Dukes of Hamilton, and now a National Trust for Scotland property. It may have inspired the Castle of Monimore, whose aristocratic chatelaine opens the fête in *Highland Holiday*. Further north along the coast, halfway between Sannox and Lochranza, is Boguillie, immortalized in Sara's play, "The Witch of Boguillie".

The bus from Brodick to Blackwaterfoot goes over the String Road (designed by the famous engineer Thomas Telford) to the flatter, more fertile, southwest of the island. A ritual described often in the books is to look quickly to either side as the car or bus reaches the summit, and see the sea on both sides of the island. High Fraoch, the farmhouse which features in *Penny Foolish*, is in real life High Feorline in the Shiskine valley, where Jean's family stayed during their holidays in Arran. For the convenience of the plot of *Susan Muddles Through*, Glen Rowan is set close to the shore at Blackwaterfoot, but it is recognisably the same farm house. Named North Feorline on the map, but called High Feorline by its owners, this farm lies between Blackwaterfoot and Shedog, east of, and higher than, the road. Opposite the house is the "summerhouse", mentioned in both books, whither the farm family would decamp over the summer while renting out the farmhouse to holidaymakers. The Murchies, the family who occupied the farm when the Patricks visited (and still farm there today), are the subject of the dedication of *Penny Foolish*. In *Highland Holiday*, the farm features as Farthinglands, which is given up in favour of staying at Renasay Lodge.

Above High Feorline, a track leads up the hill to a low ruined building housing a sheep dip. In *Penny Foolish* it is called Rashiedrum, and described as an old farmhouse: which indeed it was, since the present farm of North Feorline was once two separate farms, the other named Bruach Breac. All that remains today is the sheep-dip itself (a narrow, deep hole) and a few rows of stones up to window height. Beyond the sheep dip, a track leads up to Loch Cnoc an Loch, which must be the little loch Penny and the Macdonalds scrambled up to, roasting potatoes on the way. Energetic walkers may want to continue along the forest walk and descend via the Clauchan Water (the Clachan Burn in *Penny Foolish*). There are two or three little pools along its length, one with a waterfall where Penny and the Macdonalds swam.

Just north of High Feorline, on the main road and

visible across the fields from the farm, is the little church dedicated to St Molios. This is always called the "Red Church" in the books, from its red tiled roof and red sandstone walls, but had no nearby manse such as the Macdonalds occupy until a rather ugly bungalow was built in its grounds. The church interior is simple and unadorned, with rows of plain wooden pews facing the communion table and pulpit. In the tiny chancel, at right angles to the table, is the pew once reserved for those staying at the Dougarie shooting lodge a mile or so beyond Machrie.

The famous Tin Hall, the upkeep of whose roof was of such concern to visitors and residents alike, is now demolished. It stood on the right hand side of the road just beyond the hamlet of Shedog. It was a Nissan hut, thrown up after the First World War, and the noise of rain on its metal roof ruined any production going on inside. It was pulled down around 1960, and modern houses now occupy the site.

On the main road down from High Feorline to Blackwaterfoot is the war memorial, past which Penny urged Mr Macpherson's pony. Opposite it are the fields of Tighenfraoch (House of the Heather) farm, possibly the source of High Fraoch's name. The road through the village turns inland to Machrie, but a track to the left leads along the coast to the golf club, centre of Blackwaterfoot's holiday activities. The Macdonalds, as Penny found, are grim players of golf, although in real life Jean was less energetic. The course at Blackwaterfoot is only 12 holes, and although she was in Glasgow University's women's golf team, Jean never could accustom herself to the standard 18 holes. A board inside the clubhouse lists former captains of the club: John Patrick, Jean's father, was captain between 1936-38; and her brother William served between 1951-52, when the club was run largely by and for the summer visitors.

The grandiose Renasay Lodge in *Highland Holiday* was located along the golf course road and to the right, where the farm of Drumadoon stands, just north-west of Blackwaterfoot. Sara's mother describes it as looking "rather like a great, bristly gooseberry, the walls are so bedecked with the antlers of defunct stags". Nothing of that description has ever occupied the site, but the model for this may well have been Dougarie Lodge, a two-storey shooting lodge built for the 12th Duke of Hamilton some five or six miles along the coast to the north. Some time before 1900 its external walls were hung with numerous pairs of antlers, giving the lodge a very bizarre appearance, although this decoration has now disappeared.

Beyond the golf course is Drumadoon Point. With cliffs rising perpendicularly from the sea to a height of 300 feet, this is a formidable natural fortress, and was occupied as such by the first inhabitants of Arran. An Iron Age hill-fort or 'doon' occupies a level area of several acres on its summit. The Doon's antiquity was of little concern to Sara and Caroline, who found the sunken depressions ideal spots to catch up on snoozing and sun bathing. A path leads round its landward side, and a steep scramble takes visitors down to the shore. A mile or so along the coast is the King's Cave, where the fake Mrs Lobster hid while trying to steal Uncle Thomas's cold cure. In *Highland Holiday*, the cave has only recently been fitted with a grille and lock: this really happened in the 1920s or 1930s, when concern over vandalism led to the cave being secured in this way. There are a number of caves at this point, one reached through a rock passage, and the King's

Cave lies beyond several smaller ones. Some of the other caves are also fitted with grilles, but the King's Cave is the only one to have a soaring pointed arch reaching to the cave's roof, nearly 40 foot above the ground. The grille is locked, but an inset of curved railings allows visitors to get slightly closer to the cave interior.

Further round the coast is Machrie, where Mirren and Callum lived in *Penny Foolish*. Machrie Water meanders across a boggy plain to the sea: by the number and names of its pools, it is obviously an angling stream. There are half a dozen stone circles standing by its banks, in various stages of preservation: some are certainly large enough to hide behind, although one would feel painfully exposed on the open moor. The proximity of the stream may be responsible for the numerous small insects which congregate here to pester visiting tourists.

West of Goatfell is Cir Mhor, the great comb, pronounced Keer Vore, which is climbed in *Penny Foolish*. In a routine well known to the Patrick family, the children cycle from Blackwaterfoot over the String Road, some ten miles' journey. At its foot, on the east side of the island, a narrow road opening on the left before the junction at Brodick leads to the flat-bottomed valley of the Glenrosa Water. A walk of some four or five miles leads to the head of the valley and up to The Saddle and the summit of Cir Mhor. Once at its summit, the Macdonalds "felt as if they had conquered the world": the achievement feels the same whatever the weather, but climbers should try to make the ascent on a day when the cloud is high, so that mist does not obliterate the marvellous views of Arran, often called "Scotland in miniature".

XII: AMANDA'S SPIES

JANE SHAW

Amanda lay on her stomach under the trees, brooding over a newspaper cutting. "It's not right," she said. "It's not right. Everybody catches Nazis but me."

Her dear friend Elizabeth sighed. Amanda, Elizabeth felt, had been quite bad enough before, but now the newspapers had published the story of the woman who, with great coolness and presence of mind, had unarmed and taken into custody a stranded Nazi airman, she was rapidly becoming impossible. Such things, she supposed reluctantly, might happen elsewhere, but really, she thought, looking about her at the lovely placid waters of Loch Ard, she couldn't imagine a less likely spot for a Nazi to lurk. She mentioned some of this, and also the fact that Amanda would be in danger of developing into a bore if she didn't turn her mind, if any, to something other than spies for a bit.

"Well," Amanda didn't object to trying, "I'd put up with a parachutist if I couldn't get a spy. But *what* hope have we of either, stuck away here in the wilds? For safety! Huh! I wish we lived in the middle of a town instead of in the middle of Perthshire. Or near an aerodrome."

Elizabeth wasn't going to admit it, but she personally was more than pleased to be staying with Amanda in the remoteness of Loch Ard. She didn't think she'd care about bombs, and if that meant doing without spies too, well, she could view even that prospect with equanimity.

"Maybe," she offered the hope, rather hypocritically, she felt, "maybe something'll turn up. And, and in the meantime," she added, "don't you think — lunch?"

Amanda sniffed. Elizabeth, she thought, was all too prone to attach a false importance to mundane things like food. Was her country's fate nothing to her? But, all the same, Amanda suffered herself to be led to where their little rowing-boat was beached, and graciously permitted Elizabeth to row her down the Loch towards the house and lunch.

She scanned the horizon and the skies gloomily as she went. The sight of a low white house, standing behind smooth lawns which sloped down to the water's edge, seemed to cause her further dissatisfaction. "Even Potty," she said, nodding towards the shuttered house "is off in the A.T.S. or somewhere, while we're rotting here in disuse —"

" 'It little profits that an idle king,
By this still hearth, among these barren crags —' "

Elizabeth began unexpectedly. Amanda looked at her coldly, and Elizabeth abruptly changed her quotation into a giggle.

"I didn't hear anyone make a joke," Amanda said.

"Really!" thought Elizabeth. "Testy!" Aloud, she explained apologetically, "I was only thinking of Potty in khaki," she said.

The story of this Potty, otherwise Miss Potts, one-time science mistress at St. Bridget's (which seat of learning numbered Amanda and Elizabeth among its less hopeful pupils) was quite a romance. After years of fighting a losing battle with girls who showed an intense desire to blow up either themselves or the laboratory, she had suddenly fallen heir to a thousand a year and a house on Loch Ard, left to her by a first cousin once removed who had never set eyes on her but who wanted to spite his nearer relations, whom he disliked. Miss Potts, set free from bondage, had straightway shown the perverseness of human nature by building herself a small laboratory at the back of the house, where she devoted herself all day to what she called her inventions, with such success that once or twice she had just failed to blow herself up. It was probably this singleness of purpose which endeared her to Amanda, who felt for Miss Potts an unbounded admiration. Once, indeed, she had collaborated with her in the construction of a patent mouse-trap, but the only thing that had succeeded in trapping had been Amanda herself.

"You needn't jeer," Amanda said, "at Potty in khaki. She's terribly lucky to be able to do anything at all — not like me —"

Elizabeth did think that Amanda might ease her over-tender conscience by knitting or making bandages or something for her country's cause, but did not dare say so. She said instead, "Don't you know where Potty actually is? Didn't you see her before she left?"

"No," Amanda said. "When I came home from school she had gone — house shut up, and her housekeeper and the maids gone home to Aberfoyle." Her voice suddenly anxious, she went on, "It's just struck me — I hope it's all right. I hope nothing has happened to her —"

Here Elizabeth, who should have known better, made a tactical error. "What *could* have happened to her?" she said.

That was enough for Amanda. And her theories, gradually becoming less and less probable, ranged from fire and pestilence to lying unconscious in the house with a broken leg.

She was to go on like this for days. Elizabeth admitted it was a change from her other theme, the desire to help her country in some thoroughly dangerous and dramatic way, but she couldn't make up her mind whether it was more, or less disturbing. More, she decided suddenly, when Amanda came away with one of her best efforts, that Miss Potts had taken out her boat one day by herself, a sudden squall had arisen and she had been drowned, and her boat and her body washed far up the Loch. As Amanda and Elizabeth were out alone in their boat and a sudden squall had arisen when Amanda mentioned this, Elizabeth felt it was one of the most tactless things it had ever been her misfortune to hear. The Loch was grey and angry, and buffeted the dinghy unmercifully.

"What a bright idea to have at the present moment," she panted, battling against the waves.

"It was the present moment," murmured Amanda lugubriously, "gave me the idea. They say," she added, "that drowning's a pleasant death. I wonder how they know?"

Elizabeth said, "Oh dear. Let's get out of here. Can't we go ashore? It's beginning to pour, and we haven't made any progress in the last ten minutes. Suppose we let the wind take us back to Miss Potts' house — we could shelter until the wind dies down or get a lift on the road, or even walk home —"

They were taken by the wind, with little effort on their part, to Larachbeg, Miss Potts' house. They jumped out of the boat and dragged it up the beach and turned it over to keep it dry. The girls huddled under a couple of bushes and watched the rain on the Loch and waited for the storm to abate.

The only thing that abated was Amanda's patience. "This is foul," she said crossly, "we'll never get home and the rain's beginning to drip down my neck."

Elizabeth handed her a handkerchief, big enough

to go round her wrist, at best. "Put that round your neck," she said, "it helps."

Amanda wished it would help to hang her, but the handkerchief fortunately proved inadequate for that purpose. "Mummy will have had a stroke by now, I should think," she went on in a tone of mild interest.

"I know. I've been thinking about her. Hadn't we better walk?"

"Oh, no, it's miles. Let's go up to the house, and try to find some better shelter," suggested Amanda. "We could always spend the night there —"

"*What*! In an empty house!"

"Well, I don't honestly think you're in a position to be too fussy. Of course it would be worrying for Mummy, but think how pleased she would be to see us in the morning —"

Elizabeth was shocked, and determined that she for one would be home before morning. "But perhaps we should go up to the house for a little," she said, "this rain may go off soon. Of course the house will be locked up, but any kind of shelter would be better than this old bush —"

"Perhaps," Amanda shouted to her as they tripped and stumbled through the rain to the house, "perhaps Potty's ghost now haunts the place?"

"I'm not expecting anything more nasty," Elizabeth said hopefully, "than a few mice."

They had no success with the out-houses or back door; all were secured against such storm-stayed vagrants as themselves.

"We'll go round and try all the ground floor windows," said Amanda, as the rain pattered down on them. They prowled round the house and stopped, at last, discouraged, by a window belonging to Miss Potts' laboratory.

"I'm fed up," growled Amanda. "For two pins I'd *break* in," she said, reaching up and shaking furiously at the shutter.

The response to this attack was unexpected and alarming. From within came a confused murmur of sound; someone shrieked out, *"Donner und Blitzen!"* and a harsh voice cried, "What is the password? What is the password?"

Elizabeth jumped as if she had been shot, and gave a little squeak.

Her eyes nearly starting out of her head, Amanda whispered, "Shut up, for goodness sake. Did you hear? Did you hear? That was German, that bit about donner and blitzkrieg — it means, oh, something or other. And the other one — did you hear *him*? It's a nest of spies, Nazi spies —"

Elizabeth swallowed once or twice, then croaked out, "Let's go back to our boat," and started to run. She looked neither to right nor to left until she reached the shore, then, panting with terror, she crawled underneath the dinghy. Her heart was beating so loudly she simply did not hear approaching footsteps — heard nothing until the little boat creaked under the arrival of a heavy weight, and then her heart stopped beating altogether.

"Tut," Amanda clicked her tongue angrily and drummed her heels against the boat, "Where is the ass?"

A muffled and sepulchral voice from the depths

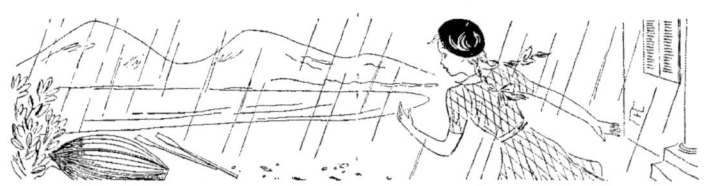

answered, "You're practically sitting on me —"

Amanda lifted the boat.

"Come in, do," said Elizabeth hospitably.

"Lily-livered knave," Amanda stormed. "What's the good of that? If they've heard us, the first thing they'll look for is a boat, if they don't see us on the road, they'll tip this up, and we'll be caught like rats."

"Let's go then," said Elizabeth, beginning to crawl rapidly away.

"Come *here*, poltroon," said Amanda, dragging her back by one pigtail. "We must have a plan."

"I have a plan," said Elizabeth, "I'm going home."

Amanda, overjoyed that at last reality was showing some resemblance to her dreams, ignored her. "What I think we should do," she whispered, "is, go back to Larachbeg —"

"Back to Larachbeg!"

"—for further evidence; then when the storm dies down a little, row back home for reinforcements. It's a pity, but I think it would be wiser than trying to capture the whole gang ourselves. There's no knowing *what* they've been getting up to, spying away. They come and go by night, I suppose, and all their nefarious doings are carried on behind shutters and drawn blinds. I expect they have a secret wireless transmitter and they send out messages to Berlin about what's going on. But not for much longer — *we*'ll cook their goose —"

"Don't you think," said Elizabeth in a voice so faint it scarcely was a voice, "that they'll cook ours first?"

"Nonsense," Amanda said briskly. "Two of us are a match for any ten Nazis."

Elizabeth thought it only fair to point out that their two was more one and a quarter, but that the quarter would do her best. "You go back to

Larachbeg," she said. "I'll stay and guard the boat."

Amanda managed to bring home to her, however, that the boat didn't need a guard, and after this discussion they advanced to the house cautiously, Amanda on her stomach. When Elizabeth objected, she pointed out that she preferred to do the thing properly, and in any case, she was wet through already.

They were crawling past the shuttered lab windows when there was a sudden crash, and the silence within the room was shattered by a very babel of sound. Harsh gutturals dinned about their ears, and never had the girls so regretted their imperfect education, for they could only make out a word here and there — *"Heinkel" "Sieg! Heil!"* — but these words they knew only too well.

Elizabeth leant against the wall, white and shaken. Amanda had a broad beam of delight on her face. "Isn't it lovely?" she said. "My chance at last."

"It's horrible," shuddered Elizabeth, as she listened. "They sound so inhuman."

Amanda said, "Now do you believe it's a nest of spies? Let's surround the place and taken them prisoner —"

Elizabeth had never doubted it was the entire Gestapo. But she did doubt their own ability to do as Amanda suggested. She moaned slightly. Amanda signed to her to come out of earshot of the window, although to judge by the noise coming from it, an elephant could have tramped round with impunity.

They halted beyond the windows, and Elizabeth, perhaps hoping to take Amanda by surprise, said, "Let's go home,"

"Oh, don't be so soft," said Amanda, exasperated. "I don't think we should wait for reinforcements. I suggest we should now go into action. I have a scheme —"

Elizabeth was to remain for ever ignorant of what Amanda's scheme might be, for at that moment from the lab came a new voice saying, in English:

"What is the password?"

Amanda looked at Elizabeth, round-eyed. "D'you hear that?" she gasped. "That's Potty's voice! Oh, the poor darling! She's being held a prisoner — in her own house — they're probably torturing her —"

Miss Potts did not sound as if she were being tortured. In fact, she sounded very much in command of the situation.

"What is the password?" she shouted again, obviously in a fine rage.

"*Ersatz*," came in a harsh voice.

"No. Password."

"*Heil Hitler*."

"No, no! The *password* —"

Amanda could stand it no longer. Before Elizabeth could stop her, she put her mouth up to the shutter and said in a low but firm and penetrating voice, "Miss Potts!"

There was a deathly silence within the room. Outside, Amanda stood tense, and Elizabeth began cautiously to edge towards the boat — if they were going to run for it, she felt, she preferred a start.

"Miss Potts," said Amanda again, "can you speak to me? It's me, Amanda —"

To their astonishment the shutter was unbolted and pushed open and a small anxious face with glasses, surmounted by rather wispy grey hair, appeared.

"It is *I*, my dear child," she said, "how often must I remind you? Why!" she added, as she surveyed them, "Quite a little gathering! This is a surprise. So kind of you to call, so kind." She suddenly recollected herself. "But you shouldn't have called. You don't know I am here. You must go away at once. At once. I'm living here in secret —"

"That's all right, Miss Potts," said Amanda, her emotion at the thought of her friend being in Nazi hands almost overcoming her, "we've come to rescue you."

"So kind of you, Amanda," said Miss Potts absently, "so kind —"

From the lab came a harsh shout of "Nuts!"

"There!" cried Miss Potts triumphantly, withdrawing her head. "The password! I have been trying for days to make him say that —"

The rescuers pulled open the shutters and gazed into the laboratory. Miss Potts, in a manner singularly unsuited to her years and dignity, was dancing round a large cage, a lump of sugar in her hand. Inside the cage a green parrot was hoping madly up and down, one eye on the lump of sugar, screaming, "Nuts. Nuts. Nuts. Nuts. Nuts."

Amanda, followed more doubtfully by Elizabeth, climbed through the window. All told, they discovered nine parrots and a cockatoo — and nothing else, neither Nazi nor human, in the whole house.

They went back to Miss Potts after their search, and, when her elation had subsided, persuaded her to talk to them. She was evasive, but they persevered. Yes, she admitted, she was living in the house, and had been for nearly a fortnight — yes, yes, of course, she had enough food, she had brought stores with her — tut! it didn't matter whether she *liked* living behind shutters and drawn blinds, that wasn't the point —

"Miss Potts," Amanda interrupted firmly, "what is the point? And what about the parrots?"

Vowing them to secrecy, Miss Potts told them then. "You know," she said, a fanatic glean in her mild blue eye, "the great and invaluable work done by pigeons in carrying messages in wartime?" They nodded. "Well," she said, a proud little smirk on her face, "I flatter myself I have hit on better messengers —"

"*Not* parrots!" said Amanda.

"Yes. Exactly. No trouble, no risk at all — no writing of notes which might so easily fall into the wrong hands — simply teach the parrot the message and send him off to Whitehall or G.H.Q., or wherever he has to go. Why! It is like having a fleet of little humans who can fly *and* speak — better, really, because no one would suspect a parrot. "Yes," and she beamed on them, "the authorities, poor short-sighted fellows, would not allow me to enlist, but I feel I am doing my little bit —"

"But Miss Potts," Amanda murmured, rather embarrassed, when she had finished, "honestly I don't think this is one of your best ideas. For one thing, when we heard the parrots they were all screeching away in *German* — "

"Oh yes, Amanda," Miss Potts' face clouded for a moment. "That was another of my ideas, a safeguard, to teach them a few simple German words or phrases — you understand, some of the things these Nazis insist on saying — so that if one of my poor parrots should fall into enemy hands he would have a little German ready to mislead his captors. But unfortunately," and she sighed, "they learn the German words so much more quickly than the passwords and codes I have been teaching them—"

"Yes," said Amanda, out of the bitterness of her heart. "Yes, they would. In fact," she said nastily, thrusting her face close up to the cage of a large bird with a particularly saturnine countenance, "I expect you are *really* a horrid old Nazi spy —"

The parrot eyed her balefully.

"Nuts," he said.

XIII: CROOKS LIMITED

JANE SHAW

Ricky slipped the newspaper cutting out of her desk and read it again. She had cut it out of the morning paper — much to her father's annoyance because he had not yet had a chance to read the paper — and she had been studying it at every suitable moment since. Not that this was a suitable moment, really, because it was in the middle of a history lesson, and she should have been listening to Miss Perry expounding the causes of the French Revolution instead of poring over a rather sensational newspaper cutting. However, it was to the cutting that she was giving all her attention:

FURNITURE VAN GANG —
DARING ROBBERIES

it was headed, and it went on to say: *Members of the public are warned of a gang operating in Glasgow and surrounding country districts. The gang drives up openly in a removal van to a house from which the owners are absent and empties the contents from the house into the van. This was the method thought to have been used when the house of Sir John McLintock in Whittingham Gardens was burgled, as a removal van, which has since not been traced, was seen standing outside the house for two hours. Sir John McLintock, a former Lord Provost of the city —* Ricky skipped that bit and hurried on to — *the house of Mr. William Lambie, the well-known Glasgow surgeon, at Killearn, was also thought to have been robbed in this way. It is significant that both Sir John and Mr. Lambie are well-known collectors of art and antiques —*

Miss Perry, glancing round the form, saw Ricky's studiously bent head, which was enough in itself to make her suspicious. She paused in what she was telling the form to say in her sarcastic way, "Erica has, I suppose, such a thorough knowledge of the causes of the French Revolution that she doesn't need to listen?"

Ricky, absorbed in her cutting, paid no attention. *Anyone*, the cutting finished, *who can give any information about this furniture van should telephone the police immediately*. Oh goodness, she thought, if only I could see this van! I'd telephone the police all right! I'd —

"*Erica!*"

Ricky jumped and looked up. "Yes, Miss Perry?"

"*Have* you a thorough knowledge of the causes of the French Revolution, Erica?"

Ricky gaped at Miss Perry. What a daft question! She didn't know the first thing about the French Revolution! Except, of course, what you could learn about it from *The Scarlet Pimpernel*. "Och, *no*, Miss Perry," she said.

"Then I suggest that as you apparently don't choose to listen in class, you can stay in this afternoon to make good the deficiency," said Miss Perry.

"Yes, Miss Perry," said Ricky, subdued. She wished that old Periwinkle didn't use such long words. Half the time Ricky didn't know what she was talking about; although, really, it wasn't difficult to understand "stay in this afternoon". It was sickening, and such a waste of time, to be kept in the very first afternoon that she had decided to hunt for that furniture van gang.

When she talked to her friends after history, they weren't particularly sympathetic.

"Furniture van! Crooks!" said Julie, who was small and round, and had red hair and freckles. "You've got crooks on the brain! Crooks, crooks, you never think of anything but crooks!"

"You should realise by this time," said Fay, "that old Periwinkle always knows what's going on. The only thing that you can safely do in her history lesson is history."

"Are you daft?" said Ricky. "How can I sit there doing nothing but history? It's so jolly dull. Besides, I've got other things to think about, such as catching those crooks."

Her friends laughed jeeringly. "Catch those crooks!" said Julie. "You've been trying for years to catch a crook, and so far you haven't even managed to *see* one, far less catch one!"

"Yes, well, I haven't been very lucky so far," Ricky admitted. "I don't know where all the crooks in Glasgow hide themselves. But just you wait! I'll catch one yet! And maybe this furniture van is my chance! I've got a feeling in my bones about this furniture van!"

"Oh, help," said Fay.

But in spite of the rude remarks of her friends, they were both waiting for her when Miss Perry eventually let her go. She beamed at them, fished in her blazer pocket, found three rather squashed and sticky toffees which she handed out, and, chewing happily, the three girls went off down the hill to catch a bus to take them home.

As no bus appeared immediately, Julie, always full of energy, suggested walking on to the next stop.

"Oh, help, *no*," said Fay, "you know what will happen. The bus will come when we're between stops."

However, it was a nice, mild June evening, the girls were in no particular hurry to reach home as they would immediately be forced by their mothers to do a lot of boring home-work when they got there, so they strolled on to the next bus-stop. Fay, of course, was right; they were mid-way between stops when the bus sailed past, and the argument started again at the next stop.

"Now that we *are* here," said Fay, "let's stop, for goodness' sake. If we go on like this, we'll find that we've walked home."

"Well, it's not far," said Julie, "and we could always buy sweets with our bus money."

This was tempting, but not quite tempting enough for Fay. She pondered for a moment, then shook her head. "Not worth it," she said. "I vote we take the bus. Ricky, what do you say?"

But Ricky was saying nothing. She was standing at the bus-stop transfixed, gazing across the road.

Julie poked her with her elbow. "What d'you say, Ricky? Do we walk home and spend the money on sweets?"

"Or," said Fay, "do we take the bus?" As she received no reply she turned and stared at Ricky. "She seems to have gone into a trance or something," she said.

Julie poked Ricky again with her elbow, a little harder this time. "Waken up," she said.

Ricky absent-mindedly brushed aside the poking elbow. "Look!" she said in an awed voice, nodding across the street.

The others looked. "Well?" said Julie. "It's only an old furniture van."

"Exactly!" said Ricky in a significant voice.

Fay shook her head and said, "I've lost the thread of this conversation," but Julie, although not so quick at spotting crooks as Ricky, was still pretty quick in the up-take.

"A *furniture* van, gosh!" she said.

Fay now turned and looked at her with a puzzled expression. Both her friends going dotty at the same moment was rather too much of a good thing, she thought. She glanced across the street at the van, hoping for some enlightenment there, but it was a perfectly ordinary furniture van, *GRANT and MURRAY, 10 PITREAVIE STREET, REMOVALS*, a perfectly well-known firm of furniture removers, she had seen their vans around Glasgow dozens of times.

Ricky and Julie were now hopping about on the pavement like a couple of demented fleas. "We must *do* something! We must stop them! Caught in the act! What shall we do? How can we stop them?" Ricky was muttering, dithering as usual.

But Julie remained calm and practical. "Do?" she said. "One of us must go for the police and the others must watch the van. We mustn't let it out of our sight for a single moment. Fay had better go for the police."

"Go for the *police*?" said Fay. "Honestly, what next? What have the police got to do with a perfectly ordinary removal?"

"Och, Fay, don't be so *dense*," said Julie impatiently, "it's not a perfectly ordinary removal. To begin with, that's Rushton's, a famous antique shop, stuffed full of valuable paintings and furniture that are now being loaded into the crook's van..."

"The crook's van?"

"Oh, *yes*. Ricky showed us the newspaper cutting to-day, don't you remember?"

"Oh, is that what you've been talking about?" asked Fay, thankful that at last she was able to follow the conversation. "But that can't be the crook's van, that's a Grant and Murray van..."

"Well, you don't think they're going to label their van Crooks Limited or something, do you?"

"No, but Grant and Murray! I mean, it's such cheek!"

Ricky, who was becoming more and more agitated, said, "Do stop blethering, Fay, and get the police. These crooks will have finished loading and be off in a minute."

But Fay was very, very reluctant to go and fetch the police. "You don't think that it's just some furniture being taken from Rushton's to the customer who has bought it?"

"Of course not," said Ricky impatiently. "Rushton's have their own van — I've seen it. And besides, it's half-past five. Why should Rushton's be open and loading furniture at half-past five when all the other shops close at five? Oh no, it's the crooks all right, what *luck* that Periwinkle kept me in and that we're here to put a spoke in their wheel! Fay, if you don't go for the police it'll be too late!"

Fay said reluctantly, "Where do I find the police?"

"Oh, gosh, Fay! There are always crowds of policemen tramping round the streets, go and get one. And there's a police station in Byres Road..."

"Byres Road! But that's miles!"

Julie said, "Don't you want to catch those crooks?"

Fay said that she supposed so, and moved off rather slowly and irresolutely. Julie said, "Better cross over, I think. We might pick up some valuable information."

"Like, say, where the hide-out is?" said Ricky, her eyes sparkling.

However, no information about the crooks' hideout was being given away. Two men in baize aprons were carrying half a bureau-bookcase into the van, and a third was standing at the door of the antique shop, apparently superintending operations. The girls stood by the tail of the van, as near as they could get, but no crumbs of information were dropped. The only things dropped were a few observations in a rich Glasgow accent from the two men.

"Well, Geordie," said the first one, who had a round, smiling face, not at all, as Fay would have thought if she had been there, like a crook's. "That's the lot except for yon wee chiffonier..."

"That's right, Wullie," said Geordie, not a man to waste words, and all three men disappeared into the shop again.

"Oh help, oh help!" whispered Ricky. "What shall we do? They've nearly finished and Fay isn't back with the police yet!" She peered up and down the street anxiously. "What shall we do? Oh help..."

"Get in," Julie whispered.

"Get *in*?"

"Yes. Into the van. Quick. We can't let them get away."

"Oh, Julie, do you think? Get in? But what will happen to us when they...?"

"Get in."

Ricky gave one wild look around. The men were still in the shop; the wide van doors screened the girls from casual passers-by on the pavement; Ricky scuttled up the ramp, crept between a tallboy and a Georgian wardrobe and crouched behind a curly sofa upholstered in yellow satin. Julie sidled in after her and crouched beside her.

Not a moment too soon: no sooner were they hidden than Geordie and Wullie came puffing up the ramp carrying the "chiffonier" which turned out to be a most elegant display cabinet in Chinese Chippendale. Then the ramp was put up, and the great doors were slammed and fastened. Wullie shouted, Geordie shouted, the cab doors were slammed, the engine was started and revved up.

Wullie shouted a few more unintelligible remarks and the great van moved ponderously off.

In the gloom of the van's interior, Ricky's blue eyes were round and scared.

"Now, where are we going?" she whispered.

"Straight into the lion's den, I should think," said Julie cheerfully.

Fay looked helplessly up and down the street for the crowds of policemen that Ricky had promised her. But it was a quiet part of town, sober and well-behaved and fortunately not often requiring the services of the law. Fay wandered up and down a couple of streets and even walked half-way back to school, but no policeman hove comfortingly in sight.

This is hopeless, Fay said to herself. We'll just have to manage without a policeman, and she made her way back to Rushton's shop.

The van, of course, had gone. Ricky and Julie had gone. Fay blinked and glanced up at the name above the door, but it was Rushton all right, and she hadn't come to the wrong corner. She peered into the shop. Of course there would be no one there, the shop had been shut long ago, Ricky had said so, and these men who had been standing about had been a bunch of crooks. But as she peered past a Hepplewhite chair and a sofa-table with a set of red and white carved chess-men on it, into the depths of the shop, she saw a small, dark man moving about. Not bound and gagged or anything like that; and not lurking about with a mask and a gun either; just a little, dark man pottering about an antique shop. Fay pushed open the door and went in.

The little man looked up inquiringly. "Good evening," he said.

"Good evening," said Fay. She really didn't know what to say next, so she said the first thing that came into her head. "Are you Mr. Rushton?" she said.

"Yes, I am," said the little man. "Can I help you?"

"I thought you were shut," said Fay fatuously.

"Och well, we are really," said Mr. Rushton, "but I had a special job on tonight. Can I help you?" he said again as Fay did not speak.

"Oh — er — Mr. Rushton — did you see a furniture van here about ten minutes ago?"

"Yes, I did," said Mr. Rushton. "That's why I'm late. My van broke down and I had to get Grant and Murray to take some stuff for me and they couldn't come till after five."

"Oh," said Fay. That ass Ricky and her crooks! She was completely round the bend. But, Fay thought, apart from being round the bend where, actually, *was* she? "Mr. Rushton," she said, "did you see two girls here? In blue and green blazers and school hats?"

"Well," said Mr. Rushton, "now you mention it, I did. But I don't know what happened to them. They were here one minute and gone the next..."

Oh, help, thought Fay, where have they gone? "Well, thank you," she said, and drifted out of the shop again.

Mr. Rushton looked after her consideringly. Queer girl, he thought. Vague —

Fay stood outside on the pavement and wondered what to do next. Where had they gone, those two idiots? It was a real furniture van so they couldn't have had any further interest in that. They couldn't have gone home; they wouldn't do that without telling her. Oh, well, she thought, what could *she* do? They must be somewhere around, she would just walk home herself and she might see them. She wouldn't take a bus or she might miss them; perhaps they had just nipped in somewhere to buy a few sweets with their bus money.

She walked on, and she was almost home when, in a terrace off Great Western Road, she saw for the second time that day a Grant and Murray removal van.

She grinned to herself. Grant and Murray's are working overtime, she thought. If Ricky were here she'd be having a cadenza. But even as she passed the van, dodging the busy men as they crossed the pavement with pictures and cases of silver in their arms, and looked up at it — *GRANT and MURRAY, 12 PITREAVIE STREET, REMOVALS* — something struck her as odd. She moved out of the way of the men, paused and looked up at the side of the van again. At first glance, she thought, something had struck her as odd. What could it have been? She looked again. *GRANT and MURRAY, 12 PITREAV* — *twelve*! That was it! Grant and Murray's address was ten! She had noticed it particularly on the other van, the real van, because she always noticed the number ten; it was her favorite number, her birthday was on the tenth of... But then, if this van had the wrong number painted on it, then it was the wrong van! It wasn't a real Grant and Murray van at all! It was — oh help, *could this* one belong to the crooks?

She began to run along the terrace. I must get home to ask mother! I must get the police, I —. She nearly bumped into a young policeman who was coming slowly along the terrace, making his way towards the van.

"Oh, I'm sorry," gasped Fay, almost grabbing at his nice blue tunic. "But that van! Do you see that removal van? There's something funny about it! It's, do you think it is, do you think it *could* be, that van that was in the papers this morning?"

If Fay had met any other policeman that evening and poured out her jumbled torrent of excitement, things might have ended very differently; but P.C. McPherson was young and eager and, like Ricky, dying to meet some crooks, not petty thieves and pickpockets and bag-snatchers and Teddy boys, but big-time crooks. "What's funny about it, my lassie?" he asked.

"The address," Fay gabbled hurriedly, "the number on the van is wrong. Grant and Murray's number is Ten Pitreavie Street — at least," she said, suddenly seized by an awful doubt, "I *think* it is, and the number on this van is twelve."

"Ugh, we'll soon find out," said P.C. McPherson and he turned and ran up the steps of the nearest house. "You wait there," he said over his shoulder, "and keep an eye on them. I'm going to look in a 'phone book. And then," he said, "if it's what you say I'm going to 'phone the Flying Squad."

So Fay stood on the pavement, trembling with terror; but after what seemed a horribly long few minutes, P.C. McPherson ran down the stairs again, the startled householder looking after him in amazement. "You were right!" he said. "Grant and Murray's number is ten, right enough. The Flying Squad's on the way. Crooks! They're all the same. They aye make one stupid mistake! Fancy not having the sense to see their van was painted right! You're a real clever wee lassie to notice it, and with any luck I'll get my promotion for this! I'm just going to stroll a wee bit nearer to get a proper look at these gentry so that I can identify them again. Coming?"

The lock of fair hair that always flopped over Fay's forehead when she was excited, flopped now. "Oh, *thanks*," she said, and she and P.C. McPherson strolled nonchalantly along the pavement in the direction of the crooks.

Ricky and Julie soon discovered that a furniture

removal van was not a very comfortable conveyance to ride in. They kept being thrown from side to side and against the sharp corners of valuable antique furniture. It was very unpleasant indeed.

"I hope... they're not... going far," panted Julie.

The van swung round a corner and Ricky put her elbow through the glass of the bureau-bookcase. "Oh blow," she panted, "now look...what I've...done."

"That's nothing," said Julie. "What's a...pane of glass...to Rushton's...when we're saving them... hundreds of pounds."

The van drew up rather suddenly and the girls nearly went head first over the curly sofa.

"Oh help, we're here," muttered Ricky picking herself up, "oh help, I wish I had a plan of campaign."

"I wish I had a gun," muttered Julie. "Shall we hide until they find us," she whispered, "or jump out on them and surprise them?"

Ricky gave a squeak of terror. Neither alternative appealed to her very much. She glanced round wildly. "Let's hide in that wardrobe," she said.

"What's the point of that?" Julie muttered.

"Oh, no point," whispered Ricky hurriedly. "It's just some place to hide until we can think what to do..."

Julie was about to demur, but the sound of Geordie beginning to open the van doors changed her mind. "All right, then," she said, and the two girls scrambled into the wardrobe. It was a tight fit, but comfortable enough in comparison with the previous journey — that is, until Geordie and Wullie began to move the wardrobe.

That was awful. The wardrobe was jerked up, heaved over sideways, tilted forward, laid on its back, dropped on the pavement — and the girls went with it.

"Michty me!" Wullie was panting. "What's the matter with this old wardrobe? What did you put in it, Geordie?"

"Nothing," said the laconic Geordie.

"First time I've known nothing to weigh half a ton." said Wullie, "Ugh well, no use grumbling, better get on; this won't pay the rent. Heave-ho, boys."

The girls once more found themselves heaved up in the air. They swayed along what seemed an interminable distance, dreading every moment that they would be hurled to the ground, and then suddenly found themselves put down with such a thump. Geordie and Wullie could be heard muttering and complaining.

Then a new voice spoke, a gentle feminine voice. "Oh, men," it said, "thank you so much, but could you please carry the wardrobe upstairs to my daughter's bedroom?"

"Upstairs!" muttered Ricky with horror.

"Up the stairs?" It was a cry of anguish from Geordie.

"Up the stairs is it!" said Wullie. "No' before I've seen what's inside!"

He flung open the doors and out fell the two girls, dishevelled, untidy, bruised and embarrassed.

"Michty me, two wee lassies!" said Wullie.

"Two big lassies," Geordie muttered bitterly. "Who ordered *them*, I'd like to know?"

Ricky said afterwards that the next ten minutes were the most uncomfortable of her life. One glance at the owner of the gentle, feminine voice convinced her that here was no crook, that here was a sweet little lady taking delivery of some antique furniture. She quite obviously was totally unable to follow Ricky's garbled, incoherent and embarrassed explanation, but taking it for some strange schoolgirl prank, she forgave the girls and even eventually plied them with glasses of milk and large pieces of shortbread.

Wullie and Geordie, inclined at first to be pretty indignant at being taken for crooks, in the end showed no ill-feeling for all the nasty suspicions that the girls had been harbouring. In fact, they gave them a lift home, riding in the cab, which was a lot better than in among the furniture and was really quite fun. As far as Ricky was concerned it was easily the best part of a rather disappointing affair.

When the girls all met at Fay's house a little later that evening, Julie and Ricky told Fay the sad tale.

"And anyway," Ricky finished, "what were *you* doing while we were suffering all those agonies?"

Fay's eyes widened innocently and her wayward lock of hair fell over her forehead as usual. "Me?" she said. "I was catching the furniture van crooks," she said.

Ricky scuttled up the ramp, followed by Julie.

XIV: THE SOUTH COUNTRY: JANE SHAW'S ENGLAND

ALISON LINDSAY

From her marriage until the family's departure for Africa, Jean Evans lived in Dulwich, once a village and now a suburb of London. Dulwich is, as mentioned in *Susan Pulls the Strings*, only five miles from St Paul's, but its wide streets with their handsome Georgian houses are an unexpected sight so near to the centre of London. In the Susan books, the Evans' home appears as the Carmichaels' house, 10 Tollgate Road, its name taken from the white-painted tollgate which crosses College Road at its southern end. This is the only remaining tollgate in London and is operated on behalf of The Dulwich Estate. An automated barrier has now been installed although the old sign with its prices in shillings, noted in *Susan Pulls the Strings*, still stands beside the road.

11 COLLEGE ROAD, DULWICH

The Evans' home, in the top flat of 11 College Road, was one of the few properties not owned by Dulwich College. This well-known public school, which boasts P G Wodehouse and Raymond Chandler amongst its former pupils, was founded in 1619 by Edward Alleyn, a Shakespearian actor and theatre manager. In *Susan Pulls the Strings*, the exhibition of theatre memorabilia which the Carmichaels visited on Boxing Day included material lent by Wichwood College, which "had been founded by an actor". *No Trouble for Susan* adds that the College "was a very powerful body which wouldn't allow people to cut down even a tree without permission", and the Estates Governors still wield considerable power; their approval is even required for exterior alterations to freehold properties in Dulwich. When the Evans moved out in 1952, their flat was taken over by Margaret Stewart, Jean's editor at Lutterworth. In the Susan books, the Carmichaels occupied the entire house; some years ago, Eric Morley (the organiser of the Miss World competition) bought the whole property and turned it back into a family home, named Rivendell House.

The Carmichaels' garden was extensive, featuring a pond, fountain, summer-house, tool-shed, vegetable garden and rockery, as well as flower beds. At its foot, across a lane, was a small orchard, which backed on to the park. The lane still exists, and according to *Susan Pulls the Strings*, led to Miss Pershore's garage. Miss Pershore lived at 14 Tollgate Road and used the empty house between, which was attached to hers, as a repository for smuggled goods. In *Susan Rushes In* the ghastly Gascoignes moved in to 12 Tollgate Road and made several alterations including transforming a cellar into their rumpus-room. On the other side of 11 College Road is the lodge and entrance gates to Dulwich Park. Beside its lake, where the Carmichaels skated in winter, is a Barbara Hepworth sculpture. Across the road is the Dulwich Picture Gallery and its surrounding garden, which

Peagreen raided for mulberry leaves for his silkworms. The gallery itself, described as "small but quite famous" in *Susan Rushes In*, was designed by Sir John Soane in the early years of the 18th century. It has a fine collection of paintings, including works by Rembrandt, Rubens and Claude. Adjoining the gallery is the chapel of Dulwich College, whose bells rang on Christmas morning in *Susan Pulls the Strings*.

To the north, along the road called Dulwich Village, is a public house, the *Crown and Greyhound*, and beyond this a row of shops. Just round the corner, at 1d Calton Avenue, there is a bookshop which the Evans family would have known well. Indeed, the building has been a bookshop since the 1920s, although the shortage of new books during the Second World War had transformed it into a lending library for the duration. In *No Trouble for Susan*, the cousins ran a bookshop in Wichwood, and its location on "the corner of the Village and the little street where the bookshop was situated" matches exactly. Across the road is "the corner by the old graveyard" from which the girls watched the battle with hooligans trying to wreck the shop.

Down Gallery Road (which has the same name in the Susan books) is Belair, built in 1785 as College Place and now a bar and restaurant. It features in *No Trouble for Susan* as the theatre used by the Wichwood Players which held such fascination for Bill and Mrs Gregson. Mrs Gregson lived at Bell Cottage, which "was in the grounds of Sir Arthur's property, and had once been the coach-house of the mansion". The real-life counterparts for these buildings may be Bell House and the adjoining Bell Cottage, 23 College Road, the latter a charming two-storey, weather-boarded, white-washed cottage which has similarities, too, with the "little doll's-house" rented by Susan's parents in *A Job for Susan*.

More cottages stand beside the pond at the junction of College Road and another curiously-named road, Dulwich Common. These are Pond Cottages (Millpond Cottages in the Susan books) where the Carmichaels' daily help Mrs Taylor lived with her policeman son. As the name suggests, a windmill once stood here although it was demolished around 1815. The pond itself never powered the mill, but was created when the local clay was dug to supply the tile kiln which stood close by. This was demolished in 1790 when the other buildings around the kiln were converted to dwelling houses. In *Susan Rushes In*, Sam Pilkington wanted to buy old Mrs Thorne's cottage despite having already knocked two of the houses into one. This really happened after the Second World War when the artist and illustrator James Fitton, who had lived at 10 Pond Cottages since 1928, converted it and No. 11 into one house.

KENT

For part of the war, Jean and her two young children stayed in Kent; unfortunately the precise location has not yet been traced, despite efforts by her family and friends to recall the address. Kent references in her books also include those places visited after the war, on motor trips from London, which add an extra level of difficulty to any identification. However, it is interesting to note that seven of Jean's books are set in this county, the highest number for a single location. These comprise *Susan's Helping Hand* (1955) and the two Susan school stories, *Willow Green Mystery* (1958), the two

Northmead books and *Paddy Turns Detective* (1967). The Evans' home in Dulwich was ideally placed for trips into the southern counties, and the run described in *Susan Rushes In*, including the stop at Lullingstone Castle, was one familiar to Jean. The silkworm farm described in the book was established there in the early 1930s and provided silk for the Coronation robes of George VI and Elizabeth II, although silk cultivation has now been moved from the castle to Dorset.

Farthing Green is first mentioned in *Susan's Helping Hand*, and is then described as being seven miles away from Apple Tree Farm. The name sounds too impossibly quaint to be true, but the village of Farthing Green does indeed exist, and lies seven miles south of Maidstone. This large town features in *Willow Green Mystery*, since the Waring children, too, livde seven miles from Maidstone and attended school there. Their home village is called Hunting Green (which also appears in *Northmead Nuisance*) although it is impossible at present to know whether this name is a disguise for Farthing Green. St Ronan's, the Kent school which Susan attends, is not given a precise location, but as half-term sees families heading for hotels in Maidstone and Tunbridge Wells, it must be in the same vicinity.

In *New House at Northmead*, much of the action centres round the great house of Claire, with its three hundred and sixty-five rooms and seven courts. These features belong in real life to Knole, close by Sevenoaks, an immense palace built in the 15th century and much remodelled in the 1600s. The Northmead girls also visited Falconshurst Place, really Penshurst Place, a 14th century Manor House which boasts superb gardens, and which lies a few miles north-west of Tunbridge Wells. The reference in New House to "the soldier-poet who was Falconhurst's most famous son" could only mean Sir Philip Sidney; it is extraordinary how often Jean gave clear clues to her locations in spite of disguising their names. The comparatively lengthy distances between these properties and others mentioned in her Kent books indicate more travel than usual on the part of their author.

CRACKINGTON HAVEN, CORNWALL

The Evans family spent several summer holidays at Crackington Haven, seven miles north of Tintagel, on the north coast of Cornwall. The village appears as Pendragon Haven in the Moochers stories, and as Hallow Haven in *The Penhallow Mystery* (1967). Its surrounding cliffs are, at 430 feet, the highest in Cornwall and form part of the South West Coast Path. Inland from the Haven is Crackington itself and south-west of that is Pengold, which according to *The Moochers* "adjoins the Pendragon land". The square church tower visible from the Moochers' bedroom at Pendragon Manor is the part-Norman St Gennys' church, on a headland above the Haven. Pendragon Manor was an Elizabethan building, according to *The Moochers*, and 1661 is the date given in *The Penhallow Mystery*; the real Crackington Manor, at the mouth of the cove, is a three-story Victorian villa although its long dining room has the exposed beams mentioned in *The Moochers*. Much older, and about a mile inland, is Crackington Manor Farm, which is now an hotel. The Pengellys' house was named 'Little Nance'; this is evidently a local name, since a guesthouse called Trenance is built in the valley.

In *The Moochers*, Mr Pengelly served on the local council which met in Carn; this name may disguise the holiday resort of Bude, some twelve miles north. It, like Crackington Haven, is popular with surfers because of the Atlantic rollers which break on its sandy beach. The references to surfing in *The Moochers Abroad* may seem surprisingly advanced in a mid-century children's book, but the Cornish coast has been long a favourite spot for this sport.

Somerset

During the war, Jean Evans and her young daughter Jane left London for Bath, where an old family friend, Jane Aitken, lived with her doctor husband. Bert Gibson had studied medicine at Glasgow along with Jean's brothers, and the proximity of a friendly doctor was one of the reasons why Jean went to the Gibsons, since she was then expecting her second child; Bert helped to deliver John (always known as Ian) on 23 June 1944. Jean had a great fondness for Bath, in large part because of its connections with her favourite writer Jane Austen, and she set three of the Penny novels there and in the surrounding countryside. When the Mallorys took Penny and Jill to the town, Laura pointed out to them the unusual angel motif on the West Front of Bath Abbey as well as the famous Roman Baths and Pump Room, but most of the action in this book is centred round the Le Roux' home at 2 Abbey Green.

Abbey Green lies to the south of the Abbey, off York Street, and Elton House at No. 2 is now owned by the Landmark Trust and available for holiday lets. The original house dates back to 1700, but alteration in the middle of the 18th century transformed it into an imposing gentleman's residence. Soon after, though, the fashionable world began moving into the splendid Regency terraces which are the glory of Bath, and the ground floor of Elton House became a shop. The upper floors were converted to flats. After the Second World War a Miss Phillipa Savery began buying up these as they became vacant, until she had secured the entire property, and around 1980 she presented this to the Trust. Until the 1970s she ran an antiques shop on the ground floor of Elton House, no doubt the inspiration for the plot of *Threepenny Bit*.

A couple of miles south of Bath is the village of Monkton Combe, called Friars Combe in the Penny books, and Thornton Combe in *A Girl With Ideas*. The school at Friars Combe plays an important role in *Threepenny Bit* and *Crooked Sixpence*, and of course is the setting for *A Girl With Ideas*; there actually is a boarding school at Monkton Combe, established in 1868 and subsequently attended by the sons of Bert and Jane Gibson, which would explain Jean's knowledge of the area. The school owns many properties in and around the village which has few other amenities; the local pub is now threatened with closure and the shop in Julian Cottages, run by a Mrs Coomes, has long since closed.

The surrounding countryside, with its deep lush valleys and open fields, must have made a deep impression on Jean, to account for her fond descriptions of it in the books. The Ealing comedy *The Titfield Thunderbolt* (1953) was filmed in the Monkton Combe valley: Titfield was Monkton Combe; and its station, closed to passenger traffic since 1925, was extended for the filming but subsequently demolished. North-east of the village is the intersection of two water systems, where the Dundas Aqueduct carries the Kennet and Avon Canal over the River Avon; this unusual feature is mentioned several times in the books. From here, a path leads north-west up Brassknocker Hill, the original of Doorknocker Hill. The derivation seems to be from the brasses once worn by horses, which clanked together as the animals laboured up the steep road from the Midford Brook. Summer Lane, where Candy's owner lived, runs south-west from the village up towards Combe Down.

St Ursula's, where the Gauntlett family lived in *Fourpenny Fair*, is in real life St Catherine's, some six miles due north of Monkton Combe. Laura told the Carters that it once been owned by a godson of Queen Elizabeth I; this is a reference to Sir John Harington, who entertained the queen in 1591 and subsequently had to part with St Catherine's. The small assemblage of buildings comprises a fifteenth century church, tithe barn, and St Catherine's Court, enlarged in the 19th century from the remains of the Bath Priory grange. In *Crooked Sixpence* the children uncover a Roman villa near to St Ursula's; traces of a Roman villa have indeed been found locally, although location information on this is scarce.

At school and at university, Jean had read and enjoyed English writers such as Jane Austen and Shakespeare, whose fondness for their familiar English surroundings is so evident. When, as a student and later as a wife, she lived in London, and travelled to England's southern counties, Jean too grew to love the town- and land-scapes so unlike the Scottish ones she had known as a child. Fortunately for her readers, she was able to recreate the lush richness of Kent and Somerset, and the tranquil bustle of Dulwich, while living in the harsher South African climate. Through her books set in England, Jean was able to recall places she had loved and make them live for readers who had never seen them.

XV: FAMILY TROUBLE

JANE SHAW

It's a terrible thing to have to admit, I thought, but I'd be a great deal better off without my family. If I hadn't any family, I wouldn't be sitting here with my life ruined. If I hadn't any family, if I were an orphan, I'd be going to the dance to-night with Edward, I wouldn't be sitting here with a broken heart...

It all happened on the day of the Carnival. That was the day that Edward came home from the university, and I saw him again for the first time in two or three years. For although we had lived next door to the Trevelyans all our lives, and had played with Edward and Don since we were two bricks high, and had had our measles and sore throats looked after by their father Dr. Trevelyan, we had seen nothing of Edward for ages, because he had been up at the university becoming a doctor and had never happened to be at home when we were. Mind you, when we were younger, before my two little sisters came along to spoil the sides (you see? Even then they were ruining my life) it was Don and I who always used to join forces against my eldest sister Louise and Edward; but this morning when I fell out of the apple-tree by our front gate and nearly flattened this boy who happened to be passing, and I sat up and looked at him, my heart turned over about six times.

"Edward!" I gasped. Honestly, he was divine! Big and broad, his dark hair a little tousled, although actually that might be because I had just landed on his head. Not that he had been too bad before he went away, but he had been so long and thin, like a weed, and though not exactly *spotty* — well... But now...

He stared at me. "Nicky?" he said. I nodded, and I could tell by the way he looked at me that I had improved too. Well, I should hope so, I'm not anything much at sixteen, I can tell you, but at fourteen I was *awful*, thin as a piece of string and almost the same colour, with the most ghastly contraptions round my teeth.

We sat where we had landed, on the grass outside our front gate, and chatted.

"How's your mother? And the Vicar?" he asked.

"Oh, Daddy's fine, thanks, both fine," I said.

"And Tubs? and Ruth?"

"Yes, fine, I said. "Now that Tubs is older she gets rather cross when we call her Tubs but of course we always do..."

"I expect that they're quite grown up young ladies now. Like you."

"Well, hardly," I said, but I was pleased that he thought I looked grown up. "They're only little kids, Ruth's only twelve and Tubs is eleven—"

"And..." he paused, "Louise? How is Louise?"

My whole life didn't depend on him at that point or I might have been more careful what I said. "Oh, haven't you seen Louise yet?" I said. "Well, you're in for a shock."

"A shock?"

"Gosh, yes. D'you remember what she used to be like?"

"Yes..." Edward paused again. "Yes, I *do* —"

"Yes. *She* should have been called Tubs. But now she's as slim as anything and — well, now she's gorgeous!" And although I *am* her sister, gorgeous she really is, I must say, with fair hair like gold silk and huge brown eyes.

"Well," said Edward, standing up and dusting bits of grass off his trousers, "when can I see them all?" He held out his hand and hauled me to my feet. "Can I come in now?"

"Of course you can," I said. "But there's no one there except Mummy and she's working like a mad thing getting our costumes ready for the Carnival. Had you forgotten that this is the day of the Carnival?"

"Oh, heavens, so it is. So that's what Don was doing in his room; getting his costume ready, moaning and groaning like anything and making a noise like a lot of tin cans."

"He's going as a knight in armour," I said with dignity.

"Oh, really? Rather a poor quality of armour, I should say."

"What are you going as?"

"Nothing. They'll have to put up with me in plain clothes. I suppose you'll all be going. By the way, where *is* Lou — where is everybody, then?"

"Gone to Bude with Daddy in the car. We ran out of crêpe paper and silver paint. But come in and say hallo to Mummy."

He came in and said hallo to Mummy, who could say all the things to him that I wanted to say, about how well he was looking — although *divine* would have been a better word — and how brilliantly he had done in his finals and did he remember that there was a dance to-night after the Carnival; his mother and she had been making savouries and sandwiches and jellies and fruit cup all morning?

"Oh, the dance, yes, of course. We must all go to that, mustn't we, Nicky? Or have you all got partners fixed up already?" And when I said that nobody was fixed up he said good and wandered off to his own house again.

Now, I thought, for by this time I was his slave, now can I count that as an invitation?

I was still wondering and going over every word that he had spoken when our car arrived back from Bude, rattling and groaning up the drive. Perhaps I should have explained that we live on the north coast of Cornwall in a tiny village not far from Bude. Edward's father is the local doctor and our father, as I expect you've gathered, is the vicar. Across the fields you can see the sea from our house and sometimes the misty shape of Lundy Island; the village lies among the folds of the hills at the top of a deep valley that leads down to a little cove where we bathe. Not that anybody was thinking about the sea or bathing that day, everybody's thoughts were concentrated on the Carnival, except mine, which were concentrated on Edward.

I rushed up to the car, which stopped with a jerk and a shudder as it usually does when Daddy is driving, to tell them all about Edward, but I couldn't get a word in edgewise because they had something to tell me.

"Oh, gosh, Nicky," Tubs yelled, nearly guillotining herself as she grabbed her parcels, talked to me and tried to get out of the car without opening the door, "we've had a real adventure at last!"

"Oh, Tubs!" I said. Tubs is hopeless, always dying for adventure.

"It's true, it's true! There's a convict escaped from Dartmoor and they're stopping all the cars and they thought he might be in our car. Oh, Nicky, you did miss yourself, such a shame. Goodness, think of a *convict*, a real dangerous escaped convict in our *car*!"

Slightly startled, I looked at the others who were grinning. "Oh, go on with you, Tubs," I said, "your imagination's running riot again. There wasn't a convict in our car!"

Louise and Ruth were helping Daddy to unload the car. "No, of course there wasn't a convict in the car," said Ruth in her calm voice. "There *is* a convict, though, on the loose, and the police did stop us outside Bude, there was a cordon across the road; but as soon as they recognised Daddy —"

But Tubs couldn't bear to have the story taken out of her hands in this very tame way. She burst in again, "And they searched every *inch* of the car—"

"Oh, Daddy, honestly?" I said.

Daddy was smiling. "Well, if you call casting a casual glance inside the car searching every inch, then they did—"

"Oh, Daddy, how *can* you?" cried Tubs. "That inspector had a most searching eye, and they wanted to look in the boot—"

"Until Sergeant Trevinnick came up," said Louise very dampeningly, "and recognised us —"

"No, but do be serious," I said, "and tell me — Ruthie, you're the only one in this family that I'll get any sense out of, you tell me, is there really an escaped convict?"

"Yes, there is," said Ruth.

"But there *can't* be!" I said. "Dartmoor is miles from here!"

Tubs was dancing with impatience and dropping parcels all round her in her anxiety to be telling the story again. "Truly, there is, Nicky," she said. "He was last seen at Launceston, the police told us, and that's only twelve miles from here, and he was still in his convict's things, only they think that he may have managed to steal other clothes by now, and they were searching all the cars because they think he might try to get a lift into Bude so as not to be so noticeable, you know —"

"Oh, sure," I said scathingly, "there are always hundreds of convicts walking about Bude."

"Well, you know what I mean," Tubs said. "If he manages to get to a town and mingle with the holiday crowds he won't stick out like a sore thumb as he would on the quiet roads or the moors."

"What chance has he anywhere, poor hunted creature?" I exclaimed with great drama and pathos.

"Now then, Nicky, don't be sentimental," Louise said crushingly. "He's a particularly nasty type, the inspector told us — robbery with violence — and yet he looks quite nice, apparently, tall and dark and good-looking —"

"Oh!" I said, suddenly remembering. "Edward's back!"

Louise, just going into the house, turned her head quickly. "Is he? Have you seen him? What's he like?"

"Oh, not bad," I said, elaborately casual. "He was asking for everybody."

Tubs had rushed into the sitting-room where Mummy was sitting surrounded by our costumes for the Carnival, sewing the swansdown tail on Louise's white rabbit costume. Tubs dumped her parcels and poured out the convict story again, delighted to have a new audience. Mummy was suitably impressed and asked all the right questions, and Tubs might have been gabbling there still if I hadn't suddenly shrieked and said, "Look at the time! We'll never be ready."

So Mummy made us try on our costumes to make sure that they were all right; and I must say that Louise in her white towelling rabbit's costume with huge pink ears and pink-lined paws and a little dab of swansdown for a tail, looked too adorable for words. We were rather proud of Tubs's too — she was a robot, with a square cardboard box for a head and another for a body and others on her legs and arms, all painted with aluminium paint. The only trouble was that it was very difficult for her to walk or use her arms, but she said that it didn't matter, and I don't suppose that it did to her. She was the kind of person who would have chopped her arms off at the shoulder if they were spoiling the effect. Fortunately that wasn't necessary. Ruth was a cracker, done up in red and green crêpe paper, not very original, I'm afraid, but we had run out of ideas by that time. She hadn't the use of her arms either, of course, and she couldn't walk very well because the tight bit of the cracker was tied below her knees. She couldn't even see because naturally the fringes of the cracker were all over her face, but she looked jolly nice all the same. I was a witch with a black cloak and pointed hat and some of my teeth blacked out, and a broomstick in my hand. By this time I was jolly sorry that I had picked on such an idiotic idea because I looked anything but appetising, and I wished that I had decided to go as a fairy or a columbine or a ballerina or something a bit more becoming now that Edward was back. I did suggest changing costumes with Louise, but she looked at me as though I had gone suddenly right out of my mind, so nothing came of that suggestion. I thought of retiring to bed with a headache, but as I had never done such a thing in the whole of my life before, far less on Carnival day, that would start all sorts of awkward questions from the family. And I must say at this point that it's very, very difficult to do anything at all out of the ordinary, such as retiring to bed on Carnival day, when you have a family like mine standing round and asking questions.

We had lunch early and set out in very good time for the Carnival. Transport was slightly difficult because neither Tubs nor Ruth could sit down. In the end Daddy took Mummy and Louise in the front of the car with him while Tubs and Ruth stood up at the back. They left them at the bottom of the field where the Carnival is always held, and then came back for me.

There is one very awkward thing about my father and that is that he seemingly likes to park his car as far away as possible from where you want to go. This afternoon was no exception. He said that it was to make it easier to get away at the end of the festivities, which didn't seem to me a very important point, and the result was that he parked the car just about as far away from the centre of things as he possibly could, right at the bottom of the huge field where the Carnival was being held. Then he rushed off to attend to his duties, which were many, and I went plodding up the hill, much impeded by my black draperies, catching round my ankles, and my broomstick. So there I was, tripping up the hill, out of sight and sound of everybody when suddenly a red and green cracker came trotting over the brow of the hill to my left, taking little anxious steps and panting. Of course she couldn't see me, on account of all that crêpe paper over her face, so I picked up my skirts and tiptoed up behind her.

"Double, double toil and trouble;
Fire, burn; and, cauldron bubble!"

I said in a very witchy way.

She yelped and jumped about two feet in the air and spun round towards me and nearly overbalanced. "Oh, Nicky! Oh, thank goodness! Oh Nicky, thank goodness it's you! Oh, Nicky, help help!"

I thought that she had gone completely round the bend, for Ruth is usually a very quiet little thing, very calm and collected. I peered at her face, what I could see of it behind the red and green fringe, and her eyes were out on sticks and she was as pale as a ghost. "Ruthie!" I gasped. "What's happened? What's the matter?"

"It's the convict!" she said.

I gaped at her. "What d'you mean, it's the convict?" I asked.

"D-d-down there!" Ruth stammered, and jerked her head in the direction of the bottom of the field. "Tubs is keeping him at bay! Or at least," she added in very ominous tones, "she was –"

This time it was I who yelped. "He may be keeping her at bay by this time!" I said. "Come *on*! Show me!"

I tore off in the direction that Ruth had indicated, tripping over my long skirts; then slowed down when Ruth wailed behind me, "Oh Nicky, wait!"

I picked up my skirts and waited for Ruth with her little mincing steps to make up on me. "It's all very well to say wait," I said impatiently. "The convict may have murdered Tubs by now!"

Ruth gave a little hysterical giggle. "More like Tubs murdering him, I'd say," she said. "She has already hit him over the head."

I was so taken aback that I stopped dead in my tracks. Ruth, who hadn't been expecting this, bumped into me. "Honestly, Nicky, you clumsy oaf," she cried, "you nearly knocked *me* out, stopping like that! I banged my nose! I think it's going to bleed, and a lot of blood won't look a bit nice down the front of a cracker! And I can't even get at a hankie!"

I ignored this tale of woe although as a matter of fact Ruth's nose-bleeds aren't things to ignore as a rule. "I think I'd better get Daddy," I said.

"Oh, Nicky, *no!*" wailed Ruth. "At least *yes* but not yet. Do come and rescue Tubs first."

So we hurried over the brow of the hill, down towards the bottom of the slope where a lane skirted the field. "Tell me what happened," I said.

"Well," Ruth said, puffing a little with her efforts to keep up with me, "Daddy dropped us in the lane to go back for you, and Mummy and Louise went haring off up the hill to the Carnival, but we couldn't hurry because of our costumes, you know, and then suddenly under a bush we saw the convict! We nearly died!"

"How did you know it was the convict?"

"Well! Convict clothes! And he was dark and tall like the inspector said, or at least he looked tall, we couldn't be sure of that because he was sitting down. He had his back to us and he was pulling on this sort of jumper thing —"

"Pulling it on?" I said slowly. "Wouldn't you expect the convict to be taking the prison clothes off, not putting them on?"

"Oh, I thought of that too," Ruth said proudly, "but Tubs explained that —"

"Oh, she did, did she?"

"Yes. It's what's called a double bluff. He's pretending to be an ordinary man pretending to be dressed up as a convict for the Carnival!"

"Oh." I thought for a second as we hurried on. "Wouldn't it be simpler to put on his other clothes and slip away?"

"He hasn't *got* other clothes, you ass, the policeman said so. No, this is a perfect disguise! He has been wandering about, trying to get other clothes and he has seen a poster advertising the Grand Carnival at Penkenna and he has decided to mingle with the crowd on the off-chance of finding food and some other clothes—"

I said doubtfully, "Mm — I suppose so. So then what happened?"

"So then Tubs — quick as a flash — picked up a great massive bit of tree that was lying there and before he could struggle clear of his jumper, she hit him over the head!"

"Gosh!" I said, impressed.

"Yes, good, wasn't it? Look! There they are!"

There, sure enough, beside a little bush, lay the figure of a convict and over him stood Tubs, looking like something from another planet, with a great club in her hands. And just at that moment, the convict began to stir. He struggled to his knees and began to claw feebly at the garment that was still over his face. With my broom grasped firmly in my hand, I tore down the hill. I reached him, raised the broom, and just as I brought it down with a dull thud, the convict managed to get clear of the folds of the jersey and turned his head. It was Edward.

I'd jolly well like to draw a veil, as they used to say in old-fashioned books, over the next bit. It was absolutely awful.

"It's Edward!" I cried in agony. "I've killed him!"

You couldn't see Tubs's face because it was hidden inside the cardboard box, but her voice sounded completely amazed. "D'you *know* this convict?" she gasped.

"Of course, I do," I said impatiently. "And so do you. It's Edward Trevelyan."

"Oh, no!" cried Ruth in a voice of horror. "Edward a convict!"

"Oh, don't be such a silly little ass," I yelled at her, thoroughly upset and exasperated, "of course he's not a convict—"

"Not a convict!" gasped Tubs. "You mean-you mean this *isn't* the convict?"

"I keep *telling* you it isn't," I said. "It's Edward!"

"Oh, no!" moaned Tubs. "But I hit him! With a stick!"

"Me too," I muttered. "With a broom."

"Oh! Oh!"

"Oh, do stop standing there moaning," I cried. "Go and get help! Get Mummy! Get water! Get *something!*"

Tubs and Ruth tottered off, obviously very weak about the knees, and by the time that they came back with Mummy, Dr. Trevelyan, Louise, jugs of water and a few carnival figures to swell the crowd, poor Edward was again struggling to his knees. He just had time to glance at me with a look of loathing before he was engulfed by Louise and his father and people giving him sips of water and bathing his forehead on which three large lumps were now rising. Three? I thought. I only know about two...

"... just parked the car in the lane there," Edward was saying in a faint but malignant voice, "when something came at me out of the blue and I didn't know any more till I came to, and my own clothes were gone and these disgusting things left in their place. I was just struggling into them, so that I could go and give the alarm, when I got *another* biff on the head that knocked me out again, and just when I was coming round from that, up comes Nicky of all people who bangs me on the head for a third time, and out I go again!"

I tiptoed away, very, very quietly....

So there I was sitting, in my room, all dressed up for the dance, with a broken heart. They had caught the convict, making for Bude in Edward's car. We had all won prizes at the Carnival, even me, with my broom which I had nearly broken over Edward's head; but all the same, my heart was broken. It certainly wasn't me whom Edward was taking to the dance. It was Louise. At least, he wasn't actually taking anybody, he was lying at home on a sofa with a bandage round his head and Louise was sitting beside him, holding his hand. She dropped it like a hot brick when I went in to apologise to him, but even before I got out of the door he had grabbed hold of it again. Between them, my family had very successfully broken my heart and ruined my life. For you must admit that to be knocked out first by one member of the family then by another is a bit off-putting. Not that it seemed to put him off Louise. Holding hands!...

There was a whistle under the window, Don's old whistle, the old war-cry whistle that he used when we formed a pretty invincible team against Louise and Edward. I ran to the window and stuck my head out. There was Don, very tidy for a change in his blazer and white flannels, looking up. "Aren't you coming to the dance, Nicky?" he called. "I've been waiting for you for ages by the gate."

Goodness, I thought, my heart isn't broken after all! Not even chipped! Not even *cracked*! I leant half-out of the window and yelled, "*Don*! Don, wait for me, I'm coming!"

Tubs and Ruth tottered off.

XVI: JUMBLE SALE

JANE SHAW

You wouldn't think that tremendous events, events that would shake our village to its foundations, could happen just because a boy is left-handed, would you?

David — he's the boy — says, "Shake our village to its foundations? That's a bit exaggerated, surely?"

"Shake our village to its foundations," I say firmly. "Don't you agree, Jill?"

"Well —" says Jill cautiously.

"Go back to the beginning," says David. "You're telling the story all upside down."

The beginning was Jill and me sitting in our old schoolroom one wet Saturday morning in the summer holidays, moaning.

I said, "Admit, Jill, that nothing ever happens in this dead-and-alive place—"

"I shouldn't say that," said Jill cautiously and thought for a moment. "Then there were all those country house robberies, especially that terrific jewel robbery at Lockesley Castle a few months ago, all those diamonds and pearls—"

"Lockesley Castle is fifty miles from here," I said. "You could hardly call that a local event."

"Well, no," said Jill, "but gosh, was it exciting! In all the papers."

That was true enough; the papers had been full of the Country House Robberies, as they were called, and full, too, of the Country House Robber who had not so far been caught; but even so, it hadn't much to do with our village—

"And then," Jill was saying, " the very next week Jennifer got engaged!"

That was true too, Jennifer is my sister and her engagement buoyed us up for weeks. Visions of weddings and clouds of white tulle and being bridesmaids whirled about in our heads. But this proved a disappointment, too, because it turned out that Jennifer and Tim Lawson, who is a struggling young doctor in our village, weren't getting married immediately at all; they were *saving up* to get married, if you please, and probably wouldn't have what they thought was enough money for years and years, when Jill and I would be eighteen or twenty and too old to care about being bridesmaids—

"Then, of course," Jill said, plodding conscientiously on, "there's Mark Lamont. It's not every little village that has a real and famous artist living there."

Well, even I had to admit that she had a point there. Mark Lamont was exciting, make no mistake about that. He came to live in our village about six months ago and brightened the place up considerably. Besides painting pictures, he also made pottery, flower-pots and jugs and plates and so on; people came from miles to buy them. In fact I was sorry that my sister Jennifer had been in such a hurry to get engaged to Tim Lawson who, while quite sweet really, is certainly not glamorous, to say nothing of all that nonsense about saving up. Mark Lamont, I thought, would have been much better. I was torn, in fact, between having him for a brother-in-law and having him for myself when I was a bit older.

Jill was still chattering on and producing compensations for living in the remote and dull village of Willow Green — pretty scenery, in the middle of all those orchards, nice people, good bus service to Maidstone — "And, of course," she finished with a quiet air of triumph, "there's the annual Jumble Sale."

I stared at her. If a Jumble Sale was her idea of excitement she was dottier than I had thought. I told her so.

"Oh, go on," she said, "you know the Jumble Sale is jolly good fun—"

"Of course," I said, " you *are* the vicar's daughter, perhaps that accounts for it."

"That's really why I came this morning," Jill went on, paying no attention to what I was saying," because Mother said would we take over the White Elephant stall this year—"

"Oh, I said, sitting up, "that might be quite fun—"

"David can help us," said Jill, "he's good at wheedling things out of the old ladies in the parish—"

David was Jill's brother. He's sixteen and a half. He used to lead Jill and me an awful life, pulling our hair and making us apple-pie beds at the drop of a hat, but since we have all grown up, more or less, he has really become much nicer and always dances with us at the Youth Club parties if we haven't got partners, which does happen sometimes because most of the boys in the Youth Club seem to be about fourteen or can't dance.

"— and I think we ought to start collecting stuff right away," Jill was saying. "You can't imagine what people are like, they promise you anything and then you have to nag away like mad for simply weeks before they finally produce the things."

I jumped to my feet, all fired with enthusiasm. "Let's start now," I said.

"Oh well," Jill was doubtful, "it's pouring with rain and I *think* my bike has a slow puncture—"

"We can start here," I said. "Poke around and see what Mother will let us have—"

Our farm-house is enormously old and had belonged to our family for hundreds of years. There is a box-room upstairs simply crammed with junk. "Come on," I said, "there must be masses of stuff up there that nobody wants—"

"If *nobody* wants it, it won't be much good for the White Elephant stall," said Jill. "We don't want to be left with a lot of rubbish on our hands."

"Oh, we shan't be," I said. "It's amazing what some people will buy."

We hauled out a splendid collection — an old table with a wobbly leg, a bird-cage, two or three pictures, a vase with only a tiny chip in it, a chestnut-roaster, a silver toast-rack, black with age and lack of polish, a fire-screen, with a picture of a King Charles spaniel sewn on it, among other things — but when my mother saw them she started hauling them all back again. "Oh, darling," she said, "you can't have *that*, it's a lovely old table, it's only waiting until your father has time to fix the leg, Jennifer might be glad of it... and *not* the bird-cage, we'll have another budgie one of these days... and that toast-rack, not that, the Mortimers gave it to us for a wedding present, Lady Mortimer would be sure to notice it on the White Elephant stall and never speak to me again... but darling, your great-great-grandmother sewed that fire-screen, I couldn't part with *that* and I can easily mend that little bit where the moths have got at it when I have time—" My mother is a bit of a hoarder.

But, eventually, she did screw herself up to part with a few things and promised when she had time to look them out.

On Monday, which was fortunately fine and Jill's bike turned out not to have a slow puncture after all

— it had a quick one and David mended it for her — on Monday, then, we started going round the village in earnest. And it was exactly as Jill had said, everybody promised us lots of things, but nobody actually gave us anything until we had badgered and pestered them right up to the day of the Jumble Sale. In fact, ten minutes before the sale was due to be opened by Lady Mortimer, I remembered we hadn't got Mark Lamont's contribution.

"Him," said David, "he won't give us any white elephants—"

"Oh, David, he will," I said, "he promised. *Do* go along to his house and collect the things, he said that he would leave them all ready, you'll be back before Lady M. has got half-way through her speech, you know that she goes on for ages once she gets started."

David grumbled like anything, but in the end he went; and he was back in no time, just as I said, long before Lady M. had got the length of declaring the Jumble Sale to be open. He was carrying two rather gay pots with things growing in them. "This is all," he whispered while people were laughing at one of Lady M.'s little jokes. "Pretty mean, I thought. He wasn't in the house, he was in that place he calls a studio, making pots, but he told me where to get them. I must say I do think that two little pots is rather a meagre contribution."

"Oh, but they're nice," I said. "He must have made them himself—"

"And they've got plants in them," said Jill. "I expect they're those famous things he grows, African daisies or something."

"They don't look much like daisies to me," said David. "They look like violets."

"They're white," I said.

"You can get white violets," David said.

"Well, whatever they are," said Jill, "we can easily charge five shillings each for those, I should think."

"Seven-and-six," I said.

People were now clapping Lady M.'s speech, and almost immediately we had our first customer. It was Tim Lawson. He would have been better employed, I thought, looking after his patients and making some money, but I suppose that he has to have some time off.

"Hallo," he said. "Any nice bargains? I'm looking for a sofa and some dining-room chairs—"

Jill started showing him some perfectly ghastly objects, some of which had come from our box-room and which he could have had for nothing any day of the week. "Hey," I said, "don't sell him those, Jennifer will kill us—"

"What about these?" said Tim, pointing to Mark Lamont's pots. "These are nice."

"Goodness, yes, they're lovely," said Jill heartily, "and they've got those very famous African daisies growing in them."

"African violets," said Tim. "Does Jennifer like indoor plants?"

"She's mad about them," I said. This wasn't strictly true because I hadn't the faintest idea what Jennifer thought about indoor plants — there are so many outdoor plants growing in the country, that people don't often bother with indoor ones. But even if she didn't particularly like them now, I thought, she could easily get fond of them.

"Yes, well, it's always a start," said Tim. "A chair or a table might have been more useful, but still, a couple of plants will be better than nothing. I'll put them in the surgery meantime and they'll cheer up the patients. How much?"

"Ten shillings each," I said before Jill could open her mouth.

Tim looked rather startled. "That's a bit steep, surely?" he said.

"Not for genuine African violets," I said, "in hand-potted pots. But seeing it's you," I said, suddenly remembering that the more money he spent the longer it would be before the wedding came off, "we'll give you a bargain. Fifteen shillings."

After a bit of arguing, we finally let him have them for twelve and six and he went off with a pot in each hand, looking pleased.

Customers came thick and fast after that, and our stall was half-empty and the toffee-tin where we were putting the money was half full when Mark Lamont suddenly appeared. He was looking anything but pleased. He glared at David. "Where are they?" he — well, snarled is the only word for the way he spoke.

David's mouth dropped open. "Wh-wh-where are wh-wh-what?" he said.

"My pots," Mark Lamont went right on snarling. "How *dare* you come into my house and help yourself to two extremely valuable pots?"

"But *sir!*" said David indignantly, getting his breath back. "You *told* me to take them!"

"*Told* you to take them? I did nothing of the kind! I told you to take a pile of old junk from the table on the right-hand side of the door. These plants were on the left-hand side. Good heavens, boy, don't you know your left hand from your right hand?"

Well, there it is. David just stood there, getting redder and redder. For the fact of the matter is that David often doesn't know his left hand from his right hand unless he stops to think. He is left-handed, you see, and naturally his left hand is the important one to him and when you say to him, turn right, he often just automatically turns left — Jill and I are always teasing him about it... Still, that didn't mean that Mark Lamont could stand there and shout at him.

"If we made a mistake, Mr. Lamont," I said coldly, "we'll get the pots back again—"

"I should think so," Mark Lamont snapped, turning and glaring at me. But I glared right back, and he must have realised that he was making an awful fuss about a trifle because he laughed in a mirthless sort of way and half apologised. "Oh, I didn't mean to make a scene," he said, "but those white violets are my pride and joy. I couldn't bear to lose them—"

"I thought it was the pots that were so valuable," murmured Jill.

"Oh, well, *valuable!*" said Mark Lamont laughing a little, his old charming self again. "It's not that; but I made them specially for a customer and she's coming for them to-morrow. A very difficult old party she is — If you can get them back, I'd be so pleased — And of course I'll give you a couple of others."

So we promised that we'd get back his pots for him, and off he went.

David wasn't quite so red in the face, but he still looked pretty upset, so I said, "What a fuss to be making about two old pots. As soon as we've sold everything and taken the cash to your mother, we'll go and ask Tim to give us the pots back."

And that was where the trouble began. When we asked Tim to give us back the pots he said no. We could hardly believe our ears. He was getting ready for his six o'clock surgery and he just stood there and grinned at us. "No," he said, "I like them. It's the second anniversary of our engagement to-morrow — two months — and I'm going to give them to Jennifer."

"But he promised to make you others," I said.

"He couldn't make them in time for to-morrow, could he?" said Tim. "Well, then—"

"But he promised this other customer," Jill said desperately.

"That's too bad," said Tim. "He shouldn't have given them to the Jumble Sale—"

Naturally we didn't want to go into that too deeply and give David away. "Well, there was a bit of a muddle," I said. "We got the wrong ones. Do let him have them back, Tim."

But Tim wouldn't. "Tell him to go and boil his head," said Tim. "Two old pots can't be so important. Now you had better buzz off, you three, because I can see Mrs. Potterton and young Bill coming. Bye."

We said good-bye sulkily and stumped crossly down the path.

"Obstinate as a mule," I said. "What *can* Jennifer see in him?"

"Well, never mind that," said David, "what are we going to do?"

"Tell Mark Lamont, I suppose," said Jill. "Perhaps he won't mind—"

Mark Lamont did mind. He was furious. "Honestly," I thought, "he's not the man I took him for at all. Cross thing. I don't think that I'll marry him after all. I don't think he'd even do for Jennifer—"

Mark Lamont, quite unconscious of the sad turn his future had taken, was saying flatly, "Well, there it is. Take it or leave it. I must have the pots. They have been paid for, so either you get them back or else you pay me five pounds out of the Jumble Sale funds."

Of *course* we couldn't get five pounds out of the Jumble Sale funds, as he very well knew. We said sulkily that we would get the pots back and stumped crossly off again in the direction of Tim's surgery. Tim glared at us through the surgery window and shook his head. We started back in the direction of the studio.

"Look here," said David, "we can't keep tramping back and forward between Mark Lamont's studio and Tim's surgery. Let's think of a plan—"

The plan we thought of, was to creep back to the surgery in the dead of night and *steal* those wretched pots. Jill thought that it was rather a bold plan and said so.

"Nothing to it," said David airily. "When Dr. Martin lived in that house, Bungo Martin and I used to be always climbing in and out of the surgery windows. I'll show you."

Jill said in a falsely hearty voice. "That's good, then, David. You climb in and out again to-night. But you don't actually need *us*, do you?"

"Of course he needs us," I said indignantly, upset at the thought of being done out of *this* adventure. "Who's going to hold the pots while he's climbing out and in?"

Well, Jill took a lot of persuading, but in the end she agreed that we should all go and steal the pots, and we arranged to meet at Tim's back gate at twelve o'clock that night.

I was delighted, a night adventure was just what I wanted, but I must admit here and now that these nocturnal excursions aren't all that they're cracked up to be. In stories people are always getting up in the middle of the night and going off and doing things, but, in case you've never done it, I can tell you that in real life it is jolly difficult. For one thing, the grown-ups go to bed so *late*. You're dead asleep before they even come upstairs and even then they often lie awake for hours, reading. And if your house is anything like ours, the stairs creak like mad and you cannot move a step without your mother shouting, "Is something the matter, dear?" However, this time I had a bit of luck. The parents and Jennifer must have been tired out after the Jumble Sale because they were in bed and sleep before you could say knife, and when everything had quite settled down, I was up and dressed and off downstairs in a jiffy.

Of course then, Mitzi, our dachshund puppy, nearly had to wreck the whole thing by insisting on coming with me. First of all I nearly fell over her, and then when I got the back door opened, she slipped out before I could stop her. I knew that it was no good pushing her back in again, she would only whine and scratch and waken the whole house. So I said, oh all right then, *come*, in a very exasperated voice and crept round to the barn to fetch my bike.

This was another difficulty. The barn was naturally pitch dark and when I wasn't falling over things that felt like sleeping elephants and which certainly weren't there in the day-time, I was falling over Mitzi. Eventually, however, I located my bike, manoeuvred it out of the big barn doors, and manoeuvred Mitzi into the basket on the handlebars. She hadn't expected a ride and kept licking my face in gratitude. As every time she did this I nearly overbalanced and fell off my bike, it turned out to be most awkward.

About fifty yards from Tim's house, I hid my bike in the ditch. I had quite forgotten Mitzi and she yelped furiously at finding herself abandoned, so I had to clamber into the ditch and fetch her out.

Unfortunately the ditch was full of nettles and although I was wearing slacks and a jersey, the number of places that slacks and a jersey don't cover is amazing.

However, bravely suffering my pain in silence, I crept round to Tim's back gate. There I made a noise like an owl, a trick that David had taught us long ago. Back came the answering call and the two dark figures of Jill and David came cautiously out from the greater darkness of the hedge.

"Hi, Lindy," they whispered and I whispered Hi, back, and felt better at once for having their company.

"We'll creep round the hedge to the surgery window," David whispered, "and then I'll show you how to –" He suddenly went headlong into the hedge.

He wasn't in a very good temper when he picked himself up. The hedge, unfortunately, was a holly hedge and from the way he was muttering and groaning and grumbling it must have hurt as much as my nettles.

"Really, David," Jill was whispering, "why don't you look where you're going? You'll waken the whole village, far less Tim."

"Look where I'm going!" David whispered back furiously. "How can I look where I'm going in pitch darkness? Besides, I fell over something. It felt like—" he bent down and fumbled with his hands and finished in a whisper of utter amazement, "It's a dog!"

"Of *course* it's a dog," I muttered impatiently. "It's Mitzi."

"Mitzi! Mitzi!" David's voice exploded in an angry whisper. "No, really, that's too much! Everybody knows that you're absolutely dotty about that dog, but really, do you have to bring her with you on an expedition like this?"

"I *didn't* bring her, she *came*," I muttered back, equally angry. "You should know Mitzi by this time, it's not easy to leave Mitzi at home when she wants to come—"

"Bringing a dog—"

"I didn't *bring* her—"

"Oh, *do* be quiet, you two and stop arguing," Jill interrupted. "Mitzi is making less noise than either of you—"

There was some truth in that, so David and I rather sulkily stopped arguing. We dodged quickly across the open bit of lawn to the surgery window.

"Now I'll creep in," David whispered, "and hand the pots out to you—"

But when David had talked so casually about climbing in and out of the surgery window with Bungo Martin, he had quite forgotten that that had been more than two years before when he was fourteen and small for his age. Now he was sixteen and a half and a front-rank forward in his school rugby fifteen... He got half-way through the window and nothing else happened.

Jill and I couldn't understand what the delay was. There was the rear end of David, kicking and struggling, and from inside the window the sound of a few strangled grunts, but that didn't seem to be getting us anywhere.

"Oh, David, *do* hurry up," I muttered impatiently at last. "It'll be morning soon and you know what an early riser Tim is—"

"Hurry up!" came back an agonised whisper. "I *can't* hurry up. I'm stuck."

"Oh, help," I said, "let's pull him out—"

"Without the pots?" said Jill, "Let's push him in."

We tried both, but neither was very successful, and all the time David was moaning and groaning away in extreme agony. "It's not good," I said eventually, "he seems to be stuck. We'll have to get one of those files or saws or whatever they are that escaping prisoners use to file through their bars. Where would I get one of those, d'you imagine?"

"Goodness, how should I know?" said Jill. "Let's try one last heave—"

Jill took one leg and I took the other and we pulled till our lungs nearly burst. Then suddenly, out he came, like a cork out of a bottle, and we all tumbled backwards on to the lawn and one of us landed on Mitzi, who yelped. However, David was free, which was the main thing, although he was still complaining like anything, insisting that all his ribs were broken.

We stood this as long as we could until I said, "Yes, well, I'm terribly sorry, David, but I expect you'll live. And meantime we still haven't got the pots."

David immediately forgot his broken ribs. "Good heavens, the pots!" he whispered. "In you go, Jill."

I can't imagine why Jill's gasp didn't waken Tim. "Who, me?" she said.

"Yes, you," said David. "You're the smallest."

"Well, I may be the smallest," Jill whispered earnestly, "but I'm jolly fat round the middle."

That was the first time she had ever admitted *that*, I can tell you, but I just grinned to myself in the darkness and whispered, "Oh, rot, you're about as fat round the middle as a piece of string. But if you think you'll stick, I'll go."

David whispered dubiously, "Well, you're not exactly *fat*, old girl, but no one could call you skinny. We don't want you getting stuck in the window, it's madly uncomfortable."

I said indignantly, "You'd think I was the Fat Woman at the fair; of *course* I shan't get stuck. Give me a leg-up—"

For one awful moment I thought that I had stuck, but I drew in my breath, and wriggled, and I was through. David handed me a torch through the window. "Be careful," he whispered.

I edged away from the window into the dark room. I switched on the torch and shone it cautiously round, looking for the pots... Desk, filing cabinet, nothing there... shiny, very hard sofa where Tim stretched out his victims... door... suddenly I screamed. Hanging outside a cupboard, stirring a little in the breeze from the window, grinning hideously, was a skeleton.

The torch dropped from my nerveless hand. I backed wildly away from the horrid sight. I knocked into something and I gasped and whimpered in terror. There was a crash behind me, like a falling bomb in that silent room. I shrank down on the

David handed me a torch through the window.

floor, my arms over my ears and my eyes tight shut...

When I dared to open my eyes again and look up, the light was on and not only Tim — in his dressing-gown — but Jill and David were standing round, looking down at me.

"Where is it? Where is it? Take it away!" I whispered.

"Where is what, take what away?" Tim said impatiently.

"The... skeleton," I whispered.

They all glanced across at the cupboard. I didn't dare look, but I knew that the grisly thing was still there, I could hear its heels tapping faintly against the wood.

"The skeleton?" asked Tim in a wondering voice. "You mean *Hector*? But that's old Hector, you've seen old Hector a thousand times when I was swotting anatomy! I had him out again to amuse young Bill Potterton and take his mind off his finger while I was lancing it. Surely you weren't frightened of Hector?"

"Well," I said, scrambling to my feet, very shame-faced. "He looked different in the dark. I didn't recognise him."

"And just look what *you've* done" David was saying accusingly, "just look!"

I looked down at my feet. There on the floor was a sad little tangle of African violets, lumps of earth scattered round, and the gay, pretty pot was smashed into twenty pieces.

I was too upset to speak. I sank down again on my heels. I picked up the poor little plant. "Perhaps this will be all right," I said at last in a small voice, "if we put it in another pot — I know that I've ruined the little pot, but perhaps we can save the plant." I gathered the lumps of earth together with my hands and rubbed one of them between my fingers and thumbs. "These feel like stones," I said.

Tim, still looking down at me in none too good a temper, said indifferently, "Perhaps he puts stones at the bottom of his pots for drainage—"

I was still rubbing the earth off the hard lumps. "He puts stones, all right," I said, giggling rather hysterically. "Rather grand stones, though. Diamonds."

Well, what a night that was! The hard lumps were diamonds, from the Lockesley Castle robbery, and at the bottom of the other pot we found more diamonds and a fabulous string of pearls. It was all too thrilling for words.

Mark Lamont was clapped into jail and later he was tried and went to prison. He was the Country House Robber, and the whole village said that they had known all the time that there was something queer about him. This of course simply wasn't true, everybody had been quite deceived in him and had liked him very much, even me, though now of course I didn't fancy him at all as a husband.

There was a perfectly enormous reward for the stolen jewels, and when we insisted on Tim's having his share, he and Jennifer decided to get married right away and Jill and I were bridesmaids. And for the rest of the holidays there was never a dull moment, what with presents pouring in, and fittings for our dresses and all the excitement of a wedding in the family. "Oh, David," I said when I got a chance to talk to him one day in the middle of the bustle, "am I *glad* that you're left-handed and never learned to distinguish between your right hand and your left!"

XVII: A GIRL WITH IDEAS

JEAN BELL

Chapter One: Dotty has an Idea

Most of the silly things that happen in our school are caused by my friend Dotty Ellis. Her real name of course isn't Dotty, it's Dorothea — can you imagine? — and that's what the staff and other grown-ups call her, but everybody else calls her Dotty, it suits her much better. There's nothing wrong with her *brain*, mind you, quite the reverse, it's just that she gets these ideas. There was one time last term, when she had spent all her pocket-money — on another of her ideas, I forget what — and she got this idea of doing everybody's maths prep for sixpence a time. It worked like anything for a while, too, and Dotty made stacks of cash, but as Dotty happens to be a sort of mathematical genius (her father really *is* a genius, top man in nuclear physics if you know what that means, we don't) we all got such good marks that eventually even Miss Parker, who isn't all that bright in the head, smelt a rat. There was a fearful row and Miss Parker wanted us all to be expelled, but after all you can hardly expel a whole form so we just had lots of boring old detentions and gatings and so on instead. It was maddening, we were all dying to be expelled and go home for an extra holiday.

Then another time Dotty thought that she would wire up the dorm so that she and I, who had been put at opposite ends for talking or something, could speak to each other in the middle of the night. So she wrote to her father for all the bits and pieces (she has no mother and he spoils her like mad) but before she had even got the thing going properly she'd got tangled up in the electricity and fused all the lights in the whole school and there was a bit of a rumpus about that.

Another of Dotty's ideas was this mad secret writing that she had heard of. We were sitting in the Common Room one day after tea when Dotty came in, carrying all sorts of things, paper, and a small bottle of lemon juice, and matches, and a stump of candle and so on. She moved two second-formers who were playing halma at a corner of the table and spread out all her stuff.

"What's this?" I said.

"A scientific experiment," said Dotty. "I read about it in a book. Don't look just yet —"

We all went back to what we had been doing, which was nothing, and Dotty busied herself with her bottle and her bit of stick and her sheet of paper.

Then she handed me the paper. "Can you read that?" she said.

"Yes," I said.

"You can?" Dotty was disappointed. "What does it say?"

"It's faint, but it says, *Have you done your prep*," I said. "Do you really want to know?"

"No, of course I don't," said Dotty. "Oh, hold on," she said, "I made a mistake, I shouldn't have used a pencil, the pencil marks show, hold on, I'll try it again —"

This time she carefully sharpened a match, but when we tried to look she hunched her shoulder and shielded what she was doing with her arm.

"There!" said Dotty. "*Now* can you read it?" She handed us what looked like a blank sheet of paper with a few wet smears on it. We told her that we couldn't. She beamed. "Well, just hold on," she said. She lit the candle and very gently began to wave the paper over it. To our amazement, letters began to appear. *This is secret writing*, it said. *Now can you* — we were absolutely fascinated, watching the writing appear, but unfortunately Dotty got carried away and held the paper too near the candle and suddenly the whole thing went up in flames.

This was very, very exciting, Dotty flapping a burning sheet of paper about, Prune shouting "Help! Help! Fire! Fire!," me trying to put out the conflagration, the two second-formers quickly moving their halma game to a safe distance and half the Common Room crowding round to see what all the fuss was about.

We got the fire out without too much trouble if you don't count Dotty's eyebrows, and Dotty repeated her scientific experiment for the third go. This time it worked like a charm; the secret writing came up beautifully. *Isn't it smashing* it said.

Dotty was delighted. "Useful, don't you think?" she said.

"Well, quite fun," I said, "but I don't know about *useful*. When could we use it?"

"Heavens," said Dotty, "in class, of course! You know how acid Nosy Parker always gets if we pass notes? Well, she can't object if we send blank bits of paper along, can she?"

There was no end to what Nosy could object to, and Dotty knew it. "Besides," I said, "what's Nosy going to be doing while we set up the apparatus? If you drop so much as a pin she knows, so can you imagine us sitting there with a burning candle deciphering secret messages?"

"Yes, I admit it's a tiny bit clumsy," said Dotty, "I'll have to work on it, these ideas in books are often a bit like that, never as easy as they look, but I'll work out something. It'll come in handy one day —"

This was to prove absolutely true, and we all had fun that afternoon writing each other secret messages, but then other things came along to occupy Dotty's mind.

It's not that Dotty is naughty — well, she's naughty too, sometimes, but that's not the point, it's just that she gets these crazy ideas; and the worst attack of ideas that she ever had was this last term.

It all began quietly enough with a new girl, a new girl and a mouse. This new girl was in our form and our dorm. On the first day of term when Dotty and I were catching up with the news, we hadn't seen each other once in the Easter hols, old Smithy the matron sent us upstairs to the dorm to find out what this new girl was doing and to bring her down to tea.

Dotty and I stood at the door of the dormitory and stared at the new girl. She was small and sort of skinny and her hair, which was very fair and straight, was hanging over her face so that we couldn't see what she was like. She was sitting on her bed looking down at something that she was holding cupped in her hands. I hoped that she wasn't howling — goodness, we were all ancient now, eleven if not twelve, and we hadn't howled on the first day of term for ages.

We had been a bit put out to discover that there was a new girl in our dorm. We were very comfortable as we were, we thought, me and Dotty and Prunella Whiting who is a bit of a prune, actually, but we can't all be perfect, I suppose, and three other bods who aren't terribly interesting, just nice dull girls, really, we usually called them the Opposition, but their names are Jennifer Lee, Flora Stewart and Angela Daly, if you want to know. And if you want to know what we look like, Dotty is small but 'wiry', according to her father. She wears glasses and has two rather short, rather mousy pigtails that somehow stick out more than any other pigtails. She is as blind as a bat without her specs and as she's always leaving them in silly places for people to sit on, or breaking them, she's as blind as a bat half the time, bumbling about in a sort of dim fog. She always begins the term with two pairs of specs and finishes it with half a pair stuck together with sticky-tape or pink elastoplast. Prune is rather *like* a prune, really, not when it's all dry and wrinkled but after it has been cooked, when it's plump and black and glossy, she has this very shiny black hair and she certainly is, well, plump. I'm three inches taller than Dotty and I've got sort of red hair; I like to think it's copper — but most people seem to think it's red.

But we couldn't stand there staring at the new girl all day so we went in. She looked up — she wasn't howling, thank goodness — and pushed her hair out of her eyes.

"Hullo," I said.

She said hullo, cautiously, and Dotty, who is like the Elephant's Child, full of 'satiable curiosity, went over to her. "What have you got there?"

The new girl had carefully cupped her two hands together again. She glanced up. "A mouse," she said.

"A mouse!" I said.

"A mouse!" Dotty cried.

The new girl looked at us rather anxiously. "There's no reason why I shouldn't have a mouse, is there?" she said. "It said in that prospectus-thing that girls in the junior school were allowed to have pets—"

"Oh, some people have pets," said Dotty. "Not horses and dogs and cats of course but things like hamsters and guinea-pigs and silkworms, I've never heard of anyone having a mouse before, have you, Denny?"

I shook my head. "But I don't suppose there's any reason why not," I said. "Heavens, a mouse is much more interesting than that boring old tortoise that Prune brought back last term. He just sat around and sulked —. I should think you'd be expected to keep him in the Pet Shed, all the same," I added.

The new girl looked anxious again. "Oh, he wouldn't like that," she said. "He lives in my pocket, actually—"

Dotty sat down beside her on the bed. "Let's see him," she said.

The new girl carefully opened her hands a tiny crack and out popped a dear little furry brown face with bright little beady eyes and pointed little ears.

"Oh, sweet," said Dotty. "Oh, let's all have mice! Let's have a mouse club!"

If I had realised at the time that Dotty had just had one of her ideas I'd have led the new girl and her mouse firmly to the Pet Shed there and then, but I wasn't thinking about Dotty at all, really, I was only thinking about that dear little mouse and dying to stroke him. "Oh, please may I hold him!" I said and held out my hands.

"Well, be careful—" said the new girl and put the mouse gently into my hands.

But I wasn't prepared for his little tickly softness and the funny little scratchy feeling of his dear little feet. "Oh, he tickles!" I yelped and dropped him on the bed.

He whisked off the bed and was out of sight in a second.

"Oh, help!" I said. "Oh, gosh, I'm sorry! Is he lost?"

"Not lost," said the new girl severely, "frightened."

"Oh, help," I said again, "I really am sorry."

"Well, he's very sensitive," said the new girl. I felt

awful.

"So now what do you do?" asked Dotty, leaning forward eagerly, her specs slipping down her nose in her excitement. She pushed them back up her nose and said to the new girl, "Shall we start looking for him?"

"No, no, keep still," said the new girl — we hadn't even had time to ask her name — "and I'll show you. I'm trying to train him. I don't know if it will work this time because he's very sensitive—" and she glared at me again.

I couldn't go on saying that I was sorry, so I just mumbled and the new girl took a bit of chocolate out of her pocket. Dotty and I looked interested, but it turned out that it wasn't for us, she broke off two or three tiny crumbs and put them on the floor. There was absolute silence for a second then, sure enough, out popped that dear little mouse from under the bed and started tucking in to the chocolate.

"Oh, *sweet*," said Dotty again. "Oh, we must all have mice—"

The new girl very gently stroked the top of his head and then gathered him up in her hand. She gave him another crumb or two as a reward. Dotty was fascinated. "Oh, we must all have mice!" she said. "We could teach them all sorts of things, send messages to each other—"

"Better than that crazy telephone that fused all the lights," I said. "Or the secret writing."

Dotty quite naturally ignored this. "Could we, do you think?" she asked the new girl, "train mice, I mean -?"

"Well, I don't know," said the new girl. "But I don't see why not. I've trained Mouse after all. A bit—"

"Is that his name?" asked Dotty. "Just Mouse?"

"What a splendid name for a mouse," I said.

"Well," said the new girl rather apologetically, "I

couldn't think of a better name for him. Beatrix Potter had already used all the good ones like Mrs. Tittlemouse and Hunca Munca and—"

"Talking about names," I said, "what's your name?"

"Lisa," she said, "Lisa Russell."

"How do you do," I said politely, "I'm Denise Wilson, only most people call me Denny, and that's—" I waved a hand at Dotty "—Dorothea Mary Ellis only everybody calls her Dotty—"

Dotty wasn't even listening. "If we could train them," she was saying, "we could work out a whole inter-com system — they could go flashing about all over the school carrying messages and nobody would even notice them, just think they were mice—"

"And all the time they were really elephants," I said sarcastically. "Have some sense, Dotty, the staff probably all loathe mice — I bet old Nosy Parker does, for one, she hates *everything* except multiplication and division and all that jazz — they'd be setting traps all over the place and having Ginger the cat working overtime—"

Lisa shuddered at the very idea and stroked Mouse gently in case all this alarming talk about traps and cats was upsetting his sensitive nerves, but Dotty just brushed aside traps, cats, staff, the lot, the way she's apt to do when she has an idea. "Well, naturally," she said, "we're going to look *after* our mice —. Could we train them, Lisa, d'you think, honestly?" So at least she had been paying enough attention to hear Lisa's name.

"I don't see why not," said Lisa. "My father trains rats in his laboratory, teaches them to run up and down stairs, in and out of the most complicated mazes, press bars to get their food — they do everything except use a knife and fork, practically—"

What a fascinating thing for a father to do, I

thought, what could he be? Dotty's father was fairly fascinating too, of course, all those secret inventions, mine was only a doctor —. Dotty was saying, "Well, if your father knows all about training rats — what does he train rats for? — wouldn't he know something about training mice? Could you write and ask him for some helpful hints?"

Lisa said that she could, of course, but that she seemed to be fairly successful with the chocolate.

All this talk about chocolate and rats getting their own food was almost too much for me. "Talking about chocolate," I said, "I could do with some tea. We'll be lucky if there's any left. Smithy will be sending out a search-party for us—"

Luckily, however, in the hurly-burly of the first day of term, Smithy hadn't had time to notice that it had taken Dotty and me a good half-hour to fetch the new girl down from the dorm. Lisa put Mouse carefully into the pocket of her djibbah — at Thornton Combe we wear the most ghastly sort of gym tunics called djibbahs, green serge in winter and green linen in summer. They're so absolutely awful that everybody eventually gets quite fond of them and a year or two ago when the school voted on whether to have very, very smart blouses and skirts or keep the vile old djibbahs, the djibbahs won by ninety-nine per cent — which means ninety-nine out of a hundred in case your maths are like mine. Anyway, djibbahs have jolly useful big deep pockets, and Lisa put Mouse carefully into her pocket with a few biscuit crumbs to keep him company and off we went down to tea.

The Junior Common Room was the usual seething mob, everybody yelling at the tops of their voices, so we didn't bother much to introduce Lisa around, only grabbed as much tea as we could — it's rather special on the first day, sandwiches *and* cake, so that the poor victims think that's how they're going to eat every day and feel quite cheered, little do they know. Prune was stuffing away quietly in a corner, so we took Lisa over to talk to her.

"Not a word about Mouse," Dotty muttered out of the side of her mouth, "Prune gets excited, before we know where we are she'll blab about the whole thing — we don't want the whole dorm in the Mouse Club with message-carrying mice rushing all over the school getting the lines of communication all tangled up. We'll tell her later—"

Well, with one thing and another, we forgot to tell Prune. First day of term is always pretty exciting, telling people all about the hols and bagging decent lockers in the Common Room and decent desks in the form-room — we did splendidly, Dotty and me in the back row, Prune and Lisa immediately in front of us. We didn't expect that it would last, Dotty and I bag the back row every term and every term one mistress after another drags her down to the front row because she can't see the board, or so she says, half the time she can see the board quite well, only it's more fun if there's a bit of fuss and bother and by the time Dotty has pottered about, finding a desk from which she *can* see, half the lesson is over.

Also we took Lisa on a quick tour of the grounds before supper. Our school is very pretty, it's not far from Bath, where I live, near the village of Thornton and it's built on the side of a valley with a jolly nice stream at the bottom and woods and fields and things on the other side. It's a great big old house which used to belong to the Thornton family before they all died out or something — there's a sort of statue of an ancient Thornton in the village church in coat-of-mail with his legs crossed which means that he went on a Crusade, or so Dotty says, I always mean to ask Miss Andross our history mistress if this is true, or if it's one of Dotty's dotty ideas but I always forget. Of course we've had some new bits built since the Thorntons' day, all the houses for instance, they're called after famous women — Brontë, Cavell, Siddons and Nightingale, ours is Nightingale, it's easily the best.

Supper is nice too on the first night, sausages and mash and ice-cream, we told Lisa to make the most of it because the next day it would be back to revolting macaroni-cheese and sago pudding. There is no prep, of course, on the first night, we arrange our things in our lockers and read, if we want to, or just natter — we all nattered; then it was time for baths and bed.

We had managed to bag jolly good beds in the dorm too — Lisa, Dotty, me and Prune in a row on the window side, so that if you screwed your neck half off you got a jolly nice view of the valley and the river. The other poor things had to make do with the opposite side — still, they needn't despair, they would know that somewhere during the term Dotty or I or both would be moved for talking after lights out and then one of them would get the best bed, I could see that Jennifer had her eye on mine already, so I told her to keep her longing glances to herself, I was a reformed character that term.

Jennifer laughed. "I bet," she said. "In fact I bet you'll be moved out of that bed in disgrace in — in — well, say, a month—"

"Done!" I said. "What do you bet?"

"A million pounds," said Jennifer.

"Talk sense," I said, "I haven't got a million pounds."

"Okay," said Jennifer, "then a — then a Mars bar."

"That's more like it," I said. "Not that it matters whether we bet a million pounds or a Mars bar because this term things are going to be different—"

Every term I mean to be super good, but something or other is always cropping up, usually Dotty, and before I know where I am, one if not more of the staff is rampaging around after my blood.

We were still laughing and arguing when Carol Young, the prefect on duty, came in to put the lights out, but she's not a bad old stick, Carol, and would never be too strict on the first night of term, so we still went on chatting quietly for a while. Lisa seemed fine, not chatting madly, I must admit, but not in floods either, so that was all right. And we were all tired after the travelling and the bustle and everything and one by one we all went off to sleep.

Chapter Two: Mouse Club

I was just drifting off when suddenly a hand was digging into my shoulder and someone was breathing in my ear in a very tickly way.

"Whasser marrer?" I murmured sleepily.

"Denny!" It was Prune, all dramatic and agitated. "Denny, wake up!"

I moved my ear out of reach and leant up on my elbow. "Well, I am awake," I whispered. "Who wouldn't be, with you yelling right in my ear-hole. What's up?"

"Denny, there's something in my bed!"

This, I must admit, was a surprise. "What sort of a something?" I asked.

"Denny, I don't know! I'm petrified—"

"Yes, well, but what size of a thing?"

"Quite small, I think, but it moves *about*. It was trying to get under my pillow at one point, scratching away like anything — what shall I do? Shall I go and get Carol?"

"Are you off your nut?" The less Carol knew about what went on in Dormitory Four the better. "I'll have a look—"

I fumbled in my locker for a torch as quietly as I could, then crept cautiously over to Prune's bed, with Prune practically treading on my heels. There was no movement in the bed that I could see and I was just beginning to think that Prune was making a fuss about nothing as usual and that a spider or some other harmless insect had got under the blankets when I heard a faint little rustling noise under the pillow. Very, very carefully I lifted the pillow. There was Mouse, attacking half a bar of chocolate with great gusto.

"Help!" said Prune. "It's a mouse! What cheek!"

"Prune!" I said in a shocked whisper, "have you been taking sweets to bed again?"

"Well of course not," said Prune virtuously, "only a tiny bit of chocolate — you *know* I get night starvation and I like to have a little something there when I wake up starving in the night, there's nothing in that —. But the cheek of that mouse! To come right into my bed, right under my pillow and pinch my chocolate! And to go right on eating it with me standing here watching him, such cheek! Just wait till I fetch Ginger, I'll fix that mouse—"

"Oh nonsense," I said, "that's not a mouse, that's Mouse, he adores chocolate—"

"That's not a mouse, that's a mouse," Prune repeated, sounding muddled. "Are you trying to be funny? When is a mouse not a mouse?"

By this time Dotty, who never misses a thing, must have heard us and wakened up, luckily the sloths on the other side of the dorm were sound asleep, snoring away like a row of little porkers. Dotty tiptoed round the end of my bed to see what was going on; as she hadn't put on her specs, she wasn't going to see much.

"What's happened?" she whispered. "What are you

doing out of bed?"

"It's Mouse," I whispered back. "That prune Prune had chocolate under her pillow and Mouse smelt it out and now he's eating himself silly, look—" I shone the torch.

Dotty was very much struck by this. "Heavens," she said, "that's a clever mouse." She peered vaguely in the direction of Prune's bed, but of course saw nothing except a dim blur. "I should think that mouse could be trained to do practically anything! One whiff of chocolate and he comes all the way from the other end of the dorm and finds it! Talk about clever—"

"That's all very well," said Prune in an injured voice. "It isn't very clever to eat all my chocolate! And as for you two! Are you just going to stand there and let him? I don't know who this mouse is that you're all talking about, but if you don't remove him pretty quick, I'm going to fetch Ginger—"

Dotty was shocked. "Prune!" she said. "What a thing to say! Fetch Ginger! This is no ordinary mouse, this is Mouse!"

"Oh help," said Prune, "now *she's* going to start! When is a mouse not a mouse — I honestly don't care whether he's a mouse or not, all I want is to get rid of him. Will you please just get him off my bed before he eats all my chocolate—?"

"Oh, if that's all you want—" said Dotty.

Of course why Dotty should ever think that she could catch a mouse I don't know, she couldn't catch an elephant without her specs; it was a great pity that she ever tried. She put out a hand vaguely in Mouse's direction, but she completely forgot (a) that she couldn't see what she was doing and (b) that Mouse had those sensitive nerves. He twitched his ears and lashed his tail like an indignant little tiger and was gone from off Prune's bed in a flash.

"Now you've done it," I said. "Now he's gone."

"Good thing too," muttered Prune, tenderly wrapping up the remains of her nibbled chocolate. She was just going to put it safely in a tin in her locker when she was apparently overcome by night starvation. She unwrapped it again. "Anyone want a bit?"

"Good heavens, Prune," I said severely, "this is no time to be standing about eating chocolate, we've got to catch that mouse!"

Well then we started. And if you think that it's easy looking for one small mouse in one large dormitory in pitch darkness in the middle of the night, you're sadly mistaken. It was chaos. But first of all, I made Dotty put her specs on — at least then there was less chance of her walking over the faces of the Opposition, but otherwise I couldn't get any sense into those two idiots at all; they wouldn't pay any attention to me and got completely carried away. They blundered and bumbled about like two bees in a jampot, they crawled under beds, they clambered over beds, they looked in lockers, they looked in sponge-bags, they had Prune's blankets all over the floor, they felt under pillows, they pulled Lisa's blankets out at the foot of her bed and giggled at the sight of her bare toes.

That was the last straw as far as I was concerned. "Oh, do shut up!" I hissed furiously. "You *know* that Mouse is very, very sensitive, you'll never catch him this way. All you'll do is have Carol in on our tops—"

It wasn't Carol we got in on our tops, it was Miss Parker. She's our house-mistress, worse luck, and I suppose that she was snooping about as usual when she heard the din coming from Dormitory Four. She came in and glared at us. Prune, her hair standing on end, poked her head out from under the heap of blankets on the floor. Her jaw dropped about a couple of feet. Dotty was lying across her bed, almost standing on her head as she tried to shine the torch underneath. When Nosy Parker came in and put the light on, Dotty tried to scramble back on her bed, lost her balance and landed with a thump on the floor. Rubbing her elbow, she grinned feebly at Miss Parker. The Opposition began to stir and sit up, blinking like owls in the light. Lisa took one bleary look at Nosy Parker and crept under the blankets again. I just stood there. Oh *drat*, I thought, there goes my Mars bar, right on the very first night.

"Prunella!" said Miss Parker in an awful voice, gazing down at the tangle of blankets and Prune that was practically under her feet. "WHAT ARE YOU DOING?"

Prune swallowed once or twice as if she were choking. "Well, actually, Miss Parker," she said in a sort of high quaver, "I'm looking for a mouse—"

This was terrible. Poor old Prune is terrified of Miss Parker and goes on like a rabbit with a stoat whenever Miss Parker comes near her, so naturally she said the first thing that came into her head, but if Miss Parker found out about Mouse — well — end of Mouse.

But Dotty had one of her ideas, and for once it was a good one.

"Actually, Miss Parker," she said confidentially in a low voice, "I think she's having a sort of a—" she turned to me, I'm supposed to be good at English, "— what's that thing called when it's something you make up in your head?"

"Hallucination?" I suggested, after a bit of thought.

"Hallucination, that's right," said Dotty. "She keeps looking for this mouse—"

Prune may be a bit of a prune but she isn't all

that dim. She was just about bursting with indignation at the very idea that Mouse was a hallucination.

"So a mouse is a hallucination now, is it?" she muttered angrily. "Just you wait. I'll show you whether it's a hallucination. Since when could a hallucination eat—" She stopped in time, having just remembered that chocolate in the dorm is Strictly Forbidden. I helped her memory still further by giving her a good hard pinch under the pretence of gathering up her blankets. "Ow!" she said, and subsided under the blankets again.

"And I suppose you're all helping her to look for this imaginary mouse?" Miss Parker was saying, she *is* a sarcastic beast.

"Yes, that's right," said Dotty cheerfully. "We didn't want to disturb anyone—"

Miss Parker raised her eyebrows. "I shouldn't say that your efforts had been entirely successful," she said. But Nosy Parker quite likes Dotty — on account of her being a mathematical genius, so instead of gating her for a month and giving her about a thousand sums to do, which is what she would have done to me, she only said coldly, "Well, seeing that it's the first night of term, I shall overlook it this time, but please all get back into bed and go to sleep *immediately*."

We said oh, thank you, Miss Parker, and of course, Miss Parker and things like that, and bundled Prune's blankets back on to her bed and got into our own beds, looking innocent, and Miss Parker gave one final glare at us and put out the light and went away.

There was intense silence for a minute or two while we listened to her clip-clopping along the corridor, and then Prune said in an indignant whisper, "Now just tell me. Is there a mouse, or isn't there?"

"Of course there's a mouse," I whispered back, "Lisa's mouse, his name's Mouse—"

"Well," Prune breathed a faint sigh of relief, "that's something, I suppose — I was beginning to wonder—"

The Opposition were twittering away, asking a lot of questions that nobody much bothered to answer and Dotty was explaining to Lisa what had happened. Lisa was horrified. "You mean Mouse got out of his box?" she asked. She dived under her bed and came up again to borrow a torch. We saw the faint light waggling about under her bed and we heard squeaks coming from Lisa. "Help!" she said. "I didn't fasten the door properly! Mouse has escaped! I must look for him! Oh *help!*"

This is where we came in, I thought, but just before they could all leap out of bed again I said, "Oh, do wait, you lunatics. Lisa can catch Mouse quite well if you'll all just shut up. Prune, give Lisa some of your chocolate—"

"Not more chocolate," said Prune rebelliously, but she was eventually persuaded to cough up a few crumbs, Lisa put them in the box that she had for Mouse and we all lay still. As usual, it worked like a charm. Mouse went into his little box — which was a very grand cage, actually, with an upstairs and a downstairs and a little wheel and all sorts of things like that for him to play with — Lisa fastened the door *securely* and we all lay back in our beds, exhausted.

"Goodnight, everybody," Dotty whispered. "Tomorrow we'll make plans for getting our own mice and starting the Mouse Club—"

"A Mouse *Club!*" Prune whispered faintly. "A whole Club of mice guzzling away at my chocolate!"

A Mouse Club, I thought, I've had enough mice to

last me for the rest of my life...

Chapter Three: We Buy our Mice

But I felt quite differently about the Mouse Club next day.

First of all, we made Lisa take Mouse to the Pet Shed and leave him there. She struggled every inch of the way but we were firm.

"He'll be lonely if we leave him there—" she said.

"Well," I said, "we'll be expelled if you don't, so you can choose—"

So she left him, and we went back to Big School for prayers and then to our form-rooms for the usual boring old round of lessons to start for another term. But at break Dotty started immediately with her plans to get ourselves mice. "First of all," she said, "who wants to join?"

"Well, do mice always eat so much chocolate?" asked Prune.

"They *like* chocolate," Lisa admitted, "that's why I'm using chocolate to train Mouse—"

"Well then," said Prune. "I don't think I will join, thank you very much."

"Good gracious, Prune, surely you can spare a tiny little bit of chocolate to give to a dear little mouse—" Dotty began, but I interrupted.

"You don't *have* to give them chocolate," I said. "Give 'em cheese or — or, well, or anything. With luck, Prune, you might get one that didn't even *like* chocolate—"

This quite cheered Prune up and she said that in that case, she *might* join, she would just think it over —.

"Well, don't take all day thinking," said Dotty, "we want to get cracking on our great School of Mouse Training. What about you, Denny?"

I had forgotten the horrors of the previous night. "Oh sure, I'll join," I said. "But where do we get the mice?"

"Pet shops are full of mice," said Dotty, "couldn't your mum get some in Bath for us?"

"No," I said firmly, "my mum is terrified of mice, she would never let us keep even white mice at home. Rabbits, yes, cats, dogs, even hamsters. Mice, no —. What about your father?"

"Well, he's in Bristol, at his lab, working on a very, very secret weapon or something, absolutely Top Secret, I can't imagine that he'd get time off to come tootling over here with a lot of mice—"

Prune, of course, was no good. She lives in Glastonbury which, as a matter of fact, isn't far from our school, but she was so jolly mean about the chocolate that we didn't think that we could trust her to bring mice from home, they'd be half-dead with starvation by the time she got them back to school.

Lisa said, "You can send them by rail, I read about it in the paper—"

We couldn't believe this, but Lisa went off to her locker to get the newspaper cutting to show us. It was a fascinating article, we kept snatching it from each other and reading bits out.

"Listen to this, there's a National Mouse Club, oh sweet—"

"Did you know that there are all sorts of different varieties? There's Blue Fox, there's Black, there's Blue Tan — what's Mouse, Lisa?"

"Well, I should have thought just mouse. But as he's sort of brown, perhaps he's a Blue Tan—"

"Oh, *do* let me see the paper—"

"All *right*, Dotty you clot, but there's no need to snatch, you'll tear it—"

I put the paper firmly on the Common Room floor,

and we all looked over each other's shoulders and read it aloud, nobody paying much attention to anyone else.

" 'The various mouse clubs hold their own shows and then there are the national shows, organised by the National Mouse Club —' oh, we *must* have a show—"

"Help, there's more to it than just sending a mouse along to a show, listen — 'Grooming is important. Mice going on show are shampooed and dried with a hair-drier!' And there's a picture of a dear little mouse being shampooed with a shaving-brush, fancy! Where can I get a shaving-brush, Daddy gave them up ages ago, he uses an electric razor—"

"Here's the bit about going by rail — 'In those open shows members living too far away to attend, send their mice in special containers by British Rail —' "

"I told you," said Lisa.

"Look, Prune, it says here that this person who had the top mouse in one show fed it on oats and soaked bread, not a word about chocolate. Linseed before shows to make its coat glossy—"

"But I haven't *got* any linseed," said Prune. "I haven't any oats for that matter—"

"Stick to chocolate, it will be easier, you always have some handy—"

"Not for mice—" said Prune.

Dotty interrupted. "There's to be an All-British mouse championship in September, sponsored by the National Mouse Club — oh, we must enter our mice!"

"How can we enter mice that we haven't got?" I asked, thinking that it was about time that some of these crazy coots came down to earth.

I should have done better to keep my mouth shut,

for Dotty said, "Yes, but we're going to get some. There's nothing else for it, Denny, you'll just have to go to the dentist—"

"Oh, Dotty, *no*," I said, "I haven't even got toothache!"

"You could raise a few twinges, couldn't you?"

"Dotty, no," I said again. "You know I'm absolutely petrified of the dentist!"

"But he'll only look at your teeth and say that there's nothing the matter, that there's nothing to be done—"

"Not my dentist," I said gloomily. "He'll find a hole—"

"Well, but Denny, I can't think of any other way to get the mice. Not even Nosy P. will make a fuss when you tell her that you have to go to the dentist—"

"My mum will make a fuss. I was at the dentist last week—"

Dotty didn't even listen. She was having one of her ideas. "And you'll trot off to Bath and on the way to the dentist you'll just slip into a pet-shop and get our mice. Nothing could be easier—"

"That's what you think," I muttered, but like an ass I let her persuade me, and went off to beard Nosy Parker in her den after lunch.

I'm the first to admit that some mistresses are quite decent, young, you know, at least young-ish, and able to crack a joke occasionally like Miss Simpson, the English mistress and Miss Lyle who teaches singing and Polly Flinders the gym mistress, they're almost human, but Nosy Parker isn't like that. She's a terror. I was shaking like a leaf when I got to her study.

"Well, Denise?" she said. Frosty, *you* know.

"Oh, Miss Parker," I said, all in a rush, "I'm very, very sorry but I think I'll have to go to the dentist on

Saturday—"

"To the *dentist*, Denise?"

"Yes, it's the only way — I mean, yes, I think I'll have to—"

"So early in the term? Didn't your mother see to all that in the holidays?"

"Yes, she did," I said, feeling indignant, "she makes us go to the dentist every holidays, it's ghastly—"

"Well, then, what's the matter? Have you got toothache? Have you got a tooth that's aching?"

By this time, not only my teeth but every bone in my body was aching madly. "Not one tooth, Miss Parker, I just sort of ache all over—"

Miss Parker looked at me sharply. "I expect that it's nothing that an aspirin wouldn't put right—" Oh *blow*, I thought, she isn't going to let me go "— but I suppose that you had better go—"

"Oh, *thank* you, Miss Parker!" I said. I could have hugged the old dragon, but then I remembered that this wasn't supposed to be a very happy occasion for me, so I quickly took the grin off my face and said, "So may I ring my mother, Miss Parker, and ask her to make an appointment for me?"

Miss Parker said yes and I scuttled off and rang my mother, who fussed like anything but finally said that she would make an appointment with Mr. Sutcliffe and should she come and fetch me in the car?

"No, no," I said, "I've got to buy some mice — I mean, something for Dotty on the way, there are sure to be people from school coming in to Bath, I'll come in the bus with them —. But if you happen to be in town that morning how about a milkshake and buns?"

"No wonder you need to go to the dentist so often," said my mother, but so it was arranged, and when the others were all going to tennis practice on Saturday morning I went off in the bus to Bath with a couple of seniors and a small thing from the Second Form.

I made a slight detour on my way to the dentist to visit a pet-shop I knew in Broad Street. Here they had a splendid selection of mice, all colours. I chose a black, a rather pretty tan and a white one. I had had a bit of a job screwing money out of Dotty and Prune who insisted that they were flat broke — how could they be, at the very beginning of term? — so one of them could have the white one, he was cheaper. I had decided on the tan one, he was a perfect pet, you could see how clever he was, it would be no trouble training him I thought. I would call him Tanny.

The girl in the shop put them in the dearest little boxes, like egg-boxes, with air-holes, and then wrapped them in brown paper because I certainly didn't want the whole Lower School to know what I had bought. She put some more holes in the brown paper, and then she said, "Have you got cages for them?"

I looked at her blankly. "Cages?" I said.

"Yes, cages, for them to live in. You can't keep them in cardboard boxes, they'd eat their way through those in no time."

I said in a very small voice, "How much are cages?"

Well, of course I hadn't nearly enough money for three cages, but I knew that I could borrow from mum, so I arranged to come back for the cages — and the mice too, because mum would have a cadenza if I took three mice to have coffee with her — and off I went quite gaily to Mr. Sutcliffe.

I wasn't gay long. That dratted man found a hole in one of my back teeth.

I looked like a Christmas tree when I staggered back to school, laden with three cages and a box of mice. The small thing from the Second Form helped me to carry the cages to the Pet Shed, I promised her a look at the mice later, then I took the parcel of mice to Nightingale. Dotty and Lisa and Prune were all waiting in the hall for me to get back; and so was Mandy Griffiths, the prefect in charge. Some pres are jolly decent when we bring tuck back to school (Strictly Forbidden) but not Mandy. She prowls about like a raging tiger and confiscates our tuck — and eats it herself, we all think. No wonder she's so fat.

Well, I had this biggish parcel in my hand and Mandy, who must have eyes in the back of her head, suddenly appeared from nowhere.

"Is that tuck?" she demanded.

"What, in this parcel?" I said. "No, it's mice."

Mandy went quite red. "I suppose you think you're funny," she said. "Just take your parcel over to that table and open it up—"

I hesitated. "But Mandy—" I began.

"Don't argue. Just take it over there and open it."

"But—"

Mandy glared at me. *"Don't argue.* Open it up."

I said oh, all right, and took the parcel over to the table. Dotty and Lisa and Prune were all giggling and nudging each other and whispering and I could hardly wait to see Mandy's face when the parcel was opened. But I took my time over the paper and string while Mandy stood there getting crosser and crosser, and when I took the paper off she grabbed one of the little boxes and opened it. Out popped a mouse. Mandy gave one terrified shriek, dropped the box and clambered up on the table. The mouse — it was Tanny — indignantly scuttered off the table and went streaking across the hall.

Mandy crouched on the table and shouted furiously at me, "It's a mouse!"

"Well, I told you it was a mouse and you wouldn't believe me," I said. "And," I kindly told her, "there are another two there on the table—" and I pointed to the two little boxes.

Mandy yelled and clambered down off the table. Tanny, who had been having a tremendous run round the hall, came darting back towards us. Mandy yelled again and clambered back on the table. She was managing that table awfully well for anyone so fat, but it was an effort, you could see, for she was puffing and panting like anything. "Catch...that...mouse! Catch...that...mouse!" she was shouting.

But of course we were all laughing far too much to do any catching; besides, Tanny, upset by all the noise that Mandy was making, had hidden under an old oak chest that sits in the hall.

"Poor little thing!" Lisa said severely when she could speak, "You've upset him—"

"*I've* upset *him*!" Mandy spluttered. "What about me?"

Well, nobody cared about Mandy, but it might have sounded rather rude to say so, so Dotty said, "If you could just stop yelling, Mandy, and keep quiet for a minute, we'll try to catch him. You know," she added helpfully, "he's much more frightened of you than you are of him—"

Mandy gritted her teeth. "I am NOT frightened," she said. "I just don't like mice—"

"'Sh!" said Lisa. Mandy meekly 'shed.

Lisa crouched down by the oak chest and held out her hand to Prune. Prune gave a gusty sigh, but obediently pulled a piece of chocolate out of her djibbah pocket. I glanced at Mandy, but she was much too far gone to care about forbidden chocolate et cetera.

Lisa put down a crumb of chocolate and — honestly, these mice are gluttons for chocolate — out Tanny crept and settled down to enjoy it. Lisa stretched out a gentle hand and scooped him up. "Would you like to hold him, Mandy?" she kindly offered. "I'm sure you would like him better if you got to know him—"

Mandy nearly fell off the table at the very idea. She climbed down rather sheepishly, but now that there were no mice in sight she began to recover rapidly. "Take these mice to the Pet Shed *at once*," she blustered. "Who said you could keep mice, anyway?"

"Well, no-one said we couldn't," I said. "I'm very, very sorry if I frightened you, Mandy, but I did tell you that it was mice I had in the parcel, didn't I?"

"We're going to have a Mouse Club," Dotty said. "Honestly, Mandy, you should get a mouse and join — I'm sure that Lisa's right. I'm sure you wouldn't be so frightened of mice if you got more used to them—"

Mandy gritted her teeth again, we could hear them grinding away. "I am *not* frightened of mice," she said, "I just don't happen to like them. And if I ever, EVER, see one of those mice in Big School or in the House again I'll tell Miss Fisher and have them confiscated."

"Yes, Mandy," we said meekly and scuttled off to the Pet Shed with our mice while I handed out the bars of chocolate that I had smuggled in, not in a great big parcel for the whole school to see, but hidden in my djibbah pocket.

Chapter Four: King Arthur Lived Here

Well, we were absolutely thrilled with our mice. Except that no-one wanted the poor little white one.

"But I bought him for you or Prune," I said indignantly. "He was cheap."

"I've got lots of money," said Dotty.

"I like the tan one much better," said Prune.

I could have knocked their heads together. "I chose the tan one," I said shortly. "His name's Tanny."

"Fanny?"

"No, TANNY. And honestly you are the limit. I go to all this trouble, have the dentist *find* a hole in my tooth, stagger home with these great parcels, have all that ghastly business with Mandy and then you don't like the mice I bring! *Look* at the poor little thing, he's sweet—"

"Well, if he's sweet," said Dotty, "*you* have him."

I glared at her and then I looked at the white mouse and honestly you would think he *knew* that nobody wanted him, he was crouched in his corner in a very dejected way, even his ears drooped. "Oh, poor little thing," I said, "he knows you're all being horrible to him, of course I'll have him, poor little thing—"

"Oh help," said Dotty, "another sensitive one."

"—he'll be the champion mouse yet and I'm going to call him Champ—"

"Champ?"

"Short for Champion," I said.

Nobody had anything to say to this. Dotty had the black mouse which she christened Sambo after Little Black Sambo, and Prune had Tanny, she thought Tanny was a good name for him too, Prune hasn't much imagination.

Dotty wrote off to Rotherham, which is a place in Yorkshire, to the National Mouse Club and asked if we could be members and we trained our mice whenever we got a chance. The Opposition were very, very jealous of our mice and we told them that if they were very good they could join the Thornton Combe Mouse Club — when they had mice, of course. The only trouble was that we didn't have nearly enough time to spend in the Pet Shed — at school, in your so-called free time, you're always being shoved off to play tennis, or do your prep, or go for a walk — it left no time for anything. We *had* to go for a walk on Sunday afternoons, and here Dotty had one of her ideas, which was a bit of luck.

"All this walking," I said, when we were changing our shoes in the dorm, "I mean, walking is all right when there's nothing better to do, but it's a frightful waste of time when we've got those mice to train—"

"Would it be a good idea," said Dotty, "to take our mice with us? We could find a nice field and train them like anything—"

Sometimes, as I've mentioned before, Dotty's ideas are an absolute danger to the community, but this seemed like a good one, for once. "Dotty," I said, giving her a hearty thump on the back, "you're a genius, like your father—"

Prune was looking anxious. "You mean just let them run all over the fields? We'd lose them—"

"Yes, there is that," I said, damped.

But Dotty's massive brain was working overtime. "Couldn't we harness them in some way?" she said slowly. "Or put a collar on them? And have a lead of — say — very, very strong nylon thread? Could we do that, Lisa?"

Lisa, of course, was still the authority on taming

mice, but she wasn't much help on this. "Well, I don't know," she said. "My father trains all his rats in the rat lab—"

"As we haven't *got* a rat lab, or rather a mouse lab, you chump, what about this idea of mine?"

"If the collar and the lead were *very* light and the nylon very strong, I should think it would be all right," said Lisa. "But it's risky."

"Nothing venture, nothing win," said Dotty enthusiastically. "What we want is nylon fishing line or something like that, and the only thing is, how are we going to get it?" and she turned and looked at me.

"No, Dotty, NO," I said. "I will NOT go to the dentist again."

"Goodness, you're selfish, Denny," said Dotty. "Never think of us. Won't sacrifice a thing for the Mouse Club. Wouldn't your dentist like to have a look at that filling he did for you last Saturday?"

"NO!"

"Okay, okay, keep your hair on. I'll write to my father, he'll get us some nylon fishing-line."

"But we won't get it for ages," said Prune sadly, "so I suppose that we'd better leave our mice behind this afternoon—"

"No, why should we, if we keep them safe in our pockets? We can go and look out a nice training-ground for them."

So we hurried off to the Pet Shed and collected our mice.

On our Sunday afternoon walks we usually made a bee-line for the village. Not that there was much to see in the village — only Mrs. Yeo's Post Office and General Store, shut naturally; and Ye Olde Copper Kettle, where cream teas were sold in the summer and ice-cream and cold drinks all the year round, which was closed to us, STRICTLY

FORBIDDEN for the Lower School, it was so unfair, the seniors could stuff themselves silly if they liked; and then there was rather a nice little antique shop, that was all, not much to see as I said, but better than the fields, really, there was always a chance that some excitement might blow up. But this Sunday we went off in the opposite direction. If we had to find a quiet field for mouse training, no use going into a densely populated area like Thornton village.

We went down through the school grounds, across the river and along by the path on the other side to the Old Camp, where the valley narrowed. There were plenty of little grassy places there with nice short smooth turf in between the bumps and mounds which I suppose were the remains of the Old Camp. It was said to be a Roman camp or something, but I don't think that anyone really knew, it had never been dug up.

I don't suppose that you've often carried a mouse around in your pocket, but I can tell you that it's jolly well not as easy as you'd think. Mouse must have been a lot better trained than any of us realised because he didn't seem to give Lisa any trouble at all, but Champ was the most restless little wriggler that you can imagine. He was just mad to get out of my pocket and every time I took my hand off him for a minute I'd look down and see his quivering pink nose sticking out. What's more, he was as cheeky as could be, he had very quickly forgotten that at one time he was the mouse that no-one wanted, you could see that he was of a very adventurous spirit and was just dying to get out of my pocket and see the world.

Tanny was just as adventurous; in fact once he got out of Prune's pocket and climbed down her leg (very ticklish, she said afterwards) and she only managed to grab him again by practically falling on him. That should have been a lesson to him, it's no joke having Prune falling on top of you. Sambo didn't try to get out of Dotty's pocket, all he did was to jump up and down like a jack-in-the-box, Dotty said that it was making her seasick.

"I don't think that these mice like pockets much," I said doubtfully, but Dotty said that of course they did, better than being in a boring old cage anyway, and that when we got to the Old Camp we'd give them a little run.

It was nice at the Old Camp, warm for an April day, sunny and sheltered by the steep hill. We found a lovely little grassy place, as smooth as a lawn, and we rather gingerly let our mice have a little exercise.

They were all perfectly well behaved except that madcap Sambo, he was off and up over a little hillock before you could say knife, we thought Dotty had lost him for ever. But of course we had armed ourselves with a spare bit of chocolate left over from yesterday. Dotty put down such a huge lump that even Sambo couldn't resist it, he came over a hummock, his nose twitching with delight, and ate himself practically into a stupor. He was no trouble, Dotty said, on the way home.

But it was too nerve-wracking trying to train the mice in those wide open spaces, so we took them home. We made Dotty write to her father that evening, and we could hardly wait for the nylon fishing line to arrive.

Meantime, while we waited impatiently, we went on with the Mouse Training School as best we could. One of Dotty's ideas was to train the mice to carry messages — "We could use that secret writing, remember?" Dotty said — but I wasn't very hopeful of that one. What I did want was to train Champ to come when I called, how would her father do that, I asked Lisa.

Lisa wasn't too sure. "If you give him a bit of chocolate every time you call *Champ*, that might do it," she said. "I mean, you can train a dog by giving him a reward each time he comes when you call, but I honestly don't know if you could train a mouse to answer to his name, I don't think that they're all that bright in the head."

I said indignantly that Champ was exceedingly bright. "And Mouse is *clever*, he always does the right thing, even Tanny comes roaring back for chocolate, not that he gets much, Prune has usually finished it by then. But I must say that Sambo seems a bit dim, even chocolate doesn't always tempt him—"

"Nonsense," said Dotty, "it's just that he's a mouse of independent character. He comes eventually."

But he didn't. Sambo was always getting lost, it was frightening. We were absolutely scared in case he would go wandering off and turn up in the Head's study, or in Nosy Parker's, or even worse, that Mandy would see him and confiscate him. So we didn't take the mice into Big School with us much. Once I did put Champ in my desk, but he made a terrible din, scratching around among my books. Luckily it was geography that lesson with Miss Greyson who never knows what's going on anyway, she's so carried away with all that jazz about trade winds.

The nylon line came from Dotty's father very quickly and it really was super, light and fine and yet very strong. We plaited little collars for the mice attached to long, long threads, and then we let them run. Then we would put down chocolate crumbs (we were getting through a stack of chocolate bars) and call them, and give a little jerk to the line and back they would all come — except Sambo, who would be off exploring some interesting smells of his own.

The only trouble was that the nylon threads were apt to get tangled up and we would be jerking away at the wrong mouse, or the mice would go running round the legs of tables and chairs and would climb over things until the lines were in a hopeless muddle and sometimes the only way to disentangle our poor mice was to cut the nylon; fortunately Dotty's father had sent plenty.

So we were dying for Sunday afternoon when we could go out to the Old Camp and our mice could run for miles without table-legs and other bits of furniture getting in the way. We never set off for our Sunday afternoon walk so eagerly in our lives.

So imagine our disgust when we got to the Old Camp and found crowds of people — well, about four — milling around. A tent had been pitched, there were piles of spades and picks and things like that lying there in heaps and one young man was actually crawling about on his hands and knees, he seemed to be measuring something.

We stopped and glared at them furiously. One of them, quite old, even older than my father, glared back, but nobody said anything, or if they did we were too far away to hear. We sat down on convenient humps and mounds and grumbled. The young man was now putting sticks into the ground here and there, the others were still standing about and talking and occasionally pointing — at first we thought that they were pointing at us but apparently not.

"What *can* they be doing?" said Dotty. "Is it some new sort of game?"

"I don't care what it is," I said, "I wish they'd go away. There's the whole of Somerset, the whole of the West Country, the whole of *England* for them to play in and they have to come here—"

Prune said nothing. She passed round acid drops to console us. They were some consolation I must admit, I love acid drops.

"They look as if they'd settled for life," said Lisa. "I mean, look at the tent and everything. Couldn't we just go on training our mice and pretend they're not there?"

It wasn't easy to pretend that four grown-up men, a tent and a great pile of spades weren't there, but we did our best, and actually we got so interested in our School of Mouse Training that we did actually forget that the trespassers were there. That was really why the trouble started. For Sambo ran away as usual with miles of nylon thread trailing out behind him. Anxiously winding up the thread as she went, Dotty gave chase; but what with her specs being halfway down her nose by this time and not really serving any useful purpose, and all those mounds and lumps on the ground, not to mention an occasional gorse bush, she was stumbling and bumbling along, and the next thing was that she stumbled and bumbled into that blessed tent and knocked it flat.

With rather trembly fingers we gathered up our mice and put them in our pockets and went leaping across the mounds and hummocks to Dotty's rescue. There the poor girl was, half smothered in piles of white canvas, Sambo vanished, her specs vanished and a horrid little man with a very cross red face standing spluttering at her in a very insulting way. "Pestilential child! Look what you've done! ... Clumsy oaf! Why couldn't you look where you were going!... Tent ruined! Valuable equipment damaged! ... Careless, clumsy girl! Why couldn't you look where you were going..." and so on and so on.

We tried to ignore all this shouting and went to

help Dotty. Fortunately her specs were still half round her neck, so we rescued these first. There was still no sign of Sambo, so we left him for the time being and tried to dig Dotty out from those folds and folds of tent. The young man who had been pushing sticks into the ground now came over, but to our fury he was laughing so much that he was absolutely no help at all. We glared at him, then began to unwind Dotty from her canvas cocoon. We got her to her feet eventually, and by this time the young man had recovered sufficiently to be able to put the tent up again. But no sooner was it up than Dotty dived through the opening again — and the whole thing collapsed on top of her once more. The tent heaved and shook and stood up and collapsed like a pantomime elephant; it was really very funny if any of us had been in the mood for laughing. But we weren't too happy and the trespassers were furious, they had by this time all gathered round. The oldest and crossest trespasser was still red in the face and muttering, and the two other rather ancient chaps were muttering a bit too. One of them kept saying, "What is this child trying to *do*?"

I felt like saying, "She's trying to catch a mouse, you silly old man," but I didn't, I devoted all my energies, as the saying is, to getting Dotty out of that tent; and as soon as the young man, with our help, had got the tent half-up again I poked my head into the opening. "Any luck?"

Dotty was beaming. "'Mm. In my pocket."

"Come out, then, and say you're sorry for goodness' sake, for they're all as mad as wet hens out here except for one chap and he's completely off his nut, he just keeps roaring with laughter."

So Dotty crept out of the tent very sheepishly and spoke to the very cross red-faced little man — his face wasn't so red now, he seemed to have simmered down a bit — and said that she was sorry, she had been looking for something and she simply hadn't noticed the tent.

The cross little man looked at her strangely. No wonder, the tent was about ten feet square.

"Is your eyesight perhaps — ah — a little deficient?" he said more sympathetically.

"Heavens yes," said Dotty, who, now that the apology was over, was her usual cheerful self again, "I'm as blind as a bat."

"May I — ah — enquire," said the little man, and that was the way he spoke, like a book, an old-fashioned book, "what you were searching for?"

"A mouse," said Dotty.

"A mouse," said the little man. "Well, well." And he looked at Dotty more strangely than ever.

"Yes, my mouse," said Dotty, and then she went on, "and I'm *really* very sorry that I sat on your tent, but we thought that this place was more or less private. It's our special Mouse Training School—"

Red-face turned, with an even more bewildered expressio,n to the young man and asked him something, it was perfectly clear that he was asking if he thought that Dotty was quite right in the head, but the young man was laughing again. I looked at them both very oddly; I was not at all sure that *they* were right in the head.

However we all cheered up — especially Prune — when the young man said, "We were just going to have some tea — if the thermos has survived — would you like some?"

We said you bet, and then these strange people laid out the most super tea — sandwiches and biscuits and rich damp fruit cake which these three old men fell on like schoolboys — or like schoolgirls, for that matter, we polished off quite a few slices ourselves. And the first old man, Red-face, who seemed to have taken quite a fancy to Dotty after all, asked about our School of Mouse Training and Dotty told him, and we showed him what our mice could do, except Sambo, you couldn't rely on him for a minute and we didn't want to knock down the tent again.

We were still of course dying to know what these trespassers were doing, apart from having a picnic, and as nobody told us, eventually Dotty asked right out.

We thought at first that they weren't going to tell us, and then Red-face said, "We are hoping to prove that King Arthur lived here—"

Chapter Five: Mice and Maths

"King Arthur? King Arthur lived here? You mean King Arthur and the Knights of the Round Table?"

"Yes—"

"But he was a chap in a story!" said Dotty.

"Yes, indeed. But we of the Arthurian Archaeological Society are convinced that he really lived — and we are going to prove it—" His face was no longer red, it was glowing with enthusiasm, his eyes were shining, he was delighted to find someone as ignorant as Dotty — not to mention Lisa, Prune and me — to whom he could explain all his ideas. It seemed to us that his ideas were about as dotty as Dotty's but it was quite interesting all the same. The bits we understood were as follows: that after the Roman legions left Britain, there lived a real person called Arthur, who was a leader of the British and who fought against the Saxons and who was buried at Glastonbury. "That's right," said Prune unexpectedly, "they've been digging away at Glastonbury Tor, looking for Arthur's grave." Fancy

Prune knowing a thing like that!

Red-face, who turned out to be really Professor Perry, an absolutely top archaeologist (and if you want to know what that means it means a person who digs up old ruins and places like that and finds old broken pots and things and puts them together and tells you when they were used and so on, even hundreds and thousands of years ago) had this idea that one of the real Arthur's castles or camps or whatever you like to call it was right here in Thornton Combe where we were sitting!

"Last year," he said, "they started a dig at Cadbury — that's about thirty miles from here, it is thought that Cadbury may really be the place that was called Camelot in the stories. Well, we think that there are also connections with Arthur in Thornton Combe—"

"Oh, well, there are," I said, "there's Arthur's Lane, do you know about it? On wild and stormy nights you're supposed to be able to hear King Arthur and his hounds riding up the lane on his way to the chase—"

Professor Perry knew all about Arthur's Lane and lots of other stories and nowadays, he said, archaeologists listened to those old stories, to local tradition and legends; if there was a local story that Arthur had lived there, then it was quite possibly true, or anyway it was worth investigating, and that was what they were doing —.

We realized then that it was time to get back to school, so we said so, and Dotty, who had been listening to all this with her mouth open, said "May we come again?"

Professor Perry went all red-faced and testy again. "We don't want the site over-run by a horde of schoolgirls," he said, not very politely in my opinion.

"Oh, heavens, not the whole school, just us," said

Dotty. "Won't you need some help?"

Professor Perry said that he certainly would but that some helpers would be joining him in a few days, when he and his son James and Professor Dickinson and Dr. Murray — and he flapped a hand at the young man who had laughed at us and the two old men — had made some preliminary investigations.

"But Professor Perry," I said, "the school does walk out this way occasionally, not much I admit, they prefer the village, but sometimes. I don't see how you can keep them away—"

"Oh, I can't," said Professor Perry, "one cannot stop curious sight-seers. But I do not want them trampling all over the site, destroying evidence."

"We want sight-seers all right," said James. "At Cadbury last year sightseers contributed half the money that was needed for the dig, they had a collecting-box—"

I couldn't imagine the school giving a penny, everybody always needed every bit of money she had, nor really could I picture them being much interested in a dig, but if they once got the idea that there was buried treasure around —. "Professor Perry," I said, "what sort of things would you be looking for? Treasure?"

"No, no!" Professor Perry barked. Really, he had a very uncertain temper. "Not treasure as you understand it at all."

"Well, what then?" asked Dotty.

"At Cadbury, for instance, they found wine-jars from the Mediterranean."

"From the *Mediterranean*?" said Dotty. "I thought you were looking for King Arthur?"

Professor Perry looked at her scornfully. "We can hardly hope for absolute proof of Arthur, his sword Excalibur for instance. But these wine-jars from the

Mediterranean proved that there were people living in Cadbury about 500 A.D. who were civilised enough — and rich enough — to have wine imported from the Mediterranean." He turned and barked at me, "Don't you think that is more interesting than foolish nonsense about buried treasure?"

Well, actually I didn't. I couldn't imagine anything more interesting than gold and diamonds and rubies and pearls, but I didn't dare say so.

We helped tidy up the picnic stuff and thanked Professor Perry and James and the ancient men, and Dotty more or less said that we'd see them next Sunday without getting her head bitten off, we made sure that our mice were safely tucked away in our djibbah pockets (they had had a few crumbs from the picnic to keep them happy) and we said goodbye and trotted off towards the river.

"Well," said Prune, "smashing tea."

"I'm sure that I've heard of Professor Perry," said Lisa. "As a matter of fact I've read about the dig at Cadbury in the colour bit of one of the Sunday papers—"

"You were lucky," I said. "You would have some idea what they were talking about."

Dotty was stumbling over the hillocks and hummocks without saying anything. She seemed to be in a bit of a daze. But when we got down to the river she turned and looked back at the Old Camp. "Wasn't it *thrilling*," she said, "meeting Professor Perry and all those archaeologists?"

"Well, I don't know if I'd have exactly called it *thrilling*," I said. "Quite interesting in a way—"

Dotty went on without even having heard me. "Ab-so-lutely thrilling," she said. "And I've got an idea—"

"Oh no, not another idea—"

"— we'll help at this dig and we'll find some

wonderful thing. King Arthur's crown, say, for instance—"

Of course we all shrieked with laughter at this, at least Lisa and I did, but Prune was worried. "What d'you mean, help? D'you mean *dig*?"

"Natch," said Dotty. "How can we find any wonderful things if we don't dig?"

"Oh, I don't think I'd like *digging*," said Prune.

"I couldn't agree more," said Lisa.

"I can think of better ways of spending a weekend, I must admit," I said.

Dotty said that we were a hopeless lot, with no interest in scientific discovery.

"You can say that again," I said, and the subject was dropped for the time being.

The following week, things went on much the same as usual, except that on Friday there was an awful row with Miss Parker who was jolly rude about us. According to her, the Lower Fourth was lazy, stupid, inattentive, unco-operative, idle and couldn't do arithmetic. We sat there shaking like jellies while she told us all this. Even that wouldn't have been so bad, although we were jolly thankful when the bell rang, but her parting shot was that we would be having a test on Monday. "And any girl who gets less than 50% will be gated for two weeks and will spend her free time doing arithmetic with me," she said and swept out, her gown flying.

Prune and I looked at each other in horror.

"Well, that's the end of me," I said hopelessly. "The best mark I've ever had in my *life* was 53% and that was when Dotty was doing my prep!"

"Fifty-three!" Prune shrieked. "I couldn't get 53% even if Nosy herself did my prep!"

"Oh, go on with you," said Dotty. "You'll be all right. If you like—"

"All very well for you," I said. "You can do

problems quicker than Nosy can—"

"I was just going to say that if you like, we could do a bit of swotting together—"

"Oh, Dotty, *no*! Not at the week-end!" I wailed.

"I think that we'll have to," said Lisa in her quiet way. Lisa usually got about 60%, sometimes rising as high as 70 or 75, but sometimes falling as low as 40, so she was as worried as the rest of us. "If Dotty can be bothered—"

"Oh, I can be *both*ered," said Dotty. "I *like* arithmetic."

That just shows you how dotty Dotty can be at times, still, it was lucky for us; it might have been French that she was good at and a lot of help that would have been.

"Well, thanks, Dot," I said. "But not on Sunday because we're going out to the dig, and not on Saturday afternoon because—"

"It'll have to be Saturday afternoon," said Dotty. "We can beg off games—"

Dotty doesn't care one way or another about games, half the time she can't see the ball anyway, but I had never begged off games in my life and I didn't know what Anne Fielding the tennis captain would say, but it couldn't be as bad as what Nosy would say on Monday, so we begged off games.

Anne thought at first that we had all gone quietly round the bend, but she quite understood when we explained about Nosy. So there we were on Saturday afternoon slaving away at those ghastly problems, it was grim. But at least by the time Dotty had finished with us, we knew what they were *about*, which was a big step in the right direction.

And then, if you can believe me, we wakened on Sunday morning to a steady downpour of rain. We had wasted a decent Saturday afternoon on those blessed problems and now we couldn't go out to the dig!

"I thought you didn't want to go out to the dig," said Dotty.

"We want to go to the dig," I said. "We just don't want to *dig*."

"Well, there will be no digging today," said Dotty. "More like swimming. Dear old Professor Perry will be up to his bald head in mud."

"It may clear by this afternoon," said Prune, "and still be too wet to dig, which would be best of all."

It didn't clear up. We splashed off to church, of course, but that was enough of the great outdoors to last us for a week. We sat moping in the Common Room.

"We could do some more problems," said Dotty. "Think what fab marks you would get."

"Not worth it," I said. "If I get 51% I've worked too hard."

"Then couldn't we give the mice a bit of indoor training?" said Dotty. "If we're going to use them for carrying messages in the form-room, we ought to give them a bit of practice in the form-room—"

Of course we're not supposed to be in our form-rooms out of school hours, but as Dotty pointed out, we could scarcely train our mice in the Common Room, they would be trampled to death.

So we got out macs and dashed out in the downpour to the Pet Shed and collected our mice, and did another dash to Big School and nobody — or so we thought — saw us.

Honestly, these mice were clever. Mouse, of course, was pretty smart already, we knew that, and would go straight to Lisa whenever she put down a crumb of chocolate, but Champ and Tanny were learning fast, and once Champ came to me when I called him, *without* any chocolate! But Sambo, he simply hadn't a clue, he was all over the place, sniffing at an interesting smell here and snuffling at a stale crumb (under Prune's desk) there. He was careering about on top of the blackboard at one point.

Well, all this was going on splendidly when suddenly Lisa said, "Sh! I can hear a noise! There's someone in the passage!"

Panic stations, then, all right. I darted to the door and opened it a crack. *Fortunately*, Lower Four form-room is right at the end of a long corridor, you can see for miles, and there, at the other end but stumping along in our direction, was Mandy!

I shut the door smartly. "It's Mandy!" I said. "Quick, quick, the mice!"

We scooped up the mice, even Sambo, who happened to be around for once.

Dotty opened the lid of Miss Parker's desk. "Quick! In here!" she said.

We popped the mice into Nosy's desk and fell into our own desks.

"Arithmetic books out!" said Dotty. That girl should be a general.

So there we all were, sitting like angels at our desks when the door was flung open and in came Mandy.

"I *thought* there was someone in Big School," she said. "What are you doing here?"

"Arithmetic problems," said Dotty, looking up at her innocently.

"We have a test on Monday," I said.

Mandy glanced over Lisa's shoulder at her exercise-book, goodness she's suspicious, that girl. "But you know quite well that you're not allowed in your form-room out of school hours!" she said. "Did you ask permission?"

"Mandy, how could we?" Dotty said. "I mean, to ask Miss Parker please may we go and do some problems, she would have thought we were sucking up—"

"She'd have thought we had a raging fever and sent us to the San," I said.

"You should be working in the Junior Common Room," said Mandy.

"Can you imagine how much work we'd get done there?" said Dotty.

"Well, you can just go there now and make the best of it," said Mandy. "I shan't give you a disorder mark this time because for once you seem to have been *trying* to behave, even if you were breaking a rule—"

"Oh, thank you, Mandy! Oh Mandy, thank you!" we said in a very hypocritical way and we gathered up our books and scampered out, breathing huge sighs of relief.

In bed that night, just before lights out, I suddenly sat up as if I had been shot. "Dotty!" I whispered. "We forgot the mice!"

Chapter Six: Alarums and Excursions

Consternation and dismay! We stared at each other in despair.

"Oh well," said Dotty, fishing for her specs and putting them on, "there's nothing else for it, we must go and get them."

I felt quite faint. Get up, creep downstairs, go outside — where it was probably still pouring streams — dash over to Big School, get in somehow for it might even be locked, rescue the mice, take them to the Pet Shed — no, we couldn't do that for it would certainly be locked — bring them up here, then, and have them scampering all over the dorm all night because we had no place to put them? No wonder I felt faint. "I think they're better where they are," I said.

"Denny, *no*, how can you be so cruel? In Nosy's desk —!"

"Well, they don't know it's Nosy's desk. *They* haven't anything against Nosy—"

"No, of course not, you ass, but how cold and uncomfortable for them in a desk! No lovely warm nest to sleep in! Nothing to *eat*!"

"Okay," I said resignedly, "I'm convinced. What do we do?"

"Are you kids going to talk all night?" Carol's voice interrupted. "Lights out now. 'Night—"

"'Night, Carol," we chorused, waited until she had shut the door, then started whispering again.

Lisa whispered to Dotty, "What's the matter?"

"We forgot the mice—"

Lisa was very, very upset. She moaned and groaned away as if we had committed a crime which of course in a way we *had*; as my mother always says, people have no right to keep animals unless they look after them properly. But Dotty cheered Lisa up as best she could and said that she and I would go down to Big School, no use all of us going.

The Opposition wanted to know what all the whispering was about. "We've left something terribly important downstairs," we told them, "and we have to go and get it — Dotty and me, anyway. You just go to sleep like good girls and if Carol comes back and asks where we are, say you don't know."

"It'll be the truth," said Flora.

We had to wait for hours, until everybody was safely in bed, and I kept dropping off to sleep. But Dotty soon fixed that, she wakened me up about eleven.

"Help," I said, "how did you manage to stay awake?"

"I read a book under my blankets," she said. (Strictly Forbidden.)

"What's the time?"

"Ten to eleven."

"Help, Dot, isn't that a bit early? Nosy will still be Nosy Parkering around — "

"Well, I can't help that, the battery of my torch is flaking out."

We put on out-door shoes, remembered to take my torch and crept out of the dorm; there was no trouble getting *out* of Nightingale, the only trouble would be getting *in* to Big School.

"Well, I don't see why it should be locked," said Dotty, as we crept carefully along the colonnade leading to Big School. "Nothing worth stealing in a school."

"Oh go on with you," I said. "There are all those pictures of ancient old Thorntons for one thing, they must be worth pots of money. And the school cups and trophies—"

Luckily the rain had almost stopped. There was a moon somewhere about, every now and then it almost came out, as the wild clouds rushed across the sky; but it wasn't cold, which was always something; and all went well until we got to the door of Big School — which of course was locked.

"Oh *bother*," said Dotty.

"Well, I told you it would be," I said, which was an annoying sort of thing to say, really.

Dotty, however, is a very good-tempered girl, and all she said was, "We'll just have to climb in a window, that's all."

I was absolutely terrified at this suggestion, but Dotty padded off quite happily. Besides being good-tempered, I think she must have a very strong character. "There's sure to be a window open somewhere along the line," she said. "Even the window of our form-room. Nosy is always shouting at us to open the window. What luck if it was open!"

What luck if it was closed, I thought. I wasn't fancying this expedition at all; if we had to start climbing in windows I'd fancy it even less. "I think it's called breaking and entering," I said in a faint voice, "and you can go to prison for it."

Dotty didn't even listen to this quavering remark, she was leading the way across the ancient stable-yard to the far end of Big School where our form-room is.

And would you believe it, the window was open. I was quite taken aback.

Dotty was delighted, naturally, and as the window is very low it was honestly no trouble climbing in. We tip-toed over to Nosy's desk, and there we did find trouble for the desk was locked.

After a moment's horrified silence Dotty exploded. "Oh, really! Isn't Nosy the limit! What does she want to go and lock her desk for?"

She started looking round, but I grabbed her arm. "*No*, Dotty!" I said. "No! You're *not* going to break open the desk, I'm not going to allow you!"

"Well, shall we just let the darling mice suffocate?" asked Dotty.

"Oh, Dotty, don't *say* those things, you'll give me heart failure. How *could* they suffocate, there must be plenty of air getting through the cracks, enough for four mice—"

"Yes, I suppose so," said Dotty, laying down the enormous ebony ruler which she had grabbed, the ruler that Nosy keeps for thumping on the desk when she's particularly cross with us. "The thing is, are the mice still there?"

"Where else would they be?" I asked.

"She might have seen them and turned them loose when she locked her desk," said Dotty.

But I simply couldn't, or wouldn't, believe this. "No, no," I said. "She just threw something in without looking and turned the key. Just let's listen—"

We put our ears up against the desk and listened like anything. Mice can keep terribly quiet when they want to, but to our great relief we could hear a little faint rustling sound. "Oh, thank goodness," I said, "at least they're alive. We'd better go back to bed now, because there's nothing else to do, but we must come down here first thing in the morning and try to get them out."

We climbed out of the window again, drew it to behind us and hurried back across the stable-yard to Nightingale. But as we crept out from the shadow of the old stables I put my hand on Dotty's arm and put my mouth close to her ear. "There's someone skulking about in the colonnade," I whispered. "What do you think he's doing here? Dotty, d'you think it's a *burglar?*"

Dotty gave a little snort of laughter, then clapped her hand over her mouth. "Of *course* it's not a burglar," she said. "It's probably someone looking for me—"

I thought that Dotty had gone quietly off her nut. "Why should anyone be looking for you in the middle of the night?" I whispered.

"Not actually looking for me this minute," said Dotty, "but looking round the place, getting the hang of the lay-out and so on. They call it casing the joint in America—"

My head began to spin, but if Dotty was going off her nut, I thought, I'd better humour her. "Why, actually, would he want to do that?"

"Because of this kidnapping of course," said Dotty. "The enemy would want to know the lie of the land."

"Dotty, *please* explain — *what* kidnapping? Who's

going to be kidnapped?"

"Me," said Dotty calmly. "I keep telling you it's possible."

I gave a great gusty sigh of relief. Of course I'd heard Dotty on this before, it was one of her silliest ideas. "Honestly, Dot, you are the limit, frightening the life out of me like that! I thought you were serious—"

Dotty suddenly stuck her great elbow into my ribs, only it missed my ribs and got me square in the tummy. "Ouch!" I said.

"'Sh!" whispered Dotty, dragging me back into the shadows, "He's moving—"

The dark figure seemed to have made up its mind. It came out of Nightingale colonnade and turned out to be two dark figures. We shrank back under the colonnade, the dark figures crossed the lawn and disappeared towards the school gates.

"Help!" Dotty whispered. "It's a gang."

I honestly didn't think that two made a gang, but I was getting beyond caring. Bed was really the only thing that interested me now. But the alarums and excursions (I got that expression out of Shakespeare) were by no means over for the night, because when we got to Nightingale front door, which we had carefully left on the latch, we found it locked.

I was really furious. "They're absolutely potty in this school," I muttered. "Everything locked! You'd think it was a prison! *Now* what are we going to do? And *don't* say climb in a window because I'm not climbing in any more windows."

"Would you rather ring the bell and have Nosy come?" Dotty whispered.

No-one in their senses would rather have that, so we trudged round the house. There wasn't a window open in the place.

Even then, believe it or not, Dotty didn't run out of ideas." Nothing for it," she whispered, "we must throw some gravel at the dorm window and somebody will waken up and let us in."

"Somebody like Nosy Parker, I suppose?"

"Well, have you a better idea?"

I hadn't, but one thing was certain. I was going to do the throwing. Dotty couldn't hit a haystack at point blank range.

So I collected some stones and gravel and Dotty located the dorm windows and although I say it myself, I did some good shooting. Bang on target. Ping! Ping! Ping! went the stones, and almost immediately the window was cautiously raised and a voice whispered, "What's going on out there? Who's there?"

"It's us!" I whispered. "The door's locked and we can't get in! Come down and let us in!"

"I certainly will!" said the whisper.

"Funny," I muttered, as we crept round to the front door, "I couldn't recognize whose voice it was. She was so quick, I thought it must be Lisa, lying awake waiting for us, but it didn't *sound* like Lisa—"

"You can't tell with a whisper."

"No, I suppose not. But I hope it wasn't one of the Opposition."

"I don't care who it was. I want to go to bed."

"Same here."

We cared a minute later. The bolt was quietly slid back, the door was opened. Miss Flinders stood there. We had been throwing stones at the wrong window.

Chapter Seven: Saved by the Mice

That was the only piece of luck about the whole awful night, that we had been throwing stones at Polly Flinders' window and not, say, for instance, Miss Parker's. It was bad enough as it was. We just stood there and gaped at her.

"Dorothea!" she said. "Denise!"

We went on gaping. She was dressed, I noticed, not in her dressing-gown, so at least we hadn't wakened her, but *hon*estly—! What were we going to say? How were we going to explain?

However, quick-witted Dotty took charge. She really will make a general one day if they have female generals by that time, and if she doesn't have to locate the enemy windows. She didn't even let Miss Flinders speak. "We're most frightfully sorry, Miss Flinders, truly we are, we didn't mean *you* to come down—"

"I can imagine," Miss Flinders murmured.

"— we didn't mean to disturb you, we meant to waken one of the other girls in our dorm, we had forgotten that your room is next to the dorm, we're most frightfully sorry, but we were worried about our pets, we had a horrible feeling that we hadn't bedded them down properly, and we know that we shouldn't have gone out, but we were so worried—"

Miss Flinders got a word in at last. "But wasn't the Pet Shed locked?" she said.

"Yes," said Dotty.

"And are you still worried?"

"More than ever," I said, thinking of that locked desk.

"Yes, well, that's a pity," said Miss Flinders crisply, "but perhaps a sleepless night and a little bit of worry will teach you to be more careful in future. It was only by luck that I was out with friends and happened to be still up—"

I nudged Dotty. Gang, indeed! Casing the joint! Polly Flinders' friends, that was all!

"— I really should give you both a disorder mark," she was saying, "but it would be a little difficult explaining to Miss Parker what you got it for, wouldn't it?"

Not half, I thought.

"All right, then, I'll let you off this time. NEVER do such a thing again and off to bed with you—"

"Yes, Miss Flinders."

"Oh, *thank* you, Miss Flinders."

We scuttled upstairs like a couple of frightened rabbits and crept into our dorm. Unluckily Lisa was awake.

"How did you get on?" she whispered.

"No dice," Dotty whispered back.

"Oh, *help*," said Lisa. "What will happen when she finds them in her desk, will she expel us?"

"No such luck," said Dotty sourly, and we fell wearily into bed.

Of course, first thing in the morning, we shot off to Big School and equally of course that dratted desk was still locked.

"Dotty," I said, "you're always having ideas. Have you any ideas about picking locks?"

"Oh sure," said Dotty. "Just hand me a bent pin, will you?"

"All right, laugh," I said, "*but what are we going to do about our mice?*"

"I don't see what we can do," said Dotty.

I was disappointed in Dotty, but I had no ideas myself, so we trailed back to breakfast at Nightingale.

None of us had a very good appetite that morning: we could see looming ever nearer the moment when Miss Parker would open her desk and four mice would jump out. And she would never believe that we hadn't done it on purpose, never. And if that wasn't enough, there was that ghastly test to follow, and whatever Dotty had put in our heads on Saturday, it had completely gone out of our heads by this time. We pushed scrambled egg mournfully round our plates.

And then a sort of miracle happened. Nosy P. got up and said grace and came over to our table where Mandy Griffiths was on duty. "Please go and put these papers in my desk in the Lower Fourth form-room, Amanda, will you—" and she handed Mandy a bundle of papers and a key. "Just leave the key in the lock—"

I had never heard such beautiful words in my life. I mean, Mandy was bad when it came to mice, but she was a thousand times better than Miss Parker. We hurried out of the dining-hall after her and were just in time to hear a most bloodcurdling shriek from Mandy and to see Sambo come scuttling out of the door and charging off down the corridor. Dotty charged off after him, and Prune, Lisa and I nipped into Upper IV next door. There was a bang as the lid of Nosy Parker's desk went down in a hurry and Mandy flashed past Upper IV doing about a mile a minute.

We hurried in to our own form-room. Lisa was muttering, "That Mandy! She probably simply threw Nosy's papers in and stunned the darling mice—"

"Just be thankful," I said, "that it was Mandy who opened the desk and not Nosy Parker."

We lifted the lid of Nosy's desk with great care. There wasn't a mouse in sight, but as usual Prune had a piece of chocolate on her and almost immediately the mice got wind of it and out they came, their dear little noses quivering. We gently captured them and hurried off to the Pet Shed. We gave them a beautiful breakfast of cheese rind and oatmeal and tucked them safely into their cages. We heaved huge sighs of relief.

We imagined that Dotty was still chasing Sambo all over Big School, but just as the bell for prayers went, she came charging in, breathless, got Sambo into his cage and gave him his breakfast.

"I must say," she panted, as we hurried off to assembly, "that mouse hasn't a clue. He ran into a crowd of second-formers, half of them had hysterics and the other half want to join the Mouse Club."

I was so thankful to have got the mice safely into their cages that I had stopped caring about the maths test. But when Nosy P. came into our form-room, the tails of her gown flying as usual, I started caring again in a hurry. To be gated for two weeks doing sums with Nosy wouldn't suit my plans at all.

Maths was first period, so it would soon be over, that was one good thing. Nosy handed out foolscap paper, just like a real exam, it was awful. Then she went to her desk to get the questions. She seemed to be scrabbling about in her desk for ages and my heart stopped again. Now what was wrong?

Nosy Parker slowly shut the lid of her desk. Instead of a big foolscap sheet of ghastly problems, she was staring at the tattered little piece of paper with jagged edges that she held in her hand. Suddenly she laughed. (Nosy Parker laughed! She couldn't have been feeling well.)

"I don't think that we'll have a test today," she said, "for the test-paper has been eaten by mice!"

We all cheered like anything; and under cover of the noise I whispered to Dotty, "What do you think of that for cleverness? I bet these are the cleverest mice in the whole of England!"

"Poor little mice," whispered Prune, "they must

have been starving to eat a maths paper!"

Well, of course, Nosy Parker didn't laugh for long, I suppose it was a mistake really, and in a minute or two we were all slogging away at ghastly algebra and the test was to be the following Monday. But that was a whole week away, anything might happen in a week if these mice went on being so clever, they might manage to burn the school down by next Monday. And if the worst came to the worst, we could get some more coaching from Dotty —.

Wednesday afternoon was our games day, but there was a tennis match on, Bath High School was playing Thornton Combe, so there was no tennis for the juniors. Of course, we were supposed to stay and watch to see how tennis should be played, but it wasn't an actual rule. Normally we *would* have watched because there was nothing better to do, but Dotty was anxious about how the dig was getting on, so we got rather reluctant permission from Miss Flinders to go for a walk, she was probably wondering if we'd be back before midnight, and off we went.

Dotty had written to her father telling him about the dig at Thornton Combe and asking him if he knew that King Arthur was a real person and how was the secret weapon getting on. He had replied that he had never given the matter much thought, but that he had made enquiries and found an old, old book that might interest her, he would send it on, and the secret weapon was coming along like a bomb.

"I'd like to get all the help I can for Professor Perry, you see," said Dotty when she was telling us this, "for honestly I think he'll have to do better than a lot of broken old pots from the Mediterranean to prove that Arthur and his knights lived there—"

But when we got to the dig, you wouldn't have known the place. A huge bit of the Old Camp had been fenced off, the lovely old smooth turf had been torn up in huge patches, there were piles of dirt and rubble and spades and wheelbarrows everywhere.

I thought it was a mess, but Dotty seemed quite fascinated. Only Professor Perry and his son James were at the dig because most of their helpers had other jobs and could only work at week-ends. So you would have thought he'd be glad to see us, but he wasn't, particularly. He glared at us with his cross face.

"Have you brought those mice?" was the first thing he asked.

We said no, and wasn't there anything we could do?

"Any menial job we'll be glad to do," said Dotty.

"Not *too* menial," Prune muttered, "we don't want to dig."

Professor Perry, who, for all his age, he must have been about fifty, had very sharp ears, said that we wouldn't be allowed to dig, digging was a skilled job. We weren't even allowed to poke about in the rubble for hidden treasure, that was another skilled job it seemed. But James, who at least seemed quite pleased to see us, got us fixed up filling wheelbarrows with rubble that had been sifted and trundling them away, I can't tell you how boring and awful it was.

The grass and turf had been cleared away from some of the humps and hillocks and there were some quite interesting bits of ruin lying about. But that didn't please Professor Perry either, because they were all Roman and what he wanted was evidence that *King Arthur* had lived there, everybody knew that the Romans had been there. At one point Dotty asked Professor Perry if he thought that he was looking in the right place, which I didn't think was a very tactful thing to say, but oddly enough, Professor Perry didn't seem to mind. He gave Dotty a whole lot of arguments about why this was the right place. Lisa, Prune and I nearly went to sleep.

Our hands were blistered and our backs were aching and our interest in archaeology was by this time very, very limited. Only Dotty was still fresh and bright, no wonder, we said, as she hadn't done any work, only talked to Professor Perry all the time. However, things cheered up later when James built a fire and made tea. We had some buns and biscuits with us and for the first time that afternoon I began to enjoy myself. James showed us one or two of the finds they had made, nothing of value, but nice, all the same. There was a coin, a *denarius*, that's a penny really, like in L.S.D., and there was a clay pot that was almost perfect except for a huge chip on one side, things like that, we all liked them much better than rubble and wheelbarrows.

So it turned out to be not a bad afternoon after all, and we went back to school quite cheerfully, promising James and Professor Perry that we would see them again on Sunday.

Little did we know what terrible things were going to happen before we did see them again ...

Chapter Eight: Dotty Vanishes

The terrible things began happening on Friday; and oddly enough the first thing that happened wasn't terrible at all, it was very, very exciting. I was picked to play in a Lower School match against Cavell. Actually, I was picked as reserve, but by a great stroke of luck Angela Daly got flu or something that day and I was to play. It was my first house-match and I was shaking like a leaf as I changed.

Dotty, Lisa and Prune had come up to the dorm with me and were full of helpful hints and encouraging remarks, most of which only made me worse but no doubt they meant well. They were all going to come along and cheer, of course, but before we could go down to the courts a third-former tracked us down with a message that Nosy P. wanted Dotty. We were all rather curious.

"Now, what have you done, Dot?" I said.

"Me?" said Dotty indignantly. "I haven't done a thing—"

Apparently she hadn't, either, for the third-former said, "I don't think there's any trouble, Dotty, it's a visitor—"

"To see me?" asked Dotty. "Who on earth can it be?"

"Well, if you'll just go down to Nosy P.'s study," said Lisa, "I dare say you'll find out."

"Don't be too long," I said, beginning to feel sick again.

"No, I shan't," said Dotty, "for I can't think who it can be—"

But she hadn't come back by the time that I was ready, and she hadn't come back by the time that we went over to the courts, where the matches between Brontë and Siddons had begun. Very soon I was too busy to pay much attention to Dotty's comings-and-goings, but I suppose that I did sort of notice out of the corner of my eye that she hadn't come back. Mean old thing, I thought, she *would* get taken out to tea on the one day that I couldn't join her; and then I stopped thinking about Dotty and concentrated on beating Mary Ferris of Cavell's, which I did, 6-4, 7-5, although it nearly killed me.

But what was really surprising was that when we

had showered and changed and gone over to Big School for the rather special tea that was always provided on match days, Dotty still wasn't to be seen. I asked the others where she was.

"*We* don't know," said Prune. "She hasn't come back since she was called to Miss Parker's study."

"Has she gone out to tea with those people who called to see her?" asked Lisa. "Would she be allowed to?"

"Oh sure," I said, "if she's not playing a match or gated or anything like that. But even so, she'd be back by this time. We have to be back by five if stray visitors should come and take us out to tea, there's just time to go down to Ye Olde Copper Kettle and fill up with cream scones and double malted milk shakes."

"But it's half-past five now!" said Prune, big-eyed.

"There will be such an unholy row if she's late," I said. "Nosy P. will skin her alive."

"Hadn't we better do something?" asked Lisa. She had brought Mouse over to the Common Room for a change of air and was brushing him with a very soft baby's brush that she had bought in the village for half-a-crown, "Isn't there anything we can do?"

"Well, we can go down to the gates and wait for her," I said. "Then when she comes she can just slip in beside us and Nosy will never notice."

"That'll be the day," said Prune, "when Nosy doesn't notice—"

"I wish she'd come," I said.

But six o'clock was roll-call and still Dotty hadn't come back. We didn't know what to do. One of us could answer for her, but there would be a *terrible* row if we were caught — and would it do any good if something had happened to her? If something had happened to her, then the sooner that Miss Parker knew the better: if something *hadn't* happened to her, then she jolly well deserved what was coming to her, for frightening us out of our wits.

Roll-call is in our form-rooms, and this night Nosy Parker took it instead of one of the prefects as it often is, so there was absolutely no hope of answering for Dotty even if we had wanted to, for Nosy would have spotted it instantly.

So when Dotty's name was called there was nothing but a horrid silence.

Miss Parker looked up. "Dorothea Ellis," she said again.

No reply.

She looked at us over the top of her glasses, she looked at Lisa, Prune and me. "Do any of you girls know where Dorothea is?" she asked.

We sat and gazed at her like hypnotised rabbits, and shook our heads vacantly.

"This is very strange," said Miss Parker. "Where can she be?"

I put up my hand. "But Miss Parker," I said, "didn't she go out to tea?"

"Out to *tea*!" exclaimed Miss Parker as if she had never heard of tea in her life before. "Why should she go out to tea?"

"Well," I said, sorry I'd mentioned it, "the people who came to see her, perhaps they took her out to tea—"

"They certainly did not! I didn't give Dorothea permission to go out to tea—"

Rachel Greenfield, who always knows everything that's going on, put up her hand. "But Miss Parker," she said, "I saw her driving off!"

Sensation!

With a face like thunder — *poor* Dotty, I thought, when she does come back — Miss Parker wanted to know all about this.

"What time was this, Rachel?"

"Oh, two-ish, I suppose. Before the matches started—"

"Two!" I said, aghast. "Has she been missing since *two*?"

I think that it was then that the really frightening thing popped into my head. Over and over again Dotty had said it might happen one day ... her father so famous and so *important*... "Miss Parker," I burst out, "d'you think that Dotty, I mean Dorothea, has been KIDNAPPED?"

Miss Parker jumped about two feet in the air. "Really, Denise," she said when she came down again, "what a *ridiculous* suggestion! Why should anyone want to kidnap Dorothea?"

"Well," I said, "because of her father, Miss Parker. He's an absolutely top scientist and he's working on this very, very important secret weapon. Couldn't some sinister Foreign Power have kidnapped Dotty and be holding her to ransom? They could write to her father, or telephone him, perhaps, 'We have your daughter. Tell us about this secret weapon or — or — or else '—" My voice faltered.

Miss Parker was looking quite dazed. "I never heard such nonsense in my life," she said, but she said it very feebly, as if she didn't think it was nonsense at all. Then she suddenly said, "I'm going to talk to Miss Fisher. You girls do your prep and then go and change for supper as usual. And when I am out of the room don't—" She obviously had been going to say don't talk but she took one look at us and decided that she was wasting her breath. "Don't make too much noise," she finished, and hurried out of the room.

The form-room fairly buzzed after she had gone, and if anyone did any prep it could only have been Sally-Anne Smith who is a swot anyway, everyone else was talking sixteen to the dozen. Lisa, Prune and I made Rachel tell us everything she knew all over again. It wasn't much. Dotty had driven off, round the back drive, in this rather ancient mini.

"But that's all I know, Denny!" she said. "I was in the hall when Dotty came out of Nosy's study with this visitor. They went out together and drove off and I went down to the courts."

"What did she look like?"

"Who, Dotty?"

"Of course not Dotty, I know what Dotty looks like. This other person—"

"Well, she was young-ish, I mean about twenty or thirty I suppose and she was wearing a bottle-green suit and—"

"Had she a gun?"

"Good heavens, of course not. At least she may have had one in her bag, she wasn't waving it at Dotty."

"And did Dotty go with her, just like that?"

"Dotty certainly wasn't kicking and screaming if that's what you mean—"

I said, "Well, I must say I'd expected Dotty of all people to put up a bit of a fight, not just tamely be kidnapped like that—"

"But Denny," said Lisa, "she didn't *know* she was being kidnapped. This person just said, well, say, for instance, would you like to come and have some tea and Dotty just said you bet—"

"But Dotty didn't ask permish—"

"Oh, this person probably told her that she had already fixed it all up with Nosy P.—"

"I suppose so," I said. "But it all sounds a jolly lot too easy if you ask me, if people can just walk into a school and kidnap people right and left—"

Well by seven o'clock Miss Parker hadn't come back so we all went off to change for supper. At least, Lisa, Prune and I had to go to the Pet Shed first to take Mouse back and to bed down the other mice.

"We had better feed Sambo," I said, "in case Dotty gets back late," and I felt very depressed and desolate. I had thought that kidnappings and sinister Foreign Powers and all that jazz might be quite exciting, but they weren't, they were horrible. It was simply ghastly and awful not knowing where in the world Dotty could be. "We'll give him an extra bit of supper in case he frets—"

Far from fretting, Sambo wasn't even there. We couldn't make head or tail of *this* new development. We wondered at first if he had just escaped, but decided that that would be beyond him because he hasn't much in the way of brains, poor old Sambo. Besides, his cage was securely fastened.

"Dotty must have taken him with her," said Prune. "What a funny thing to do!"

"It is a funny thing to do, to take a mouse with you when you're being kidnapped," I said.

"She didn't *know* that she was being kidnapped, I keep telling you," Lisa said again. "She thought she was going out to tea—"

"Well, that's even funnier," I said, "taking a mouse out to tea—"

"Oh, I don't know," said Lisa, "I often take Mouse with me."

"Yes, but Mouse is a well-trained mouse and Sambo, let's face it, is a stupid clot," I said. "Honestly I can't think why Dotty would take him out to tea—"

"Well, she has—" said Lisa.

"And if she really has been kidnapped," said Prune, her round face all woebegone, "then Sambo will be company for her—"

That was a little bit of comfort, I suppose, but just the same, we went up to the dorm to change for supper feeling very, very miserable. There was a blank sheet of paper lying on my bed, I couldn't imagine where it had come from, I pushed it into the waste-paper basket and we trooped downstairs in gloomy silence.

It wasn't silent downstairs, the whole house was buzzing with Dotty's disappearance. Rumours were flying like mad. Miss Fisher had telephoned Dotty's father, she had telephoned Sergeant Garrett in the village, she had telephoned Scotland Yard — none of them seemed to think it at all likely that Dotty had been kidnapped, and everybody looked at me as if it was my fault.

Still no news by bed-time — and the sight of Dotty's empty bed made us feel quite sick. There was no larking and chatting, there was no whispering after lights out. We said goodnight to each other in subdued voices. "Good night," I said, "I ask you, we're not likely to close an eye—"

But we did, I suppose, although it didn't feel like it; I kept wakening and wondering what was happening, if there was any news. By about five o'clock the dawn chorus had started and the birds were making a fearful din, and I just gave up trying to sleep. As soon as it was light I'd get a book — and perhaps by rising-bell there would be some news. I was jolly sure in my own mind that even if Dotty *had* been kidnapped, she would soon have some ideas about escaping... old Dotty and her ideas... ideas... IDEAS! Secret writing!

CHAPTER NINE: SECRET WRITING

I fell out of bed so quickly that I stubbed my toe on my locker and didn't even notice it. I felt about in the dark for a torch, I shone it on the waste-paper basket, I took out the blank sheet of paper.

It could be, it just could be a message from Dotty in her famous secret writing; the paper looked as if it might easily have lemon juice smeared all over it; and if it was, then she wrote it before she disappeared! This blank sheet of paper was a CLUE!

At least — it was a clue if I could find a bit of candle and read it. And the only hope I had of finding a bit of candle was in Dotty's locker. It was ages since we had practised secret writing, but still there was just a chance that she had kept the stump of candle. I went and rummaged in her locker — and there was a stump of candle and some matches.

I was very, very excited as I lit the candle and stood it on the floor. I was terrified that I'd set the whole thing alight as Dotty had once done, but with great care I waved the paper gently over the flame — and writing began to appear! The writing said *GONE TO THE OLD CAMP*.

Good gracious, I thought, did the kidnappers take her to the Old Camp? Then my head cleared a bit and I realized that it would be very funny kidnappers who would sit around waiting while Dotty wrote me messages in secret writing. Then — then — had she not been kidnapped at all? Had she gone to the Old Camp of her own free will? And if so, *why hadn't she come back?*

Well, I thought, that was our job, to find out. I wakened Prune and Lisa.

Prune groaned. "It *can't* be time to wake up. I've only just got to sleep for worrying—"

"What is it?" growled Lisa. "Has Dotty been found?"

"'Sh! No, but I know where she is!"

Lisa sat up and Prune padded over to hear what was going on. I showed them the paper with the secret message. "So she went to the Old Camp," I said, "and she hasn't come back, so something must have happened to her, so let's go out there and find out!"

We quickly pulled on slacks and jerseys — it was none too warm at that time of the morning — and we crept out with our torches.

As we were passing Nosy Parker's door, Lisa stopped. "We must tell her," she said.

"Yes, of course," I said and lifted my hand to knock.

"Will she stop us going?"

"I expect so," I said, "she's always stopping someone doing something. Better not tell her."

"Oh, we must," whispered Lisa. "The staff must be frantic, search parties out, the lot. Besides, they can get help to Dotty if she has broken her leg or something. I tell you what, you two go on and I'll wait and tell her. She can't stop you if you're not here. I'll come on afterwards—"

Goodness, I thought, this was noble of Lisa! "Good show," I said, "just let us get downstairs and then knock—"

So Prune and I crept off, and as we reached the bottom of the stairs we heard Lisa knock; and Nosy can't have been asleep either because she opened her door immediately only we didn't wait to hear what they said to each other.

The sky is the east was beginning to lighten as we ran down to the river, across the bridge and along the river-path, and when we got to the Old Camp with stitches in our sides and no breath left, the sun was rising.

But the sun didn't rise on Dotty, the dig was quite deserted. We ran all over the place, we clambered over hummocks and mounds, we stood and called. I could have howled.

"Oh, Prune!" I said. "I was so sure that she'd be here—"

Then Prune, and I wouldn't have thought that she'd have so much sense, said, "Well, Denny, she could easily be lying behind one of those old bits of Roman remains and we'd never see her if we searched all day. But if we climb up the hill—"

I gave old Prune a great thump on the back that nearly sent her flying. "Prune," I said, "you're a genius. Come on—"

So we began to climb up the hill, stopping frequently to look below us and calling, calling all the time. But there was no call in reply, there was no sign of Dotty anywhere.

At last Prune said despondently, "I suppose this is silly, I suppose we ought to go back to school and let the grown-ups take over. Telephone Professor Perry and find out if Dotty did appear at the dig yesterday afternoon—"

"I suppose so," I said equally despondently if not more so, but even as I spoke the words, I suddenly clutched Prune's arm and pointed. "Look!" I said.

"Oh, what? Where? What is it? Is it Dotty?" cried Prune, looking everywhere at once.

"No, it's not Dotty," I said, "but I'm jolly sure it's Sambo!"

With great care we crept closer to the tiny black dot that I'd seen against the smooth green turf, we didn't want that madcap Sambo scampering off in his usual carefree way. He didn't scamper off, however, he just sat there; and we were able to come quite close to him. "Got any chocolate?" I said.

"Well," said Prune reluctantly, "a tiny little bit—"

We put the chocolate down on a convenient stone, but although Sambo's nose quivered, he didn't come near.

"Well there's a thing," said Prune, rather pleased, "gone off chocolate, has he?"

"I shouldn't think that's very likely," I said. "Let's

see if we can get any closer—"

We inched our way forward and still Sambo didn't move. Finally we put the chocolate right in front of him, almost touching his nose, and still he didn't come and get it.

"He's caught in some way," I whispered, "look, you can see he's trying to get to the chocolate—"

Very, very cautiously I put out my hand and gathered him up. Round his neck was the famous fishing-line that Dotty's father had sent us.

"Oh!" said Prune. "Do you think — if we follow the line — do you think that Dotty's at the other end?"

"She'd better be," I said, "because I don't know where else to look—"

We put Sambo in my pocket along with the chocolate and we began to unravel that line like What's-his-name, Theseus, finding his way through the labyrinth in the old Greek tale; and Sambo must have been having a high old time, because the line was twisted round rocks, tangled in gorse-bushes — until at last it simply seemed to disappear into the earth. There was a clump of bushes and stunted hawthorn trees, rather knocked about as if someone had sat on them, and the line simply vanished.

"It's broken!" said Prune. "Oh help, it's broken!"

"I don't think so," I said, "there's no end, it's still taut—"

I very carefully parted the bushes and a large hole appeared. "Dotty!" I shouted. "*Dotty!*"

And Dotty's voice answered eerily, hollowly from somewhere under our feet. "You certainly didn't hurry yourselves!" she said.

Rather gingerly we pulled aside the bushes, we didn't fancy disappearing into the bowels of the earth like Dotty. "Dotty, where are you?" I said.

"Well, I'm down in a sort of cave-thing—"

I whispered, "Where are they?"

"Who?"

"The kidnappers."

"What kidnappers?"

"Haven't you been kidnapped?"

"Are you off your rocker? I came out here to tell Professor Perry what I had discovered and I fell into this hole—"

"Can't you get out?"

"Of course not, you ass, or I'd have been out long ago. Why didn't you come yesterday?"

"We didn't know where you were yesterday, we thought that you had been kidnapped."

"Kidnapped? Why on earth should I be kidnapped? Who would kidnap *me*?"

"Goodness!" I said indignantly. "The sinister Foreign Power, of course. You said yourself that you might be kidnapped one day!"

"Oh, that was just one of my ideas," Dotty said airily. "Didn't you get my note?"

"Of course I got your note, but I threw it in the waste-paper basket. It wasn't until this morning that I guessed it might be your dotty secret writing. Why didn't you write a proper note, then we could have found you sooner?"

"And get a disorder mark for bunking games, if it had Fallen into the Wrong Hands? Besides, *I* didn't know I was going to fall into this dratted hole! I thought the secret writing would be a bit of fun—"

"A bit of fun! Everybody's having a thousand cadenzas! Miss Fisher rang your father, and the police—"

"Help!" said Dotty. "*Not* one of my better ideas —. Did you find Sambo?"

"You bet, that was how we found *you*—"

Prune leant carefully over the hole. "Dotty," she said, "are you hurt?"

"No, not really — lots of bruises. I bet I'm black

and blue—"

"And Dotty," Prune was really worried about this, "are you *hungry*?"

"What do you think? I haven't had a bite since lunch yesterday—"

"How do you know whether it's yesterday or today in that dark hole?" I asked.

"Well, I can see the sky a little bit."

"Dotty," Prune was saying, "I've got the tiniest little bit of chocolate — it's only a tiny little bit because we had to give Sambo some — but how do I get it down to you?"

"You could lower it down on the fishing-line, perhaps?"

But I had a better idea. We tied the chocolate in Prune's handkerchief — a trifle grubby — and then we tied the line firmly round both the hanky and my torch and lowered them down the hole. They seemed to go down a very long way, and then Dotty shouted, "Bang on. Thanks tons —." We leant over and saw a faint glow. Then Dotty said, and she sounded very excited, "Denny! This isn't a cave at all! It's more like a cellar, it's all built up with stone, it's a building — oh, do go and get Professor Perry, oh heavens, d'you think I've discovered King Arthur's castle?"

Prune and I very guiltily realized that we should have gone to fetch help long ago and relieve the minds of Dotty's father, Lisa, Nosy Parker, Miss Fisher, Sergeant Garrett, Scotland Yard, et cetera et cetera. So I left Prune to mark the spot and to keep Dotty's spirits up and I went careering joyfully down the hill. The rescue party, led by Lisa, were just coming along the river-path. Professor Perry was there and James and Sergeant Garrett, not to mention Nosy P. and Miss Fisher. Dotty's father was on his way from Bristol.

"We've found her, we've found her!" I yelled and they cheered like anything. I must say I never thought to see Nosy Parker waving and cheering as wildly as anyone; she must have a heart after all, hidden away under all those maths.

James went down into the cavity with a rope and up came Dotty, then the rope went down again and up came James. He was very, very excited, he could hardly speak for excitement but he didn't need to, because Dotty was explaining to Professor Perry what it was like down there in the hole. "I'm sure it's King Arthur's place," she was saying, "it's mentioned in this ancient old book that my father sent me, he marked the place where it says, '*At Thornestoun on the hill standith this place, sumtyme a famous toun or castelle. The people ther telle that they have hard say that Arture much resortid to Thornestoun.*' I told you that I didn't think you were looking in the right place, didn't I?"

I turned away, because I honestly didn't want to see Professor Perry strangling Dotty — not after all the trouble we'd had rescuing her. I whispered to Lisa, "Did they bring out any food on the off-chance?"

"Oh, yes," said Lisa, "a huge thermos and sandwiches—"

"Well," I said, "I could do with some and so could Prune and as for Dotty, she has only had half a bar of chocolate since lunch-time yesterday."

Chapter Ten: Dotty has an Idea

So we had this mad sort of picnic out there on the hillside. And the explanation of Dotty's disappearance was really quite simple. "Well, it was this book that my father sent me," she said. "I had asked him if he knew anything about King Arthur and he found this book. It's very, very old, I'll show you the bit, the spelling's all wrong and it's difficult to read, so of course I came out here to have a look, you were all playing tennis—"

"But Dotty!" I said. "Rachel Greenfield saw you drive away in a car with a strange woman!"

"Good gracious how could she? Rachel is always seeing things—"

"So you didn't drive away in a mini with a strange woman?"

"Heavens, yes, so I did! It was the girl in the bookshop where Daddy bought this book, she brought it to me because she passed the school on her way home, it was sweet of her, it was her half-day. I got into her car to show her the quick way round the village. And then I read the book, Daddy had marked the place, and as you were all playing tennis I roared away out here to show it to Professor Perry, I was sure he wasn't digging in the right place —"

"Dotty Ellis, the famous archaeologist."

"Oh, archaeology is so boring, all that digging and then you're in the wrong place. So I went further up the hill to have a look for the right place, and the next thing I knew, I had crashed through those bushes and fallen down that hole and couldn't climb up. Dear old Sambo could climb, though. I had brought him with me to give him a little training, but I don't think I'll ever train him, he hasn't got the brains."

"How can you talk like that about darling Sambo?" I said indignantly. "If it hadn't been for Sambo we'd never have found you—"

"Well, Denny, I shall present him to you, because when I was down that hole I had another idea—"

XVIII: SANDS ACROSS THE SEA: JANE SHAW'S FRANCE

ALISON J. LINDSAY

Jane Shaw first visited Brittany around 1930, as an undergraduate student of French: she last wrote of it in *Susan's Kind Heart*, published in 1965. The very vivid image of it she retained means that her readers can easily identify the St Clos of *Susan's Kind Heart* (1965) with the St Brioc featured in her first book *Breton Holiday* (1939) and *The Moochers Abroad* (1951), and with Kerdic in *Twopence Coloured* (1954). In March 2001 I made my own journey to Binic in the company of Rosemary Auchmuty, another admirer of Jane Shaw. I had already realised that Jane Shaw only wrote about places she knew well, and our Binic visit was a trip from which I expected much. *Breton Holiday* was the first Jane Shaw title I read, and regular re-readings had left me feeling I knew the town already. Fortunately, we were not disappointed: we felt instantly at home there; and interspersed our many walks with regular cries of "That must be..."

The characters in these books travel direct from Britain, by-passing Paris: the Storms and the Moochers take the ferry across the Channel to St Malo; while the Carters and Carmichaels go by aeroplane. Once in France, and usually at the mercy of public transport, they find the journey to Binic takes a long time. Nonetheless, they find plenty to see: most typical of Brittany are the stone representations of crucifixions, called Calvaries, which are found throughout the region. Nowadays, the narrow roads remain, but a new motorway links Binic with St Brieuc.

Binic

Jean Evans brought her family to Binic in 1950, a year before *The Moochers Abroad* was published; which, however, has far less of the sense of immediacy communicated by *Twopence Coloured*, obviously based on this holiday. *Twopence Coloured* also contains the fullest description of Binic itself, and most of the names mentioned in it can be traced on a modern town plan. Binic is now a popular holiday spot with the French themselves, but in the nineteenth century it was one of the ports from which tall-masted ships left for the cod-fishing off Iceland. The hard lives of these men are immortalised in Pierre Loti's *Pêcheur D'Islande* (1886), a deeply depressing book in which all the main characters either die or go mad. The harbour now holds mainly pleasure craft, but the importance of fishing to the economy is indicated in the town's coat of arms, which features two cod, and a Fête de la Morue (Festival of Cod) is held in Binic each May.

Binic boasts two large sandy beaches, on either side of the old harbour. South is the Plage de la Banche, and to the north, reached through a cleft in the rocks called Le Goulet, is the Plage de L'Avant-Port. Set behind this beach are green-roofed bathing huts. The harbour is almost encircled by two long quays: the Quai de Pordic to the south of the harbour; and the Jetée de Penthièvre to the north, with a lighthouse at its end. A *piscine* or swimming pool is constructed along the south side of the Quai de Pordic and is designed to fill with water at high tide. Across the other side of the inner harbour, facing the Quai de Pordic, is the row of buildings which Fiona Auchenvole thought looked "quite like a Scottish village". This is the Quai Jean Bart, where the weekly Thursday market is held. Halfway along it is the *Mairie* or *Hotel de Ville* with its sheaf of notices and French flag hung outside.

The shops on the Quai Jean Bart have back entrances on to the narrow Rue Joffre, and although the frontages have been modernised, the backs are much as they were when the Evans knew them. Over the rear doorway of one named *Passage du Port*, faded paint declares it to be a *Bazar*, one of the shops mentioned in *Twopence Coloured*. Leading north-east off the Quai Jean Bail is the Rue des Falaises (Rue de la Falaise in *Twopence Coloured* — *falaise* means cliff), where the painter and waiter Armand Brossollet lived. The Brossollets occupied "a rather big, gracious eighteenth-century house, looking over the houses below to the harbour", which has recently been opened as the Musée Vasserot Cueff.

Eating plays a major part in the French books, and Binic is described as being well provided with cake shops and cafes. There is only one *pâtisserie* there now, but this sells the most lavish confections, prepared by a Serge Nabucet and of an almost Parisian quality. In *The Moochers Abroad* there were two cake shops, the *Bon Accueil* and the *Pâtisserie Desmoulins* (which served superior cakes). Monsieur Nabucet's *pâtisserie* sits at the west end of the Rue Joffre, on the corner of the Rue des Moulins, so perhaps this is the site of the *Pâtisserie Desmoulins*. *Pierrot Gourmand*, Sara's favourite sweet, and the large rocher pralines beloved by the Carters, can still be bought today, and *citron pressé*, a favourite drink of many characters, is served in some *cafés* as well as the local mineral water, Plancoët.

Near the *Mairie*, a pedestrian suspension bridge crosses the Ic. Just over the bridge is a patch of land where mud from the river is dredged to be sold as fertiliser. Beside this is the Square de la Libération with its painted bollard marking the Allies' route through here in 1944. Names on the war memorial include some from Jane Shaw's French books: Martin, DuClos and Berthelot (Madame Bertholet in *Anything Can Happen*).

THE PETIT TRAIN

The little train which ran between Binic and St Brieuc plays a significant role in *Twopence Coloured*, although it does not feature in any modern guide, and Jane Shaw's books may be one of the few places where it is still remembered. It formed part of a much larger system of narrow-gauge railcars operated by the *Compagnie des Chemins de Fer des Côtes du Nord*, known to locals as the *michelin*. In Binic, the michelin station was beside the road overlooking the Plage de la Banche. A large car park was created there following the closure of the line in 1956.

An immense expanse of beach is visible here at low tide, proving one frequent assertion of the books: the tendency of the sea to disappear over the horizon at the most inconvenient moment. Low tide also reveals 'the islands', the Roches de St Quay, where the Storms and the Moochers hunted for shrimps after a depressingly early start.

In their forays abroad, the Storms, the Moochers and the Carmichaels all stay at a *château* outside the village, while the Carters stay at the Hôtel de la Plage. The Evans family too stayed in the Hôtel de la Plage, where Sara and Caroline provided afternoon tea for the Duvals. The hotel building still stands, at the southern end of the Plage de la Banche, but it has been converted to holiday apartments called *Vacanciel Armor*.

THE CHÂTEAUX

Disentangling the various châteaux in the books and on the ground is a major exercise. Madame's *château* on the cliffs above Binic appears in all four books, although under a multitude of names. In its initial appearance, as Petit Chose in *Breton Holiday*, it lay on the south side of the town. It was in the same location as the Villa Rosette in *The Moochers Abroad* and the St Clos' *château* in *Susan's Kind Heart*. The first two books described it as being tall and white-painted, with green shutters, but in the latter it had "grey stone walls and pepper-pot towers". Confusingly, there are three *châteaux* in *Twopence Coloured*: on the south cliffs were Mrs Carter's Madame's *château*, painted white and green like Petit Chose, and the *petit château* of the pigeon fancier with its pepper-pot turrets. The Manoir de la Falaise, where Louise was imprisoned, is described as lying to the north, above the Plage de l'Avant-Port.

This last is the easiest to identify — it stands above the cliff top path beyond the Plage de l'Avant-Port and Les Fauvettes camping ground, surrounded by pine trees, and clearly visible from the path. The house was built in 1900 by Jean Vasserot, a painter, some of whose works are on display at the Musée Vasserot Cueff. These include views of the house in the 1900s, when the trellis in front of the house was smothered in plants. Inside was a dining room with dark wooden panelling, and a tall hall, and all the rooms had views out to sea.

The family sold the house in 1941 and bought the one which now contains the museum. The house was originally named Les Doudelins (now Ker Anick), and is reached via the Rue des Doudelins, at the end of the Rue des Falaises. It is a sizeable house of three storeys, not really a *château*, although it does have two round turrets at its northern end. The southern side, which is visible from the cliff path, is painted a faded cream, and it has grey shutters at most of the windows.

Two other *châteaux* lie in the town itself, and though both are worth viewing they are unconvincing candidates, since it is a feature of Jean Shaw's Breton stories that all the settings are close by the sea. In the centre of town, on the Avenue Foch, is a classic turreted château, very smartly refurbished and now a workers' holiday centre. Further up Le Saulnier de Saint Jouan is an older and much ruined building of three storeys, with French windows on the two main floors and surrounded by a tall creeper-clad wall. This wall, and its handsome wrought-iron gates, correspond to the description in *Breton Holiday*, but this building is situated inland, some twenty minutes' walk from the beach.

Madame's *château* is not easy to identify, despite the directions to (or rather from it) being clear enough. The Carters "set off up by the little path that climbed up the cliff behind the hotel", which now bears the name *Sentiers des Douaniers*, or Path of the Customs Officers. In *Susan's Kind Heart*, the little road which ran past the *château* was called by this name, but according to present-day maps the *Sentiers des Douaniers* runs along the coast on either side of Binic. The path is easy to find behind the hotel, and after some ten minutes' walk it reaches an intersection with a wider track. Below, but invisible, is the continuation of the cliff-top path, while uphill is the local council's recycling centre. Immediately beyond this is a turreted building, occupied by a family called Martin (the name of the faithful servants in *Breton Holiday*). This road leads to the hamlet of Courtel, beyond which a grassy track continues over fields before joining another road. Down this road to the left is the little rocky *grève* which features in all the books. The cliff top path, meanwhile, continues round the coast to the *grève*, then along the spur of land which rises between this valley and the sea.

The road which leads up from the *grève* continues to another hamlet, La Ville Évêque, just before which, on the left hand side of the road, is a three-storey building, pink with white shutters, and with a two-storey stone extension. In *Breton Holiday*, Sara cried disappointedly on seeing Petit Chose "but it's no *château*", and this building is certainly no *château* despite being in the appropriate location. It can also be seen, half-hidden in trees, from the coastal path beyond the *grève*. In La Ville Évêque there is a much more convincing *château*, three storeys, stone-built, with symmetrical wings and a stone wall dividing it from the road, but Petit Chose enjoyed a greater isolation and the pink villa seems the likeliest candidate so far for Madame's home.

Around Binic

Although Binic is the centre of activities in the Breton books, various characters made excursions to surrounding places of interest. Some five miles north of Binic is St Quay Portrieux, with its outdoor swimming pool. The Île de Brehat, the island of rose-red rocks just north of Paimpol, was visited in *Twopence Coloured* and *Susan's Kind Heart*.

Excursion boats run to it from St Quay and Binic. Along the coast to the east is Dinard, where the Carmichaels and Carters caught the bus to start their holiday, and where they and the Storms enjoyed looking in the luxurious shops. Inland from Dinard is Dinan, with its pretty medieval buildings, which the Carmichaels visited in the company of Jean-Louis. Even further east, about 80 miles from Binic, is Mont St Michel, described in detail in *Breton Holiday* and *Susan's Kind Heart*. Aside from the incident of la petite Jacqueline, the girls' activities were those of typical tourists, including the consumption of the famous Mont St Michel omelettes.

PARIS

In *Twopence Coloured*, Penny, Jill and Louise made the long journey to Paris, the only Breton holidaymakers to visit the capital. *Anything Can Happen* (1964) and *Looking After Thomas* (1957) take place in Paris, and the latter part of *Crooks Tour* (1962) is also set there. Aunt Sophie and her nieces, like the earlier *Crooks Tour* party, stayed in an hotel in the Rue du Mont Thabor. This street lies parallel to the Rue de Rivoli, north of the Jardin de Tuilleries. The hotel is unnamed, but as Dizzy takes a short cut through the expensive and exclusive *Hôtel Meurice* (which still exists today), they are evidently not staying there. There are now two large hotels at the east end of the street, but these do not correspond with the small hotel Jane Shaw describes. However, on the north side of the street, midway between the Rue Cambon and the Rue de Castiglione, is the *Hôtel du Continent*, with 26 rooms and a tiny hall. This has been an hotel since the start of the 20th century and until its recent refurbishment boasted a small, odd-shaped lift, so this may be the one Jane Shaw had in mind. The "funny little restaurant round the corner" where Alison and Dizzy enjoyed their first French lunch may have been *Chez Flottes* in the Rue Cambon. Also in the Rue Cambon is the Piccadilly (sic) Tea Room, with a daintily-painted but now derelict frontage. Might this have been the "place in the Rue Cambon that has heavenly cakes" where Alison and Dizzy treated "les petites"?

The Rue St Honoré and the Rue de Rivoli, with their fascinating (and expensive) shops, exerted a hypnotic fascination over all female characters, and still specialise in souvenirs for the tourist. At the corner of the Rue de Rivoli and the Place des Pyramides is a gilded statue of Joan of Arc, and the *café* where the characters in *Anything Can Happen* enjoyed citron pressé. Off Rue St Honoré was the un-named (and unidentifiable) restaurant where the *Crooks Tour* party had dinner on their first night, and where Pierre took Alison and Dizzy out to dinner: *Twopence Coloured* names it as *La Bonne Fourchette*, a name which now belongs to a restaurant on the Boulevard St Michel. Confusingly, *The Picture* places *La Bonne Fourchette* in Montmartre.

Printemps, the department store mentioned in *Crooks Tour*, lies on the Boulevard Haussmann at its junction with the Rue de Caumartin. Another store, Les Grand Magasins du Louvre, where Alison and Dizzy bought their wigs, stood opposite the Louvre Museum. It closed in 1973 and was converted into an antiques supermarket called *Louvre des Antiquaires*. Museums visited in the various books include the Louvre, the Musée Carnavalet, and the Musée Grévin on the Boulevard Montmartre, home to a dazzling arrangement of waxwork tableaux.

Around Paris

All Jane Shaw's characters visit Montmartre, and eat at the restaurant whose real name is La Mère Catherine in the Place du Tertre. In *Looking After Thomas*, Tish was given a painting showing the shop *Au Singe qui Lit* where it was bought. A gift shop of this name still occupies a site in the square next to the restaurant. Aunt Sophie's flat is described as lying near the Parc Monceau, off one of the streets radiating from the Place de l'Étoile. The flat itself is impossible to identify, but the Monceau is a delightful park in a pretty neighbourhood. The family's hotel in *Looking After Thomas* is situated in the Rue Vernet, a narrow street running parallel to the Champs Élysées. There are two hotels on the Rue Vernet today, both four star: the *Hôtel Vernet*, at no. 25, and the *Élysées Star* at no. 19.

In *Looking After Thomas* the children found it hard to forsake the fascinating light-up map which indicated routes — there is still a working example at the Concorde *Métro* station. Cité is the *Métro* stop for Nôtre Dame and the Bird Market where Thomas acquired his pets. Behind Île de la Cité lies the quieter Île St Louis, its narrow streets lined with tall grey apartments, in one of which Pierre lived.

Madame Bertholet's flat in *Anything Can Happen* lies in the district of St Germain des Prés, named after the white sandstone church on the corner of the Rue Bonaparte. Opposite it is *Les Deux Magots*, one of the intellectual havens of Parisian society, where Alison and Dizzy plotted the rescue of Madame Bertholet. The name means The Two Images, for the two statues of Chinese philosophers which can be seen in the centre of the room. Just round the corner, although the direction is unspecified, is Madame Bertholet's flat. If this is identical with Miss Mason's flat in *Looking After Thomas*, it should be somewhere off the Rue Jacob, where the big double doors do indeed have neat little wicket gates cut in them.

In hot pursuit of Madame Bertholet, the girls learned that she has gone to the Hôtel des Fleurs at Saint Martin-en-Laye. Aunt Sophie helpfully observed that she had watched fireworks from the terrace there on Bastille Day: this is the clue to its real identity as St Germain-en-Laye, the final stop on the eastbound express *Métro*. Its two-mile *Grande Terrasse*, which offers superb views across Paris, was laid out by Le Nôtre before he began work on Versailles. The Hôtel des Fleurs, placed some two miles outside St Germain, is from its external description a variant of Les Doudelins at Binic: the current local guide does not include any hotel or restaurant with this name.

If you visit Paris in order to see all of the places Jane Shaw described, you will take in many of the traditional tourist venues — but you will also find some unexpected pleasures: in the comparative silence of the Rue du Mont Thabor, despite its proximity to the bustling Rue de Rivoli; in the quiet charm of the Parc Monceau; or in the stunning vista of Paris from the *Grande Terrasse* at St Germain-en-Laye. Binic, by contrast, is almost entirely unknown to British visitors (and to many French) but its charm was manifest even on a rainy out-of-season March day. The pleasure of mapping a literary landscape on to a real one will be known already to many of the readers of this book, but I found a particular delight in doing so in Binic, because of my long connection with Jane Shaw's books, and because relatively few changes have occurred since she visited and wrote of it.

XIX: SARA'S ADVENTURE

JANE SHAW

Sara and Caroline were sitting in the waiting-room of the air terminal at Les Invalides in Paris. There were big, comfortable chairs to sit in, with little tables beside them; round the walls were miniature shop windows, little, brightly-lighted, tempting squares, filled with scarves, bags, gay bunches of artificial flowers, scent-bottles and souvenirs of Paris. Sara had had a good prowl round them all before collapsing beside Caroline to wait for the others. She and Caroline had been having a holiday in Paris with Vanessa, who was Caroline's grown-up sister, and Vanessa's husband, John. Vanessa and John had gone to see about the luggage or something. Caroline was sitting doing nothing, which just suited her: Sara was fidgeting up and down; at all the movement and bustle of the waiting-room she darted interested but rather hazy glances because she hadn't put on her glasses. A blurred voice came over the loud-speaker, making an announcement in French. Sara jumped to her feet. "This is us!" she cried. "Where's John? Where's Vanessa? We'll miss the plane!"

"Sit down!" said Caroline in a bored voice. "That's the plane for Rome being announced." The loud-speaker voice, repeating the announcement in English, confirmed this.

"Oh, so it is," said Sara, sitting down and blushing a little. "Funny, I thought she said *Londres*, not Rome". She slumped down in her chair and sighed. "Oh dear, oh dear!" she said. "I wish we *were* going to Rome. It is *so* sad to be going home. And nothing accomplished, as it were — "

"I don't know what you mean," said Caroline. "We've had ten days in Paris and seen the Sacré Coeur floodlit and the Eiffel Tower and the Louvre, and been to Versailles and gone up the Seine in a boat, and been to the Bird Market and the Flea Market, and seen the marionettes in the Tuileries Gardens, and we managed to cross the Champs Élysées without being killed and climbed to the top of Notre Dame, and if you don't call *that* an accomplishment — "

"I call it a rotten swindle," said Sara. "Whole ten days in Paris and nothing to show for it."

Caroline turned her head slowly and gazed at her red-headed cousin. She said in her lazy voice, "I'm sure I don't know what more you want — all these things I've just mentioned *and* the most heavenly food — "

"Oh gosh, yes!" said Sara, "the food!"

"Well, then," said Caroline, "what more do you want?"

"Adventure!" said Sara, with what she thought was a rather interesting and faraway look in her eyes.

"For goodness' sake take that vacant look off your face," said Caroline. "You look half-witted. I mean, it's bad enough to *be* half-witted without looking it. Especially when you're with me. Adventure indeed! Isn't ten days in Paris an adventure?"

"Oh, yes, of a sort," Sara admitted. "But not exactly the sort I want."

"Really, Sara!" said Caroline. "One of these days you'll grow up."

Sara couldn't think of a suitable reply to this. She changed the subject. "Where d'you think Vanessa and John have got to?" she said. "They could have dealt with ten tons of luggage by this time — "

"Well, you know John," said Caroline. "He always manages to make things a little more complicated than they really are."

Sara glanced round at the glowing, if dim, squares of temptation round the walls. "You don't think Vanessa is buying anything else, do you?" she said. "Because if she is I'd like to be in on it."

"If she is I'd like to stop it," said Caroline, who sometimes thought that she was the only member of the family, grown-up or otherwise, with a grain of common sense. "She has spent all her money and John said that he was down to his last thousand francs. I suppose," she sighed, "that I'd better go and see what she's doing." She rose and slouched slowly off in the direction of the little shops.

The little old woman in black who was sitting at the next table and who had been listening to the girls' conversation with a half smile, turned now to Sara and said, in English but with a charming French accent, "Ah, *mademoiselle*, I see that you have the brave heart!"

"Oh, have I?" said Sara, pleased.

"*Mais oui, mais oui*! The heart for adventure!" said the little woman in black. "It is such a splendid thing to have!" Sara sat up straighter, preening herself a little. Half-witted, indeed! It was a good thing that somebody could recognise her for what she was! The little woman in black smiled again, wistfully. "I cannot offer you adventure," she said. "*Hélas*, I fear that those thrilling days are over. But you could do me a great kindness, if you would — "

"Anything, anything, *madame*?" cried Sara, her lance practically rattling as she prepared to go to the defence of this sweet and helpless, but obviously intelligent, lady.

"Ah," said the little woman in black, "*comme vous

êtes gentille! Alors, mademoiselle, would you have the goodness to carry this little parcel of butter to my daughter in London?"

"Oh gosh, *butter!*" said Sara.

"But, *mademoiselle,* " said the little woman in black, misunderstanding Sara's dismay, "I would not ask you to smuggle the butter through your English customs! *Jamais, jamais*! You will declare the butter and pay what duty monsieur the customs officer demands, the skinflint! I give you the money."

"Oh, that's all right, *madame*," said Sara, a little uncomfortably. "I shouldn't expect it will be much, if anything."

"But I insist," said the woman in black. "Ah, I cannot tell you what joy this will give to my daughter! She so misses her *petit déjeuner* of *croissants* and butter! Sometimes there in London she can get the *croissants*, and she can get her so little bit of butter, but a-a-a-ah, it is not like the French butter! A friend, she has promised to take the butter, but she has not — how you say — turned over?"

"Turned up?" Sara suggested, after thought.

"*Oui, oui, oui, c'est ca*, tur-r-r-ned oop! And me, I cannot afford to buy a kilo of butter and have it wasted — "

"Oh no, of *course* not, *madame!*" cried Sara, her tender heart wrung. "Of course I'll take the butter. But where shall I find your daughter and how shall I know her?"

"She is meeting the aeroplane at the airport," said the little woman in black. "She expect my friend and she will be wearing a red rose to distinguish herself—"and thanking Sara a thousand times for her kindness, the woman in black put a parcel into her hands and hurried off.

At that moment the others came back. John was

The woman put a parcel into Sara's hands.

fuming, Vanessa was looking guilty and Caroline was grinning. "You were right, Sara," she said. "She *was* buying something."

"Would you *believe* it?" said John. "My last thousand francs spent on a bunch of artificial daisies! When I'm busy with the luggage she says lend me some money, just a franc or two, so like a fool I hand her my last thousand-franc note and off she goes and buys a bunch of daisies!"

"Oh but aren't they sweet?" said Vanessa. "And they'll look perfectly wonderful on that old black dress of mine. In fact, John, I've really *saved* you the price of a new dress — "

"And meantime," John growled, "We've got about seven francs between us and starvation."

"But shall we need any more money?" said Sara soothingly. She had a fellow-feeling towards Vanessa because she was a reckless spender herself when she got the chance. "We'll get dinner on the plane and you said your old car would be waiting for us at the airport."

John opened his mouth to speak, but his reply was drowned by the loud-speaker requesting the passengers for Flight 506 B.E.A. to London to take their seats in the bus.

In the bus, Sara was crowded in beside John. She didn't stop to put her parcels on the rack because she was anxious for a last glimpse of the Eiffel

Tower in the distance and the Arc de Triomphe as they swept past it at speed and went up the Avenue de Wagram. Paris *was* nice — and she had had a *little* adventure, talking to that sweet old lady…

John interrupted her thoughts. "Sara, what's this tatty-looking bag," he said peremptorily, "that keeps bumping me?"

Sometimes Sara found John a thoroughly unsatisfactory person. "It's a bag of *croissants* that I'm taking home to mother," she said with dignity. "Mother adores *croissants*."

"And what's this parcel, oozing grease? Don't tell me, I can guess, it's butter, and any minute now it will be on my trousers. No really, Sara, it's too much."

"Put them up on the rack then," said Sara anxious to keep the peace.

Muttering crossly, "*Croissants*! *Butter*!" John put the rather sordid parcels on the rack. "And if that butter comes down on my hat, Sara, I'll kill you."

Sara smiled and said nothing. Butter! It wasn't really butter that she was carrying. It was secret information through the enemy lines — the safety of the whole army, the whole country, depended on her getting through. Butter!

She might not have smiled if she had known exactly what she was carrying.

At the airport a surprise announcement awaited them. For reasons unspecified, Flight B.E.A. 506 had been delayed.

Sara's eyes gleamed. This was better! This was more like the thing! Their aircraft would burst into flames in mid-air and she would have a wonderful time rescuing everybody! Or maybe there was a fog in the Channel and they would be lost in the fog and she would find the way to London for the pilot! Oh yes, this was certainly better!

Two hours later, when they were still sitting at Le Bourget, she wasn't so sure.

"John," she said, "really I'll *die* if I don't get something to eat! It's nearly nine o'clock and we haven't had a bite since that cake we had in the pâtisserie in the Rue St. Honoré and that was at four o'clock."

"For the three hundredth time, Sara," said John, "we have no money. Our last thousand francs went on that, that bunch of daisies." Vanessa pretended not to hear.

"Let's trade in the daisies," said Caroline, looking sourly at them.

"Nobody with any sense would give you a *croissant* for them," said John.

"Hey!" said Caroline, "croissants! Sara's got *croissants*!"

"Well, I have," said Sara, "but they're for my mother. Mother adores *croissants*."

"Our need is greater than your mother's" said Caroline. "Come on, pet, unload — "

"Well, darling," said Vanessa, "I really like butter with my *croissants* so you needn't give me one — "

A great beam spread over John's face, for the first time in the last hour. "But Sara has butter too!" he said.

"Well, I have," said Sara again, "but it's not mine—"

"What d'you mean, it's not yours?" said John. "I suppose it's for your father?"

Sara hesitated and prevaricated — but in the end she was obliged to tell them the story of the butter and the little French-woman in black. The others felt that the whole transaction was unfortunate and a bit of a nuisance, but as Caroline said, it was an ill wind that blew nobody good and could they all stop talking and get into a corner with the *croissants* and butter, some place where nobody could see them?

But Sara was obstinate — they couldn't eat somebody else's butter, especially that sweet little lady's, because she didn't seem to have too much money. The others thought that if she was as sweet as Sara said she was she wouldn't grudge them a little bit of butter. So Sara gave in at last. "All right then," she said. "As a matter of fact, I've just remembered that she forgot to give me the money for the customs, so perhaps we could have just a little."

Feeling quite cheered again, they fetched the parcels of rolls and butter from among the luggage and found a quiet corner of the waiting-room. They could look with equanimity now at the other delayed passengers drinking and eating to their hearts' content; they even heard the announcement of another hour's delay with comparative calm. John produced a large penknife and they joyfully spread the *croissants* with the good French butter and sighed blissfully as they ate.

"Ow!" said Sara suddenly, "I've broken a tooth or bitten on some foreign body or something! No, it doesn't seem to be a tooth. Oh, well, I've swallowed it now —"

But a second later Caroline also bit on something hard. She took it out of her mouth and wiped it on her handkerchief. "What horrible butter," she said. "It's got stones in it."

"Stones!" said John suspiciously. "Let me see."

Caroline held out her hand. "Stones!" said John again. "I think they're diamonds!"

"Really, John," said Sara, "you do blether sometimes. Funny-looking diamonds! Dull! I know what diamonds look like. All bright and sparkling."

John was poking with his penknife in the butter and finding more little stones. "I'm certain they're diamonds," he said, "commercial diamonds, which aren't so bright as the other kind because they're not cut and polished. There you are, Sara," he went on, nastily, "that's what you get for talking to strangers."

"What do I get?" said Sara indignantly.

"You get roped into a smuggling gang!"

At first Sara simply couldn't take it in. She refused to believe that that sweet old lady had been using her shamelessly to smuggle. But when she was convinced, she was furious. She had been completely hoodwinked, a mean advantage had been taken of her good nature.

"Well, she said, "there's one good thing. Thank goodness we *did* eat the creature's butter! Let's all have another *croissant* with simply *piles* of butter!"

The others agreed to this with acclamation.

"We must hand the butter — and the diamonds — to the customs officers at London," said Vanessa.

"Oughtn't we to go to the police here?" said Caroline, but there was an outcry at that. John said that he couldn't possibly miss the plane because he had to be in London the following day, although at this rate he wouldn't get there anyway. Sara said that she wanted to meet the woman with the red rose as arranged, so that she could have the pleasure of handing her over to the English police. But then John said, "Perhaps we *ought* to go to the French police. Could you describe the woman in black, Sara? Would you know her again?"

"Well," Sara admitted, "I hadn't my glasses on — "

"Darlings," said Vanessa, "the whole thing is, have any of us sufficient command of the French language to explain this extraordinary business to the French police?"

That settled *that* point. They must take the diamonds to England and hand them over to the customs there. But to this Sara refused to agree.

She was out for blood. She was going to catch the woman with the red rose if it was the last thing she did. "If we hand over the parcel to the customs," she said "she'll get away."

"I don't see why — " Caroline began.

"Well, I do," said Sara. "She'll run like a hare if she sees a posse of customs men advancing. I must meet her with the butter — "

"All right then," said John. "There's only one thing to do if we want to catch the other woman — we must try to pass this — this dynamite through the customs as butter."

"John," Vanessa said gently, thinking the excitement had turned his brain, "it's not dynamite, it's diamonds!"

Sara's eyes sparkled. "It's adventure!" she said, and at that moment the loudspeaker announced their flight.

"One thing," said Caroline, hastily gathering up the parcel of butter and the bag of rolls, "this adventure racket passes the time, I'll say that for it!"

They stood in the customs shed at Northolt and Sara's teeth, for one, were quite frankly chattering with terror. Adventure was all very well, heavenly really, but it was rather upsetting. She had been too upset to enjoy the intriguing dinner provided on the plane, very neatly done up in a box, or to enjoy the flight itself, or the sight of London by night as they flew in — a magical fairyland of coloured lights.

"Now remember," John muttered fiercely in her ear, "don't say a word! Leave it all to me. Are you all right?"

Oh yes," said Sara, glancing round nervously. "Tra-la-la," she hummed, jumping up and down a little to show how much at ease she was.

"Do stop jigging like that," said Caroline. "A blind

man three miles away could see that you're in the fidgets about something."

"Me in the fidgets!" said Sara. "I'm as cool as a — as a — well, jolly cool anyway."

"Yeah," said Caroline. "About as cool as an active volcano — "

And then it was their turn. Their bags were heaved up on the long counter. A weary-looking customs official handed them a most terrifying card which threatened all sorts of unpleasantness if they didn't declare every single thing they had bought.

"Surely we don't have to declare *everything*," said Vanessa, "only cigarettes and scent and things like that?"

"Everything you bought," said the customs officer harshly.

"Oh goodness," said Sara, losing her head and disobeying John's instructions. "I didn't buy a thing, scarcely, only a wee picture and some scent for Mother and a hankie for Daddy and, and some butter and — "

"Butter, eh?" Suddenly, along the whole counter, stillness seemed to descend. The tired customs men stopped rummaging in cases or chalking indifferent marks on luggage and looked up. "Butter, eh?" said the customs officer again. "You come along inside and show me your butter."

John began to babble foolishly, "Officer, I can explain everything — "

"Explain inside," said the official. "Come along." He grasped Sara firmly and led her away, amid the stares of their fellow-passengers. Caroline followed, burning with shame; John was still trying to get a hearing; Vanessa had no thoughts but for her loved ones, being carted off to gaol wholesale.

The customs official pushed open a door and pushed Sara inside. A great big man, the biggest man that Sara had ever seen, rose as they entered. With the deepest satisfaction, the customs official said, "We've got her, sir!"

Sara nearly fainted.

In spite of her love of adventure, Sara never really liked to think afterwards of the next ten minutes. The great big man was Inspector Roberts of Scotland Yard, called in by the Customs and Excise Department. It turned out that commercial diamonds were being smuggled from Holland to England via Paris in a big way; and the Customs had had a tip that they were being brought through in the innocent disguise of butter. Inspector Roberts took some convincing that Sara was as innocent as the butter.

Yes, you seem innocent enough," he said eventually, "but why did you try to pass the stuff? You knew very well that there were diamonds in the butter."

"If you would only let me *speak*," said Sara, who had been talking steadily for ten minutes. "We wanted to catch the woman with the red rose."

"Who's she?" said Inspector Roberts. "Another of your gang?"

Sara was affronted; and she indignantly, but a little more coherently this time, went over the whole story again.

"Okay," said Inspector Roberts, "I'll take a chance — go and catch her."

So the now rather soggy-looking parcel of butter — minus the diamonds — was done up again, a porter was summoned to bring up the luggage, the four, now about as limp as the parcel of butter, went through the customs shed to where the public were allowed to wait for the plane passengers. A woman in a neat black suit with a red rose in her lapel was standing there. Sara went up to her.

"Oh, hallo, Miss — *Mademoiselle*. Er — er — were you expecting some butter?"

The woman with the red rose smiled broadly. "But yes, yes!" she said. "How worried I have been for you! The plane so late, and everything! Is this my butter? Thank you very much — "

Sara handed the butter to the woman with the red rose. Inspector Roberts loomed up from nowhere and firmly took her by the arm.

And so Sara was a kind of heroine after all. Inspector Roberts, who had hopes that he would be able to round up the whole smuggling organisation from his capture of the woman with the red rose and Sara's description of the little woman in black, was in high good humour and congratulated them all; and it was long past midnight when the weary four eventually tottered off to John's ancient and battered car.

Suddenly Sara gave a yell and clutched her stomach.

"Sara!" said Vanessa in a panic, "what is it *now*?"

Sara said, wide-eyed, "I've just remembered! I *swallowed* one of those diamonds!"

Inspector Roberts loomed up from nowhere and took her firmly by the arm.

XX: THE PICTURE

JANE SHAW

That day I was meeting Carol at the Georges V Métro. It was a glorious spring day, the sun was shining, and almost warm, and there was a film of green on the chestnut trees in the Champs-Élysées. Carol and I were both having six months in Paris, living with French families: my family were perfectly sweet and kind and took me everywhere with them; Carol's family, the Bossuets, were rather rich and important and inclined to give her all the washing-up to do, but kind too; M. Bossuet was an art-dealer, he had a very grand gallery in the Faubourg St Honoré near the British Embassy where, Carol said, he sold Old Masters and Impressionist pictures for fabulous sums.

Carol and I met as often as we could. Sometimes we went up to Montmartre to our favourite little restaurant, sometimes we bought *paté* and rolls and had a picnic in the Bois de Boulogne, sometimes we went to a film, sometimes we wandered down the Champs-Élysées to the Place de la Concorde and the Rue de Rivoli looking in the shops; sometimes, when we felt that we *must* improve our minds a little or when the letters from home hoped rather plaintively that we were *making the most of our opportunities* during this six months in Paris, we would go to the Louvre or some boring museum or other and improve our minds.

That morning when Carol said "Where to?" I said "Oh, let's go up to Montmartre, to Madame Legrand's" (that was our favourite restaurant).

Carol, who is apt to pay rather too much attention to her conscience, said, "What about our minds?"

"Oh, fiddle," I said. "Besides, we were at the Cluny Museum last week, and if we have time we'll have a quick glance at the Sacré Coeur when we're up there. Montmartre," I said firmly, "is madly cultural."

So we took the Métro so far and then toiled up the steps (I wanted to take the funicular but Carol said that it was a waste of money) to the Sacré Coeur where it stood shining in the sun like some gorgeous eastern palace instead of the quite modern church that it really is. We circled round to the Place du Tertre, which was looking very picturesque that morning, full of artists painting busily and people sitting outside cafés in the sun, round to the little street where our restaurant is. This little cobbled street goes winding down towards Paris, but at the top is *La Bonne Fourchette*, two steps up off the street, behind a little railing.

Madame Legrand allowed the young artists to lean their pictures against this railing and if any of the passing tourists took a fancy to one and wanted to buy it, she would negotiate the sale. This happened oftener than you might think by looking at them for some of the pictures were pretty terrible, although not those of Jean-Jaques Durand, who practically lived at Madame Legrand's. He was a great friend of ours and we liked his pictures very much.

The restaurant was sweet: it had blue and white checked curtains and pieces of polished copper round the walls, and window-boxes filled with pink and white double daisies. It was run by Madame Legrand and her daughter Angélique, who was about twenty and very, very pretty. Monsieur Legrand was dead, and sometimes I think it was a very hard struggle for the two women, because Madame Legrand cooked such wonderful food and charged so little for it that we didn't see how it could possibly pay. Besides, she was always giving free meals to all those artists who hung around. One day, when we thought that Angélique looked rather worried, we mentioned this and she agreed with us. "We shall certainly be ruined," she said. "Every day the rent goes up and the price of meat and butter and wine goes up but our takings go down. The best of everything goes into Maman's cooking and the best of everything goes into the empty stomachs of those artists, but nothing goes into the till. I tell Maman that we will be ruined but she doesn't listen — my father was just the same, he was the friend of all the penniless artists in Montmartre — ." All the same, Angélique might talk in this severe way but we had seen her heaping the plates of those same artists – especially Jean-Jacques – when everyone knew that there wasn't the faintest chance that they would be able to pay for their dinner.

Anyway, this sunny morning when we climbed up to Montmartre and arrived at La Bonne Fourchette rather out of breath it was soon clear that a crisis of some sort was going on.

The first thing that we noticed – not that that was very unusual – was that there was a new picture leaning against the railing, a picture of a narrow street in Montmartre with the Sacré Coeur looming up at the end as usual. The next thing we noticed – and this was *very* unusual – was that Angélique had been crying. (I may say in passing that she looked just as pretty, if not prettier, when she was crying as when she wasn't, which is a great gift for a girl to have. Carol and I, for instance, look perfectly ghastly when we have been crying, red and swollen and blotchy.) Jean-Jaques was sitting gloomily in the window. He made room for us at his table and told us what it was all about.

What with Monsieur Legrand's illness before he died, and the good things that Madame put in her cooking and the free meals for the young artists there was an awful lot of money going out and not so much coming in and the bills were piling up. "So," Jean-Jacques finished, "Madame Legrand and Angélique, they decided to sell The Picture."

"That picture?" said Carol, waving her hand towards the railing. "What's so special about that picture?"

"Well," Jean-Jacques lifted one shoulder. "To you, to me, nothing, but to Madame and Angélique a great deal. The great friend of Angélique's father painted that picture. 'He painted it for me,' said Angélique's father. 'Never sell it!' he said. 'Unless, of course, you are starving — .' "

"Oh, horrors!" Carol shrieked. "They're not starving!"

"No, no," Jean-Jacques said reassuringly, "but there are the bills, always the bills, and an American tourist wants to buy it. He is coming back at dinner-time for Madame's decision. He has offered her sixty thousand francs for The Picture— ."

We nearly fainted — until we remembered that francs didn't cost as much as pounds. In fact, sixty thousand francs was only worth about sixty pounds at this time. Still, as Carol said, sixty pounds was a lot of money.

After lunch and after Jean-Jacques had gone gloomily off to his horrid little studio in somebody's garret, wishing that *he* could sell a picture and help the Legrands, we went and had a look at The Picture.

With all our trotting round picture galleries and museums and so on we knew quite a bit about art

by this time, I can tell you. We stared at this picture and Carol said, "You know what? This picture reminds me of something. What does it remind you of?"

"Well," I said, "it reminds me of all those pictures of Montmartre by Utrillo." And Utrillo, in case you didn't know – we didn't, until very recently – is a very famous painter indeed.

"Oh, gosh!" said Carol, her eyes sparkling. "Me too! You don't think – ," she lowered her voice and glanced over her shoulder at the restaurant, but Angélique was still busy rushing round serving luncheons, " – that it possibly *could* be — ?"

"A Utrillo, you mean?" I said, trying to sound calm but really quite dizzy with excitement.

"Well, it would account for old Monsieur Legrand telling his wife not to sell it," Carol said, "wouldn't it? And if it is," she went on, "that American tourist is cheating the Legrands like anything. I suppose a Utrillo would be worth sixty thousand *pounds* far less sixty thousand francs — ."

I was absolutely carried away by this dazzling vision of wealth for the Legrands, but I tried to keep calm. "If only we could be *sure* — ," I said.

"Well," said Carol in a considering voice, "there is Monsieur Bossuet, he would know— ."

"Gosh, Carol, what a brainwave!" I said. "Get him up here, you mean?"

"Heavens, no!" said Carol, shocked, "he's *much* too important. No, we should have to take The Picture to him — ."

I glanced at The Picture again: it was a fair size, in a frame too, but still, it was a good cause — . "All right," I said, "let's do it!"

"No use buoying up the Legrands' hopes in case we're making a mistake, " said Carol. "We'll just sneak it away — ."

We left a note stuck on the railings because we didn't want the Legrands getting into a panic and thinking that The Picture had been stolen; and while I kept an eye on the restaurant, Carol gently lifted down The Picture. "Jill," she said, "there's an awfully nice little still-life of Jean-Jacques here – let's take that too. Monsieur Bossuet might give us a couple of guineas for it — ."

"Well, hardly," I said, "when he goes in for Old Masters and Moderns worth thousands of pounds, but we might as well take it if it's not too heavy and I suppose that Monsieur Bossuet might tell us what he thinks of it. If it's no good Jean-Jacques had better know that and start being a plumber or something instead — ."

So we lifted Jean-Jacques' little picture too and shot off round the corner without anyone from *La Bonne Fourchette* noticing us.

You might not know if you haven't done it, but it's extraordinarily difficult carrying a large framed oil through the streets of Paris and especially in the Métro, which is crowded at all times, with people standing ten deep (at least in the second-class it is; the first class may be half-empty and very comfortable, we haven't tried it) but that afternoon seemed worse than usual. Nor do French people hesitate to tell you when you have bumped into them with the hard and knobbly corner of a large picture-frame. I had wanted to take a taxi but Carol wouldn't let me. She's very careful of our money – and sometimes downright mean. So by the time that we had reached the Faubourg St Honoré we were nearly dead with embarrassment, heat and exhaustion and The Picture felt about the size of Notre-Dame. I carefully lowered it to the ground in the doorway of Monsieur Bossuet's gallery and peered in.

"Goodness, this place looks a bit grand," I said doubtfully. There was one very small Old Master leaning against a fold of blue velvet in the window and nothing else at all. Inside there was nothing much either, except an air of quiet opulence, a picture or two on the walls, thick grey carpets and a stair leading up to the gallery above.

"Well, it *is* grand," said Carol. "Monsieur Bossuet is rolling in money and he's a *world-famous* authority on pictures."

This made me even more doubtful. "Then will he want to be bothered with us and our troubles?" I asked.

"He will if The Picture is a Utrillo," Carol said.

This was doubtless true, but I should have felt more hopeful if I'd been a little tidier. I had just caught a faint reflection of myself in the glass and the sight was by no means reassuring – my hat was on the back of my head, and it wasn't my best one, it wasn't even my second best. Carol wasn't much better, her nose was shining and she had no lipstick left on. However, we couldn't stand at the entrance to Monsieur Bossuet's grand little gallery titivating ourselves, so I took a deep breath; and I had just picked up The Picture and Carol had opened the door when things began to happen.

A man, carrying a picture about as big as The Picture, came charging downstairs and because he was glancing over his shoulder and not looking where he was going he charged straight into us. I dropped The Picture, he dropped his picture, there was a scrum and a muddle. He seized his picture and was off through the door like a bullet from a gun.

"Really!" I said crossly (my hat was on the floor by this time). "This may be a very grand place, but the people don't have very grand manners." I bent down to get my hat and then I yelled. "Carol!" I shrieked. "He's taken the wrong picture!"

Carol bent down. "What's this, then?"

"Oh, some dingy old daub. Carol! The Picture!"

"After him!" yelled Carol.

I leant the dingy old daub against the wall and we sprang to the door. Man – and Picture – was hurrying up the Faubourg St Honoré.

"I'll get him!" shouted Carol and ran.

Carol hadn't been right wing in the school hockey eleven for nothing. She was making up on him rapidly when more extraordinary things began to happen in the shop. Down the stairs staggered a little fat man. He was most elegantly dressed but blood was streaming from a cut above his eye and he was yelling the most amazing nonsense, which sounded like *Help! Thieves! Murder! Help!* – all in French, of course. He stopped when he saw me. "Where is he? Where has he gone?" he gasped.

I pointed vaguely towards the Faubourg in the general direction that the man had taken. The little man tried to push past me to the door, but he was obviously half-fainting for he staggered again and clung on to the door. "But you are wounded!" I exclaimed.

In a very dazed way the little man put his hand up to his head and looked astounded when he brought his hand away, covered with blood. He pulled out a beautiful silk handkerchief and mopped at the cut.

"Hadn't you better sit down, Monsieur?" I said, glancing anxiously round for a chair.

The elegant little fat man looked round too and the dingy daub leaning against the door caught his eye. I thought he was going to drop in a dead faint right there and then at my feet, and I wasn't best pleased because I felt that I had enough on my plate just at that moment. He picked up the daub in a trembling hand. "But it is here!" he exclaimed. "He did not take my picture!"

"No," I said, glancing balefully at the daub. "He took ours!"

For the first time the little man seemed to realize that I was there. "Your picture?" he said. "What is your picture?"

"A Utrillo," I said proudly. "I think."

"Merciful heaven," said the little man, "we must pursue him — ." He bravely tried to reach the door, but had to hang on to something again to save himself from falling – me, this time. I tottered with him to a very frail and exquisite gilt chair and put him into that, hoping that it would stand the strain, and I was just looking round rather wildly for help or water or brandy or something when Carol staggered back into the shop. What *is* going on? I thought. Everybody looks semi-conscious — . But I was mightily relieved to see that she was clutching The Picture – the weight of which I must admit was enough to make anyone stagger.

When the little fat man saw Carol he nearly fell off his chair. "Carol!" he explained. "What are you doing here, *ma p'tite?*"

"Well, I'm not very sure," said Carol. "Everybody seems to have gone mad. I run after this man and I make up on him at the corner and he's just getting into a taxi and I say, very politely, excuse me

Monsieur, but you have taken my picture by mistake, and he looks down at The Picture and then – " Carol was nearly choking with indignation " – and then what d'you think he did? He picked up The Picture and hit me over the head with it!" She put up her hand to her head. "I have a lump like an egg on my forehead and –" she added, anxiously looking at The Picture, "if you ask me it hasn't done The Picture any good either — ."

Well, we got everything straightened out eventually. We got a doctor for the little man who, of course, was Monsieur Bossuet, and Carol, and when they were both nicely bandaged up Monsieur Bossuet told us that what we had got mixed up in was the most daring, but *the most daring* robbery that he had ever heard of. This wicked man, this burglar, this assassin, calling himself by a very famous English name, the Earl of Dulwich, no less, makes an appointment and comes to see a picture. Monsieur Bossuet's assistant is sent off on an errand, a wild-goose chase, Monsieur Bossuet is struck down and when he comes to himself the "Earl" is gone, the picture is gone and the telephone wires have been cut. "My dear young ladies," he finished, "what luck that you were in the doorway when he came downstairs! You have saved my life, my reputation, my picture!"

I glanced scornfully at the dingy daub. "Why, is it a valuable picture, Monsieur Bossuet?" I asked.

Monsieur Bossuet closed his eyes for a second and shuddered delicately. "Valuable!" he began in his fiery way, and then remembering presumably that we had saved his life, his reputation, his picture, he took a grip on himself. He said in a hushed voice, "It is an El Greco!"

"Worth a – a – lot of money?" Carol asked carelessly.

"Worth...a...lot...of...money!" Monsieur Bossuet said solemnly.

Well, when this was all over Monsieur Bossuet got round to the reason of *our* visit and tremblingly we produced The Picture.

And I'm sure you will scarcely believe this, but The Picture was not by Utrillo at all!

"Ah, pouf! I know this man's work," said Monsieur Bossuet. "He was a pupil of Utrillo for a time and slavishly copied the master — ."

Carol gulped. "And – er – Monsieur – er – how much would this picture be worth?"

"How *much*?" Monsieur Bossuet said contemptuously. "Twenty thousand francs. Nothing. The price of the canvas."

Twenty thousand francs! Twenty pounds! I thought. We'd better rush that dratted Picture back to the American tourist pretty smartly.

Monsieur Bossuet was talking about rewards and bravery and courage and such-like blah but we were too disheartened to listen. We picked up The Picture and turned sadly away.

But Monsieur Bossuet's eagle eye had caught sight of Jean-Jacques little still-life which, to be honest, we had quite forgotten in the general hurly-burly. "Ha!" he said. "But you have something else to show me?"

"Oh, that," said Carol, in a thoroughly dispirited way, "that's just a little thing by a friend of ours in Montmartre — ."

Monsieur Bossuet took Jean-Jacques' picture from the floor and propped it up on a little easel; then he stood a little way back from it and looked at it with his head on one side, then with his head on the other, then with his eyes more or less shut – he'll be looking at it through his legs soon, I thought, like Peter Pan and the wolves. I wish he'd hurry up, I want to get back to that American.

But Monsieur Bossuet was muttering, "Charming...charming...more than charming: form, line, colour, strength, major talent..." Then abruptly, "I will give you fifty thousand francs for this picture. Will he sell, your friend in Montmartre? Are you authorised to sell his picture?"

Fifty thousand francs! Would he sell! Were we authorised to sell! Jean-Jacques had never sold a picture in his life.

We forgot our bitter disappointment over The Picture. We even forgot how heavy it was. We went back to Montmartre on wings.

We descended to earth with a bump when we reached *La Bonne Fourchette*. Madame was in tears. Angélique was in tears. It could even be that Jean-Jacques was in tears. The American had come – and gone.

We felt like murderers. "Can't we take The Picture to his hotel?" Carol faltered.

"He changed his plans," Angélique sobbed, her great dark eyes drowned in tears and more beautiful than ever. "He leaves on this afternoon's plane for New York."

"We were trying to help," I choked. "We thought that The Picture was a Utrillo. We thought we should get an expert opinion on it. We thought that the American wasn't offering you enough."

"Enough!" Jean-Jacques laughed in the midst of all the woe. "Three times too much!"

"Yes," we gulped, "we know that now. We're desperately, desperately sorry — ."

We turned to go. I fumbled blindly in my bag for my hankie, and my fingers touched Jean-Jacques' cheque. "Oh," I sniffed, "Jean-Jacques, this is yours. We sold your picture."

Jean-Jacques looked up sharply. "You sold my

picture? How much?"

I swallowed nervously. "F-f-fifty thousand francs," I stammered and handed him the cheque.

"Fifty thousand francs!" he whispered. "BOSSUET!" he yelled. "Is this true?"

"Yes, it's true," we said. "Are you terribly angry with us too?"

"Bossuet! Fifty thousand francs!" Jean-Jacques seemed to be virtually speechless.

"And he said that you were to show him any other things you've done, Jean-Jacques," Carol said nervously. "Are you pleased?"

"*Pleased!*" Jean-Jacques gave a wild yell, did a little dance across the cobbles and hugged us all in turn. "*Bossuet!* If Bossuet buys my pictures, my fortune is made!" He hugged Angélique again. "Now at last you will marry me, Angélique," he cried. "And I will sell my pictures and help pay the bills!"

This was a little disappointing for us because we had rather hoped to marry Jean-Jacques ourselves. But, as Carol pointed out, when the celebrations were over and Madame's extra special dinner had been cooked and eaten and we were on our way home – in a taxi I'm thankful to say, Carol having given in for once – but, as she pointed out, we couldn't both marry him, so perhaps it was better that Angélique should have him and save any argument. "And anyway," she said, "we helped him. At least it was us who started him on his road to fame!"

"Yes," I agreed with deep satisfaction. "One way and another we seem to have given things a push in the right direction today!"

XXI: ADVENTURES IN THE ALPS — AUSTRIA, SWITZERLAND AND ITALY

BEVERLEY GARMSTON

Jean Evans put to good use memories of holidays in Switzerland and Austria, with five titles set there. They are: *Susan Interferes* (1957), featuring Lake Lucerne and its surroundings; *Fivepenny Mystery* (1958), set in the Austrian Tyrol, near Innsbruck; and *Bernese Holiday* (1940), *Crooks Tour* (1962) and *The Tall Man* (1960) all set around Interlaken and Grindelwald in Switzerland, but featuring different characters. Lake Como is the setting for an unpublished work, *The Man at the Villa Carlotta*, of which she wrote only the first two chapters, and Susan and Midge visit Venice in *Where is Susan?* (1968).

SUSAN INTERFERES (1957)

Many readers will first have encountered Jane Shaw through the colourful Children's Press reprints of *Susan Interferes*, one of the easiest titles to find. It opens with Susan and her cousins, the Carmichaels, hurrying to catch the lake steamer immediately outside Lucerne railway station (wonderful Swiss efficiency!) to their destination, the village of 'Rosendorf'. Swans still swim on the lake by the steamers, whilst tourists arrive in exactly the same way at the station and then catch lake steamers to the various resorts on Lake Lucerne.

Weggis

The small lakeside resort of Weggis on a promontory east of Lucerne seems to be in the right location for Rosendorf. In 1926 the first Weggis Rose Festival was held, which may have given Jean the idea of calling her village "Little Town of Roses" (p27). Even now Weggis is just a small village, with few shops but a number of hotels. As further corroboration, a little train runs from the ferry landing dropping people off at their hotels and also runs to Weggis' Lido — the Carmichaels took it in turn to travel on a little train from the Lido to meet the ferries on the day the Ghastly Gascoignes were due to arrive. They also enjoyed evenings at the café Confiserie Hoffmann, overlooking the lake — in Weggis there is a café by the lake with a dance area where small bands play. Their hotel, the Chalet du Lac, was right by the lakeside, and their rooms were in an old chalet in the grounds. Dr Carmichael mentioned a monument to Mark Twain in the garden: this can be found by the lake near the Buhlegg restaurant. The Hotel Buhlegg was demolished around 1967 and replaced by flats. Mark Twain stayed at the Hotel Buhlegg in 1897 and wrote "this is the most charming place we have ever lived in for repose and restfulness", as Uncle Charles told the girls (p90).

Mount Rigi

During their stay the Carmichaels visited various places around Lucerne; trips which can easily be followed today. On their first day they visited Mount Rigi, travelling to Vitznau by ferry and "the little red train" up the mountain. The family walked down to the village of Kaltbad. Here Midge and Susan took the train again to save walking down the rest of the mountain. In 1968 a cable car link between Kaltbad and Weggis opened, which is far quicker than travelling via the train and ferry route. During the Rigi trip Susan realised she disliked heights — unsurprisingly, as Mount Rigi is 1800m (or 6000 ft).

Lucerne

Lucerne town is excellently described, bringing to life the medieval side of the city with its old squares, streets and bridges. The Carmichaels indulged in cream cakes at a restaurant near one of the bridges (there are two or three restaurants located by the river Reuss) and lunched at "a most delightful little café which overlooks a quiet backwater of the river, near one of the old bridges and the town mill". In the penultimate chapter Bill provided further details: "[once over the] second old funny wooden bridge, which was called the Spreuerbrücke, I think, we come to the Mühlenplatz"; adding that this was where they lunched earlier in their holiday. He led them to the wine market and then the Kornmarkt where Fraulein Amacher's flat was located, with its fresco decoration of a family tree. This building, originally a guildhall, stands in the south-west corner of the Kornmarkt, and is now a restaurant.

On the first day, the family crossed the Reuss by "the footbridge between the old Rathaus (Town Hall) and Fraulein Amacher's medieval palace". This is the footbridge adjacent to the Kappellbrücke (Chapel Bridge), which joins with the Bahnhofstrasse on the other side of the river. From this footbridge Susan saw someone watching from the flat next to Fraulein Amacher's. Susan and the Carmichaels revisited Lucerne the next day to deliver Fraulein Amacher's sought-after parcel of tea. Bill suggested they visit the Lion of Lucerne monument to the Swiss Guard and gave a good synopsis reading from his guidebook! Although they don't actually visit this monument all the relevant information has been neatly included. Further detail is given on Fraulein Amacher's flat's location, as they left via the Kornmarkt and then into the Kapellgasse (Chapel Street) which is described as 'an ancient, very narrow, very busy little street which led into the Kornmarkt and Schwanenplatz'. At the busiest, narrowest part Susan was almost pushed under a car by Herr Gruber. The medieval quarter of Lucerne has since been pedestrianised, and is probably much pleasanter and easier to walk around nowadays. They had a café glacé at a café to recover, then walked to the Haldenstrasse, "that promenade by the side of the lake where the big hotels and grand shops are", which appears to be almost unchanged today, to investigate the parcel of tea. Lucerne at night features in the final chapter. The narrow medieval streets and squares, filled with jostling crowds, took on a nightmarish quality as Susan and the Carmichaels desperately searched for Rudi, Peagreen and Herr Gruber during a major firework display.

As Fraulein Amacher seemed to have disappeared, Susan and her cousins searched for her, embarking on a terrifying trip via Vitznau in a tiny cable car up the mountainside to a place called Wissifluh; Jean details in her journal the trip she undertook to this location.

Mount Pilatus

The Gascoignes and Carmichaels together visited Mount Pilatus, one of the largest mountains in the region. They travelled via ferryboat to Kehrsiten and changed boats — whilst waiting, Gabrielle and Adrian jived to American jazz from a jukebox, much to everyone's surprise and the Carmichaels' embarrassment. A second ferry took them to the village of Alpnachstadt, and from here they travelled up Mount Pilatus in a red funicular (described as "built in steps") which still runs today. On arrival they lunched at a hotel located between the peaks of Mount Pilatus.

Around the Lake

More happy sightseeing with the Gascoignes occurred for the Carmichaels during their steamer trip around Lake Lucerne. This is a particularly good way of seeing all the lakeside villages, as one can disembark and board another ferry later on. They lunched at Brunnen and then went on to Flüelen. They saw the Rütli with the meadow where the idea for a Swiss Republic was first mooted. Peagreen wandered off and missed the ferry, so the rest of the party waited at Treib for him, where they admired an attractive house built in 1639.

The Carmichaels and Susan also visited the Joch Pass, which they agreed was one of their best trips. They went via ferry to Stansstad, then mountain railway to Engelberg, followed by a funicular and a cable car, which held at least 40 people, so Susan had no qualms about this. She even managed a chairlift quite happily.

Crooks Tour (1962); *The Tall Man* (1960); *Bernese Holiday* (1940)

These titles are set in the area around Interlaken, Lakes Thun and Brienz, and Grindelwald. *Crooks Tour* features three Scottish schoolgirls — Ricky,

Julie and Fay — on a summer school trip to Switzerland and Paris. *The Tall Man* features the four Waring children — Clarissa, twins David and Patricia (Tish), and Thomas — travelling to Böningberg on Lake Brienz to meet their Aunt and Uncle. In *Bernese Holiday* (its original title, slightly revised as *Bernese Adventure*) Sara and Caroline Storm, the cousins from *Breton Holiday*, accompany Caroline's sister Vanessa, and her husband John on a touring holiday to Switzerland.

Interlaken

The Waring children began their holiday rather luxuriously for 1960, by flying to Zurich. As their Aunt and Uncle failed to appear they travelled to Interlaken by train, passing Lake Lucerne on the way. At Interlaken Ost they caught a lake steamer, the *Jungfrau*, and journeyed along the river Aare, which joins the lakes Brienz and Thun, onto Lake Brienz itself, to the lakeside village of Böningberg. Böningberg was the second stop of their steamer's journey — whilst the real-life lakeside village with the similar name of Bönigen is the first stop. The Warings stayed at a *pension* named Chalet du Lac, an old brown chalet set by the lakeside.

Ricky, Fay and Julie stayed in the village of 'Rosenberg' above Interlaken, which from its location under the north face of the Eiger would seem to be a disguised Grindelwald. They travelled by train from Paris to Basle where they changed trains, and compared the station to Glasgow's Central Station. On the way to Interlaken the scenery (just fields) was rather uninteresting, but once through Berne the mountains, including the Jungfrau, began to appear, with Lake Thun on their left. At Interlaken they changed trains for the mountain railway to Rosenberg.

Sara and Caroline travelled from Basle via train for Interlaken and thence to Grindelwald. In the original edition of *Bernese Holiday* there is an extra paragraph detailing Vanessa's mistaken idea that they must change trains at Interlaken and they therefore reboarded after realising they should actually change at Interlaken Ost, the next station. They were thrilled with their first sight of the mountains and, as in *Crooks Tour*, mention is made of the rather dull, flat scenery around Berne. The edited version of this story, *Bernese Adventure*, omits Sara's fascination with the peaked cap of the train guard. *Bernese Holiday* relates that she thought his name "BOB" is recorded on his cap — Caroline corrected her, explaining that it stands for "Bernese Oberland Bahn"!

Grindelwald

Rosenberg in *Crooks Tour*, overlooking a "little jade-green lake", is described as a fairytale village, with their hotel, the Alpenblick, "the most fairytale of all"; it had gentians and edelweiss carved on its old wooden walls, with the Eiger's north face visible from the hotel. The hotelkeeper suggested places to visit including Grindelwald, and Interlaken with its famous floral clock and spectacular shops. In their rooms, the girls encountered "great billowing quilts" known as duvets. In *Susan Interferes* they are described as "enormous great white billowing sort of eiderdowns".

Once at Grindelwald, in *Bernese Holiday*, Sara and Caroline discovered they were actually staying at a village down the valley from Grindelwald. This village isn't named in the book, although Alison Lindsay thinks it may be the village of Schmendi, where the author spent her honeymoon. The Storms' hotel was the Alpenrose. The Eiger, Mettenberg and Wetterhorn mountains can be seen from the village, but the better-known Mönch and Jungfrau are hidden from Schmendi by a lower hill. As it was May, most of Grindelwald's best hotels were closed — unlikely nowadays, as the tourist season in Switzerland continues year round. However, there were postcards for sale and a café open for cakes and hot chocolate. The girls explored the surrounding area, seeing avalanches taking place on the Eiger. They located the Abbach waterfall on their way back to the hotel.

The following day a mountain mist obliterated the views, so they caught the 2.15pm train to Interlaken. They enjoyed the shops, presumably on the Hoheweg, Interlaken's main shopping street. The Swiss weather was beginning to change, with heavy rain in Interlaken, and it was sleeting on their return to the Alpenrose. The next morning they found it had snowed and was extremely cold. Caroline took the chance to write postcards — very economically with the same message on each card! *Bernese Holiday* added a description of Sara "borrowing" the hotel owner's skis (not to mention John's boots and trousers) and Caroline found her attempting to ski — Caroline eventually had to come to her aid by digging her out of a snowdrift! For some reason in *Bernese Adventure* Sara's skiing session is completely omitted, with just a paragraph stating that "Two days later, the snow had gone". Perhaps the publishers decided a snowscene was inappropriate in what is otherwise a book with an early summer setting.

In all three books Grindelwald's glaciers are mentioned. In *Bernese Holiday* Caroline, Sara and Vanessa crossed the Lütschine stream and walked along the valley to Grindelwald's Lower Glacier — Sara was very disappointed because of the stones and rubble in it. They returned to their village by a steep lane, which took them towards the hamlet of Duftbach (Tuftbach on the map). They also visited the Upper Glacier, with its ice-grotto; Sara (and David Waring) was pleased as this was more like her idea of a glacier. Ricky, Fay and Julie made various excursions including Grindelwald and Mürren: these trips are mentioned in passing.

AROUND THE REGION

Other trips in *Crooks Tour* have detailed descriptions. The school group visited the Schynige Platte, via Wilderswil where they changed trains. Interlaken was visible as the train climbed higher, and further up were the three main mountains of the Bernese Oberland, the Eiger, Mönch and Jungfrau. The Schynige Platte with the Alpine Garden is a popular tourist attraction nowadays. The schoolgirls appreciated the wonderful view of the mountains from it. Another trip was to the Rhône Glacier and its ice grotto, and they saw the Devil's Bridge and the River Reuss during their travels. The return journey was via the Grimsel Pass where they stopped for lunch, by which time the rain had turned to snow, and they passed through deep snow on their homeward journey.

BÖNIGEN AND EXCURSIONS FROM LAKE BRIENZ

In *The Tall Man*, the names of two of the lakeside villages have been conflated — Ringgenberg and Bönigen have become Rinigen and Böningberg. The Warings rowed across to the small village of Rinigen to see its turreted castle. A woodcarver told them about Grindelwald and its glaciers, which they decided to visit. They went to the castle (Schloss Rinigen) where they met Meieli Rinigen, who told them about the famous ruby and gold necklace, an heirloom of the Rinigen family, known as the "Red Roses of Rinigen".

At this point "The Tall Man" of the title is mentioned, who is an infamous burglar. The Warings' attempts to track down "The Tall Man" make up a large part of this book. They thought he might have been staying at their hotel, and split up for a complete day to observe the other guests. David and Tish followed a Dr Maclaren up to Grindelwald; at Interlaken Ost they boarded the mountain railway and enjoyed the view of the Jungfrau. Part way up the railway changed to rack-and-pinion. Once at Grindelwald Dr Maclaren bought a ticket for the chairlift to First, and they did likewise. The chairlift to First was at one time the longest chairlift in Europe, but this has been replaced with small gondolas, each of which carries six passengers — the trip takes approximately 25 minutes. One of the chairlift's original chairs is in the Museum of Tourism at Unterseen, in Interlaken. At First they found a hotel and various paths leading off into the mountains. The twins nearly became stuck on the cable car for the night,

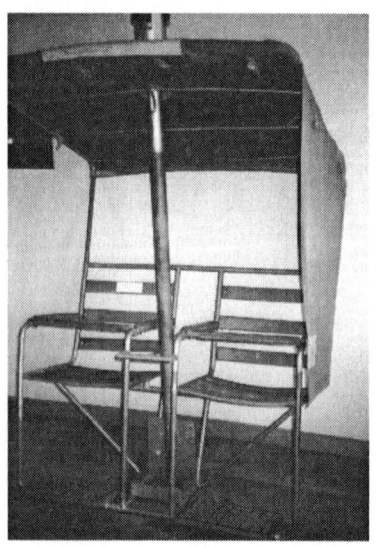

after falling asleep following lunch, with the result that they were the last people on the chairlift back down to Grindelwald: the attendants didn't know they were on it and closed it for the night. Luckily Dr Maclaren alerted the attendants to start up the ride again. The three enjoyed the trip down the Lütschine valley in the dark and, Dr Maclaren treated the twins to dinner at Interlaken in a restaurant overlooking the river Aare. Clarissa spent an enjoyable day at Mürren, a village perched 1650m high on a valley shelf in the next valley to Grindelwald, with a sheer drop hundreds of feet to the valley floor.

Berne

Thomas visited Berne and described the famous old sixteenth century clock with its figures, bears and a man holding a staff and hour-glass, and knight in armour who strikes the hours. He saw some fountains, his favourite being one of an ogre eating little children: this was to scare children away from a deep ditch, which existed in earlier times. He also saw the famous bearpit of Berne. Tish expressed concern about the bears being kept in a pit, but Thomas replied that it was a very nice pit and the bears had a wonderful time, just eating nuts and carrots all day long, although he thought they looked overfed. Today visitors can still feed the bears carrots.

During the Warings' visit Swiss National Day on the first of August was celebrated. In the evening there were speeches and the Swiss children wore their national dress and carried lighted lanterns. At night there were bonfires round the lake and mountain villages, paper lanterns displayed from boats on the lake and fireworks. Nowadays, evening cruises are advertised on Lake Brienz during the National Day celebrations.

FIVEPENNY MYSTERY (1958)

In the fifth of the Penny series, Penny, her family, friends John and Laura Mallory and their cousin, Stephen, holiday in the Austrian Tyrol.

INNSBRUCK

At Innsbruck Airport they met Penny and Jill's cousin Deborah, arrived from South Africa, to escort her back to their guesthouse in the village of Adlerhorst. In the centre of Innsbruck they saw the famous Maria Theresienstrasse with the Anna-Saule column. At Adlerhorst (which means Eagle's Nest) they stayed in the Gasthof Alpenrose, set in a cobbled square. From the village the mountains of the Nordkette range were visible, and another village with a church with the typical 'onion' spire. About ten minutes away was a small green lake and, halfway between the village and lake, a white-walled castle. The castle or 'Schloss' plays a significant role in the book, as Penny was quarantined there whilst she has chickenpox. When Penny was recovering and able to go out, they revisited Innsbruck where they saw the Goldene Dachl ('golden roof') — actually quite a small roofed balcony in the Herzog Friederichstrasse, but extremely famous and a "must-see" for all visitors to Innsbruck. Later Penny created mayhem on the road into Innsbruck when kidnapped in a caravan, by throwing its contents onto the road as a 'trail' for the others, and further havoc on the Maria Theresienstrasse when she entangled a policeman on point duty in a sheet causing major disruption to the town's traffic! Penny and Agamemnon were taken through the Rennweg Square and then the Herzog Friedrichstrasse, where there are ancient inns with fascinating old wrought-iron signs.

ACHENSEE

They also visited the Achensee — a place of great significance to any collector of Elinor Brent-Dyer's Chalet School series — via the old town of Hall, which at one time had its own mint. On reaching the village of Jenbach they left the main road for the mountain road up to the Achensee. Unfortunately, other than mentioning that the lake is green and blue in turn, there is little description of the setting. Later Penny's parents were stranded in the village of Pertisau on the Achensee when their car broke down. The Achensee is an easy day trip from Innsbruck, by train to Jenbach, where there is the option of travelling on the mountain road by bus, or more interestingly via the little mountain steam train which is over one hundred years old.

SHOPPING

Jean Evans was clearly interested in the Swiss woodcarvings, embroideries and lace offered for sale, which would have been very different from the goods then obtainable in the UK. In *Crooks Tour*, during their first walk around Rosenberg village, the girls encountered shops selling the usual range of items including carved bears, the symbol of the Bernese Oberland. Later on they visited the woodcarving village of Brienz, reached via lake steamer from Interlaken. Nowadays at Brienz there is the Living Museum, which has a large collection of Swiss woodcarving and musical boxes. Interlaken provided the girls with more shopping opportunities — possibly the exchange rate was more favourable to the pound at this time than nowadays as these schoolgirls seem able to shop constantly on what would have been limited budgets.

In *Susan Interferes*, at the top of Mount Rigi, little stalls selling musical boxes, toy chalets and other items are mentioned. In *Fivepenny Mystery* the village shops sold woodcarvings and embroideries, Tyrolean hats and braces embroidered with edelweiss.

In *The Tall Man* the shops in Böningberg sold, amongst other items, ivory brooches, embroidered hankies, musical boxes and many wooden bears. At this point Thomas, like Caroline and Susan, opened all the musical boxes, although only Susan got her ears boxed by an irate schoolmaster by mistake! In *Bernese Holiday*, whilst at Grindelwald Sara bought a book on Alpine flowers and gentian-embroidered handkerchiefs for her mother.

Food

In *Susan Interferes*, Bill was shocked with his introduction to the continental breakfast of hot rolls, croissants, swieback — a type of sweet rusk — and jam. As schoolchildren nowadays are accustomed to cereal and toast (if anything at all!), this would not be such a big surprise today. The Warings' Swiss breakfast of cherry jam, honey, rolls and hot chocolate presented no problem as they had experienced the continental breakfast whilst in Paris. The Carmichaels' and Susan's first Swiss meal was roast veal with vegetables — excepting breakfast, veal features in almost every meal mentioned in the books with a Swiss setting. In *Crooks Tour* the girls' first meal comprised veal again, followed by a sumptuous chocolate pudding. In *Fivepenny Mystery* Penny was joined at the Castle by Jill, John and Laura for a dinner of Wiener Schnitzel (veal cutlet) although another meal of Kummelbraten (roast beef with caraway seeds) is mentioned later on — followed by the ever-popular Apfelstrudel.

In *Susan Interferes*, on their trip to Mount Rigi, the family's packed lunch provided by the hotel had cold veal (!), cheese, hard-boiled egg, roll and butter, twist of salt, apple, orange and biscuits which seems fairly generous. David and Tish's packed lunch at First; was similar, but also had cheese triangles. Bill and Dr Carmichael bought chocolate whilst the girls and Aunt Lucy were preoccupied in the shops; Bill was thrilled with all the different varieties on offer, as were the Warings who, when faced with varieties such as praline, pistachio and orange fourré, eventually settled for milk chocolate after all!

Whilst at Wissifluh the Carmichaels and Susan had drinks at the Hotel Alpenblick — Bill and Midge had apple juice, Susan had coffee to recover after the nerve-wracking cable car ride, and Charlotte ordered tea — as did Fay in *Crooks Tour*, to the disgust of her friends who thought it made her look like a tourist. In both instances it arrived in a glass with a muslin bag floating in it — Charlotte said it was ghastly.

VENICE

In Susan's journeys round Venice in *Where is Susan?*, she and Midge took in most of the well-known sights as well as a private visit to a palazzo on the Grand Canal lent to the Gascoignes. The three hotels mentioned in the book are Soldati's, the Ambasciata and the Venezia: none appears in current guides to Venice. Soldati's was "an ancient palace" at the corner of the Calle delle Rasse and therefore a little to the east of Piazza San Marco, off the Riva degli Schiavoni. The Ambasciata or Embassy Hotel, where Susan and Midge found accommodation, lay beside the Rio San Trovaso, a narrow canal running south from the Grand Canal just west of the Accademia. At its foot, on the Zattere, was the squero, where gondolas were brought for repair. The Hotel Venezia, where Susan caught the hotel thief, was on Calle Largo XXII Marzo, which runs parallel to the Grand Canal just west of Piazza San Marco. It had "a stately doorway with bay trees on either side": the street is now home mainly to bank headquarters.

Of course, major differences have occurred in these countries since the books were written forty to sixty years ago. However, in most cases it is still possible to visit the places described and appreciate the atmosphere of the books. They are well worth reading prior to a visit to any of the locations (take them with you for handy reference!).

XXII: WITH JANE SHAW IN SOUTH AFRICA

POLLY WHIBLEY

Assessing Jane Shaw's work on South Africa and her experiences there inevitably lit a spark for me. My love for this beautiful land with its deep perplexities of "Black" and "White" is as solidly in my blood as if I had been born there or had earlier settler forebears.

I do not know the Jane Shaw of the *Susans*, but am content to browse among her backcloths in Johannesburg and Cape Town, where her footprints cross with mine, over and over. She wrote two full-length books about South Africa, *Venture to South Africa* and *Nothing Happened After All*. *The Matchmakers*, elsewhere in this volume, is set in South Africa's Drakensberg mountains; and *Fivepenny Mystery* starts off in Johannesburg before moving on to Europe.

When I went to South Africa for the first time, on holiday and only a few years after the end of World War II, it was to fall in love with a city. Not with Cape Town, the "Cape of Storms" christened by Bartholomew Diaz in 1488, where our Union-Castle liner had docked on a sharp winter morning in July, and where sunlight banished shadows from the deep blueness of Table Mountain and the sea was a rich turquoise as we approached. I fell in love with Johannesburg, where beauty was not to be found in buildings or places, but in the vibrancy of the people, Black and White, and their mix of laughter and pain. It was a profound and sharp study in contrasts. Even the sunshine, striking between stark city buildings in typically symmetrical Johannesburg streets, produced either dazzling white light or pools of black shadow.

Jane Shaw's novel, *Venture to South Africa*, sparked off many memories, from the Eliots' first drive round Table Mountain (I had also done it with a car full of impatient children) to the long haul up to Johannesburg. In following years we did that and similar journeys in the need to get away from the rarefied atmosphere of the high veld, 7000 ft above sea level, where the blood gets thin after living there for a while.

The Eliot family "roundly condemned the Orange Free State" and its miles and miles of "nothing". Perhaps a natural reaction if you had been in thickly populated London suburbia all your life (like the Eliots), but I was surprised at this, well remembering my own appreciation of all that wonderful space after a childhood and girlhood on Merseyside. I was a little depressed at derogatory references to this and that and comparisons to Scotland for most of the journey up-country. Then they arrived in Johannesburg and "the city was a disappointment". Jane Shaw argues that it had really been started as a shanty town, less than a hundred years before, as somewhere to house those pioneering goldminers, but then her interest quickly diverts to the lovely northern suburb where the Eliots eventually make their home, and where the shops are frankly more to their taste than the city ones, likened to "the wrong end of Oxford Street" in London.

These lovely suburbs, including Rosebank which is mentioned several times, were always a show-piece of Johannesburg, with their banks of flowers, velvet lawns and vivid semi-tropical shrubs, kept immaculate by Black gardeners who worked long hours for very little money. Many of the gardens had a palm tree in the midst of their splendour, and there were always roses – the giant blooms produced by the African climate, which, though stunning to look at, lack the fragrance of those growing in a damp cooler climate like that of the British Isles. The houses were low and widespread and generally one-storey, as is normal in South Africa and other southern hemisphere countries, and were kept cool in the hottest weather by a wide, shady, open veranda, sometimes right round the building and known as the stoep (pronounced "stoop").

I think Jane Shaw possibly never ventured to the southern suburbs of Johannesburg which Mrs Eliot dismissed as being "nearer the mines". The apartheid question is well described, and leaves the reader in no doubt as to the inequality and injustice which existed in South Africa at that time. It was indeed as she describes, as was the standard of living for Whites in just those northern suburbs, but there is no attempt to catch the atmosphere of those to the south, and she completely missed the homely and historic districts built to house ongoing generations of gold miners. The mines and mine-dumps were truly ever present (and not beautiful!), but my own love for this pioneering city was always stirred by the very starkness of the yellow dumps – the waste from those excavations of long ago – and the old shabby houses and air of this-was-where-it-all-began. In later years when I went back to Europe several times, returning by jumbo jets which flew in low over those southern approaches, the sight of the dumps never failed to bring a lump to my throat and a gladness to be back.

Jane Shaw describes vividly all facets of life in this very hot land, thousands of miles from her native shores, and that of her family of Eliots. My experience of returning to Southern Africa as part of an immigrant family in 1958 led me in similar ways, except that my children were younger than even her smallest Eliot (Blinky aged 10), and I arrived there pregnant with my second. Mrs Eliot was spared such traumas, although I would hardly have envied her moving hemispheres with a crowd of teenagers.

The settling down of my own experience, after a few initial weeks in Johannesburg, was in the pleasant town of Germiston, 10 miles to the east, where I had my baby, and later a third one. But my expatriate experiences were so much the same as Jane Shaw's that memories return starkly as her book unfolds. Finding a flat – having a baby in a strange hospital – finding a house – meeting (and liking) people of all races – learning in fact to be a happy South African and to make it our home, it was all, in essence, as Jane Shaw described. Not easy, but worth all the ups and downs of the years.

Five years after *Venture to South Africa*, in 1965 came her second full-length book set in Africa. Two English girls are invited to stay with a family of cousins, who live in Johannesburg, but are keen on travelling everywhere under the African sun. Johannesburg is given only scant attention in this book, although some enthusiasm for the same northern suburbs is once more evident, and the same dislike of those parts of the city she describes as "ugly".

Jane Shaw's former lack of enthusiasm for the long stretches of the Orange Free State (or simply "the Free State" as it is known in South Africa) is again clearly seen as Dizzy and Alison and their cousins travel north-east to the Kruger National Park. "… just great stretches of wan, yellowish-brown nothing, with only tall, dusty olive-green trees called blue-gums to relieve the monotony…"

She allowed Rob, one of the cousins, to put the point of view of the sweep of sky and wide horizons being breathable landscape, but obviously was not herself convinced. Great relief all round when they arrived at a place called Machadadorp where the scenery "took a marked turn for the better when hills and valleys and rivers and trees appeared"!

But once the writer went with her "family" of cousins through the Numbi Gate of the Kruger National Park, she was swept up into that age-old fascination for wild animals in their natural state. The camp where they would be eating and sleeping consisted of round thatched huts known as rondavels in shady rows, and a place for a car beside each one. In the ablution block were baths and toilets, and plain simple kitchens in areas where one could either cook over a crackling fire or on a proper stove.

Their next camp was Olifants, somewhat differently arranged, but in essence the same, and where they saw the Letaba River. But it was at their last camp in the northern reserve that the "grey-green, greasy Limpopo" became hugely real to them, and where indeed the Rudyard Kipling of *Jungle Book* must constantly live again, especially for English tourists who can picnic beside it, and if so inclined, picture the man himself.

When Dizzy and Alison went on to Zimbabwe it was then Rhodesia, and Mozambique still Portuguese East Africa. It was hotter and steamier here, and perhaps in tourists' eyes more of the real Africa.

Jane Shaw's English teenagers liked Johannesburg no better when they returned from their travels in the wild (I am beginning to believe there are those who don't!), but if the Golden City was her *bête noir* — except obviously her own home patch — she had certainly adopted the rest of South Africa into a close relationship which came through her books with the ease of great familiarity. As with most expatriates of long standing, names and phrases in Afrikaans, and even Zulu Venda and Sotho, tripped off her tongue unthinkingly. I confess to being mildly irritated by comparisons with the British Isles, feeling that Africa in all its wild grandeur does not need comparison with anywhere on earth! – but I have long learned to accept that the English (perhaps I should say British) have a peculiar way of eulogising the beauty of their own land by comparing it glowingly with "abroad".

But when the action of *Nothing Happened After All* moved to the country of the Drakensberg, the long, snaking mountain ranges which border Natal, the Orange Free State and East Griqualand, and what was then Basutoland, and is now Lesotho, it was evident that here was Jane Shaw's chief delight. The brilliant winter in this southern region, with its bright sunshine and clear blue skies comes tumbling from her pen, and if bitingly cold mornings and nights needed every jersey and blanket one possessed, what of it? The air was like champagne and one felt ready to conquer Everest, let alone that doyen of the Drakensberg range, Mount aux Sources.

It was softer, greener, time to relax when they came down from the jagged peaks and felt the old world graciousness of Cape Town. Here it was mellow, and if they were back to making comparisons again, it was now between aspects of the different cities they had seen, and the widely differing terrain rather than references to what it was like at "home". Maybe by now the mental picture of Africa was more strongly printed, and England beginning to take on a slightly faded perspective. But this happens, so it is no great wonder.

Jane Shaw returns to the Drakensberg briefly in *The Matchmakers*, but beyond taking place on the steep rocky slopes above a wide rushing river, there is no real indication where this could be.

Fivepenny Mystery opens at an evening *braaiveleis* (barbecue) in Johannesburg, and introduces Deborah who has just left school. The South African connection is broken next day when her plane leaves for Athens. *New Girl at Northmead* gives only a slender look at the background to Lynette du Toit's home life in South Africa.

I would have liked to see a further novel set in South Africa, and to have my own set opinions challenged once again by Jane Shaw with her frank appraisals of a country we both made our own for a number of years, and to have seen it all again through her eyes.

Johannesburg today is very different from the one Jane Shaw knew and talked about. Shops and people have moved away to the outer suburbs. It still preserves its business and learning centres, but has become the ethnic hub. Market sellers take up their places on main street pavements. But it is full of lovely people, just the same; smiling Black faces and cheerful greetings in a variety of African tongues. And the magic is still there.

Thank you, Jane Shaw, for rekindling my memories.

XXIII: THE MATCHMAKERS

JANE SHAW

The three girls were lying on a flat rock overhanging the river. The hot African sun warmed their backs, below them the clear waters of the Umlambonja rushed by, round them towered the great mountains of the Drakensberg, the Horns, the Bell, Cathedral Peak and opposite them the Baboon Rock: well-named, for the girls had often seen an old baboon crouching in just such a way on the mountain slopes while the flightier members of his family played around him. There were no houses in this remote spot among the mountains, only the hotel hidden in a fold of the hills, and, up and down the valley, the native kraals with their round thatched huts like old-fashioned bee-hives. The sky was a deep and cloudless blue, nothing disturbed the stillness and the peace except the noisy brawling of the stream below, and far across the valley, a native boy on a Basuto pony was threading his way up a tiny mountain path.

Things were not quite so peaceful with the girls, who had other things on their minds besides the beauty of the mountains. They stared moodily at their sister Elizabeth, who was sun-bathing on the other side of the river, and at the young man who was sitting hunched beside her, his hands round his ankles, his chin on his knees. He was staring moodily at Elizabeth too. Sisters! Jennifer thought. The young ones aren't so bad, she thought, glancing at Jill and Tina, because mostly they do what they're told — eventually. But the ones old enough to get married give you nothing but trouble. "We'll have to prod her on," she said aloud.

"I should think so," said Jill. "She could have been married twenty times over by now. I could have been a bridesmaid ages ago."

"That's all you think about," said Jennifer. "Ever since you were about two years old, and that's nearly thirteen years, you've been desperate to be a bridesmaid. Elizabeth could have married the king of the Cannibal Islands as far as you were concerned, just as long as you were a bridesmaid at the wedding —."

"Oh, James isn't as bad as the King of the Cannibal Islands," said Tina, "he's rather a decent old stick, actually, if a trifle on the slow side. Poor old thing, he'll have one foot in the grave if they don't hurry up and make up their minds. He's *ancient*, gosh! Twenty-seven!"

"At this rate," Jill was grumbling on, "we won't be bridesmaids until we're about a thousand years old and past caring."

"I must say," said Jennifer, "that when James arrived up here I thought that Elizabeth would get engaged on the turn."

"And now if *he* doesn't hurry up she will — only it won't be to him, it will be to this new one who has turned up, this Paul — ."

"I shouldn't mind Paul for a brother-in-law," Jennifer said dreamily. "Tall and dark and handsome —."

"Handsome is as handsome does," said Jill, snappily. " Why doesn't *he* marry her? Why doesn't *one* of them marry her?"

"We must prod James on," Jennifer said again.

Tina, with vague ideas of knight-errants and damsels in distress running in her head, said: "We must get James to do something terribly brave for her. We must think of something —."

There was a deep silence while they all thought.

"D'you think," said Tina, gazing down into the water, "that he could rescue her from drowning?"

"Well, hardly," Jennifer said, " seeing that she is practically South African free-style champion. But," she added slowly, "he could rescue one of us — ," and she and Jill both turned and stared at Tina.

"Oh, not me!" said Tina. "Please, Jennifer, not me this time!"

"You'll be all right," Jennifer said absently. "I have an idea. And we can do it now, this minute. We'll go across the river to Elizabeth — ."

"She'll be jolly glad to see us after being alone with that bore James not proposing all morning," Jill muttered under her breath.

" — only," Jennifer said, frowning at Jill, "we'll cross *above* the pool, where we were told not to, and poor little Tina will slip and fall into the deep part. James will dive in and save her — and Elizabeth will be so overcome with gratitude that she'll — she'll fall into his arms or something and James will beg her to marry him and she will — ."

"And supposing he doesn't?" asked Tina.

"Doesn't what?"

"Doesn't rescue me," said Tina.

"Of course he'll rescue you," Jennifer said impatiently. "Really, Tina, you are awfully selfish, always thinking of yourself. Well, come on, let's do it — ."

The clear waters of the river sparkled in the sunshine and rushed madly between the stones. Holding hands the girls stepped cautiously into the stream.

"Goodness, it's coming down fast today," said Jennifer.

"Mm. Lucky," Jill said.

Tina said nothing. She had enough to do to keep her balance.

When they were about the middle of the stream, Elizabeth noticed them. "Jennifer! Go back! The current's much too strong to cross there! Go back!"

Jennifer dropped the others' hands and cupped her own hands round her mouth. "Can't hear. What did you say?" she shouted back over the din of the river. "Now, Tina," she muttered, "now's your chance. Take a deep breath and slip — ."

Tina, as a matter of fact, had slipped already. As she had not had time to take a deep breath, she came to the surface in the middle of the pool, gasping and spluttering and scared nearly out of her wits. "Help!" she yelled. "Help!" She tried to swim, but the current hurled her on towards the rocks. "*Help!*" she yelled.

"Gee, man," said Jill, bracing her legs against the rush of water and gazing downstream at Tina admiringly, "Tina's doing it awfully well!"

"So is James," Jennifer said.

Elizabeth and James had plunged down the bank to the water's edge, shouting encouragement to Tina. James flung himself towards the pool, but his haste was his undoing.

"Now *he's* down," said Jill. "What a splash! Knocked himself unconscious, I shouldn't wonder. We'll have to rescue both of them, seems to me."

But a lean, tanned figure had appeared from nowhere. Somehow or other, he grabbed Tina in one hand and James in the other and deposited them both at Elizabeth's feet.

Elizabeth gazed up at him in admiration. "Oh, Paul, *thank* you," she said...

Jill now came out openly on the side of Paul. Even if it meant another six months before she could hope to follow Elizabeth up the aisle she still, she said, preferred Paul. So did Tina, tenderly nursing her bruises.

So, apparently, did Elizabeth. At least at the hotel that evening she danced with him half the night. Tina and Jill, who weren't allowed to stay up for the dancing, hung about the wide and shadowy stoep, peering round the open doors at the dancers. Jennifer abandoned her partner, who had been hacking her on the shins rather a lot in any case, and went over to talk to them. Elizabeth and Paul were doing some very brilliant and complicated steps in a corner, James was ambling unhappily around with a fat girl in glasses.

"You must admit," said Jennifer, "that James has a kind heart."

"She's probably the only person who would dance with him" said Jill.

"Well, I quite *like* James," said Tina, "I always have, but he wasn't much good at rescuing me."

"Let's face it," said Jill. "Now I wouldn't lift a finger to help James."

Jennifer did not approve of this desertion of James. Besides, she was beginning to think that Paul was rather wasted on Elizabeth. "You *both* liked James before Paul arrived," she said severely. "Let's stick to James. Let's give him one more chance."

"With me as the victim again?" said Tina in a hopeless voice.

"Yes, of course," Jennifer said. "You could get lost on the mountains or something and James could rescue you — ."

Tina was saying that she hoped that James was better at rescuing people from mountains that he was at rescuing people from rivers, when the girls' mother appeared and chased Jill and Tina off to bed. They went, slowly and reluctantly and grumbling all the way.

"Cheer up, you can be thinking of a good *plan*," Jennifer muttered to them. "And anyway, being old enough to stay up for the dances isn't all bliss, I can tell you," she said and went back to her shin-hacker...

The perfect opportunity, it seemed, to put their plan into action came the next day when the girls and Elizabeth, with Paul and James in attendance, set off to walk to the Rainbow Gorge. They didn't reach the Rainbow Gorge, because after walking and scrambling for what seemed like miles over the shoulder of a mountain and down through a damp and dense forest and in and out of a rushing stream, James developed a blister on his heel which made walking extremely uncomfortable and they all turned back.

"Liz," said Jennifer, an inspiration having darted into her head, "Jill and Tina and I are so hot, we're going to run on and have a swim before lunch."

"If you run you'll be hotter," said Elizabeth.

"Yes, but we'll have longer to cool off in the pool," said Jennifer.

"Good idea," said Paul heartily. He preferred Elizabeth without all those sisters hanging round; and without James too, for that matter. He didn't see how he could get rid of him, a limpet was easier to dislodge in his opinion, but to push the girls off was a step in the right direction. "Good idea to go and have a swim," he said.

"Well, all right," said Elizabeth. "Don't slip and twist your ankles on the path, don't stay in the pool too long, don't — ."

Really, thought the girls as they ran off, it was time that Elizabeth was married she was getting so boring. She was as bad as the grown-ups with her *don't, don't, don't...*!

When Elizabeth and Paul and James, hobbling painfully, reached the hotel, they paused by the swimming-pool. Jennifer was practising butterfly, and Jill was doing back-stroke, rather badly, disappearing under the surface every now and then.

Elizabeth, who was finding her two sulky cavaliers rather a trial, stopped and called, "Hallo!" She added, "Where's Tina?"

Jennifer swam to the side and climbed out, shaking the water out of her eyes and hair like a little dog. "Tina? Isn't she with you?" she said innocently.

"Well, you know she isn't," said Elizabeth. "She ran on with you."

"Yes, but she didn't come with us after all," said Jill, who had now climbed out of the pool to join the others. "She was hot, she said, so she waited beside the path for you — ."

"But she wasn't there when we passed!" said Elizabeth. "We didn't see her — ."

Jennifer and Jill glanced at each other. Good old Tina!

"I'd better go back," said Elizabeth, her mind still running in that boring grown-up way on sprained ankles, "I'd better go back and look for her — ."

"I'll go," said James.

"But James," said Elizabeth, "your foot!"

"Oh, that doesn't matter," said James. "I'll take my shoes off. I'll certainly go — ."

"I'll go too," said Paul, with a small, small sigh which was heard only by Jennifer.

The two young men hurried off. "Get dressed, you two," said Elizabeth and went after the men . . .

It was all very well for Jennifer, Tina thought, making all those schemes, but it was very boring for her. She rose from the rock behind which she had crouched until Elizabeth and James and Paul were well out of sight. It had been extremely dull behind the rock, but now at least, she thought, I can go up the mountain a little way and lose myself properly.

She climbed steadily up from the path, picking her way through the long coarse grass, between boulders, by the side of a tiny stream where cool, white arum lilies were growing. Here, of course, in Natal arum lilies are practically weeds, she thought, but in Britain wedding bouquets are made of them. Let's hope that Liz will soon be carrying a wedding bouquet and we'll all get a bit of peace. The hillside was steep here and very soon she decided that she was much too tired to climb any further. This would have to do, she thought, she would just have to be lost here.

Suddenly, to her right, she heard a strange noise, a sort of angry chattering. She stopped climbing and looked round. Below her was a troop of baboons; and unless Tina was very much mistaken, these baboons weren't in the best of tempers.

Oh, bother it all, thought Tina. I don't want to get mixed up with a crowd of angry baboons just at the moment. It was well known that baboons sometimes carried off small children; she had read in the paper once how a little girl had been stolen away by baboons in the Megaliesberg mountains; and while it was fairly unlikely that baboons could carry a big lump of twelve like herself, she supposed that they could attack her and knock her about quite a lot. And she didn't at all fancy being attacked and knocked about by baboons just to help Jill to be a bridesmaid.

At this point the baboons apparently became aware of Tina. They forgot their private quarrel, and in the inquisitive way of their kind came up the mountainside to have a look at her. An old grandfather baboon led them, and the babies rode on their mothers' backs, like jockeys. Under happier circumstances — at the zoo, for instance, or from the safety of a car in the Game Reserve — Tina would have enjoyed watching their antics, but just at this moment she wished that they would go away. She threw a stone down among them. The baboons chattered crossly. She climbed higher, as quickly as she could. The mountain was very steep now, she was clinging with hands and knees and panting; suddenly she found that beneath her was a sheer drop to the path below, above her the mountainside rose high and unscaleable; in her anxiety to escape from the baboons she had taken a wrong direction and now found herself on a shelf of rock and unable to go any farther. Oh bother these blessed baboons, she thought, if I'd paid less attention to them I shouldn't be stuck out here on this horrid little ledge. I'd better go back —. She glanced back and down — and her head began to swim and she felt sick.

In nearly everything else, as her sisters would have agreed, Tina was fairly intrepid, but she had a very poor head for heights. It was one thing going up, with her face comfortably turned to the mountain — but when she looked down and saw how far she had climbed, how steep was the drop, how far below in the dizzy distance was the winding path, her knees felt as if they had turned to cotton-wool. She collapsed on the ledge, clung hard and turned her face away from the horrifying height. Oh help, oh help, she thought, now I really *do* need to be rescued — "Help! *Help!* HELP!"

The baboons, who had found something else to divert them, ran across the hill-side below, forgetting Tina...

James and Paul hurried across the little stream and along the Rainbow Gorge path, soon outdistancing Elizabeth and her parents and the people from the hotel who, egged on by the lurid tales of Jill and Jennifer, had flocked out to help in the rescue.

"All the better," said Jennifer. "All the more people to watch James being a hero."

"Paul," Jill said.

Before very long James and Paul could hear Tina's shouts for help, and when they came round the shoulder of the hill they could see her, a tiny dot, her red shorts bright against the rocks, high up on the face of the cliff. James climbed quickly up the steep mountain-side towards her; Paul circled round, using the same route that Tina had taken to reach the ledge.

James shouted encouragingly to Tina, who, flat on her face on the ledge, cautiously leant an inch over the edge to see how he was getting on. I never thought, she said to herself, that I would be so glad to see old James; and, greatly daring, she leant over a little farther to watch his progress. But unfortunately the rock against which she leant was not as firm as it looked. Tina's weight dislodged it and it went hurtling down the cliff. It whistled past James's right ear, but crashed on his bare foot. He gave a yell of pain and surprise, lost his grip and went slithering down the slope rather more quickly than he had come up.

Willing onlookers hurried up to him and helped him back to the hotel; and it was Paul who rescued Tina, carefully guiding her along the ledge, down the mountain-side and back to the hotel...

Jennifer was furious. Tina, she said, had bungled the whole thing. "Now Paul's the hero again! Dropping boulders on James's feet!" she said disgustedly. "You might have killed him. As a matter of fact," she went on, "I don't know why you wanted to go climbing away up there anyway. It was a good idea to climb a little way, but to go clambering on to a ledge — !"

"The baboons —" poor Tina began.

"The baboons!" said Jennifer with scorn. "Baboons can climb a jolly lot better than you can, you might have thought of that — ."

"Well, I'm glad I didn't," retorted Tina, "because I was quite frightened enough as it was. And I am not going to be rescued again, Jennifer, not by *any*one, so you needn't think I am — ."

They were in their bedroom. Tina was supposed to be resting after all the excitements of the morning, and the others were cheering her up.

Jill said, "I quite agree. James has had it. We've given him two glorious opportunities to be a hero and impress Elizabeth and look what he does. From now on he can look after himself as far as I'm concerned. I'd much rather have Paul —."

The door burst open and Elizabeth came in. Her sisters could see at once that something had happened. She looked about twice as pretty as usual, which was saying something; she sat on Tina's bed and positively glowed. She nonchalantly waved her left hand backwards and forwards in front of her face until even a blind bat, far less three anxious girls, would have noticed the ring.

"You're engaged!" they yelled, and there was a wild flurry of hugging and kissing and dancing round the room.

Elizabeth eventually collapsed on one of the beds. "I'll be needing some bridesmaids soon," she said.

"At last!" said Jill. "But gosh, that was quick work!"

"I don't know about quick work," said Elizabeth, stretching out her hand and waggling it so that the light caught the diamond and made it sparkle.

"We've really been engaged for ages but James said that we couldn't announce it until he had a better job, and today he's got a better job — the letter has just come — ."

"*James?*"

"Well, naturally, James! Who else? I thought you three gossips would have tumbled to that long ago — ."

"Well, of course, we did — ," Jennifer began.

"Only —," said Jill, uncomfortably, "we thought that you liked Paul better now — after all," she accused, "you *danced* with him rather a lot — !"

"And he saved my life, sort of," said Tina. "Twice."

"Yes, well, I don't expect that Tina will need to have her life saved as a general rule," said Elizabeth, "and as James just suits me and Paul doesn't — ."

"Gosh!" said Jennifer. "He would suit me!"

"Then," said Elizabeth, grinning, "you'd better marry him yourself. Later on."

"Oh, help," said Tina, "let's get one wedding over first before we have to start on another — !"

"*Tina's doing it awfully well,*" said *Jill*.

XXIV: A JANE SHAW BIBLIOGRAPHY

ALISON J. LINDSAY

Titles in square brackets indicate unpublished material

SARA AND CAROLINE

Breton Holiday (reissued as *Breton Adventure*) (Collins, 1939)
Bernese Holiday (reissued as *Bernese Adventure*) (Collins, 1940)
Highland Holiday (Collins, 1942)

THE MOOCHERS

The Moochers (Lutterworth, 1950)
The Moochers Abroad (Lutterworth, 1951)
[*Moochers and Prefects*] Completed and sent to Lutterworth in 1951, but subsequently lost while under consideration by West Regional TV.

SUSAN LYLE

Susan Pulls the Strings (Collins, 1952)
Susan's Helping Hand (Collins, 1955)
Susan Rushes In (Collins, 1956)
Susan Interferes (Collins, 1957)
Susan at School (this and the following three were illustrated by R.A. Branton) (Collins, 1958)
Susan Muddles Through (Collins, 1960)
Susan's Trying Term (Collins, 1961)
No Trouble for Susan (Collins, 1962)
Susan's Kind Heart (Collins, 1965)

Where is Susan? (Collins, 1968)
A Job for Susan (Collins, 1969)
[*Susan in Trouble*] *A manuscript draft of the first chapter was found amongst Jean Evans' papers after her death, and is included in this book.*

PENNY (illustrated by Gilbert Dunlop)

Penny Foolish (Nelson, 1953)
Twopence Coloured (Nelson, 1954)
Threepenny Bit (Nelson, 1955)
Fourpenny Fair (Nelson, 1956)
Fivepenny Mystery (Nelson, 1958)
Crooked Sixpence (Nelson, 1958)

THOMAS (illustrated by Gilbert Dunlop)

Looking After Thomas (Nelson, 1957)
Willow Green Mystery (Nelson, 1958)
The Tall Man (Nelson, 1960)

NORTHMEAD (illustrated by Robert Hodgson)

New House at Northmead (Nelson, 1961)
Northmead Nuisance (Nelson, 1963)

DIZZY AND ALISON

Anything Can Happen (illustrated by Thelma Lambert) (Nelson, 1964)
Nothing Happened After All (Nelson, 1965)

SINGLE TITLES

The House of the Glimmering Light (Collins, 1943)
The Crew of the Belinda (Collins, 1945)
Venture to South Africa (illustrated by Gilbert

Dunlop) (Nelson, 1960)
Crooks Tour (Collins, 1962)
[*The Man at the Villa Carlotta*] *An untitled manuscript draft of the first two chapters was found amongst Jean Evans' papers after her death; the title has been added by the editor. The manuscript indicates that it was Jean's practice to decide on the names of her characters once the writing was completed, since these are left as blanks.*

For Younger Children

Magic Ships (Collins, 1943)
Farm Friends (illustrated by 'Lindy') (Collins, 1953)
Puppy Tales (illustrated by 'Lindy') (Collins, 1953)
Uncle Remus Stories Retold by Jane Shaw (illustrated by William Backhouse) (Collins, 1960)
Heidi Grows Up Retold by Jane Shaw (Collins, 1961)
Left handed Tumfy (illustrated by Gwyneth Mamlock) (Lutterworth, 1962)
Brer Rabbit and Brer Fox Retold by Jane Shaw (illustrated by William Backhouse) (Collins, 1969)

As Jean Patrick

Builders of Books in the *Park Chronicle*, 1937 (included in this book)
My Own Book of Baby Beasts (Collins, 1938)
My Own Book of Other Lands (Collins, 1938)

As Jean Evans

Letter from Africa, in the *Park Chronicle*, 1954
Encounter in S. Africa, in the *Park Chronicle*, 1964

As Jean Bell

Paddy Turns Detective and *The Penhallow Mystery* (paperback) (Collins: 'Spitfire' series, 1967)

Articles

In *The Glories of Britain* (Collins, 1939)
William Shakespeare by Jane Shaw
The Fighting Téméraire by JBSE.

Short Stories

It is impossible at present to produce a complete list of every appearance of Jane Shaw's short stories, since many were reprinted several times in Collins' various annuals and compendiums. Listed below is every known short story.

Amanda's Spies (*Collins' Girls' Annual*, 1941)
Sara's Adventure (*Collins' Girls' Annual*, 1953; reprinted in *The Crackerjack Book for Girls*, Collins, 1959)
The Adventures of a Snowman (*Collins' Girls' Annual*, 1954; reprinted in *The Crackerjack Book for Girls*, Collins, 1959)
The Wilson's Won't Mind (*Collins' Girls' Annual*, 1955; reprinted in *The Treasure Book for Girls,* Collins, 1958, and *Ballet Stories*, edited by Ian Woodward, 1982)
Susan's School Play (*Collins' Girls' Annual*, 1957; reprinted in *The Crackerjack Girls Own Book*, Collins, nd)
Susan and the Home-Made Bomb (*Collins' Girls' Annual*, 1958)
The Matchmakers (*Collins' Girls' Annual*, 1959)
Susan and the Spae-Wife (*Collins' Girls' Annual*,

1960)
Family Trouble (*Collins' Girls' Annual*, 1961)
Crooks Limited (*Collins' Girls' Annual*, 1962)
Jumble Sale (*Collins' Girls' Annual*, 1963)
[*The Picture*] *The typescript was found amongst Jean Evans' papers after her death, and is included in this book.*
[*Adventures of a Mouse*] *The typescript was found amongst Jean Evans' papers after her death. It was written at Jean's first South African address, 7 Congo Road, and so must predate her 1967 move to Rosebank. It does not appear to have been published and Jean evidently drew on her for her later and much longer novella,* A Girl With Ideas. *It has therefore not been included in this book.*

DIE BRANDWAG

*This was an Afrikaans newspaper, whose editor lived next door to the Evans in Johannesburg. In 1954 Jean contributed several short stories to it, which the paper arranged to be translated into Afrikaans. It is not known how many were actually published, since only one cutting (*Die Man Langsaan*) was found amongst Jean's papers.*

The Man Next Door (*Die Man Langsaan*), in *Die Brandwag*, 10 December 1954
The Matchmakers
Birthday
Patchwork Quilt
Two's Company
The Quarrel

Stories for Lutterworth

The notebook in which Jean kept records of payments from publishers lists these five short stories or articles as being sold to Lutterworth. None has yet been found published, but they are included here for the sake of completeness.

[*A Pony of Your Own*], sold 10 March 1950
[*No Robbery*], sold 10 March 1950
[*I rode with the Covenanters*], sold 17 August 1950
[*Mere and Moorland*], sold [-] January 1951
[*Heather Mixture*], sold [-] December 1951

For Younger Children

The following appeared in various *Collins' Children's Annuals* and are not dated:
Aladdin's Lamp Grows Old
The Giant's Washing [a Griselda story]
Tiger Kitten
The Magic Basket [a Griselda story]
The Cat's Grandmother [a Griselda story]
Griselda and the Goblin
Griselda and the Baby Elf
The Onion Man
The Cat and the Cabin Boy (*Treasure Trove for Boys and Girls*, Collins, nd)
Griselda and the Rain Fairies (*Treasure Book for Boys and Girls*, Collins, nd)
The Lonely Giant (*Treasure Book for Boys and Girls*, Collins, nd)
Visiting a Fairy (*My Book of Elves and Fairies*, Collins, nd)
The Tale of Three Puppies in *Five Listen With Mother Tales Number 6*, BBC books, nd

Broadcast Material

Wullie, BBC Children's Hour, 21.2.1949
Wullie visits the Peat Moss, BBC Children's Hour, 28.2.1949
Wullie & the Tinkers, BBC Children's Hour, 7.3.1949
Wullie's Hallowe'en Party, BBC Children's Hour, 14.3.1949
The Church Mouse, BBC Listen With Mother, 2.5.1950, repeated 6.6.1950
Christine and the Left-handed Brownie, BBC Children's Hour, 5.5.1950
The Goblin of the Black Loch, BBC [-], 13.5.1950
The Cookie Bun, BBC Listen With Mother, 10.11.1950, repeated 2.3.1951, 11.1.1952, 2.7.1954, 3.8.1956, 22.9.1958
The Gentle Dragon, BBC [-], 4.5.1951
The Teddy Bear Who Lost his Growl, BBC [-], 5.2.1952
Taddy's Tail, BBC Listen With Mother, [-] August 1952, repeated 23.3.1955, 1.5.1956, 28.8.1958, 9.8.1960, and on Australian Broadcasting Commission's Schools programme on 4.7.1960
Janet's Easter Egg, BBC Listen With Mother, 21.4.1954, repeated 11.4.1955, 27.3.1959
A Tale of Three Puppies, BBC Listen With Mother, 24.5.1951, repeated 3.4.1952, 12.7.1957, 6.7.1959
The Cat, the Owl and the Scottie Dog, on BBC [-], 17.3.1954, repeated 28.10.1964
The Elves and the Shoemaker, and *The Cock and the Mouse and the Little Red Hen*, accepted by South African Broadcasting Corporation in a letter dated 12 August 1953 but no further information on whether or not they were broadcast

PHOTOGRAPH ALBUM

Jean Patrick (far left) and Robert Evans (far right) with friends on holiday in Arran. Photograph: Joyce Aitken

No 9 Newtown Place, Glasgow, Jean's home from birth until marriage.

The entrance gates to Park School at No 25 Lynedoch Street, Glasgow, which Jean attended from 1919-1928.

Jean Patrick (front row, second left) with Glasgow University Women's Golf Section, in Glasgow University Magazine, 1931-32. Photograph: Department of Special Collections, Glasgow University Library

Rhona Stern, Professor A. C. Partridge, and Jean Evans at a P.E.N. Centre Luncheon, Johannesburg, 1969.